"For the record, I think that was probably up there with the best kisses of my life."

He could feel Makena smiling.

"Okay, I lied. That was the best kiss of my life. And it gets me in trouble because I don't want to stop there. I want more. And when I say more, I don't just mean physical." He could almost hear the wheels spinning in her brain and could sense she was about to do some major backpedaling.

"I hear what you're saying, Colton. I feel whatever this is happening between us, too. I don't exactly have anything to give right now."

"You don't have to explain any of that to me. I feel the same."

TEXAS LAW

———

USA TODAY Bestselling Author

BARB HAN

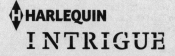

HARLEQUIN
INTRIGUE

All my love to Brandon, Jacob and Tori,
the three great loves of my life.

To Babe, my hero, for being my best friend, my greatest love
and my place to call home.

I love you all with everything that I am.

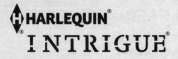

Recycling programs
for this product may
not exist in your area.

ISBN-13: 978-1-335-13688-6

Texas Law

Copyright © 2020 by Barb Han

This edition published by arrangement with Harlequin Books S.A.

For questions and comments about the quality of this book,
please contact us at CustomerService@Harlequin.com.

Harlequin Enterprises ULC
22 Adelaide St. West, 40th Floor
Toronto, Ontario M5H 4E3, Canada
www.Harlequin.com

Printed in U.S.A.

USA TODAY bestselling author **Barb Han** lives in north Texas with her very own hero-worthy husband, three beautiful children, a spunky golden retriever/ standard poodle mix and too many books in her to-read pile. In her downtime, she plays video games and spends much of her time on or around a basketball court. She loves interacting with readers and is grateful for their support. You can reach her at barbhan.com.

Books by Barb Han

Harlequin Intrigue

An O'Connor Family Mystery

Texas Kidnapping
Texas Target
Texas Law

Rushing Creek Crime Spree

Cornered at Christmas
Ransom at Christmas
Ambushed at Christmas
What She Did
What She Knew
What She Saw

Crisis: Cattle Barge

Sudden Setup
Endangered Heiress
Texas Grit
Kidnapped at Christmas
Murder and Mistletoe
Bulletproof Christmas

Visit the Author Profile page at Harlequin.com.

CAST OF CHARACTERS

Makena Eden—She has outlasted her bank account and exhausted her resources, but can she keep going long enough to outrun her ex?

Colton O'Connor—This sheriff runs into someone from his past who needs his professional help despite her pleas otherwise.

River Myers—This cop has a temper and seems fixated on his ex.

Randol Bic—This sharpshooter has a clean record on the job, so why does his name keep coming up?

Jimmy Stitch—Who is this officer who seems to be protecting River Myers?

Chapter One

Sheriff Colton O'Connor took a sip of coffee and gripped the steering wheel of his SUV. Thunder boomed and rain came down in sheets. Seeing much past the front bumper was basically impossible. He'd had three stranded vehicle calls already—one of those cars had been actually submerged—and the worst of this spring thunderstorm hadn't happened yet. The storm wreaking havoc on the small town of Katy Gulch, Texas, was just getting started.

On top of everything, Colton's babysitter had quit last night. Miss Marla's niece had been in a car crash in Austin and needed her aunt to care for her during her recovery. The spry sixty-five-year-old was the only living relative of the girl, who was a student at the University of Texas at Austin.

Colton pinched the bridge of his nose to stem the thundering headache working up behind his eyelids. His mother was pinch-hitting with his twin boys, Silas and Sebastian, but she was still reeling from the loss of her husband, as was Colton and the rest of the family.

A recent kidnapping attempt had dredged up the unsolved, decades-old mystery of his sister's abduction, and his father was murdered after deciding to take it upon himself to take up the investigation on his own again. Colton was just getting started untangling his father's murder.

Considering all that was going on at the ranch, Colton didn't want to add to his mother's stress. As much as his one-year-olds were angels, taking care of little ones with more energy than brain development was a lot for anyone to handle. His mother had enough on her plate already, but she'd convinced him the distraction would be good for her.

And now a storm threatened to turn the town upside down with tornadoes and flash floods.

So, no, Colton didn't feel right about leaving his mother to care for his children, although Margaret O'Connor was strong, one of the toughest women he'd ever met.

He took another sip of coffee and nearly spit it out. It was cold. Bitter. The convenience-store kind that he was certain had been made hours ago and left to burn. That tacky, unpleasant taste stuck to the roof of his mouth.

This might be a good time to stop by the ranch to check on his mother and the twins. He could get a decent cup of coffee there and he wanted to check on his boys. His stomach growled. A reminder that he'd been working emergencies most of the night and had skipped dinner. He always brought food with him on nights like these, but he could save it for later. It was getting late.

Colton banked a U-turn at the corner of Misty Creek and Apple Blossom Drive, and then headed toward the ranch. He hadn't made it a block when he got the next call. The distinct voice belonging to his secretary, Gert Francis, came through the radio.

"What do you have for me?" He pulled his vehicle onto the side of the road. At least there were no cars on the streets. He hoped folks listened to the emergency alerts and stayed put.

"A call just came in from Mrs. Dillon. Flood waters are rising near the river. She's evacuating. Her concern is about a vagrant who has been sleeping in her old RV. She doesn't want the person to be caught unaware if the water keeps rising, and she's scared to disturb whoever it is on her own." Mrs. Dillon, widowed last year at the age of seventy-eight, had a son in Little Rock who'd been trying to convince her to move closer to him. She had refused. Katy Gulch was home.

Colton always made a point of stopping by her place on his way home to check on one of his favorite residents. It was the happiest part of his job, the fact that he kept all the residents in his town and county safe. He took great pride in his work and had a special place in his heart for the senior residents in his community.

He was a rancher by birth and a sheriff by choice. Both jobs had ingrained in him a commitment to help others, along with a healthy respect for Mother Nature.

Colton heaved a sigh. Thinking about ranching brought him back to his family's situation. With his father, the patriarch of Katy Bull Ranch, now gone, Colton and his brothers had some hard decisions to make about keeping their legacy running.

"Let Mrs. Dillon know I'm on my way." Actually, there was no reason he couldn't call her himself. "Never mind, Gert. I've got her number right here. I've been meaning to ask her how she's been getting around after foot surgery last week."

"Will do, Sheriff." There was so much pride in her voice. She'd always been vocal about how much she appreciated the fact he looked after the town's residents. The last sheriff hadn't been so diligent. Gert had made her opinion known about him, as well.

"After I make this call, I need to check out for a little while to stop by the ranch and see about things there," he informed her.

"Sounds like a plan, sir." More of that admiration came through the line.

Colton hoped he could live up to it.

"Be safe out there," Gert warned.

"You know I will. I better ring her now." Colton ended the call. Using Bluetooth technology, he called Mrs. Dillon. She picked up on the first ring.

"I hear you have a new tenant in the RV. I'm on my way over." Colton didn't need to identify himself. He was pretty certain Mrs. Dillon had his cell number on speed dial. He didn't mind. If a quick call to him or Gert could give her peace of mind, inconvenience was a small price to pay.

"Thank you for checking it out for me. This one showed up three nights ago, I think." Concern came through in Mrs. Dillon's voice. "I know it's a woman because MaryBeth's dog kept barking and I heard her tell him to shush."

"Well, if she stays any longer you'll have to start charging rent," he teased, trying to lighten the mood.

The older woman's heart was as big as the great state they lived in.

"If I started doing that, I'd end up a rich lady. Then all the young bachelors would come to town to court me. We can't have that, can we?" Her smile came through in her voice.

"No, ma'am. We sure can't."

"I hope she's okay." She said on a sigh. "Not a peep from her. I wouldn't have heard her at all if it hadn't been for MaryBeth's dog." Mrs. Dillon clucked her tongue in disapproval. Normally, her neighbor's dog was a thorn in her side. This time, Cooper seemed to have served a purpose.

"Sounds like we have a quiet one on our hands. I'll perform a wellness check and make sure she gets out before the water rises."

"I always complained to my husband that he put the parking pad to the RV way too close to the water's edge. But do you think he listened?" Her tone was half-teasing, half-wistful. Mr. and Mrs. Dillon had been high school sweethearts and had, much like Colton's parents, beaten the odds of divorce and gone the distance. The Dillons had been schoolteachers who'd spent their summers touring the country in their RV. Anyone who knew them could see how much they loved each other. They were almost obnoxiously adorable, much like his own parents had been.

Losing Mr. Dillon had to have been the hardest thing she'd gone through. Colton's heart went out to her.

"I just didn't want her to be caught off guard. If this storm is as bad as they say it's going to be, the RV will be flooded again." She heaved a concerned-sounding sigh. "I probably should've gotten rid of that thing ten years ago after the first time it flooded. But Mr. Dillon loved his camping so he could throw out a line first thing with his morning coffee." Her voice was nothing but melancholy now at the memory.

"He was one of the best fishermen in the county." Colton swerved to miss a puddle on the road that was forming a small lake. Flash flooding was a real problem in the spring. This storm was just beginning to dish out its wrath. Mother Nature had a temper and it was becoming apparent she was gearing up to show them just how angry she could become.

"That he was," she agreed.

"Who is driving you to Little Rock?" He changed the subject, hoping to redirect her from a conversation that would bring back the pain of losing her husband. After seeing the look on his mother's face at hearing the news her husband was dead, Colton didn't want to cause that kind of hurt for anyone, certainly not for someone as kind as Mrs. Dillon. His second grade teacher deserved more brightness in her day, and especially after putting up with him and his brothers when they were young. They'd been good kids by most standards. And yet they'd also been a handful. After having twins, Colton was more aware of the responsibility and sacrifice that came with the parenting job.

"Netty. You know her from my knitting club. She's heading that way to stay with her daughter, so I'm hitching a ride with her." He could almost see the twinkle in Mrs. Dillon's eye when she said the word *hitched*.

"Tell Netty to drive safe." He could barely see in the driving rain and needed to close the call in order to concentrate on the road ahead.

"I will do it, Sheriff. Thank you for checking on

my *tenant*." He could envision her making air quotes when she said the last word.

"You're welcome. In fact, I'll head to your house now." After exchanging goodbyes, he ended the call.

The rain was so thick he could barely see the end of his vehicle now, let alone the road. The weather had definitely turned in the last couple of minutes since he'd started the conversation.

It was a miracle he could see at all. His headlights were almost useless. If he didn't know the area so well, he'd pull over and wait it out. These kinds of storms usually came in waves. Radar didn't look promising on this one.

As he turned right onto Mrs. Dillon's street, a flash of lightning streaked across the sky, and a dark object cut in front of him so suddenly he couldn't stop himself from tapping it with his service vehicle.

A *thunk* sounded and then a squeal. The noise was quickly drowned out by the driving rain.

Colton cursed his luck, wondering if he'd been struck by debris. He hopped out of his vehicle to check. Rain pelted his face. He pulled up his collar and shivered against the cold front, praying whatever he'd hit wasn't an animal. Deer sometimes cut through town. At least he was on his way to the ranch. He could scoop it up, put it in the back and see what he could do about nursing it back to health.

Pulling his flashlight from his belt, he shined it around the area. It was next to impossible to see.

Hell, he could barely see his hand in front of his face for the rain.

Squinting, he caught sight of something moving a few feet from his passenger-side bumper. Hell's bells. He hadn't nicked an animal at all…it was a person.

Colton dashed to the victim. He took a knee beside the woman, who was curled in a tight ball. Her dark clothing covered her from nearly head to toe. She was drenched and lying in a puddle.

"My name is Colton O'Connor. I'm the sheriff and I'm here to help." He knew better than to touch her in case she was injured.

"I'm okay. You can go." He didn't recognize the voice, but then it was next to impossible to hear over the sounds of the rain. She kept her face turned in the opposite direction, away from him.

Considering she seemed anxious to not show her face to him, he wondered if she had something to hide.

"I'm not going anywhere until I know you're okay. And that means being able to stand up and walk away from here on your own," he said, figuring she might as well know where he stood.

"I already said that I'm okay. Go away," the woman shouted, and he heard her loud and clear this time. Her voice was somewhat familiar and yet he couldn't place it.

He dashed toward his vehicle and retrieved an

umbrella. It wouldn't do much good against the torrent. Water was building up on the sidewalk and gushing over faster than the gutter could handle it. But it was something and might help with some of the onslaught.

And he believed that right up until he opened the umbrella and it nearly shot out of his hands. A gust of wind forced him to fight to hold on to it and keep it steady over the victim. Finally, it was doing a good job offering some shelter from the rain.

"Like I said, I need to see that you can walk away from here on your own and answer a few questions. I'm the one who hit you and there's no way I'm leaving. What's your name?" He bent down lower so she could hear without him shouting at her.

She didn't answer and that sent up more warning flares. Anyone could see she was injured. She'd taken a pretty hard hit. She might be in shock or maybe suffering head trauma. From his position, it was impossible to see if she was bleeding, and because of the way she'd fallen, he couldn't rule out a broken arm or leg.

Colton stood up and walked around to where she was facing. He dropped down on his knees to get a better look. Rain was everywhere—his eyes, his ears, his face. He shook his head, trying to shake off the flood.

"I'm calling an ambulance. I'm going to get some help." He strained to see her face, still unable to reach back to his memory and find a name that matched the voice. In a small town like Katy Gulch, Colton knew most everyone, which meant she was someone who'd passed through town.

She lifted her arm to wave him away.

"No can do. Sorry." He tilted his mouth toward the radio clipped to his shoulder. With his free hand, he pressed the talk button. "Gert, can you read me?"

There was a moment of crackling. He feared he might not be able to hear her response. And yet going to his SUV wasn't an option. He didn't want to leave the woman alone in the street in the soaking rain again. She looked like she needed a hand-up and he had no plans to leave her.

With the wind, his umbrella was doing very little, but it was something.

The woman, who had been curled up on her side, shielding her face, pushed up to sit. "See, I'm okay. I'm not hurt. I just need a minute to catch my breath and I'll be fine."

Colton wasn't convinced she was able to think clearly. Often after experiencing trauma, it took a while for the brain to catch up. That was how shock worked. She might not even realize it.

"What's your name?" he asked again, trying to assess her mental state.

She shook her head, which either meant she didn't want to disclose it or she couldn't remember. Neither was a good sign.

Since she hadn't answered his question, there was no choice but to have her cleared medically before he could let her go, even if she could walk away on her own, which he highly doubted at the moment.

"I'm just going to get somebody here to take a look at you, and if everything's okay, you'll be cleared in no time. In the meantime, you can wait inside my vehicle and get out of this weather." He'd noticed that she'd started shivering.

He slipped out of his rain jacket and placed it over her shoulders.

The woman looked up at him and their gazes locked. His heart stirred and his breath caught.

"Makena?"

WATER WAS EVERYWHERE, flooding Makena Eden's eyes and ears. Rain hit her face, stinging like fire-ant bites. She blinked up and stared into the eyes of the last man she'd expected to see again—Colton O'Connor.

Still reeling from taking a wrong turn into the road and being clipped by his sport utility, she felt around on her hip.

Ouch. That hurt. She could already feel her side bruising. Mentally, she tried to dust herself off and stand up. Her hip, however, had other plans, so she sat there, trying to ride out the pain.

"I just need a minute." There was no other option but to get up and fake being well. She had no job, no medical insurance and no money. And she couldn't afford to let her identity get out, especially not on a peace officer's radio. Then there was the other shock, the fact that Colton was kneeling down in front of her. How long had it been?

"Not so fast." Colton's eyebrow shot up and he seemed unconvinced. He was one of the most devastatingly handsome men she'd ever met, and her body picked that moment to react to him *and* remind her. This was turning out to be one red-letter day stacked on the back end of months of agony. One she'd survived by hiding and sliding under the radar.

"I don't want you to try to move. We need to get you checked out first." He snapped into action, tilting his chin toward his left shoulder to speak into his radio. She could hear him requesting an ambulance. For a split second, she wondered if she could run away and get far enough out of sight for him to forget this whole situation. *Wishful thinking.* It was so not good that he knew her personally. Granted, he knew her before she'd become Mrs. River Myers, but still…

Panic squeezed her lungs as she tried to breathe through the building anxiety. She couldn't let her name go down on record. She couldn't have anything that would identify her over the radio.

"I promise that I'm not broken. I'm shaken up." Before she could say anything else, he put a hand up to stop her.

Water was dripping everywhere, and yet looking into those cobalt blue eyes sent her flashing back to her sophomore year of college. The two of them had been randomly hooked up as partners in biology lab. Even at nineteen years old, it was easy to see Colton was going to be strong and muscled when he finally filled out.

Now, just seeing him released a dozen butterflies in her chest along with a free-falling sensation she hadn't felt since college. She could stare into his eyes for days. He had a face of hard angles and planes. Full lips covered perfectly straight, white teeth.

Looking at him was like staring at one of those billboard models. The man was tall. Six feet four inches of solid steel and ripped muscle. The only reason she noticed was the survival need at its most basic, she told herself. She was in trouble and had to assess whether or not Colton could defend her.

Icy fingers gripped her spine as she thought about the past, about *her* past. About *River.* Stand still long enough and it would catch up to her. He *would* find her.

Colton might look good. Better than good, but she wouldn't let her mind go there for long. There were two things that would keep her from the attraction she felt, other than the obvious fact they'd had one class and a flirtation that hadn't gone anywhere. A badge and a gun.

Chapter Two

Makena needed to convince Colton that she wasn't injured so she could get far away from him and Katy Gulch. Coming here had turned out to be a huge mistake—one that could get her killed.

How had she not remembered this was his hometown?

Being on the road for months on end had a way of mixing up weeks. Towns were starting to run together, too. They fell into one of two categories, big and small.

Dallas, Houston and Austin fit into the big-city category. They all had basically the same chain restaurants if a slightly differing view on life. Small towns, on the other hand, seemed to share a few characteristics. In those, she was beginning to realize, it was a little harder to go unnoticed.

Getting seen was bad for her longevity.

The other thing she'd noticed about small towns in her home state of Texas was the food. Some of the best cooking came from diners and mom-and-pop shops. Since she'd run out of money, she'd been forced to live on other people's generosity.

Makena hadn't eaten a real meal in the past three days. She'd sustained herself on scraps. The owner of the RV where she'd been staying had been kind enough to leave a few supplies and leftovers a couple of days ago, and Makena had stretched them out to make them last. Hunger had caught up to her, forcing her to seek out food.

The fact that the owner knew Makena was staying on her property *and* Makena had remained there anyway signaled just how much she'd been slipping lately. Starvation had a way of breeding desperation. Not to mention it had been so very long since she'd slept on a real bed in a real room or in a real house that she could scarcely remember how it felt. The RV was the closest she'd come and she hadn't wanted to give it up.

Makena was drenched. She shivered despite having the sheriff's windbreaker wrapped around her. She could sit there and be stubborn and cold. Or, she could get Colton's help inside the SUV and wring herself out. And at least maybe have him turn the heat on.

"If you help me up, I can make it to your vehicle," she said to him.

Colton's eyebrow shot up. "You sure it's a good idea to move? I didn't realize how badly you were hurt when I offered before."

"I'm so cold my teeth are chattering. You look pretty miserable. There's no reason for me to sit here in a puddle when I can be warm inside your vehicle." She had to practically shout to be heard. She put her hands up in the surrender position, palms up. "All I need is a hand up and maybe a little help walking."

He opened his mouth to protest.

"Sitting out here, I may end up with the death of cold." She realized she was going to have to give him a little bit more than that. "I'm pretty sure that I have a nasty bruise working up on my left hip. It was stupid of me to run into the street. I didn't even see you."

"You must've darted out from in between the parked vehicles right when I turned." There was so much torment in his voice now.

"Sorry. I was just trying to stay out of the rain but I'm okay. Really." It wasn't a total lie. Mostly, a half-truth. Being dishonest pained Makena. She hated that she'd become the kind of person who had to cover her tracks like a criminal.

"What are you doing out on a night like this?" he asked.

"I-um…was trying to get back to my rental over by the river." The way she stammered was giving her away based on the look on his face.

He nodded as he studied her, but she could see that he wasn't convinced.

"My name is Makena. You already know that. It's Wednesday. At least, I think it is."

"Do you know where you are right now?" The worry lines on his forehead were easing up.

"Katy Gulch, Texas," she said. "And I've been out of work for a little while. That's the reason I've lost track of the days of the week."

It was her turn to look carefully at him.

"What do you think?" she asked. "Did I pass?"

Colton surveyed her for a long moment. Lightning raced sideways across the sky and thunder boomed.

"Lean on me and let me do the heavy lifting." He put his arm out.

"Deal." She grabbed hold of his arm, ignoring the electrical impulses vibrating up her arm from contact. This wasn't the time for an inappropriate attraction and especially not with a man who had a gun and a badge on his hip. She'd been there. Done that. And had the emotional scars to prove it.

Not taking Colton's help was out of the question. She had no car. No money. No choices.

Makena held onto his arm for dear life. As soon as she was pulled up to her feet, her left leg gave out under the pain from her hip.

"Whoa there." Colton's strong arms wrapped around her, and the next thing she knew he'd picked her up. He carried her over to his SUV and managed to open the passenger door and help her inside.

She eased onto the seat and immediately felt around for the adjuster lever. Her fingers landed on the control and she adjusted her seat back, easing some of the pressure from her sitting bones. Her hip rewarded her by lightening up on some of the pain.

Colton opened the back hatch, closed it and was in the driver's seat a few seconds later.

He then leaned over and tucked a warm blanket around her. "Is that better?"

"Much." She said the word on a sigh, releasing the breath she'd been holding.

"Be honest. How badly does it hurt?" he asked, looking at her with those cobalt blues.

"On a scale of one to ten? I'd say this has to be a solid sixteen."

The engine was still humming and at least she'd stopped shivering. She could also finally hear him over the roar of the weather, even though it seemed the rain was driving down even harder than a few minutes ago.

"I couldn't hear a word Gert said earlier." He flashed his eyes at her. "Gert is my secretary in case you hadn't sorted it out for yourself. And she's a lot more than that. She's more like my right arm. I'm the sheriff."

She glanced down at the word *SHERIFF* written in bold yellow letters running down her left sleeve. Even if he hadn't told her earlier, she would've figured it out. With a small smile, she said, "I put that together for myself."

"Is your car around here somewhere? I can call a tow."

"No." Talking about herself wasn't good. The less information she gave, the better. She hoped he would just drop the subject, let her warm up and then let her get back to her temporary shelter in the RV.

Her stomach growled, and surprisingly, it could be heard over the thunder boom outside.

"There's someone I need to check on. Are you hungry?" Colton asked.

"Yes. I didn't get a chance to eat dinner yet." She followed his gaze to the clock on the dashboard. It read 8:30 p.m.

With his left hand, he tucked his chin to his left shoulder and hit some type of button. "Gert, can you read me?"

Crackling noises came through the radio. And then a voice.

"Copy that, Sheriff. Loud and clear." The woman sounded older, mid-sixties if Makena had to guess.

"I need an ambulance on the corner of Misty Creek and Apple Blossom. Stat. A pedestrian was struck by my vehicle and needs immediate medical attention. She is alert and communicative, with a possible injury to her left hip. She's lucid, but a concussion can't be ruled out," he said.

"Roger that, Sheriff. You must not have heard me earlier. There's flooding on several roads. Both of my EMTs are on calls and even if they weren't, the streets aren't clear. No one can get to you for at least the next hour."

Relief washed over Makena. However, Colton didn't look thrilled.

"Roger that." He blew out a frustrated-sounding breath. "I'll drive the victim to the hospital myself."

"County road isn't clear. There's been a lot of flooding. I don't advise making that trip unless it's life-threatening," Gert said.

Flash floods in Texas were nothing to take lightly. They were the leading cause of weather-related deaths in the state.

"We probably need to close the road since the water's rising," she continued.

Colton smacked his flat palm against the steering wheel. "Roger that."

"As soon as I warm up, you can drop me off. I think my hip just needs a little chance to rest." Embarrassingly enough, her stomach picked that moment to gurgle and growl again.

Colton's gaze dropped to her stomach as he reached under the center console of his SUV and pulled something around. A lunchbox?

He unzipped the black box and produced what looked like a sandwich. He opened the Ziploc bag and held it out toward her. "I knew I'd be working late tonight with the storms. So I made extra. You're welcome to this one."

When she didn't immediately reach for the offering, he locked gazes with her. "Go ahead. Take it. I have more."

"I really can't take all your food." Her mouth was practically watering.

"It's no big deal. I can always swing by my house and get more. It's on the way to my office, not far from here."

"Are you sure about that, Colton?" The last thing she wanted to do was take his food and leave him with nothing. The sandwich looked good, though. And she was pretty certain she'd started drooling.

"It's fine," he reassured her with that silky masculine voice that trailed all over her, warming her better than any blanket could.

He urged her to take it, so she did.

"Thank you." She wasted no time demolishing the sandwich. Ham. Delicious.

He barely looked away from the screen on the laptop mounted inside his vehicle as he handed her an apple next.

This time, she didn't argue. Instead, she polished off the fruit in a matter of seconds while he studied the map on the screen. Just as she wrapped the remains of the apple in the paper towel he'd given her, he pulled out a thermos and handed her a spoon.

"Soup," was all he said.

Angel was all she thought.

COLTON ENTERED the hospital's location into his computer. The screen showed red triangles with exclamation points in the center of them on more roads than not, indicating flooding or hazardous road conditions. Gert was a lifeline, going well above and beyond typical secretary duties. She'd become Colton's right arm and he had no idea what he'd do without her.

Makena needed medical attention. That part was obvious. The tricky part was going to be getting her looked at. He was still trying to wrap his mind around the fact Makena Eden was sitting in his SUV.

Talk about a blast from the past and a missed opportunity. But he couldn't think about that right now when she was injured. At least she was eating. That had to be a good sign.

When she'd tried to stand, she'd gone down pretty fast and hard. She'd winced in pain and he'd scooped her up and brought her to his vehicle. He knew better than to move an injured person. In this case, however, there was no choice.

The victim was alert and cognizant of what was going on. A quick visual scan of her body revealed nothing obviously broken. No bones were sticking out. She complained about her hip and he figured there could be something there. At the very least, she needed an X-ray.

Since getting to the county hospital looked impossible at least in the short run and his apartment was close by, he decided taking her there might be for the best until the roads cleared. He could get her out of his uncomfortable vehicle and onto a soft couch.

Normally, he wouldn't take a stranger to his home, but this was Makena. And even though he hadn't seen her in forever, she'd been special to him at one time.

He still needed to check on the RV for Mrs. Dillon…and then it dawned on him. Was Makena the 'tenant' the widow had been talking about earlier?

"Are you staying in town?" he asked, hoping to get her to volunteer the information. It was possible that she'd fallen on hard times and needed a place to hang her head for a couple of nights.

"I've been staying in a friend's RV," she said. So, she was the 'tenant' Mrs. Dillon mentioned.

It was good seeing Makena again. At five feet five inches, she had a body made for sinning, underneath a thick head of black hair. He remembered how shiny and wavy her hair used to be. Even soaked with water, it didn't look much different now.

She had the most honest set of pale blue eyes— eyes the color of the sky on an early summer morning. She had the kind of eyes that he could stare into all day. It had been like that before, too.

But that was a long time ago. And despite the lightning bolt that had struck him square in the chest when she turned to face him, this relationship was purely professional.

Colton wasn't in the market to replace his wife,

Rebecca, anytime soon. He was still reeling from the loss almost year later. He bit back a remark on the irony of running into someone he'd had a crush on in college but not enough confidence to ask out. He'd been with Makena for all of fifteen or twenty minutes now and the surge of attraction he'd felt before had returned with full force, much like the out-of-control thunderstorm bearing down on them.

He refocused. His medical experience amounted to knowing how to perform CPR and that was about it.

Even soaked to the bone, Makena was still stunning—just as stunning as he remembered from twelve years ago in biology lab.

However, it was troublesome just how quickly she'd munched down on the sandwich and apple that he'd given her. She'd practically mewled with pleasure when she'd taken the first sip of soup, which she'd destroyed just as quickly.

Colton glanced at the third finger on her left hand. There was no ring and no tan line. For reasons he couldn't explain, given the fact he hadn't seen Makena in years, relief washed over him and more of that inconvenient attraction surged.

No ring, no husband.

It didn't exactly mean she was single. He told himself the reason he wanted to know was for the investigation. Here she'd shown up in town out of nowhere. She was staying in an RV and, based on the brightness in her eyes, he was certain she was sober. He hadn't expected her to be doing drugs or drinking. However, his job had trained him to look for those reasons first when dealing with uncharacteristic behavior.

Darting across the road without looking, in the middle of one of the worst thunderstorms so far this year, definitely qualified as uncharacteristic. Now that he'd determined she fell into that camp without a simple explanation, it was time to investigate what she was really doing in town and why.

Again, the questions he was about to ask were all for the sake of the investigation, he told himself, despite a little voice in the back of his head calling him out on the lie.

For now, he was able to quiet that annoyance.

Chapter Three

In the dome light, Colton could see that Makena's face was sheet-white and her lips were purple. Color was slowly beginning to return to her creamy cheeks. He took that as a good sign she was starting to warm up and was in overall good health.

"I thought you were in school to study business so you could come back and work on your family's ranch." She turned the tables.

"I realized midway through my degree that my heart was not in business. I switched to criminal justice and never looked back." Colton figured it couldn't hurt to give a little information about himself considering she looked frightened of him and everything else. As much as he didn't like the idea, she might be on the run to something or *from* something. Either way, he planned to get to the bottom of it and give her a hand up. "How about you? Did you stay an education major?"

"I stayed in my field," she said.

He would've thought that he'd just asked for her social security number and her bank passwords for the reaction he got. She crossed her ankles and then her arms. She hugged her elbows tightly against her chest. To say she'd just closed up was a lot like saying dogs liked table scraps over dry food.

"Did I say something wrong?" Colton may as well put it out on the table. He didn't like the idea of stepping on a land mine, and the response he'd gotten from her was like a sucker punch that he didn't want to take twice.

"No. You d-didn't say anything wrong. You j-just caught me off guard." The way she stammered over every other word told him that she wasn't being completely honest. It also made him feel like she was afraid of him, which was strange. Innocent people might get nervous around law enforcement, but straight-up scared? He wasn't used to that with victims.

"Okay. We better get on the road and out of this weather. I promised one of our elderly residents that I would stop by and check on her property. The rain isn't letting up and we're not going too far from here. Her home is nearby. Mind if we—"

"It's okay. You can just let me out. I don't want to get in the way of you doing your job." Panic caused her voice to shake. Colton didn't want to read too much into her reaction.

"Makena, I hit you with my SUV and the fact is

going to bother me to no end until I make absolute certain that you're okay. Check that. I want you to be better than okay. In fact, I'd like to help you out if I can, no matter what you need." He meant those words.

Makena blew out a slow breath. "I'm sorry. You've been nothing but kind. I wasn't trying to put you off. Honest. I'm just shaken up and a little thrown off balance." She turned to look at him, and those clear blue eyes pierced right through him. "Don't take any of this the wrong way. It's just been…" she seemed to be searching for the right words "…a really long time since I've had anyone help me."

Well, he sure as hell hoped she didn't plan on stopping there. If anything, he wanted to know more about her. He chalked it up to nostalgia and the feelings he'd experienced when he was nineteen, the minute he sat beside her in the bio lab, too chicken to pluck up the courage to ask her out.

He'd waited for weeks to see if she felt the same attraction. She was shy back then and he was even shyer. When he finally found his courage, a kid had beaten him to the punch. Dane Kilroy had moved in.

Colton couldn't say he'd ever had the best timing when it came to him and the opposite sex. Missed opportunity had him wanting to help her now. Or maybe it was that lost look in her eyes that appealed to a place deep inside him.

He knew what it was to be broken. His family had experienced a horrific tragedy before he was born. One that had left an echo so strong it could still be heard to this day.

A decades-old kidnapping had impacted the O'Connor family so deeply that they could never be the same again. The hole could never be filled after his six-month-old sister was abducted.

Colton figured the best place to start with Makena was the basics. "Is your last name still Eden?"

He opened up a file report on his laptop.

"What are you doing?" She seemed shocked.

"Filing a report." Colton forgot that she was a civilian. She would have no idea about the process of filling out an incident report. "I need to file an accident report."

"No. That's really not necessary. I mean, I didn't get a good look at your car but there didn't seem to be any damage to your bumper. As far as me? I'll be okay in a couple of days. There's really no need to file any type of report. Won't that get you in trouble with your job?"

She was worried about him?

"My job isn't going to be on the line over a freak accident. This is what I do. This is my job, my responsibility."

"What can I say to stop you from filing that report?"

Colton couldn't quite put his finger on what he

heard in her tone when she asked the question, but it was enough to send a warning shot through his system.

"Are you in some type of trouble?" he asked.

Part of him wished he could reel those words back in when he heard her gasp. Too late. They were already out there. And consequences be damned, he wanted to know the answer. Maybe he shouldn't have asked the question so directly.

"Colton, this is a bad idea. My hip is hurting right now, but it's going to be fine. There's really no reason to make a huge ordeal out of this. Despite what you said it can't be all that good for your career for you to have a car crash on your record. I can't imagine someone who drives around as part of his job wouldn't be hurt by a report being filed. I promise you, I would tell you if this was a big deal. It's so not."

The old saying, "The lady doth protest too much," came to mind. Colton realized what he heard in her voice. Fear.

And there was no way he was going to walk away from that. "Makena, I can't help you if I don't know what's going on. Do you trust me?"

Colton put it out there. As it was, everything about her body language said she'd closed up. There was no way he was getting any information out of her while she sat like that, unwilling to open up. And since the person closest to a woman was the one most likely to hurt her, as angry as that made him, his first thought went to her hiding out from a relationship that had soured.

Domestic disturbances were also among the most dangerous calls for anyone working law enforcement.

"It's really nothing, Colton. We're making too big a deal out of this. I'm just passing through town." She heaved a sigh and pulled the blanket up to her neck. "You asked if I stayed with teaching as my degree and the answer is yes. I did. Until the music program was cut from the school where I worked, and I decided to see if I could make it as a musician on my own."

"Really?"

"I've been traveling across the state playing gigs as often as I can set them up. I don't have a manager and I've been living in an RV without the owner's permission, but I planned to leave a note and some money as soon as I'm able to." He noticed her fingers working the hem of the blanket. "I've fallen on hard times recently and jobs have been in short supply. Really, it's only a matter of time before I get back on my feet."

"Sounds like a hard life and one that's causing you to make tough choices. And the owner knows you've been staying there. She asked me to make sure you're okay." Colton nodded his head. Her explanation nearly covered all the ground of any question he could've thought of. She'd pretty much wrapped up her lifestyle in a bow and the reason she would be moving around the state. But was her story tied up a little too neatly?

He decided to play along for just a minute.

"I thought I remembered seeing you on campus a million years ago picking at a guitar." He tried not to be obvious about watching her response.

"You saw me?" The flush to her cheeks was sexy as hell. She was even more beautiful when she was embarrassed. But that physical beauty was only a small part of her draw. She was intelligent and funny and talented, from what he remembered years ago.

He wondered how much of that had changed… how much she'd changed.

Thunder rumbled and it felt like the sky literally opened up and dumped buckets of rain on them.

Tornado alarms blared. He owed his former father-in-law a call. It was impossible to know if there was an actual tornado or if this was another severe thunderstorm drill. Colton had warned Preston Ellison that overusing the alarm would lead people to disregard it, creating a dangerous situation for residents.

Had the mayor listened?

Clearly not. He hadn't listened to his daughter, Rebecca, either. The single father and mayor of Katy Gulch had overprotected his daughter to the point of smothering her. She'd rebelled. No shock there.

Down deep, Rebecca had always been a good person. She and Colton had been best friends since they were kids and married for less than a year when she'd died. Damned if he didn't miss her to the core some days.

But being with Makena again reminded him why he hadn't married Rebecca straight out of high school.

"ARE YOU COMFORTABLE?" Colton's question felt out of the blue to Makena, but she'd noticed that he'd lost himself in thought for a few minutes as he slogged through the flooded street. This must be his way of rejoining the conversation.

The windshield washers were working double time and had yet to be able to keep up with the onslaught.

"I'm better now that I'm inside your vehicle and we're moving toward safety. Why?" Luckily, the height of the SUV kept the undercarriage of the vehicle above water. The engine sat high enough on the chassis not to flood.

Makena strained to see past the hood. The sirens stopped wailing. The sound would've been earsplitting if it hadn't been for the driving rain drowning out nearly every other sound outside of the SUV.

"The storm's predicted to get worse." He wheeled right and water sloshed as his tires cut a path where he made the turn. The sidewalks of the downtown area and the cobblestoned streets had to be completely flooded now.

"Really?" Makena tried to shift position in her seat so that she could get a good look at the screen he motioned toward. Movement only hurt her hip even more. She winced and bit out a curse.

Colton's laptop was angled toward the driver's side and the only thing she could see was the reflection from the screen in his side window.

He seemed to catch on and said, "Sorry. I can't tilt it any closer to you."

"No need to apologize. Believe it or not, I'm not usually so clumsy, and I don't make a habit of running out in front of vehicles. Like I already said, give this hip a few days and she'll be good as new." Makena forced a smile.

"I hope you weren't planning on going anywhere tonight." There was an ominous quality to his voice, and he didn't pick up on her attempt to lighten the mood.

"Why is that?" Actually, she had hoped to figure out her next move and get back on the road. She'd ducked into the RV to ditch a few friends of her ex-husband, who was the real reason she'd been on the run. Her marriage to an abusive Dallas cop had ended badly. Hunger had caused her to leave the relative safety of the RV. She assumed it would be safer to travel in the rain and easier to cover herself up so she could travel incognito.

It was most likely paranoia, but she could've sworn she'd seen the pair of guys she'd caught in their garage late one night, huddled up and whispering with River. She'd surprised the trio and River had absolutely lost his cool. He'd demanded she go back inside the house and to bed, where he told her to wait for him.

River's decline had become even more apparent after that night. He was almost constantly angry with her over something. Yelling at her instead of talking. Not that he'd been great at it before. Gone was the charm of the early days in their relationship.

When River's attention was turned on, everyone noticed him in the room and he could make the most enigmatic person come to life. River's shadow was a different story altogether. It was a cold, dark cave. His temper had become more and more aggressive to the point she'd had to get out.

"According to radar, this storm's about to get a whole helluva lot worse." Colton's voice cut through her heavy thoughts.

Leaving her husband, River, one year ago had been the best decision she'd ever made. Not a night went by that she didn't fear that he'd find her.

"How is that even possible?" she asked as a tree branch flew in front of the windshield.

"Apparently, Mother Nature isn't done with us yet. We're about to see just about how big this temper tantrum is going to get."

And just when she thought things couldn't get any worse than they already were this evening, the tornado alarms blared again. Rain pounded the front windshield, the roof. And in another moment of pure shock, she realized the winds had shifted. Gusts slammed into the vehicle, rocking it from side to side.

"Normally, I wouldn't leave the scene of an accident. However, if we want to live to see the light of day, we better get out of here." Colton placed the gearshift into Drive and turned his vehicle around. Water sloshed everywhere.

"Where to? You mentioned an elderly neighbor that you need to check on." Another gust of wind blasted the front windshield. Makena gasped.

"She asked me to check on her 'guest' who was staying in her RV. Since you're right here, a change of plans is in order. My place isn't far from here. The parking structure is sound and partially underground. We should be safe there."

Before she could respond, Colton had his secretary on the radio again, updating her on his new destination. Makena figured she could ride out the storm with Colton, giving away as little personal information as she could. Their shared history might work in her favor. Any other law enforcement officer in this situation would most certainly haul her in. Her name would get out.

Makena couldn't risk River figuring out where

she was. With his jealous tendencies, it wouldn't be good for him to see her around Colton, either. The Dallas cop would pick up on her attraction faster than a bee could sting.

Colton stopped at the red light on an otherwise empty street. Everyone seemed to have enough sense to stay off the roads tonight. The only reason she'd left the RV at all was to find scraps of food while everyone hunkered down.

Makena had thrown away her phone months ago, so she'd had no idea a storm was on its way. The cloudy sky and humidity had been a dead giveaway but spring thunderstorms in Texas were notorious for popping up seemingly out of nowhere. In general, they retreated just as fast.

This one, however, was just getting started.

Chapter Four

"What do you think?" Colton asked a second time. He'd blame the rain for Makena not hearing him, but she'd been lost to him for a moment.

The prospect of her disappearing on him wasn't especially pleasing. After being in the vehicle with her for half an hour already, he barely knew any more about her or her situation than he had at the start of the conversation.

The fact that she deflected most of his questions and then overexplained told him the storm brewing outside wasn't the only one.

Since she seemed ready to jump if someone said boo, he figured some things were better left alone. Besides, they were trapped together in a storm that didn't seem to have any intention of letting up over the next twenty-four hours. That would give him enough time to dig around in her story.

Colton relaxed his shoulders. He needed to check in with his mother and see if she was okay with having the twins sleep over. Again, he really didn't like doing that to her under the circumstances no matter how many times she reassured him the twins were nothing but pure joy.

"About what?" Makena asked.

"Staying at my apartment at least until this storm blows over." Colton banked right to avoid a tree limb that was flying through the air.

"When exactly might that be?"

Colton shouldn't laugh but he did. "I'm going to try not to be offended at the fact that you seemed pretty upset about the prospect of spending a couple of hours alone with me. I promise that I'm a decent person."

"No. Don't get me wrong. You've been a godsend and I appreciate the food. I was a drowned rat out there." She blew out another breath. "I wasn't aware there was a big storm coming today. And especially not one of this magnitude. I got caught off guard without an umbrella."

He didn't feel the need to add, without a decent coat. The roads were making it increasingly unsafe to drive to Mrs. Dillon's place. It looked like there were more funnel systems on the way. A tornado watch had just been issued for this and four surrounding counties. He'd like to say the weather was a shock but it seemed folks were glued to the news more and more often every year and some supercell ended up on the radar.

"You didn't answer my question." The reminder came as she stared at the door handle.

Makena sat still, shifting her gaze to the windshield, where she stared for a long moment. She heaved another sigh and her shoulders seemed to deflate. "I appreciate your hospitality, Colton. I really do. And since it doesn't seem safe to travel in this weather, going to your place seems like the best option. I have one question, though."

"And that is?"

"It's really more of a request." She glanced at the half-full coffee sitting in the cupholder.

He knew exactly what she wanted. "I have plenty of coffee in my apartment. I basically live off the stuff."

"I haven't had a good cup of coffee in longer than I care to count."

His eyebrow must've shot up, because she seemed to feel the need to qualify her statement. "I mean like a really good cup of coffee. Not like that stuff." She motioned toward the cupholder and wrinkled her nose.

He laughed. At least some of the tension between them was breaking up. There was no relief on the chemistry pinging between them, though. But he'd take lighter tension because he was actually pretty worried about her. He couldn't imagine why she would be living even temporarily in an RV that didn't belong to her in a town she didn't know. She was from Dallas and they'd met in Austin. Again, his thoughts drifted toward her running away from something—he wasn't buying the broke musician excuse. And since he hadn't seen her in well over a decade, he couldn't be one hundred percent certain she hadn't done something wrong, no matter how much his heart protested.

Something about the fear in her eyes told him that she was on the run from someone. Who that would be was anyone's guess. She wasn't giving up any information. Keeping tight-lipped might have been the thing that kept her alive. Didn't she say that she'd been on the road for months with her music? There were more holes in that story than in a dozen doughnuts. The very obvious ones had to do with the fact that she had no instrument and no band. He figured it was probably customary to bring at least one of those things on tour.

"To my place then," he said.

The light changed to green. He proceeded through the intersection, doing his level best to keep the questions at bay.

His apartment would normally be a five-minute drive. Battling this weather system, he took a solid fifteen and that was without anyone else on the road. A call home was in order and he needed to prepare Makena for the fact he had children.

As he pulled into the garage and the rain stopped

battering his windshield, he parked in his assigned parking spot, number 4, and shut off the engine.

"Before we go inside, I need to make you aware of something—"

Makena scooted up to sit straighter and winced. His gaze dropped to her hip and he figured he had no business letting it linger there.

"Now, there's no reason to panic." It was clear she'd already done just that.

"Was this a bad idea? Do you have a girlfriend or wife in there waiting? I know what you already said but—"

"Before you get too twisted up, hear me out. I have twin sons. They're with my mother because the woman who usually lives with me and takes care of them while I work got called away on a family emergency and had to quit. She hated doing it but was torn, and blood is thicker than water. Besides, I told her to go. She'd regret it if she wasn't there for her niece after the young woman was in a car crash."

"I'm sorry." Much to his surprise, Makena reached over and touched his hand. Electricity pinged. Turned out that the old crush was still alive and well.

"Don't be. It was the right thing for her to do." He debated these next words because he never spoke about his wife to anyone. "I was married. I didn't lie to you before about that. My wife died not long after the babies were born."

"Oh no. I really am sorry, Colton. I had no idea." She looked at him. The pain in her eyes and the compassion in her voice sent a ripple of warmth through him.

He had to look away or risk taking a hit to his heart.

"Why would you?" He'd gotten real good about stuffing his grief down in a place so deep that even he couldn't find it anymore.

When he glanced over at Makena, he saw a tear escape. She ducked her head, chin to chest, and turned her face away from him.

"I'm not trying to upset you…" This was harder than he wanted it to be. "I just didn't want you to walk into my place and be shocked. You've been through enough tonight—" longer if he was right about her situation "—and I didn't want to catch you off guard."

She sat perfectly still, perfectly quiet for a few more long moments. "You have twin boys?"

"Yes, I do. Silas and Sebastian. They are great boys."

When she seemed able to look at him without giving away her emotions, she turned to face him, wincing with movement and then covering. "I bet they're amazing kids, Colton."

It was his turn to smile. "They are."

"Are they at your house?"

"My mom is watching them for me at the family's ranch while I work. She'll be worried with all the weather. I need to check in with her and make sure the boys are asleep."

"How old did you say your boys were?" She seemed to be processing the fact that he was a father.

"One year old. They're great kids." He needed to contact his mother. But first, he needed to get Makena inside his apartment with the least amount of trauma to the hip she'd been favoring. "How about we head inside now?"

He half expected her to change her mind, especially with how squirrelly she'd been so far.

"It would be nice to dry off."

Colton shut off the vehicle's engine and came around to the passenger side. He opened the door. She had her seat belt off despite keeping the blanket around her. Color was returning to her creamy skin, which was an encouraging sign.

"It might be easier if I just carry you up."

"I think I got it. I definitely need some help walking but I want to try to put some weight on this hip."

Considering Makena knew her identity and didn't slur her speech—a couple of key signs she was lucid—his suspicion that she might have a concussion passed. Although, he'd keep an eye on her to be safe. He figured it wouldn't hurt to let her try to walk; he had to trust her judgment to be able to do that.

"Okay, I'm right here." He put his arm out and

she grabbed onto it. More of that electricity, along with warmth, fired through him. Again, he chalked it up to nostalgia. The past. Simpler times.

Makena eased out of the passenger seat, leaning into him to walk. He positioned himself on her left side to make it easier for her. With some effort, she took the first couple of steps, stopping long enough for him to close the car door.

His parking spot was three spaces from the elevator bank, so at least she didn't have far to go.

"You're doing great," he encouraged. He couldn't ignore the awareness that this was the first time in a very long time that he'd felt this strong a draw toward someone. He hadn't been out on a date since losing Rebecca. He'd been too busy missing his wife and taking care of their boys. Twelve months since the kiddos had been born and soon after that, he'd lost his best friend and wife in one fell swoop. He never knew how much twelve months could change his life.

MAKENA LEANED HEAVILY on Colton. She couldn't help but wonder if he felt that same electrical impulse between them. If he did, he was a master at concealment.

Thankfully, the elevator bank was only a few more steps. Pain shot through her if she put any weight on her left leg. But she managed with Colton's help. Despite having told him repeatedly that she'd be fine, this was the first time she felt like it might be true.

The elevator did nothing to prepare her for the largeness of Colton's penthouse apartment. Stepping into the apartment, she realized it took up the entire top floor of the building, which was three stories on top of the parking level.

It felt like she'd been transported into a world of soft, contemporary luxury. "This place is beautiful, Colton."

She pictured him sharing the place with his wife and children. Losing the woman he loved must have been a crushing blow for a man like him. Colton was the kind of person who, once he loved you, would love you forever.

Why did that hurt so much to think about?

Was it because she'd never experienced that kind of unconditional love?

It was impossible not to compare Colton to River. She'd been so young when she and River had gotten together. Too naive to realize he was all charm and no substance. He'd swept her off her feet and asked her to marry him. She'd wanted to believe the fairy tale. She would never make that mistake again.

Colton's apartment comprised one great room and was built in the loft style, complete with a brick wall and lots of windows. The rain thrashed around outside, but the inside felt like a safe haven. In the space cordoned off as the living room, two massive brown leather sofas faced each other in front of a fireplace. In between the sofas was a very soft-looking ottoman in the place of a coffee table. It was tufted, cream-colored and stood on wooden pegs. She noticed all the furniture had soft edges. The light wood flooring was covered by cream rugs, as well.

There was a pair of toy walkers that were perfect for little kids to explore various spots in the room. A large kitchen, separated from the living room by a huge granite island, was to her right. Instead of a formal table, there were chairs tucked around the white granite island, along with a pair of highchairs.

Seeing the kid paraphernalia made it hit home that Colton was a dad. Wow. She took a moment to let that sink in. He gave new meaning to the words *hot dad bod.*

The worry creases in his forehead made more sense now that she knew that he'd lost his wife and was navigating single parenthood alone.

Makena had once believed that she would be a mother by now. A pang of regret stabbed at the thought. She'd known better than to start a family with River once she saw the other side of him. She was by no means too old to start a family except that the pain was still too raw from dealing with a divorce. The dream she'd once had of a husband and kids was the furthest thing from her thoughts as she literally ran for her life. She still felt the bitter betrayal of discovering that the person she'd trusted had turned out to be a monster.

It had taken her years to extract herself from him. Now she'd be damned if she let that man break her. Her definition of happiness had changed sometime in the last few years. She couldn't pinpoint the exact moment her opinion had shifted. Rather than a husband and kids, all she now wanted was a small plot of land, a cozy home and maybe a couple of dogs.

"Are you okay?" His voice brought her back to the present.

"Yes. Your home is beautiful, Colton," she said again.

Now it was his turn to be embarrassed. His cheeks flamed and it was sexy on him.

"I can't take the credit for the decorating. That was my mother." Not his wife? Why did hearing those words send more of those butterflies flittering around in her chest again?

"She did an amazing job. The colors are incredible." There were large-scale art pieces hanging on the walls in the most beautiful teal colors, cream and beige. The woman had decorating skills. The best part was how the place matched Colton's personality to a T. Strong, solid and calm. He was the calm in the storm. It was just his nature.

She took a few more steps inside with his help.

"Can I ask a personal question?" she asked.

He nodded.

"Didn't your wife want to decorate?"

"She's never been here." She felt a wall go up when it came to that subject.

"How about we get you settled on the couch and I get working on that cup of coffee?" he asked, changing the subject. His tone said, case closed.

"Are you kidding me right now? That sounds like heaven." She gripped his arm a little tighter and felt nothing but solid muscle.

He helped her to the couch before moving over to the fireplace wall and flipping a switch that turned it on. There were blue crystals that the fire danced on top of. It was mesmerizing.

She tried to keep her jaw from dropping on the carpet at the sheer beauty of the place. It was selfish, but she liked the fact that he'd only lived here as a bachelor, which was weird because it wasn't like she and Colton had ever dated, despite the signals he'd sent back in the bio lab. She had probably even misread that situation, because he'd never asked her out. The semester had ended and that was that.

Makena again wanted to express to Colton how sorry she was for the loss of his wife. Considering he had one-year-old twins, his wife couldn't have died all that long ago. The emotional scars were probably still very raw.

"If you want to get out of those wet clothes, I can probably find something dry for you to wear for the time being." He seemed to realize how that might sound, because he put his hands up in the air. "I just mean that I have a spare bathrobe of mine you can wear while I throw your clothes through the wash."

She couldn't help herself. She smiled at him. And chuckled just a little bit. "I didn't take it the wrong way and that would be fantastic. Dry clothes and coffee? I'm pretty certain at this point you've reached angel status in my book."

He caught her stare for just a moment. "I can assure you I will never be accused of being an angel."

A thrill of awareness skittered across her skin. A nervous laugh escaped because she hoped that she wasn't giving away her body's reaction to him. "I wouldn't accuse you of that, but I do remember what a good person you are. I wouldn't be here alone with you right now otherwise."

She surprised herself with the comment as he fired off a wink. He motioned toward an adjacent room before disappearing there. He returned a few moments later with a big white plush bathrobe that had some fancy hotel's name embroidered on the left-hand side.

Colton held out the robe. When she took it, their fingers grazed. Big mistake. More of that inconvenient attraction surged. She felt her cheeks flush as warmth traveled through her.

He cleared his throat and said, "I'll go make that coffee now. You can change in here. I promise not to look."

Again, those words shouldn't cause her chest to deflate. She should be grateful, and she was, on some level, that she could trust him not to look when she changed. Was it wrong that she wanted him to at least consider it?

Now she really was being punchy.

Makena took in a deep breath and then slowly exhaled. Colton made a show of turning his back to her and walking toward the kitchen. Despite pain shooting through her with every movement, she slipped out of her clothes and into the bathrobe while seated on the couch. The wreck could've been a whole lot worse, she thought as she managed to slip out of her soaked clothing and then ball it all up along with her undergarments, careful to keep the last part tucked in the center of the wad of clothing.

"Do you still take your coffee with a little bit of sugar and cream?"

"Yes. How did you remember after all this time?"

He mumbled something about having a good memory. Was it wrong to hope that it was a bit more than that? That maybe she'd been somewhat special to Colton? Special enough for him to remember the little things about her, like the fact she took her coffee with cream and sugar?

Logic said yes, but her heart went the opposite route.

Chapter Five

"I'm surprised you don't live on the ranch." Makena watched as Colton crossed the room. He walked with athletic grace. If it was at all possible, he was even hotter than he'd been in college. He'd cornered the market on that whole granite jawline, strong nose and piercing cobalt blue eyes look. Based on the ripples on his chest and arms, he was no stranger to working hard or hitting the gym. His jeans fit snug on lean hips.

"I have a place there where I spend time with the boys on my days off." He handed over a fresh cup of warm coffee. She took it with both hands and immediately took a sip.

"Mmm. This is quite possibly the best cup of coffee I've ever had."

Colton laughed and took a seat on the opposite couch. He toed off his boots and shook his head, which sent water flying everywhere. He raked his free hand through his hair. He was good-looking in that casual, effortless way. "I got this apartment so I could be closer to my office, after…"

The way his voice trailed off made her think he was going to tell her more about his wife. He shook his head again and recovered with a smile that was a little too forced. He took a sip of coffee. "You don't want to hear my sad story."

Before she could respond, he checked his phone.

"I do, actually," she said softly, but he didn't seem to hear. Strangely, she wanted to hear all about what had happened to him since college. Even then, he'd been too serious for a nineteen-year-old. He'd seemed like he carried the weight of the world on his shoulders. His eyes had always been a little too intense, but when they'd been focused on her they'd caused her body to hum with need—a need she'd been too inexperienced to understand at the time.

He picked up the remote and clicked a button, causing one of the paintings to turn into a massive TV screen. Makena had known his family was successful, but she had no idea they had the kind of money that made TVs appear out of artworks on the wall.

Color her impressed.

It was a shock for many reasons, not the least of which was the fact that Colton was one of the most down-to-earth people she'd ever met. She was vaguely aware of the O'Connor name, having grown up in Texas herself. But being a big-city girl, she had never really been part of the ranching community and had no idea until she'd seen an article about his family years ago. That had been her first hint that they might be wealthier than she'd realized.

Makena had had the opposite kind of childhood. She'd been brought up by a single mother who'd made plenty of sacrifices so that Makena could go to college without having to go into massive debt. And then a couple of years into Makena's marriage with River, long after the shine had worn off and she realized there was no other choice but to get out, her beloved mother had become sick.

Leaving her husband was no longer the number one priority. Her mother had taken precedence over everything else, despite River's protests that helping her ill mother took up too much of her time. He'd had similar complaints about her work, but her job had kept her sanity in check while she watched the woman she loved, the woman whose sacrifices were great, dwindle into nothingness.

Makena reached up and ran her finger along the rose gold flower necklace she wore—a final gift from her mother.

Despite River's protests, Makena remained firm. But with a sick mother who needed almost round-the-clock care in her final months, Makena had been in no position to disappear. And she'd known that was exactly what she had to do, when she walked away from River after his threats.

When Makena looked up, she realized that Colton had been studying her.

"What's his name?" he asked. Those three words slammed into her. They were so on point it took her back for a second.

She opened her mouth to protest the question, but Colton waved her off before she could get a word out.

"Makena, you don't have to tell me his name. I'll leave that up to you. Just don't lie to me about him existing at all."

Well, now she really felt bad. She sat there for a long moment and contemplated her next move. Having lived alone for six months after losing her mother, barely saying a word to anyone and focusing on the basest level of survival, she now wanted to open up to someone.

She just wanted to be honest with someone and with herself for a change.

"River."

She didn't look up at Colton right then. She wouldn't be able to bear a look of pity. She didn't want him to feel sorry for her. It was her mistake. She'd made it. She'd owned it. She would've moved on a long time ago if it hadn't been for her mother's illness.

"Was he abusive? Did he lay a hand on you?" The seriousness and calmness in Colton's tone didn't convey pity at all. It sounded more like compassion and understanding. Two words that were so foreign to her when it came to her relationship with a man.

"No." She risked a glance at him. "He would've. We started off with arguments that escalated. He always took it too far. He'd say the most hurtful things meant to cut me to the quick. I didn't grow up with a father in the house. So I didn't know how abnormal that was in a relationship."

"No one should have to." There was no judgment in his voice but there was anger.

"Things escalated pretty badly, and one day when we were arguing I stomped into the bedroom. He followed and when I wouldn't stop, he grabbed my wrist like he was a vise on the tightest notch. He whirled me around so hard that the back of my head smacked against the wall. I was too prideful to let him know how much it hurt. It wasn't intentional on his part. Not that part. But he immediately balled his fist and reared it back."

Makena had to breathe slowly in order to continue. Her heart raced at hearing the words spoken aloud that she'd bottled up for so long. Panic tightened her chest.

"What did you do to stop him from hitting you?" Colton's jaw muscle clenched.

"I looked him dead in the eyes, refusing to buckle or let him know that I was afraid. And then I told him to go ahead and do it. Hit me. But I cautioned him with this. I told him that if he did throw that punch he'd better sleep with one eye open for the rest of his life because we had a fireplace with a fireplace poker and I told him that he would wake up one morning to find it buried right in between his eyes."

A small smile ghosted Colton's lips. "Good for you. I bet he thought twice about ever putting a hand on you again."

"Honestly, I don't think I could ever hurt another human being unless my life depended on it. But I needed him to believe every word of that. And he did. That was the first and last time he raised a fist to me. But his words were worse in some ways. They cut deep and he tried to keep a tight rein on who I saw and where I went."

"Can I ask you a question?"

"Go ahead." She'd shared a lot more about her situation than she'd ever thought she would with anyone. Part of her needed to talk about it with someone. She'd never told her mom because she didn't want her to worry.

"Why did you stay?"

"My mom. She was sick for a couple of years and then she passed away." Makena paused long enough to catch her breath. She tucked her chin to her chest so he wouldn't see the tears welling in her eyes. "That's when I left him. Before that, honestly, she needed me to be stable for her. She needed someone to take care of her and she needed to stay with the same doctors. I couldn't relocate her." Makena decided not to share the rest of that story. And especially not the part where River had threatened her life if she ever left him. He seemed to catch onto the fact that she'd at the very least been thinking about leaving.

But Makena didn't want to think about that anymore, and she sure as hell didn't want to talk about herself. She'd done enough of that for one night. She picked up her coffee and took a sip before turning the tables.

Catching Colton's gaze, she asked, "How about you? Tell me about your wife."

"There isn't much to tell. Rebecca and I were best friends. She lived across the street and we grew up together. Her father is the mayor. We dated in high school and broke up to go to different colleges. Her older sister had married her high school sweetheart and the relationship fell apart in college, so Rebecca was concerned the same thing would happen to us."

"And what did you think?"

"That I was ready for a break. I looked at our relationship a lot like most people look at religion. When someone grows up in a certain church, it's all they know. Part of growing up and becoming independent is testing different waters and making certain it's the right thing for you and not just what's ingrained. You know?"

"Makes a lot of sense to me." She nodded.

"Before I committed the rest of my life to someone, I wanted to make damn sure I was making the right call and not acting out of habit. That's what the break meant to me."

"Since the two of you married, I'm guessing you realized she was the one." Why did that make Makena's heart hurt?

"You could say that. I guess I figured there were worse things than marrying my best friend."

Makena picked up on the fact that he hadn't described Rebecca as the love of his life or the woman he wanted to spend the rest of his life with, or said the two of them had realized they were perfect for each other.

"We got married and the twins came soon after. And then almost immediately after, she was hit by a drunk driver on the highway coming home from visiting her sister in Austin. She died instantly. I'd kept the twins home with me that day to give her a break."

"I'm so sorry, Colton."

"I rented this apartment after not really wanting to live on the ranch in our home. The place just seemed so empty without her. I go there on my days off with the twins because we still have pictures of her hanging up there and I want the twins to have some memories of growing up in a house surrounded by their mother's things."

"Being a single dad must be hard. You seem like

you're doing a really great job with your boys. I bet she'd be really proud of you."

"It really means a lot to hear you say that. I'd like to think she would be proud. I want to make her proud. She deserved that." A storm brewed behind his eyes when he spoke about his wife.

"How long were the two of you married?" Makena asked, wanting to know more about his life after college.

"We got married after she told me that she was pregnant."

Was that the reason he'd said he could've done worse than marrying his best friend? Had she gotten pregnant and they'd married? Asking him seemed too personal. If he wanted her to know, he probably would've told her by now. The questions seemed off-limits even though they'd both shared more than either of them had probably set out to at the beginning of this conversation.

Despite the boost of caffeine, Makena had never felt more tired. It was probably the rain, which had settled into a steady, driving rhythm, coupled with the fact that she hadn't really slept since almost running into the pair of men she'd seen with River, not to mention she'd been clipped by an SUV. She bit back another yawn and tried to rally.

"Losing her must've been hard for you, Colton. I couldn't be sorrier that happened. You deserve so much more. You deserved a life together."

COLTON HADN'T EXPECTED to talk so much about Rebecca. Words couldn't describe how much he missed his best friend. There was something about telling their story that eased some of the pain in his chest. He was coming up on a year without her in a few days. And even though theirs hadn't been an epic love that made his heart race every time she was near, it had been built on friendship. He could've done a lot worse.

Being with Makena had woken up his heart and stirred feelings in him that he'd thought were long since dead. In fact, he hadn't felt this way since meeting her sophomore year. He'd known something different was up the minute he'd seen Makena. Rebecca had texted him that day to see how he was doing and it was the first time he hadn't responded right away.

Rebecca had picked up on the reason. Hell, there were times when he could've sworn she knew him better than he knew himself.

Being here, with Makena, felt right on so many levels. It eased some of the ache of losing his best friend. Not that his feelings for Makena were anything like his marriage to Rebecca. He and Rebecca were about shared history, loyalty and a promise to have each other's back until the very end.

Colton felt a lot of pride in following through on his promise. He'd had Rebecca's back. He'd always have her back. And in bringing up the twins, he was given an opportunity to prove his loyalty to his best friend every day. Those boys looked like their mother and reminded him of her in so many ways. A piece of her, a very large piece, would always be with him.

He reminded himself of the fact every day.

Right now, his focus was on making certain the residents in his county were safe and that fearful look that showed up on Makena's face every once in a while for the briefest moment subsided. She'd opened up to him about living with a verbally abusive ex. Colton had a lot of experience with domestic situations. More than he cared to. He'd seen firsthand the collateral damage from relationships that became abusive and felt boiling hot anger run through his veins.

He flexed and released his fingers to try to ease out some of the tension building in him at the thought of Makena in a similar predicament. He'd also witnessed the hold an abusive spouse could have over the other person. Men tended to be the more physically aggressive, although there were times when he saw abuse the other way around. Women tended to use verbal assaults to break a partner down. He'd seen that, too. Except that the law didn't provide for abuse that couldn't be seen.

Texas law protected against bruises and bloody noses, ignoring the fact that verbal abuse could rank right up there in damage. The mental toll was enormous. Studying Makena now and knowing what she'd been like in the past, he couldn't imagine her living like that.

"How long were you married?" he asked.

"Nine years." The shock of that sat with him for a long minute as he took another sip of fresh brew.

"Was your mother the only reason you stayed?" he asked.

"Honestly?"

He nodded.

"Yes. She got sick and couldn't seem to shake it. I took her to a doctor and then a specialist, and then another specialist. By the time they figured out what was wrong with her, she had a stroke. It was too late to save her." She ran her finger along the rim of her coffee cup.

The look of loss on Makena's face when she spoke about her mother was a gut punch. She didn't have that same look when she talked about her ex. With him, there was sometimes a flash of fear and most definitely defiance. Her chin would jut out and resolve would darken her features.

"I miss her every day," she admitted.

Since the words *I'm sorry* seemed to fall short, he set his coffee down and pushed up to standing. He took the couple of steps to the other couch and sat beside her. Taking her hand in his, he hoped to convey his sympathy for the loss of her mother.

"She's the reason that I got to go to college. She,

and a very determined college counselor. It was just me and my mom for so long. She sacrificed everything for me."

"Your mother sounds like an incredible person."

"She was." Makena ducked her head down, chin to chest, and he realized she was hiding the fact that a tear had rolled down her face.

"I can imagine how difficult it was for her to bring you up alone. There are days when I feel like my butt is being kicked bringing up my boys. Without my family by my side, I don't even see how it's possible to do it. I don't know what I'd do without my tribe and their help."

"Whoever said it takes a village to bring up a child was right. We just had two people in ours and it was always just kind of us against the world. It wasn't all bad. I mean, I didn't even realize how many sacrifices my mom made for me until I was grown and had my first real job out of college. Then I started realizing how expensive things were and how much she covered. I saw what it took to get by financially. She didn't have a college education and insisted that I get one. She worked long hours to make sure that it could happen without me going into a ridiculous amount of debt. I never told her when I had to take out student loans because I wanted her to feel like she was able to do it all."

"It sounds like you gave her a remarkable gift. Again, I can only compare it to my boys but I also know that I want to give them the world just like I'm sure your mom wanted to with you. The fact that she was able to do as much as she did with very little resources and no support is nothing short of a miracle. It blows me away."

He paused long enough for her to lift her gaze up to meet his, and when it did, that jolt of electricity coursed through him.

"It's easy to see where you get your strength from now." Colton was rewarded with a smile that sent warmth spiraling through him before zeroing in on his heart.

"Colton…" Whatever Makena was about to say seemed to die on her lips.

"For what it's worth, you deserve better, with what you got from your marriage and the loss of your mother so young," he said.

She squeezed his arm in a move that was probably meant to be reassuring but sent another charge jolting through him, lighting up his senses and making him even more aware of her. This close, he breathed in her unique scent, roses in spring. The mood changed from sadness and sharing to awareness—awareness of her pulse pounding at the base of her throat, awareness of the chemistry that was impossible to ignore.

He reached up and brushed the backs of his fingers against her cheek and then her jawline. She took hold of his forearm and then pulled him closer, their gazes locked the entire time.

When she tugged him so close, their lips were inches apart, and his tongue darted across his lips. He could only imagine how incredible she would taste. A moment of caution settled over him as his pulse skyrocketed. His caution had nothing to do with how badly he wanted to close the distance between them and everything to do with a stab of guilt. It was impossible not to feel like he was betraying Rebecca in some small measure, especially since his feelings for Makena were a runaway train.

He reminded himself that his wife was gone and had been for almost a year. It was a long time since he'd been with someone other than her, and that would mess with anyone's mind. Not to mention the fact he hadn't felt this strong an attraction to anyone. In fact, the last time he had was with the woman whose lips were inches from his.

Makena brought her hands up to touch his face, silently urging him to close that gap.

Colton closed his eyes and breathed in her flowery scent. He leaned forward and pressed his lips to hers. Hers were delicate and soft despite the fiery and confident woman behind them.

All logic and reason flew out the window the second their mouths fused. He drove the tip of his tongue inside her mouth. She tasted like sweet coffee. Normally, he took his black. Sweet was his new favorite flavor.

Makena moved toward him and broke into the moment with a wince. She pulled back. "Sorry."

"Don't be." He wanted to offer more reassurance than that but couldn't find the right words. Either way, this was just the shot of reality that he needed before he let things get out of hand. Doing any of this with her right now was the worst of bad ideas.

They were two broken souls connecting and that was it. So why did the sentiment feel hollow? Why did his mind try to argue the opposite? Why did it insist these feelings were very real? The attraction was different? And it was still very much alive between them?

"I'm sorry if I hurt you," he finally said.

"You couldn't have. It was my fault. I got a little carried away." Her breathing was raspy, much like his own.

He'd never experienced going from zero to one hundred miles an hour from what started as a slow burn. Don't get him wrong, he'd experienced great sex. This was somehow different. The draw toward Makena was sun to earth.

Colton was certain of one thing. Sex with Makena would be mind-blowing and a game changer. With her hip in the condition it was, there was no threat it was going to happen anytime soon. That shouldn't make his chest deflate like someone had just let the air out of a balloon. He chalked it up to the lack of sex in his life and, even more than that, the lack of companionship.

This was the first time he realized how much he missed having someone to talk to when he walked in the door at night. Having the twins was amazing but one-year-olds weren't exactly known for their conversation skills.

Colton took the interruption from the hip pain as a sign he was headed down the wrong path. Granted, it didn't feel misguided, and nothing inside him wanted to stop, but doing anything to cause her more pain was out of the question.

A voice in the back of his mind picked that time to remind him of the fact he'd struck her with his vehicle. He was the reason she was in pain in the first place.

The idea that she'd been adamant about not filing a report crept into his thoughts. As much as she'd insisted not doing so was for his benefit, he'd quickly ascertained that she didn't want her name attached to a report. Colton had already put two and two together and guessed she was hiding out from her ex. But living in a random trailer and hiding her name meant her situation was more complicated than he'd first realized. No matter what else, this was a good time to take a break and regroup.

"I'm sorry. That whole kissing thing was my fault. I don't know what came over me." Makena's cheeks flushed with embarrassment and that only poured gasoline onto the fire of attraction burning in him.

"Last I checked, I was a pretty willing participant." He winked and she smiled. He hadn't meant to make her feel bad by regrouping. In fact, the last thing he wanted to do was add to her stress. Based on what she'd shared so far, her marriage had done very little to lift her up and inspire confidence.

Was it wrong that he wanted to be the person who did that for her?

Chapter Six

Embarrassment didn't begin to cover the emotion Makena should be feeling after practically throwing herself at Colton. It was impossible to regret her actions, though. She hadn't been so thoroughly kissed by any man in her entire life. That was a sad statement considering she'd been married, but wow, Colton could kiss. He brought parts of her to life that had been dormant for so long she'd forgotten they existed.

She wanted to chalk up the thrill of the kiss to the fact that it had been more than a decade in the making, but that would sell it short. He'd barely dipped the tip of his tongue in her mouth and yet it was the most erotic kiss she'd ever experienced. She could only imagine what it would feel like to take the next step with him.

And since those thoughts were about as productive as spending all her paycheck on a pair of shoes, she shelved them. For now, at least.

Makena blew out an awkward breath. Yes, dwelling on their attraction was off the table, because not only was it futile, but there was no way she could compete with a ghost. Colton had said so himself. He'd married his best friend. His beloved wife had died shortly after giving birth to their twins and making a family.

Despite the fact that he hadn't described his relationship with his wife as anything other than a deep friendship, it would be impossible to stack up to that level of love.

Colton's gaze darted to his coffee cup. "Mine's empty. How are you on a refill?"

"I'm good. I think I've had enough." She bit back a yawn. "If it's okay, I'd like to just curl up here and rest my eyes for a few minutes."

"Make yourself at home." Colton stood. The couch felt immediately cold to her, after his warmth from a few moments ago. He scooped up his coffee mug and headed toward the kitchen. She could've sworn she heard him mumble phrases like "another time and place and things might be different," and "bad timing." She couldn't be certain. It might've just been wishful thinking on her part to believe there was something real going on between them.

An awkward laugh escaped. She'd never been the type to latch onto someone, but then this wasn't just anyone. Was she seriously that lonely?

This was Colton O'Connor and they shared history. And based on the enthusiasm in his kiss, an attraction that hadn't completely run its course.

Makena counted herself lucky that embarrassment couldn't kill a person. Actually, maybe it wasn't embarrassment she felt. Maybe it was that strong attraction that caused her cheeks to heat. When she really thought about it, she hadn't done anything to be embarrassed about.

The past six months, being alone, had done a number on her mindset. That was certain. But it hadn't knocked her out. And it wouldn't. She would get through this, rebound and pick her life up again. A life that seemed a little bit colder now that she'd been around warmth again.

Makena figured it was too much to hope that she'd find her feet rooted in the real world again. And real world started with a few basics. "Hey, Colton. Any chance you have a spare toothbrush and a washcloth I could use?"

Her clothes were in the dryer, so she might as well go all in wishing for a real shower rather than a bowl of warm soapy water by the river like she'd done the past few days at the RV.

"Like I said, make yourself at home." He tilted his head toward the hallway where he'd disappeared earlier to bring her the robe. "You'll find a full bathroom in there. Spare toothbrushes are still in the wrappers in the cabinet."

With some effort, Makena was able to stand.

Colton turned around and a look of shock stamped his features.

"Hold on there. I can help you get to the bathroom."

"It still hurts, I'm not going to lie. But it's not as bad as it was an hour ago. I'd like to see if I can make it myself." She wasn't exactly fast and couldn't outrun an ant, but she was proud of the fact that she made it to the bathroom on her own. She closed the toilet seat, folded a towel and paused a moment to catch her breath. It was progress and she'd take it.

As she sat in the bathroom waiting for the pain in her hip to subside, she couldn't help but inhale a deep breath, filling her senses with Colton's scent. The bathrobe she wore smelled like him, all campfire and outdoors and spice. It was masculine and everything she'd remembered about sitting next to him in biology lab. His scent was all over the robe.

She needed to get her head on straight and refocus. Thinking much more about Colton and how amazing and masculine he smelled wasn't going to help her come up with a plan of what to do next.

It would probably be best for all concerned if she could put Colton out of her head altogether. She appreciated his help, though.

Taking another deep breath, Makena reached over and turned on the water. Using the one-step-at-a-time method, she peeled off the bathrobe and then took baby steps until she was standing in the massive shower. She had no idea what materials actually were used, but the entire shower enclosure looked like it was made of white marble. There were two showerheads. The place was obviously meant for a couple to be able to shower together. However, a half dozen people would fit inside there at the very least.

Now that really made Makena laugh. Images of single father and town sheriff Colton in a wild shower party with a half dozen people didn't really fit well together.

They tickled her anyway.

And maybe she was just that giddy. Exhaustion started wearing her thin, and her nerves, nerves that had been fried for a solid year and really longer than that if she thought back, eased with being around Colton.

The soap might smell clean and a little spicy, but it was the warm water that got her. Amazing didn't begin to cover it. She showered as quickly as possible, though, not wanting to keep too much pressure on that hip. Her left side bit back with pain any time she put pressure on it.

After toweling off and slipping back into the robe, she brushed her teeth. She had a toothbrush at the RV, in the small bag of shower supplies she kept with her at all times while on the move. But this was a luxury. It was crazy how the simple things felt so good after being deprived. Simple things like a real shower and a real bathroom.

Speaking of which, the cup of coffee that she'd had a little while ago had been in a league of its own.

Makena reminded herself not to get too comfortable here. It was dangerous to let her guard down or stick around longer than absolutely necessary. Being in one place for too long was a hazard, made more so by the fact her identity could be so easily revealed by Colton.

She tightened the tie on the bathrobe before exiting the bathroom and making her way back into the living room. She might move slow, but this was progress. If she could rest that hip for a couple of hours and let the worst of the storm pass, she could get back to the RV and then…go where?

Thinking about her next step was her new priority. She'd been so focused on surviving one hour at a time that she'd forgotten there was a big picture—an end game that had her collecting evidence against her ex. Time had run out for her in Katy Gulch.

Inside the living room, Colton was in mission control mode. He was so deep in thought with what was going on and talking into his radio that he didn't even seem to hear her when she walked into the room.

Rather than disturb him, she moved as stealthily as possible, reclaiming her spot opposite him on the couch. He glanced up and another shot of warmth rocketed through her body, settling low in her stomach. Colton's deep, masculine voice spoke in hushed tones as she curled up on her side on the sofa. He almost immediately shifted the laptop off his lap and grabbed the blanket draped on the back of the sofa.

He walked over and placed it over her before offering her an extra throw pillow. She took it, laid her head on it and closed her eyes.

With all the stress that had been building the six months and especially in the past couple of days since she thought she'd seen River's associates, there was no way she could sleep.

Resting her eyes felt good. That was the last thought she had before she must've passed out.

Makena woke with a start. She immediately pushed up to sit and glanced around, trying to get her bearings. Her left hip screamed at her with movement, so she eased pressure from it, shifting to the right side instead.

Daylight streamed through the large windows in the loft-style apartment. She rubbed blurry eyes and yawned.

Looking around, she searched for any signs of Colton as the memory of last night became more focused. She strained to listen for him and was pretty sure she heard the shower going in the other room. The image of a naked, muscled Colton standing in the same shower she'd showered in just a few hours ago probably wasn't the best start to her morning. Or it was. Depending on how she looked at it. Makena chuckled nervously.

The events from the past twelve hours or so came back to her, bringing down her mood. She opened up the robe to examine her hip on the left side. Sure enough, a bruise the size of a bowling ball stared back at her. Pain had reminded her it was there before she'd even looked.

Movement hurt. She sucked in a breath and pushed past the soreness and pain as she closed her robe and stood. Then she remembered that Colton had some of the best coffee she'd ever tasted. Since he'd instructed her to make herself at home, she figured he wouldn't mind if she made a cup.

Her stomach growled despite the sandwich, apple and soup he'd given her. She glanced at the clock. That had been a solid ten hours ago. How had she slept so long?

Makena hadn't had that much sleep at one time in the past year. Of that she was certain. She cautioned herself against getting too comfortable around Colton. She'd already let way too much slip about her personal life, not that it hadn't felt good to finally open up to someone she trusted and talk about her mother and other parts of her life. It had. But it was also dangerous.

A part of her wanted to resurface just to see if River had let his anger toward her go by now. If he'd let *her* go by now. Being on the run, hiding out, had always made her feel like she'd done something wrong, not the other way around.

Standing up to fight a Dallas police officer who ran in a circle just like him could wreak complete havoc on her life, so she had erred on the side of caution.

But should she start over now, after she'd found Colton again? There was something almost thrilling about seeing him, about finding a piece of herself that had been alive before she'd lost her mother... before River.

If Makena was being completely honest with herself, she could admit that part of her disappearing act had to do with wanting to shut out the world after losing her mother. She'd succumbed to grief and allowed fear to override rational thought.

But where to start over? Dallas was out. Houston was a couple hours' drive away. Maybe she could make a life there? Get back to teaching music. It was worth a shot.

Living like she had been over the past few months, although necessary, wasn't really being alive.

Makena saw a coffee machine sitting on a countertop. It was easy to spot in the neat kitchen. There were drawers next to it and so she went ahead and made the wild assumption that she'd find coffee in one of them.

She didn't. But she did find some in the cupboard above. It was the pod kind. She helped herself to one that said Regular Coffee and placed it in the fancy-looking steel machine. She glanced to the side and saw a plastic carafe already filled with water.

There was only one button, so that was easy. The round metal button made the machine come to life. It was then that she realized she hadn't put a coffee cup underneath the spout.

"Oh no. Where are you?" She opened a couple of cupboards until she found the one that housed the mugs. She grabbed one and placed it under the spout just in time for the first droplets of brown liquid to sputter out. "Good save." She mumbled the words out loud and, for the second time since opening her eyes, chuckled.

Her lighter mood had everything to do with being around Colton again. The kiss they'd shared had left the memory of his taste on her lips. And even though their relationship couldn't go anywhere, the attraction between them was a nice change of pace from what she usually felt around men. After being with River, she'd become uneasy interacting with the opposite sex.

Makena slowly made her way to the fridge. Quick movement hurt. Walking hurt. But she was doing it and was certain she could push through the pain.

In the fridge, she found cups of her favorite thing in the world, vanilla yogurt. She took one and managed to find a spoon. She polished it off before the coffee could stop dripping.

The carton of eggs was tempting, but she needed

to take it easy on the hip. Standing in front of the stove was probably not the best idea. The yogurt would hold her over until she could rest enough to gather the energy to find something else to eat or cook.

Cup of coffee in hand, she slowly made her way to one of the chairs at the granite island. It would be too much to ask for sugar and cream at this hour, especially with the amount of pain she was in. She hadn't asked for ibuprofen last night, not wanting to mask her injury. Today, however, she realized the injury was superficial and she would ask for a couple of pain relievers once Colton returned from the shower.

Speaking of which, she was pretty certain the water spigot had been turned off for a while now.

Nothing could have quite prepared her for the sight of Colton O'Connor when he waltzed into the room wearing nothing but a towel. The white cloth was wrapped around lean hips and tucked into one side.

"Good morning." The low timbre of his voice traveled all over her body, bringing a ripple of awareness.

"Morning to you." She diverted her gaze from the tiny droplets of water rolling down his muscled chest.

"I see you managed to find a cup of coffee. It's good to see you up and around. How's that hip today?" His smile—a show of perfectly straight, white teeth—made him devastatingly hot.

"It's better. I managed the coffee minus the cream." She decided it was best to redirect the conversation away from her injury. "This coffee is amazing straight out of the pot. Or whatever that thing is." She motioned toward the stainless-steel appliance.

Colton's eyebrow shot up and a small smile crossed his lips—lips she had no business staring at, but they were a distraction all the same.

"You want cream and sugar?"

"It's really no big deal." She'd barely finished her protest when Colton moved over to the fridge and came back with cream that he set on the counter in front of her. He located sugar next and tossed a few packets in her direction.

She thanked him.

"You seemed pretty busy last night. Is everyone okay?" she asked.

"The storm was all bark and no bite thankfully. Roads were messy, but folks respected Mother Nature and she backed off without any casualties."

"That's lucky," she said.

"There were a few close calls with stranded vehicles. Nothing I could get to, but my deputies could."

"That's a relief." She took a sip of coffee and groaned. "This is so good."

He shot her a look before shaking his head. "That's a nice sound. But not one I need in my head all day and especially not after…never mind."

The words on the tip of his tongue had to be *that kiss*. She'd thought the same thing when she saw him half-naked in the kitchen.

"I can't remember the last time I slept as well as I did last night." She stretched her arms out.

"If you slept that well on the couch, imagine what it would be like in a real bed." He seemed to hear those words as they came out and shot her a look that said he wanted to reel them back in.

The image that had popped into her thoughts was one of her in bed with him. Considering he still stood there in a towel, she needed to wipe all those thoughts from her head.

Seeing him again was making a difference in her mood and her outlook. Somewhere in the past six months after losing her mother, she'd given up a little bit on life. Looking back, she could see that so clearly now.

This morning, she felt a new lease on life and was ready to start making plans for a future. She hadn't felt like she would have one, in so long.

She took another sip of coffee. "I know that I said last night was the best cup of coffee I'd had in a long time, but this beats it."

He practically beamed with pride. "Are you hungry?"

"I already helped myself to yogurt. I hope that's okay."

"Of course it is. I make a pretty mean spinach omelet if you're game."

The man was the definition of hotness. He cared about others, hence his job as sheriff. And now he decided to tell her that he could cook?

"You're not playing fair," she teased. "I really don't want you to go to any trouble."

"If it makes you feel any better, I plan to make some for myself. No bacon, though. I'm out."

"Well, in that case, forget it. What kind of house runs out of bacon?" She laughed at her own joke and was relieved when he did, too. It was nice to be around someone who was so easy to be with. Conversation was light. This was exactly what she remembered about biology lab and why she'd been so attracted to him all those years ago. Sure, he was basically billboard material on the outside, with those features she could stare at all day. But how many people did she know who were good-looking on the outside and empty shells on the inside? A conversation with a ten on the outside and a three on substance made her want to fall asleep thinking about it.

Physical attraction was nice. It was one thing. It was important. But she'd learned a long time ago that someone's intelligence, sense of humor and wit could sway their looks one way or the other for her.

On a scale of one to ten, Colton was a thirty-five in every area.

Chapter Seven

Colton whipped up a pair of omelets and threw a couple slices of bread into the toaster while Makena finished up her cup of coffee at the granite island.

"Is there any chance I can have some pain reliever?" she asked.

"I have a bottle right here." He moved to the cabinet at the end of the counter. Medicine was kept on the top shelf even though his sons had only just taken their first steps recently. "Ibuprofen okay?"

"It's the only thing I take and that's rare."

"Same here." He grabbed a couple of tablets and then put a plate of food in front of her. "You probably want to eat that first. Ibuprofen on an empty stomach is not good."

She nodded and smiled at the plate. Tension still tightened the muscles of her face but sometime in the past twelve hours they'd been together, she'd relaxed just a bit. Given her history with men, it was wonderful that she could be this comfortable

around him so quickly, and Colton let his chest fill
with pride at that, although her ease was tentative,
as he could tell from her eyes.

"Are you serious about these eggs?" She made a
show of appreciating them after taking another bite.

Colton laughed. He realized it had been a really
long time since he'd laughed this much. The roller
coaster he'd been on since losing Rebecca and then
his father had been awful to say the least.

To say that Colton hadn't had a whole lot to smile
about recently was a lot like saying The New Texas
Giant was just a roller coaster.

The exception was his twin boys. When he was
with them, he did his level best to set everything else
aside and just be with them. He might only have an
hour or so to play with them before nighttime routine kicked in, but he treasured every moment of
it. The last year had taught him that kids grew up
way too fast.

"I'm glad you like the eggs."

"*Like* is too weak a word for how I feel about this
omelet." Her words broke into more of that thick,
heavy fog that had filled his chest for too long.

"The roads are clearing up. After you eat, I should
make a few rounds."

"Can you give me a ride to the RV?" she asked.

"Happy to oblige," he teased. "I just need to get
dressed."

Her cheeks flushed and he wondered if it had

anything to do with the fact that he was still in a towel. A rumble of a laugh started inside his chest and rolled out. "I just realized that I'm walking about like I don't have company. Pardon me. I'll just go get dressed now."

"Well, it hasn't exactly been hard on the eyes." Now it was her turn to burst out laughing. "I can't believe I just said that out loud."

He excused himself and headed into his bedroom, where he threw on a pair of boxers, jeans and a dark, collared button-down shirt. He pulled his belt from the safe and clipped it on. It held his badge and gun.

Colton located one of his navy windbreakers that had the word *SHERIFF* written in bright, bold letters down the left sleeve. He finger-combed his hair and was ready to go. Walking out into the living room and seeing Makena still sitting there in his robe was a punch to the chest.

"I'll go and grab your clothes from the dryer." His offer was met with a smile.

"I can go with you. Or you could just point me in a direction. I think I can find my way around," she said.

"Down the hall. Open the door in the bathroom. You probably thought it was a closet, but it's actually a laundry room."

"That's really convenient." She tightened her grip on her robe and disappeared down the hallway.

He was relieved to see that her hip seemed in better condition today. She was barely walking with a limp. Even so, he wondered if he could talk her into making a trip to the ER for an X-ray.

Ten minutes later, she emerged from the hallway. She'd brushed her hair and dressed in the jeans and blouse she'd had on yesterday. "Ready?"

"Are the pain pills kicking in yet?" he asked.

"It's actually much better. I mean, I have a pretty big bruise, but overall, I'm in good shape. The ibuprofen is already helping. I won't be riding any bucking broncos in the next few days, but it'll heal up fine."

"I like the fact that you're walking more easily, but I would feel a whole lot better if we stopped off at the county hospital to get it checked out. The roads are clear on that route." He hoped she'd listen to reason.

She opened her mouth to protest, but he put his hand up to stop her.

"Hear me out. You won't have to pay for the cost of the X-ray. It's the least I can do considering the fact that I hit you."

"Technically, I ran out in front of your car and you didn't have enough time to stop. You also couldn't see me because of the rain. So, technically, I hit you."

Well, Colton really did laugh out loud now. That was a new one and he thought he'd heard just about every line imaginable in his profession. He couldn't help himself, and chuckled again. It was a sign she was winning him over, and he didn't normally give away his tells.

"I'm glad you're laughing, because you could be writing me up right now or arresting me for striking an official vehicle. Does that count as striking an officer?" She seemed pretty pleased with that last comment.

"All right. You got me. I laughed. It was funny. But what wouldn't be funny is if there's something seriously wrong with your hip and it got worse because we didn't get it checked out." Was it him or had he just turned into his old man? He could've sworn he'd heard those same words coming out of Finn O'Connor's mouth for most of Colton's life. His dad was great at coaxing others to get checked out. He didn't seem to think he fell into the same category.

And it was only recently that Colton and his brothers had found out his father had been dealing with a health issue that he'd kept quiet about until his death.

"Don't you think we would know by now? Plus, what's the worst it could be? A hairline fracture? I had one of those in my wrist in eighth grade PE. It's an incident I don't talk about because it highlights my general inability to perform athletics of any kind. But there wasn't much they could do with it except wrap it and put it in a sling. It wasn't like I needed a cast. I'm sure my hip falls into the same category. I need to rest. I need to take it easy. Other than that, I think I'm good to go."

What she said made a whole lot of sense, and Colton knew in the back of his mind she was right on some level. The thought of dropping her off at the RV to fend for herself after witnessing the way she'd gobbled down food last night and cleaned her plate this morning wasn't something he could stomach doing.

He wanted to help her, but he didn't want to hurt her pride. He needed to be tactful. "Since you're going to be resting for a few days anyway, why not do it here?"

The question surprised even him. But it was the logical thing to do. He had plenty of room here. He could sleep on the sofa. He'd done that countless times before, unable and unwilling to face an empty bedroom.

"That's a really kind offer. Maybe under different circumstances I could take you up on it…"

"I didn't want to have to pull this card out, but since you mentioned it, you're leaving me no choice." He caught hold of her gaze and tried his level best not to give himself away by laughing. "If you don't stay here and let me help you heal, I might be forced to handcuff you."

He mustered up his most serious expression.

Makena's jaw nearly dropped to the floor, and a twinge of guilt struck him at tricking her.

"That's blackmail. You wouldn't do that to me. Would you?" Her question was uncertain and he suspected she'd figured out his prank.

"I don't know." He shrugged. "Is it working?"

She walked straight toward him with her slight limp on the left side and gave him a playful jab on the shoulder. "That wasn't funny."

"Actually, I thought it was ingenious of me." Seeing the lighter side of Makena and her quick wit reminded him of why he'd been willing to walk away from the relationship he'd known his entire life, for someone he'd met in biology lab.

Deep down, behind those sad and suspicious eyes, she was still in there. Still the playful, intelligent, perceptive woman he'd fallen for.

"I'm probably going to regret this, but I'll think about staying here until I get better. Maybe just a day or two. But…"

"Why is there always a *but*?" He rubbed the day-old scruff on his chin.

"But I sleep on the couch. You only have two bedrooms here. One is yours and the other has two cribs in it. The door was open on the way to the bathroom. I couldn't help but notice," she said in her defense.

"Yes, you can stay here. Thank you for asking. And who sleeps on the couch is up for debate. We'll figure out a fair way to decide." There was no way he was going to let her curl up on the sofa when he had a king-size bed in the other room. Most of the time, he nodded off with a laptop open next to him and a phone in his hand anyway. It was easier than facing an empty bed on his own.

"And hey, thanks for considering my proposal," he added.

Colton appreciated how difficult her situation must be for her to feel the need to hide in a random stranger's RV, and he appreciated the confidence she put in him by staying with him last night.

In the ultimate display of trust, she'd fallen deeply asleep.

She didn't speak, but he could see the impact of his words. Sometimes, silence said more than a thousand words ever could.

Colton put his hand on the small of Makena's back as he escorted her to the elevator. Emotions seemed to be getting the best of her, because she'd gotten all serious and quiet on him again. The lighter mood was gone and he wondered if it had something to do with what he'd said or the simple fact they were going back to the RV where she'd been staying.

There were so many unanswered questions bubbling up in his mind about Makena and her need to hide. Abusive exes he understood. But she'd been in hiding for months, and he wondered how much of it had to do with losing her mother. He knew first-hand what it was like to have a close bond with a parent who died. Colton and his siblings were still reeling from the loss of their father. Worsened by the fact none of them could solve the decades-old mystery about their only sister's abduction from her bedroom window.

Frustration was building with each passing day, along with the realization their father had gone to his deathbed never knowing what had happened to Caroline. Plus, there was the whole mess of Caroline's kidnapping being dredged up in the news ever since there'd been a kidnapping attempt in town a couple of months ago.

Renee Smith, now Renee O'Connor after marrying his brother Cash, had moved to Katy Gulch with her six-month-old daughter, Abby, in order to start a new life. Her past had come with her and it was a haunting reminder of what could happen when a relationship went sour.

Renee's ex had followed her to Katy Gulch unbeknownst to her and tried to take away the one thing she loved most, in order to frighten her into coming home.

Was Makena in the same boat?

At least in Makena's case, she knew what she was dealing with. Renee had been caught off guard because her ex had cheated on her and was having a child with a coworker before deciding no one else could have Renee. That was pretty much where the comparisons between the two ended.

He'd brought up a good point, though. Colton wanted to know more about Makena's ex so he could determine just how much danger she might be in.

The fact she'd left the man a year ago stuck in Colton's craw. The way he'd found her and discovered how she'd been living made him think that she'd either run out of money or couldn't get to hers.

But then, he didn't know many people who could go a year without working and survive. Colton may have come from one of the wealthiest cattle ranching families in Texas, but all the O'Connors had grown up with their feet on the ground and their heads out of the clouds. Each one was determined to make a mark on this life and not rely on the good graces of their family to earn a living despite loving the land and the family business.

Colton helped Makena into the passenger seat, where she buckled herself in. The drive to Mrs. Dillon's place was short. Colton checked in with Gert on the way and the rest of the car ride he spent mulling over what he already knew.

He hoped Makena was seriously considering his offer to let her stay at his apartment. He couldn't think of a safer place for her to heal. It dawned on him that he hadn't even asked her if she liked children. He just assumed she did.

That was one of the funny things about becoming a parent: he was guilty of thinking that everyone loved kids. Growing up in Katy Gulch didn't help, because most people were kind to children in his hometown.

Colton had to stop a couple of times to clear the road of debris. So far, it was looking like Katy Gulch had been spared the storm's fury.

Gert had reported in several times last night and first thing this morning to let him know that very few people had lost power. Neighbors were pitching in to make sure food didn't spoil and people had what they needed. It was one of the many reasons Colton couldn't imagine bringing up his boys in any other place.

The twins were fifth-generation O'Connors, but whether or not they took up ranching would be up to them. Both seemed happiest when they were outdoors. Colton prayed he could give them half the childhood he'd been fortunate to have. He and his brothers had had the best. Of course, they'd also had their fair share of squabbles over the years.

Garrett and Cash seemed to rub each other the wrong way from just about the day Garrett was born. Make no mistake about it, though. Either one would be there for the other in a snap. Help needed? No questions asked.

Was it strange that Colton wished the same for Makena? He wished she could experience being part of a big family. It sounded like since losing her mother, she'd lost all the family she had. He couldn't even imagine what that would be like.

She'd remained quiet on the way over. They were getting close to Mrs. Dillon's and the river.

"Everything all right over there?" he asked her.

"Yeah, I'm good." The words were spoken with no conviction.

From the way she drawled out those three words, he could tell she was deep in thought. Her voice always had that sound when she was deep in concentration. He'd once accidentally interrupted her studying and heard that same sound.

He'd given her a lot to think about. To him, it was a no-brainer decision. Knowing Makena, she wouldn't want to live off him for free even for a few days.

It occurred to him that he was momentarily without a sitter. He wasn't even sure if she was up for the job, considering her left hip. She was walking better today, but she would know better than anyone else if she'd be able to keep up with the boys.

For the time being, it was a lot of bending over and letting them hold your fingers while they practiced walking. They also had swings and walkers and every other kid device his mother could think to buy for them.

He could put gates up to make it easier for her. More and more, he liked the idea. It would give her some pocket money and a legitimate place to stay. She wouldn't have to feel like she was imposing, if she took a short-term job with him just until he found someone permanent.

"How are you with children?"

"They seem to like me. I have been a music teacher in an elementary school. I don't know about little-littles. I don't have much experience with anyone younger than the age of five. But I do seem to be popular with eight-year-olds." Hearing her voice light up when she talked about her career warmed his heart. "Why?"

"It's just an idea. I already told you my babysitter had an emergency in Austin and had to quit. I also mentioned having my boys with my mom at the ranch isn't ideal for anything less than short-term. We have a lot going on in our family right now with our father passing recently. I was just wondering if you'd be interested in helping me out of a pinch. Would you consider taking care of the boys until I could find someone else full-time?"

He gripped the steering wheel until his knuckles went white, as he waited for an answer.

"When would you need me to start?"

Was she seriously considering this? Before she could change her mind, he added, "Now would be good. My mom can hang on for a couple more days if needed."

"Can you give me a few hours to think about it?"

"Take all the time you need, Makena. I don't have any interviews set up just yet. Mom is on board with helping for a few days. I'm just trying to lighten her load."

"Okay." She nodded, giving him the impression that she liked the idea. "It's definitely something to think about. Maybe I could just meet the boys and see if they even like me."

"That's a good first step. I'm sure they will, though. They're easygoing babies. It might be good for you to see if that age scares you, without the pressure of signing on for a commitment." He liked the idea of taking some of the burden off his mother, considering everything she was going through. And the thought of Makena sticking around for a while.

"I've been so focused on my situation that I haven't considered what your family must be going through," she said. The conversation ended when Colton parked at Mrs. Dillon's house.

Makena had opened the passenger door and was out of the vehicle before Colton could get around to help her. "I just want to pick up the few things I always have with me."

As she walked toward the RV, a bad feeling gripped him.

He glanced around, unable to find the source that was causing the hairs on the back of his neck to tingle.

Why did it feel like they were walking into a trap?

Chapter Eight

The silver bullet–style RV sat on a parking pad behind the farmhouse and near the river. Makena had placed a foot on the step leading into the RV when she heard Colton's voice in the background, warning her. She craned her neck to get a good look at him.

"Stop." That one word was spoken with the kind of authority she'd never heard from him before. It was the same commanding cop voice she'd heard from River.

Colton locked gazes with her. "Take your hand off the handle slowly. Don't put any pressure on the latch. And then freeze."

Makena stood fixed to the spot as a chill raced up her spine at the forceful tone. The "cop voice" brought back a flood of bad memories.

Would it always remind her of River when she heard Colton talk like that? Even a simple friendship, let alone anything more, was out of the ques-

tion if her body started trembling when she heard
him give an order.

She also knew better than to argue with him.
He'd obviously seen something and was warning her.

"Stay right where you are. Don't move." He was
by her side in a matter of seconds.

Makena's heart hammered against her rib cage,
beating out a staccato rhythm. Panic squeezed her
chest, making inhaling air hurt.

"Stay steady. Don't shift your weight." Colton
dropped down to all fours. In that moment, she knew
exactly what he was looking for.

A bomb.

Sweat beaded on her forehead and rolled down
her cheek. She focused on her breathing and willed
herself not to flinch. She reminded herself to slowly
breathe in and out. Her hands felt cold and clammy.

Although she couldn't exactly say she'd been living the past six months, she didn't want to die, either. And especially not here.

Her mouth tried to open but her throat was dry,
and she couldn't seem to form words. Fear was replaced with anger. Anger at the fact that by hiding, she'd allowed River to run her life all these
months. She'd been miserable and lonely, and had
nearly starved because of him. But she'd survived.
Now there'd be no going back.

Makena decided by sheer force of will that she
would live. No matter what else happened, she

would make it through this. It was the only choice she would allow herself to consider.

"There's a device strapped to the bottom of this step. Stay as still as you possibly can. We're going to get through this." Colton pushed up to standing and quickly scanned the area. Based on the expression on his face, which was calmer than she felt, she knew the situation was bad. He was too calm.

From the few action movies she'd seen, it seemed like if she moved, she'd be blown sky-high. She was afraid even to ask, because a slight shift in her weight, no matter how subconsciously she did it, would scatter her into a thousand tiny bits. More of that ice in her veins was replaced by fire.

River didn't get to do this. If anything happened to her, she needed Colton to know who was responsible. "My ex." She slowly exhaled, careful not to move so much as an inch.

"His name is River Myers. He works at the Dallas Police Department as an officer. He's the reason I've been on the run for the past six months. He has threatened me on numerous occasions. I walked away from a man who is armed and dangerous. He's calculating. He'll destroy me if he finds me before I locate evidence against him," she said in a voice as steady as the current in the river next to them.

"Don't you give up on me now. You're going to be fine. But the clock is ticking. I have no idea how much explosive is here and we're running out of options."

With that, he literally dove on top of her, knocking her off the step and covering her with his own body. When a blast didn't immediately occur, he said, "Let's get out of here."

With one arm hooked under her armpit, he scrambled toward a tree near the riverbank. He rounded the tree, placing it in between them and the RV. He hauled her back against his chest. He leaned back against the tree and dropped down, wrapping his arms around her.

Not two seconds later, an explosion sounded.

Her first thought was that she was thankful for Colton. If he hadn't been there, she'd be dead. Her brain couldn't process that information. It was going to take a while for that to sink in. Her second thought, as Colton's arms hugged her in a protective embrace, was that everything she'd owned in the past few months was gone.

The guitar her mother had given her had been blown to smithereens. The few clothes she had were gone along with it. It wasn't much but it was all she owned in the world.

A few tears of loss leaked out of her eyes. She sniffed them back, reminding herself this could've been a whole lot worse. It was hard to imagine, though. She had so little left from her mother.

She brought her right hand up, tracing the rose

necklace with her fingers. Thankfully, she had at least one thing left from her mother.

A little voice in the back of her head pointed out that she had someone in her corner for the first time in a very long time. It wasn't the security of her mother's guitar or the few articles of clothing that meant something to her. But she had the necklace and she had Colton.

She would have to rebuild from there.

And then another thought struck. She was in danger. Real danger. Colton had a young family, and because of her, his twins had been almost orphaned. She'd never been more certain of the fact that she couldn't accept his help any longer.

Moving forward, she planned to ask him for a loan, some kind of cover identity and a ticket out of town. She'd been crazy to stay in Texas. It was only a matter of time before River and his buddies would find her there. She'd adopted the hiding-in-plain-sight strategy and it had backfired big time.

Staying in the country was no longer an option. Since Mexico bordered Texas, she could slip across the border and make a new life. Maybe she could get down to one of the resorts and work in a kitchen or someplace where she'd be hidden from view.

A ringing noise in her ear covered the sound of Colton's voice. The only reason she realized he was talking at all was because she felt his chest vibrate against her back. The blast had been deafening. And at least temporarily, she'd lost hearing. Bits of metal had blown past her and the last thing she'd heard was the bomb detonate.

Everything felt like it was moving in slow motion. It was like time had stopped and everything around her moved in those old-fashioned movie frames and some mastermind stood behind a curtain clicking slides.

When the last of the debris seemed to have flown past and everything was still, Colton scooted out from underneath her and whirled around to check the damage.

Her heart went out to the owner, the sweet woman who'd just lost a remnant from her past.

Makena balled her fists and slammed them into the unforgiving earth in frustration.

Colton had disappeared from view. She rolled around onto all fours to see for herself. The door had been blown completely off its hinges. Many of the contents had gone flying. The RV was on fire. Colton had raced to his sport utility and returned with a fire extinguisher before she was able to get to her feet.

River hadn't just sent a potent message. His intention had been to kill her. All those times he'd threatened her came racing back. And so did the memory of the pair of men she'd seen the other day.

WITHIN THE HOUR, Colton had cordoned off the crime scene. A few of his deputies arrived on-site to aid in the investigation. There was no need to call in a bomb expert. The one that had caused the kind of damage the RV had sustained was a simple job. One that anyone could've logged onto the internet and bought materials to make.

Hell, any person old enough to know how to use a phone and have access to a credit card could grab the materials used here. The bomb was crude but would've done the job of killing Makena if he hadn't been there.

A ringing noise still sounded in Colton's ears, but his hearing was coming back at least. People didn't have to shout at him anymore for him to hear what they were saying.

Deputy Fletcher walked over. He had on gloves. His palm was out, and a key chain was on top. It was a classic hotel style, with the words *Home sweet home* inscribed on the black plastic.

"What's this?" Colton asked his deputy.

Fletcher shrugged. "Found it about fifteen feet from the RV."

"Let's check with Makena to see if she recognizes it." He led Fletcher over to the spot where she was being examined by EMT Samantha Rodriguez. There were no visible signs of bleeding, so she'd been spared being impaled by debris. Colton, on the other hand, hadn't been so lucky. He'd taken a nick to his shoulder, and he was holding a T-shirt pressed to the wound to stem the bleeding.

Samantha's partner, Oliver Matthew, had tried to get Colton to stop long enough for treatment, but he had a crime scene to manage and wouldn't take any chance that evidence could end up trampled on.

"Does this look familiar to you?" he asked Makena, pointing toward the key chain on Fletcher's palm.

She gasped.

"I bought one just like that for River after moving in together. He kept losing his key, so I ordered a key chain for him. That looks exactly like the one I bought," she stated.

"Bag it and see if you can lift a print," he said to Fletcher.

"Yes, sir." Fletcher turned and walked toward his service vehicle after thanking Makena for her confirmation.

Although any Joe Schmo could make this bomb, Colton had zeroed in on one name: River Myers. And now he might have proof. Colton was a little too familiar with the law enforcement statistics. Police officers battered their spouses in shockingly high numbers. The stress of the job was partly to blame and the reason why Colton, as a law enforcement leader, went to great lengths to offer programs and resources to help combat a pervasive issue with his deputies and employees. He saw it as his responsibility to ensure the mental and physical fitness of the men and women who served under him.

However, he could only keep an eye on his employees and do his level best to ensure they had plenty of tools to manage the stress that came with a career like theirs. He couldn't force them to take advantage of a program. An old saying came to mind: "You can lead a horse to water but you can't make it drink."

One of the advantages of running a smaller department like his office came in the form of being able to be up-front and personal with each one of his employees. A large department like Dallas wouldn't have that same benefit. Running an organization that large presented challenges.

In no way, shape or form was Colton condoning or justifying what a cop under duress might do. He held his people to the highest standards. Part of the reason why he was so selective in the hiring process. In a bigger setup, it would be easier to slip through the cracks.

When the site had been secured and medical attention given, he made his way back to Makena. Samantha turned to him.

"Her hearing should return to normal in a few days. Other than that, she was very lucky."

The last word Colton would use to describe Makena was *lucky.* Bad things happened to good people sometimes. But he understood what Samantha meant. The situation could've been a whole lot worse, with neither one of them walking away from it.

They'd also been fortunate that the pressure on the step had set off a timer and not a detonator. Those critical fifteen seconds had saved both of their lives.

"I'm so sorry, Colton. I should've known something like this would happen." Makena's pale blue eyes were wide. Fear flashed across them for a moment, followed by anger and determination. Two emotions that could get her in trouble.

"You know this isn't your fault." He needed to reassure her of the fact. He thanked Samantha.

The EMT folded her arms, put her feet in an athletic stance and shot him a death glare. "You are going to let me check out that shoulder now. Right?"

Samantha knew him well enough to realize he would put up a fight. Colton always made sure everyone around him was okay first.

"I'm standing here right now, aren't I?"

"Good." She didn't bother to hide the shock in her voice. She bent down to her medical bag and ordered him to take off his shirt, which he did.

"This is the only injury I sustained other than the ears, just like Makena."

Samantha stood up and made quick work tending to the cut in his shoulder. Within minutes, she'd cleaned the wound, applied antibiotic ointment and patched it up with a butterfly bandage.

"This should help it heal up nicely. I'd try to talk

you into stopping by the ER for a few stitches, but I didn't want to push my luck."

"I appreciate the recommendation. This should be good." He'd grown up working a cattle ranch, so it wasn't the first time he'd ended up with a scar on his body. Nor would it be the last. He thanked Samantha for doing a fine job, which she had.

She told him it was no trouble at all before closing up her bag and heading toward the driver's seat of her ambulance. He would've just patched himself up but didn't want to appear a hypocrite in front of Makena after urging her to seek care.

Before he could open his mouth to speak, Makena threw herself into his chest and buried her face. He stroked her long, silky hair, figuring this was a rare show of emotion for her.

He couldn't be certain how long they stood there. Being with her, it was like time had stopped, and nothing else mattered except making sure she was okay.

When she pulled back, his heart clenched as he looked at her. She wore the same expression as she had that last day of biology lab. He'd been so tempted to ask her out despite the fact that it had been made clear she was with someone else. It would've gone against everything he believed in. Honor. Decency. He'd never break the code of asking someone out who was married, in a relationship, or dating someone else.

He'd cleaned up his own relationship at home, realizing that he and Rebecca would never have the kind of spark that he'd felt with Makena. He'd decided right then and there, with his nineteen-year-old self, that he'd hold out for that feeling to come around again. Little did he know just how rare it could be.

All these years later, he'd never felt it again until recently. It was then he realized what he and Makena had had was special.

"It's not safe for me to be here anymore, Colton. I know you need a statement from me, but I'd like to keep my name as quiet as possible. He obviously found me here and he'll find me again. I'll be ready next time. I took his threats too lightly. Not anymore."

"I do need a statement from you. And I have no authority to force you to stay in Katy Gulch. Whether or not you do, a crime happened here in my jurisdiction. Someone's property was damaged and there was an attempted murder and that makes it my responsibility. So, whether you're here or not, I plan to investigate." Why did the news of her wanting to run away impale him?

She had every right to do what she felt was necessary to protect herself. Now that he knew her ex was in law enforcement, so many of her reactions made sense to him. That fact alone made a relationship between them practically impossible.

Given Colton's line of work, she would always be reminded of her ex.

Makena shook her head furiously. "I understand you have to file a report. Believe me when I say you don't want to chase this guy down. Look what he's capable of, Colton. You have a family. You have young boys who depend on you. I won't have your life taken away from them because of something I did."

"Is that what you believe? That any of this is somehow your fault?"

"I didn't mean it like that. I know what River did in the past and now is completely on him. I didn't deserve it then and I don't deserve it now. I won't take responsibility for any of his actions. That's all on him. But *I* brought that man to your doorstep. That's the responsibility I feel."

"You're right about one thing. You did nothing wrong."

Her chin quivered at hearing those words, so he repeated them. "You did nothing wrong."

She was nodding her head and looked to be fighting back tears. "I know."

"Sometimes we just need to hear it from someone else."

"Thank you, Colton. You have no idea what you've done for me in the past twenty-four hours and how much that has truly meant to me, which is why I can't burden you any more than I have."

Colton had his hands up, stopping her from going down that road again. "In case you hadn't noticed, Makena, this is my job. This is what I do. And yes, there are personal risks. Believe me when I say that I don't take them lightly. Also, know that I take safety very personally. I have every intention of walking through the door every night to my boys as I watch them grow up. There is no other option in my mind. And if this had been anyone else but you in this situation, I would still be following the same protocol. Most law enforcement officials are there for all the right reasons. It's rare for them to go completely rogue or off the chain. But when they do, they aren't just a danger to one person. They will be a threat to women, to children and to men. That's not something I can live with on my conscience. Not to mention the fact that I'm a law enforcement officer. Being on this job is in my blood."

He stopped there. He'd said enough. He gave her a few moments to let that sink in while he walked her over to his SUV.

Makena took in a deep breath. "Okay."

She blew the breath out.

Colton hoped that meant she'd heard what he said and was ready for him to continue his investigation.

"Let's do this. Let's make sure that River Myers never hurts another soul again. I'll tell you everything I know about him."

Colton helped her into the passenger seat before

closing the door and claiming his spot. Pride filled his chest. It wasn't easy for anyone to go against someone they'd cared about or, worse yet, someone they were afraid of. It took incredible courage to do what she was doing, and he couldn't be prouder of her than he was right then.

After giving Colton a description of her ex, his badge number, his social security and his license plate, she dropped another bomb on him.

"Abuse is not the only thing he's guilty of. I don't know the names of the people he was talking to one night in my garage but I'd heard a noise and when I went to investigate, River flipped out. He rushed me back inside the house and threatened me. He told me that I had no idea what I'd just done. All I can figure is that I walked in on some kind of meeting between the three of them."

"Did you hear what they were talking about, by chance?"

"I wish I had. He rushed me out of there too early and I was too chicken to go back." Her hands were balled fists on her legs. "I guess they were planning something or talking about something they didn't want anyone else to know about. They sounded threatening and there was a handprint around River's throat. I thought I overheard something about getting someone to pay but I have no idea what that means."

"Were the other men in uniform?"

"No. They weren't. They were in regular street clothes but they acted like cops." That didn't mean they weren't officers.

"Did you get a good look at them?"

"Yes. As a matter of fact, I did. And I saw them here three days ago. It's the reason I ducked into the RV and didn't leave for three days straight."

That explained why she'd practically starved to death by the time she'd walked out to find food. So many things clicked in the back of his mind. Like the fact that she'd gone out in a driving rain when there were no cars out. It must have been to forage for food. The way she'd gobbled down that sandwich and apple made more sense to him now.

He'd wondered how long it had been since she'd had a meal.

"I knew I'd stuck around too long and I was pre-paring to move on. Seeing them scared me to the core. River had always been clear. If I left him, he would hunt me down and kill me. He would see the divorce as the ultimate betrayal."

Another thought dawned on Colton. River may not have been trying to kill her. His cohorts, on the other hand, seemed ready to do the job.

They could be in league with River. They may or may not be cops themselves, but they definitely could be doing his dirty work.

"Describe them to me in as much detail as you can remember."

Chapter Nine

"The first one I saw was around six feet tall. He had a football-player build, with a clean-shaven face. His hair was light red…kind of strawberry blond. He had a thick neck and big hands. Other than that, I remember that he had light skin and freckles." Makena remembered the men vividly because they were so different.

Colton nodded.

"The second guy had one of those 1970s mustaches on an otherwise clean face. Black hair with big bushy eyebrows. He had these puffed-out cheeks like he had a big wad of gum or tobacco in his jaws. His hair was short and thick and a little wavy. I remember that he was several inches shorter than Red. They were so distinct-looking and oddly matched. Opposites. That's what I remember about them from that night."

"Did you have a chance to hear their voices? Would you recognize them if you heard them?"

She shook her head.

"Cops?" he asked.

"I don't know for certain. I can't be one hundred percent sure. They looked like they were law enforcement. They had that cop carriage, if you know what I mean."

Colton nodded. He seemed to know exactly what she was talking about. There was just a cop swagger. Being on the job, wearing a holster for long shifts day in and day out caused them to hold their arms out a little more than usual. They also walked with the kind of confidence that said they could handle themselves in almost any situation. They had the training to back it up.

"What shift did your ex work?" Colton asked.

"Deep nights. He requested them. Said he liked to be out and about when everyone else was asleep." She couldn't imagine anything had changed in the past few months since she'd been gone, considering the fact that River had been on deep nights for almost fifteen years.

"A couple of my brothers work in law enforcement," he said.

"Oh yeah?"

"U.S. Marshals. They would help if we brought them up to speed." Colton had scribbled down descriptions of Red and Mustache Man. He also made notes about River's shift preference. Considering it was only ten thirty in the morning, River would be home and still asleep.

"I'm not sure it's such a good idea." A lot was coming at her, fast. She needed a minute to process. "Can I think about it first?"

He nodded and then moved on. "Could he afford the residence you shared on his own?"

"I moved into his bachelor pad and fixed it up. It's likely that he's still there. He doesn't really like change."

Colton checked the clock on his dashboard. It was almost like he read her thoughts. He started the engine of his sport utility. "I have a few calls to make that might go a little easier in my office. You okay with that?"

What he was really asking was would she stay with him? She could read between the lines. Since she had nowhere to go, literally, and no friends in town, she nodded. The honest truth was that she didn't feel safe with anyone but Colton. Being with him was warmth and campfires despite the dangers all around.

She leaned her head back and brought her hands up to rub her temples. Her head hurt. A dull ache was forming between her eyes. The headache distracted her from her hip pain. Now, there was something. She was getting punchy.

Makena appreciated the fact that the ride to Colton's office was short. She climbed out of the sport utility, her hip reminding her that it wasn't quite finished with her yet.

The driver's-side door of a blue sports sedan popped open two spots down, the driver having cut off the engine almost the minute she stepped out of the SUV. Makena flinched.

The person held something toward Colton. As the youngish man, early thirties if she had to guess, bum-rushed them, Colton tensed. His gaze bounced from being locked onto the guy he seemed to recognize and then across the rest of the cars in the lot. The way he watched anything that moved reminded her just how out in the open they were in the parking lot.

The jerk with what she recognized as his phone in his hand caught up to them. "Sheriff O'Connor."

"Mike."

"Sir, do you care to comment on your sister's kidnapping and the recent crime wave in Katy Gulch?"

Colton stopped dead in his tracks. He turned to face the guy named Mike, who Makena assumed was a reporter. "That story has been dead for decades, Mike. What's wrong? Slow news week?"

"Sir, I—I—I…"

"I accept your apology, Mike. Now, if you don't mind, I have business to attend to in my office." Colton turned his back on the reporter and started walking toward the building. He said out the side of his mouth, "But if there are any new leads, you'll be the first to know."

Considering Colton's stiff demeanor, it was clear to Makena the story about his sister's kidnapping was off-limits.

Mike stood there, looking dumbfounded.

Makena heard what was said, and she couldn't help but think about the fact that Colton's father had just died. She wondered if the two incidents were connected in some way. That had to be unlikely, given that Colton himself had said his sister's kidnapping was decades old. Colton had also mentioned a kidnapping attempt on his newly minted sister-in-law's adopted daughter and then there was his father's death. A family like the O'Connors could be a target for any twisted individual who wanted to make a buck. A shudder raced through her. She could only imagine based on her experience of living in fear for the months on end what it must be like living on guard at all times.

Colton had mentioned that a couple of his brothers had gone on to become US marshals. He was sheriff. She had to wonder if their choices to go into law enforcement had anything to do with a need to protect each other and keep their family safe.

The minute Colton walked through the front door and into the lobby, a woman who seemed to be in her late sixties popped up from her desk, set the phone call she'd been on down, and ran over to give Colton a warm hug. The moment was sweet and the action seemed to come from a genuine place.

"Thank heavens you're okay." The woman had to be Gert, Makena guessed from the sound of her voice. It also made sense that she would be at Colton's office.

When Gert finally released him from the hug, he introduced her to Makena.

"I'm pleased as punch to meet you. I'm sorry for the day you've had. Can I get you anything? Coffee? Water?"

"Coffee sounds great. Just point me in a direction and I can get my own cup." Makena echoed Gert's sentiments. Now that she'd had a minute to process the fact that her ex had tried to blow her to smithereens, she needed a strong cup of coffee.

"Don't be silly. I'd be happy to get you a cup. I just put on a fresh pot."

"If you're offering, I'll take a cup of that coffee, too." He placed his hand on the small of Makena's back and led her through a glass door that he had to scan his badge to enter. He hooked a right in what looked to be a U-shaped building and then led her halfway down the hall. His office was on the right.

"Make yourself comfortable," Colton said. "Is there anything else you'd like besides coffee?"

"No, thank you." The shock of the day's events was starting to wear off. The annoying ringing noise was a constant companion as she moved to the leather sofa and then took a seat.

Colton moved behind his desk. "Professional courtesy dictates that I make a call to Mr. Myers's chief before questioning him."

"Won't that give River a heads-up that you want to speak to him?" The thought of being in the same room again with her ex fired more of that anger through her veins. It needed to be a courtroom, the next time. And he needed to be going to jail for a very long time. One way or another, she would find a way for justice to be served and keep him from harming other innocent people. But the River she knew wouldn't exactly lie down and take what was coming his way. Without a doubt, he'd deny any involvement.

The explosion and fire would have made certain there were no fingerprints. When she really thought about the crime, it was an easy way on his part to get away with murder. No one would know her in Katy Gulch. That meant she would most likely have ended up a Jane Doe. She'd quit her job and disappeared. No one would miss her.

She could vanish and there was no one to notice. How sad had her life become since marrying him, since her mother's drawn-out illness, that Makena could die at the hands of her ex and no one would know?

The only person she knew in Katy Gulch was

Colton. He would have had no reason to suspect a blast from the past. He wouldn't have been looking for her. And if she'd been badly burned, which seemed like the plan, her face would have been unrecognizable anyway. It had been a near-perfect setup.

She flexed and released her fingers a couple of times to work out some of the tension. She rolled her shoulders back and took in a couple of deep breaths. She couldn't imagine trying to hurt someone she supposedly cared about.

Colton's voice broke through her heavy thoughts. She realized he was on a call.

"Yes, sir. My name is Sheriff Colton O'Connor and I need to speak with Chief Shelton. This is a professional courtesy call and I need to speak to him about one of his officers." Colton was silent for a few beats. And then came, "Thank you, sir."

A few more beats of silence, and then someone must've picked up on the other line. Gert walked in about that same moment with two mugs of coffee in her hands. She set the first one down on Colton's desk, which was the closest to her. The other one she brought over to Makena, who accepted the offering and thanked Colton's secretary for her kindness.

Gert produced a couple packets of sugar and a pack of creamer from her pocket and set them down on the coffee table along with a stir stick. Gert made eye contact and nodded. The sincerity, warmth and compassion in her gaze settled over Makena. It was easy to see the woman had a heart of gold. She disappeared out of the room after Makena mouthed a thank-you.

"As I said before, this is a professional courtesy call to let you know that the name of one of your police officers came up in the course of an investigation today." Colton was silent for a moment. "Yes, sir. The officer's name is River Myers. A few more seconds of silence followed. "Is that right?" A longer pause. This time the silence dragged on. Colton glanced at her, caught her eye and then nodded. She could tell there was a storm brewing behind his cobalt eyes.

After Colton explained to the Dallas police chief that he wanted to speak to River in connection with an attempted murder case, there was even more silence.

Colton ended the call by thanking the chief for his time and by promising that he would keep him abreast of his investigation.

"What did he say?" She waited for Colton to hang up before asking the question.

"He wished me luck with my investigation. He said his office was fully prepared to cooperate. And then he informed me that River Myers is on administrative leave pending an investigation."

Makena gasped as all kinds of horrible thoughts

crossed her mind. "Did he say what River was being investigated for?"

Colton's earlier words that she needed to speak up so she could prevent anyone else from getting hurt slammed into her. Had River done something to another woman he was in a relationship with?

"The chief said he really can't share a lot of details for an ongoing investigation, but in the spirit of reciprocity, he said an internal affairs division investigation was underway on two counts of police brutality and one count of extortion."

Relief washed over Makena that River wasn't already being looked at for murder. He was, now. "What does being placed on administrative leave mean?"

"It's basically where he would be required to hand in his department-issued weapons along with his badge until the investigation is over and it's decided whether or not any criminal charges would be filed." Colton took a sip of coffee.

Makena brought her hand up to her mouth. If River had still been on the job, they would know exactly where to find him. "Does this mean what I think? That he's out there somewhere? Going rogue?"

"That is a distinct possibility." Colton's grip on his coffee mug caused his knuckles to go white. With his free hand, he drummed his fingers on his desk. "I need to issue a BOLO with his name and description. I don't want my deputies being caught unawares if they happen to run into him personally or on a traffic stop."

Colton mentioned a couple of other things before jumping into action. Not five minutes later, he'd had Gert issue the BOLO, he'd started the report on the explosion, and he'd nearly polished off his second cup of coffee. Once he'd taken care of those preliminary details, he looked at her. "My next call needs to be to my mother. But first, I want to know where you stand. Will you stay with me until the investigation runs its course?"

The look on his face suggested he expected an argument. She had none.

"I appreciate the offer. You already know my concerns about bringing danger to your doorstep. And then there's your boys to consider."

"Don't worry about my sons. For the time being, they'll be safe at the ranch. I know my mom will pull through and yet she's the one I worry about the most. I have two new sisters-in-law I forgot about before, who I can ask to pitch in. The ranch has a lot of security in place already, and I don't mind adding to it. In fact, it might not be a bad idea for me to take you to my home there. Times will come up when I have to leave for the investigation or for work, and I want to know that you're safe."

Makena could stay on the ranch safely with all the extra security. She could not live with bringing danger around Colton and his children. "I'll stay with you at your apartment or I'll wait here at your office if you need to investigate someone without me there. But I won't go to the ranch. It's too dangerous for the people."

Colton rubbed the scruff on his chin. He took a sip of coffee. "That's fair."

She hoped so, because it was the only offer on the table. If she had to sit in the office for an entire day, she would. There was no way in hell she was going to risk his family. Granted, River wanted her. But she couldn't be certain that he wouldn't use one of them to draw her out. It was a gamble she had no intention of taking.

Makena rolled up her sleeves and drained her cup. She set the mug down on the coffee table. She placed her flat palms on her thighs and looked at Colton.

"What's next?"

"You tell me everything you can think of about your ex. His favorite restaurant. Whether or not he's a fisherman and has a fishing lease. Is he a hunter? Does he have a hunting license? Who are his friends? And then, I go track him down."

"Hold on there. I'm the best person to help find him. I want to go to Dallas with you."

"Not a chance. The agreement we just made was that you would stay here while I investigate. It's either here or my apartment. I need to know that I can trust you to do what you say you're going to do."

"I wouldn't lie to you. I just thought it would be easier to track him down with me involved."

"If you're his target and he sees you, it could be game over."

"I'm not arguing. However, trying to blow me to pieces on a timer once I thought I was safely inside an RV doesn't exactly make me feel like he wants to be connected to my murder in any way. In fact, he seems to be taking great pains to kill me without leaving any trail back to him."

"True enough. The explosion was most likely meant to cover his tracks. We also have to broaden the scope. You saw his friends…or…acquaintances might be a better word. You said yourself they were speaking in hushed tones. We can go after them, too. They might be acting on his behalf or they might be on their own."

"Oh, I doubt anyone would do that. Not with River's temper. He never struck me as the type to step aside."

"We have to keep unbiased eyes on the case and we have to follow the evidence. Right now, you saw two people from your past in town three days ago and that spawned you to disappear into the RV."

"Allegedly saw. I mean, they were far away and I can't be one hundred percent certain it was them."

"Okay. What are the chances the two guys you saw, even at a distance, weren't the men you saw in your garage?" He was playing devil's advocate. She could see that. Looking at the case from every angle probably made him a good investigator.

It was impossible for Makena not to lead with emotions in this case. For one, the explosion was targeted at her. And for another, River's threats echoed in her mind. To her thinking, he was delivering on threats he'd made six months ago.

Chapter Ten

Colton spent the next hour getting to know River Myers. He then made a quick call to his mother, and she agreed the twins staying on with her would be for the best, at least for a couple of days.

He knew better than anyone that investigations often took far longer than that, but he hoped for a break in this one. If Makena's ex was determined to erase her and she was constantly at Colton's side, he would have to get through Colton first. Makena had made a list of River's known hangouts. Colton had handed the list over to Gert, who'd meticulously called each one to ask when the last time River had been in.

So far, no one had seen or heard from River for the past month. Of course, the couple of places that were known cop hangouts most likely wouldn't admit to seeing him if he was standing in front of their faces.

Other than that, he frequented a popular Tex-Mex

restaurant and a couple of taco chains. None of the managers or employees admitted to seeing the man in the past few weeks if not a month.

The timing of River sticking to himself coincided with when he was put on leave according to the chief. It was odd, since the guy would've had more free time on his hands. Usually, that meant being seen in his favorite haunts more often. In River's case, he seemed to be hunkering down.

A call to one of his neighbors revealed that it didn't seem like he'd been home, either. There were no lights left on in the evenings, and the neighbor hadn't seen his truck in a couple of weeks.

"What are the chances he has a new girlfriend?" Colton asked Makena.

She looked up from her notebook, where she'd been trying to recall and write down all the places he could've possibly gone to.

"Anything is possible. Right?" She tapped her pencil on the pad. "I mean, he's not really the type to be alone and he was served with divorce papers not long after I disappeared. I worked through my lawyer to finish up the paperwork."

"If River is spending all his time at a new girl-friend's house, it might be harder to track him down." His personal phone number had changed. Colton had his guess as to why that might have happened.

As word spread about the morning's incident,

Colton's phone started ringing off the hook. Everyone in the community wanted to pitch in and help find the person responsible for blowing up Mrs. Dillon's RV. Colton couldn't give any more details than that and it was impossible to keep this story completely quiet considering how much neighbors watched out for each other in Katy Gulch.

After hours of receiving and making phone calls, Colton realized it was past dinnertime. Not a minute later, Gert knocked on the office door. It was a courtesy knock because Colton had a long-standing open-door policy.

"It might be time to take a break," Gert said. They both knew she would go home and continue working on the case, but it was her signal she was heading out.

"Let me know if you get any leads or figure out anything that I've missed," Colton said. He stretched out his arms and yawned, realizing he'd been sitting in the same position for hours. It was no wonder his back was stiff. His ears were still ringing from the explosion this morning but there was improvement there, too.

"You know I will, sir." Gert waved to Makena before exiting the room. Before she got more than a few steps down the hall she shouted back at them. "I'll lock the front door."

Colton turned to Makena. "What do you think about taking this back to my apartment? We should probably get up and get our blood moving. And then there's dinner. You must be starved by now."

"That's probably a good idea. I'm not starving, but I could eat. The bags of nuts and trail mix that Gert has been bringing me have tided me over."

"I'll just close up a couple of files and log out and then we can go." Colton tried not to notice when Makena stood up and stretched just how long her legs were. She had just the right amount of soft curves, and all he could think about was running his hand along those gorgeous lines...

He forced his gaze away from her hips—a place he had no business thinking about. He straightened up his desk and then closed out of the files on his desktop. His laptop had access to the same system, and he could get just as much done at home. He figured Makena would be more comfortable there anyway.

It also occurred to him that she'd lost everything she owned except the clothes on her back. He stood up and pushed his chair in. He gripped the back of his chair with both hands. "We can stop off anywhere you need on the way to my house. I'm sure you want a change of clothes and something to sleep in."

"I appreciate the offer, but pretty much everything I own was blown up. I don't have any ID or credit cards with me." He realized that she wouldn't want to carry ID in case she got picked up. Now that he knew her ex was a cop, he understood why she'd gone to the lengths she had to keep her identity a secret.

"How about I take care of it for you? It really wouldn't be any trouble—"

"You're already doing so much for me, Colton. It's too much to ask. I'll be fine with what I have."

"I promise it isn't. We don't have to do anything fancy. We can stop off at one of those big-box stores. There's one on the way home. We can let you pick up a few supplies. It would be a loan. Just until you get back on your feet. I have a feeling once we lock this jerk away for good, you'll get back on your feet in no time. For old times' sake, I'd like to be the one to give you a temporary hand up."

Colton hoped he'd put that in a way that didn't offend her. He wasn't trying to give her a handout. All he wanted was to give her a few comfort supplies while they located the bastard who'd tried to kill her.

She raked her top teeth over her bottom lip, a sure sign she was considering his offer. Then again, with her back against the wall, she might not feel like she had any options.

"I promise it's no trouble, and if you don't want to take the stuff with you, you could always leave it at my place. One of my new sisters-in-law will probably fit the same clothes. Renee looks to be about your size, if leaving them would make you feel better. It would certainly make me feel better to be able to help you out. Besides, you're probably the only reason I passed biology lab."

That really made her laugh. "I was terrible at biology lab. If you hadn't helped me, I would've failed and I'm pretty certain I dragged your grade down."

"I might have been better at the actual work than you were, but you were the only reason I kept going to class."

Her smile practically lit up the room. It was nice to make her smile for a change after all she'd been through. She deserved so much better.

"I tell you what. I'll let you buy me some new clothes. But once this is over, maybe I can stick around a few days and watch the boys for you as a way to pay you back. I'm not sure I'm any good with kids that age and they might not even like me, but I'm willing to try. And who knows, we might actually have some fun. It would make me feel so much better if I can do something nice for you."

"Deal." He wouldn't look a gift horse in the mouth. This was something nice, and she made a good point. He was halting his nanny search so he could throw himself completely into this investigation. As much as the process would take time, he was also keenly aware that the colder the trail, the colder the leads. His best bet at nailing the bastard would come in a window of opportunity he had in the next seventy-two hours. If the investigation dragged on longer than that, the apprehension rate would drop drastically.

Unless there was another attempt. Colton didn't even want to consider that option.

"Do you want to take a minute to order a few things on the laptop? We can put a rush on the order, and they'll have it ready by the time we swing through. I just need to turn off a few lights and double-check the break room." He handed his laptop over.

"Sure." She sat down in one of the leather club chairs across from his desk and studied the screen as he headed down the hallway.

Turning off the lights had been an excuse to give her a few minutes alone to order. In reality, he didn't like the idea of her going out in public where she'd be exposed. A skilled rifleman could take her out from the top of a building or beside a vehicle.

And then there was the gossip mill to consider. Most of the time, he didn't mind it. For the most part, people were trying to be helpful by sharing information. Being seen with him would be news. Like it or not, the O'Connors were in the public eye and people seemed to enjoy discussing the details of his family's private lives.

He took his time checking rooms before returning. The laptop was closed. She stood up the minute she heard him come in the room. "Ready?"

"All set," she said, handing over the device. He

tucked it under one arm before placing his hand on the small of her back and leading her out the rear of the building. He guided her down the hall and outside, deciding it would be safer to take his personal vehicle home.

His pickup truck was parked out back.

"I don't want to run into Mike or anyone else sniffing around for a story." It was true. But he also didn't want to risk going out the same way he'd come in, just in case River or one of his cohorts was watching. That part Colton decided to keep to himself.

Colton finally exhaled the breath he'd been holding when they were safely inside his truck and on the road. It was past seven o'clock, and it wouldn't be dark for another hour and a half this time of year.

Being out in the daylight made him feel exposed. He kept his guard up, searching the face of every driver as he passed them. He stopped off at the box store and pulled into the pickup lane. A quick text later, an employee came running out to the designated curbside area.

Colton thanked the guy and handed him a five-dollar bill. The rest of the ride to his apartment took all of ten minutes. He pulled up to the garage and punched in the security code before zipping through the opened gate.

From a security standpoint, the place wouldn't be that difficult to breech on foot. But the gate kept other drivers from coming in and closed quickly enough after he pulled through that it would be impossible to backdraft him.

Colton had spent part of the drive thinking through something that had been bugging him since he'd gotten off the phone with the DPD chief. If River was being investigated for serious charges like police brutality and extortion, there had to be a reasonable complainant involved. Considering there were several charges against him, he wondered what kind of huddle Makena could've walked into that night, when she'd interrupted River and the other two men.

It was obviously a meeting of some kind. The fact that River had ushered her away so fast meant that he was trying to protect his group, or her. Possibly both. In his twisted mind, he probably believed that he loved his wife.

Abusers usually thought they cared for their partners. Forget that their version of caring was tied up with control and abuse, sometimes physical. When they realized that, they seemed to have some sense of remorse. For others, it was just a way of life.

Thinking back, Colton wondered if Makena's life would've turned out differently if he'd somehow plucked up the courage to ask her out.

But then, his own life might've turned out differently, too. Having the twins was one of the best things that had ever happened to him. He wouldn't trade his boys for the world. And even though his wife had died, he wouldn't trade the years of friendship they'd had, either.

Since regret was about as productive as stalking an ant to find cheese, he didn't go there often. Life happened. He'd lost Rebecca. He'd gained two boys out of their relationship.

Makena's life might not have turned out differently even if they had dated. There was no way to go back and find out. And even if they could…change one thing and the ripple effect could be far-reaching.

Returning his focus to the case, he thought about Red and Mustache Man. The what-if questions started popping into his mind.

What if Red and Mustache had been working to shake someone down? Considering one of the charges against River was extortion, it was a definite possibility.

If Mustache and Red had come to Katy Gulch, were they sticking around? Were they acting alone? Were they after her because they thought she'd heard something in her garage that night?

Alarm bells sounded at the thought. He felt like he was onto something there.

This could've been an attempt to…what?

Hold on. Colton had it. If River had gone into hiding and the guys blew up Makena, would that be enough to bring him out?

COLTON THREW A PIZZA in the oven while Makena mixed together a salad from contents she'd found in the fridge. Working in the kitchen with her was a nice change to a frozen dinner in front of his laptop after the boys were in bed.

They'd just sat down at the island to eat when his cell phone buzzed. He glanced at the screen and saw Gert's name. Makena was sitting next to him, so he tilted the screen in her direction before taking the call. He held the phone to his ear.

"This is Colton. I'm going to put you on speaker. Is that okay?" There was some information that was sensitive enough that Makena shouldn't hear.

"Fine by me, sir."

Colton put the call on speaker and set it in between him and Makena on the island. "Okay. Makena and I are listening."

"Sir, Deputy Fletcher was canvassing in Birchwood and stopped off at a motel along the highway. He got a hit." Her voice practically vibrated with excitement. Gert loved the investigation process. "The clerk told Deputy Fletcher a man matching River Myers's description had been staying at her motel for the past four days. The clerk's name is Gloria Beecham and this place is a rent-by-the-hour type, if you know what I mean. She said he was a cash customer. Given the amount of time he'd been there and the fact that he kept the Do Not Disturb sign on the door the whole time, housekeeping was freaked out by the guy."

Colton wasn't surprised. Hotels and motels had tightened up their processes to ensure every room was checked.

"Housekeeping alerted the clerk to the fact. She made a call to let him know that housekeeping had to check his room every twenty-four hours by law. She said that when they came to clean, he would stand in the corner of the room with the door open and his arms crossed over his chest."

"Odd behavior," Colton noted.

"It sure is." She made a tsk noise. "They never did find anything suspicious, and honestly, admitted to getting in and out of there just as fast as they could."

"And this mystery man matched River's description?" he asked.

"Yes, sir."

"He was staying in the room alone?" This could be a solid lead. Colton looked at Makena, who was on the edge of her seat.

"Yes, sir."

"Did they say whether anyone else ever came in or out of the room?"

"No. No one to her knowledge. She started keeping an eye on the room by the camera mounted outside. This place has no interior spaces. It's the kind of place where you park right in front of your door and use a key to go straight inside. So there are cameras along the exterior overhangs. She said it was something the owner had insisted on installing over a year ago. The funny thing is, he struck her as odd because his face was always pointed the opposite direction of the nearest camera."

"He was smart enough to realize that cameras might be in use."

"So much so, in fact, he wore a ball cap most of the time. He kept his chin tucked to his chest as he walked in and out of the building."

"Did they, by chance, get a make and model on his vehicle?" Colton asked.

"No, sir. They did not. He never parked close enough to the door for the cameras to pick up his vehicle."

Colton wished there were parking lot cameras. Even a grainy picture would give him some idea of the kind of vehicle River was driving, if that was in fact him. The coincidence was almost too uncanny.

The possibility the clerk could've picked up on any details of the bombing case from the media was nil. He'd kept a very tight rein on the details of the morning's event on purpose. He'd released a statement that said there had been an incident involving an RV and a homemade explosive device, and there'd been no casualties or injuries. Technically, that part was true. The scratch on his arm would be fine and his hearing would return to normal in a few days. The ringing was already easing.

Evidence was mounting against River.

"And this witness was certain, without a shadow of a doubt, that the man at the motel matched the BOLO?"

"Not one hundred percent," Gert admitted. "She said she wouldn't exactly bet her life on it, but it was probably him."

Colton cursed under his breath. He needed a witness who would testify they were certain it was River, not someone who *thought* it might be him.

"This is something. At least we have someone who can most likely place him in town or at least near town. Birchwood is a half-hour drive from here."

"That's right, sir."

"Is he still there, by chance?" He probably should've asked this already, except that Gert would've known to lead with it.

"That's a negative sir." Gert's frustration came through the line in her sigh. "You're going to love this one. He checked out first thing this morning, at around six thirty."

Colton had figured as much, even though he'd hoped for a miracle. River, or anyone in law enforcement, would be smart enough to stay on the move. "You mentioned the place was basically a cash-and-carry operation. Is that right?"

"Yes, sir. And I confirmed that the person who'd stayed in room 11 paid with cash."

"Good work, Gert." Colton pressed his lips together to keep from swearing.

Makena issued a sharp sigh. "So close."

"Thanks for the information, Gert. It gives us confirmation that we're on the right track."

"My pleasure, sir. And you know me. Once I'm on a trail, I stick with it."

"I've never been sure who was the better investigator between the two of us. I appreciate all your efforts." He knew it made Gert's chest swell with pride to hear those words. He meant them, too. She was a formidable investigator and she'd proven to be invaluable in many cases.

Colton thanked her again before ending the call.

"I knew it was only a matter of time before he caught up to me." Makena's voice was a study in calm as she stabbed her fork into her salad. Almost too calm. And yet, Colton figured she was much like the surface of the river. Calm on top with a storm raging below the surface.

If River checked out at six o'clock this morning, he could've set the bomb at the RV. He'd had a specific detonation in mind. It made sense to Colton that he'd wanted Makena to be stepping on the platform as she headed inside the RV to blow her up. Otherwise, if she stepped on the platform to go outside, then the bomb could've been a warning. It was possible, maybe unlikely, the ordeal was meant to be a scare tactic.

Without knowing much about River, it was difficult to ascertain which. But what would he have to gain by scaring her months later?

River had had some time on his hands recently to stew on his situation. It was clear the guy had a temper. He'd used that on Makena during their marriage. And yet a hothead didn't tend to be as calculating. That type was usually more spontaneous.

In Colton's years of investigating domestic violence cases, of which there'd been sadly too many, it was generally a crime of passion that led to murder. A spouse walked in on another spouse having an affair. The unsuspecting spouse got caught up in the moment, grabbed a weapon and committed murder.

Makena had not had an affair in this case. She'd left. That was a betrayal someone like River wouldn't take lightly.

Chapter Eleven

Makena pushed around a piece of lettuce on her plate. The fact that River had been in town at the very least on the morning someone had attempted to take her life sat heavy on her chest. It wouldn't do any good to look back and question how on earth she'd ever trusted him in the first place.

It was time to move forward. And then something dawned on her. "Did I hear right? Did Gert say River checked into that hotel four nights ago?"

"That's the same thing I heard. Gert will write it all up in a report, but yeah, that's what I heard." Colton rocked his head. He pushed the phone away from their plates.

"So River shows up four days ago. It's now been four days since I saw Red and Mustache Man." A picture was taking shape, but it was still too fuzzy to make out all the details.

"So these three have met in your garage and now they are in town at the same time without staying in the same room. We don't know if they rented a room next door." Colton got up, found a notepad and pen and then reclaimed his seat. He scratched out a note for them to check with the early-morning-shift clerk to see if anyone matching the description of Red or Mustache had checked in or been seen coming into or out of River's room.

"Gert said River had no visitors," she corrected, distinctly remembering Gert's words.

"True." He scratched out the last part. "Which didn't mean they didn't meet up somewhere."

She was already thinking the same thing.

"Maybe they thought I overhead them and that's why I left my husband. Maybe in their twisted-up minds they think I know something, which meant the meeting in the garage could've been some kind of planning meeting."

Colton was already nodding his head. "It makes sense. When we look at murder or an attempted murder case, we're always looking for the motive. In your case, one could make the argument that River was still jealous months after you left and that it took him that long to hunt you down. That would make sense. It's a story that, unfortunately, has been told before. The twist in this case is Mustache and Red. If River was here because of a jealousy that he couldn't let go of or because he didn't want you to ever be with anyone else, which is another motive in domestic cases, there wouldn't have been anyone else with him."

"That's exactly my thinking. So if I did walk in on a meeting that day and they think I know something, which I assure you I don't no matter how much I wish I did, they're willing to kill me to make sure I'm silenced. River has already gotten in trouble with his department for extortion. At least, he's under investigation for it." They were finally on a path that made some sense to her. Granted, it was still twisted and unfair, and she didn't like anything about it, period, but it made sense. "Okay, what do we do next?"

"Tonight? We eat. We try to set the case aside at least for a little while. Overly focusing on something and overthinking it only creates more questions. Tomorrow, six a.m., we pay a visit to Gloria Beecham and see if she remembers seeing Red or Mustache anywhere in the area. If we can link those three up, it's a story that makes sense."

Colton was holding something back.

"What is it?"

"There's another story that says all three of them are in town and in a race to see who gets to you first."

Makena shuddered at the thought. It was a theory that couldn't be ignored. It would still take a while to wrap her thoughts around the fact that anyone would want her dead, let alone three people. But it was possible each person was acting on his own, trying to be the one to get to her first to see what she knew and if she had evidence against any one of them.

"Think you can eat something?" Colton motioned toward her plate. "It's important to keep up your strength."

"I can try." She surprised herself by finishing the plate a few minutes later. Colton was right about one thing—overthinking the case would most likely drive her insane.

When the plates were empty, she picked up hers and headed toward the sink. She stopped midway. "I can clean yours while I'm up." At least the ringing noise in her ears was substantially better if not her left hip. The bruise was screaming at her, making its presence known. Colton was right. All she wanted was to stand under a warm shower and to curl up on the couch and watch TV to take her mind off the situation.

Colton was on his feet in the next second, plate in hand. He was such a contrast to River, who, in all the years she spent with him, basically set a plate down wherever he was and got up and walked away without a thought about how it got cleaned and ended up back in the cabinet the next day. He'd blamed his disinclination to do the house chores on being tired after working the deep night shift. The truth was that he thrived on that schedule. And the other truth was that he was lazy.

"It's not that hard for me to rinse off a second dish and put it in the dishwasher."

Colton set his dish down next to the sink. "For the last year, I've done everything for myself. Well, for myself and two little ones. I'm not trying to be annoying by doing everything myself, but I can see how that might get on someone's nerves. Especially someone who is strong and independent, and also used to doing things for herself. The truth is, being in the kitchen together making dinner tonight, even though it was literally nothing but pizza and salad, was probably my favorite time in this kitchen since I moved in."

Well, damn. Colton sure had a way with words. His had just touched her heart in the best possible way and sent warmth rocketing through her. She stopped what she was doing, turned off the spigot and leaned into him.

"It's been a pretty crazy twenty-four hours since we literally ran into each other, but it's really good to see you again, Colton."

It was so easy in that moment to turn slightly until her body was flush with his and tilt her face toward him. She pushed up on her tiptoes and pressed a kiss to his soft, thick lips. Being around Colton again was the easiest thing despite the electricity constantly pinging between them. Instead of fighting it…she was so very tired of fighting…she leaned into it.

Colton took a deep breath. And then he brought

his hands up to cup her face. He ran his thumb along her jawline and then her chin as he trailed his lips in a line down her neck. He feathered a trail of hot kisses down her neck and across her shoulder. She placed the flat of her palms against his solid-walled chest, letting her fingers roam.

She smoothed her hands toward his shoulders and then up his neck, letting her fingers get lost in that thick mane of his as he deepened the kiss.

There was so much fire and energy and passion in the kiss. Her breath quickened and her pulse raced. Kissing Colton was better than she'd imagined it could be. No man had ever kissed her so thoroughly or made her need from a place so deep inside her.

He splayed one of his hands across the small of her back and pressed her body against his. Then his hands dropped, and she lifted her legs up and with help wrapped them around his midsection. He dropped his head to the crook of her neck.

Colton held onto her for a long minute in that position before he released a slow, guttural groan and found her lips again.

He fit perfectly and all she wanted to do was get lost with him.

THE ATTRACTION THAT had been simmering between Colton and Makena ignited into a full-blown blaze. He wanted nothing more than to strip down and bury himself deep inside her.

Her fingernails dug into the flesh of his shoulders. Considering her injury, this was about as far as he could let things go between them. There was another reason. A more obvious one. He knew without a doubt that taking their relationship to the next level would be a game changer for him, and he hoped it would be for her, too.

But she had trust issues and he still hadn't gotten over the loss of his best friend. Besides, as much as Makena fit him in every possible way, he had zero time to commit to a new relationship. He had the boys to think about and the fact that they might not be comfortable with him moving a stranger into the house. Somewhere in the back of his mind, his brain tried to convince him these were excuses. Maybe they were.

But if he was ready, he doubted his mind would try to come up with reasons they shouldn't be together. The biggest of which was the fact that she hadn't gotten over the experience with her ex.

Colton had seen that fear in her eyes one too many times. Granted, her anxiety had never been aimed at him and he would never do anything knowingly to hurt her. He wouldn't have to. His badge and gun might prove to be a problem for her.

Plus, she'd changed her life in every sense of the word. She needed to reemerge and find a footing in her new life.

Makena moaned against his lips, and it was about

the sexiest damn thing he'd ever heard. Let this go on too much longer and no cold shower in the world would be able to tame the blaze. Because he was just getting started.

He dropped his hands from her face, running his finger down to the base of her neck. He lowered his hand to her full breast and then ran his thumb along her nipple. It beaded under his touch and sent rockets of awareness through his body. Every single one of his muscles cried out for the sweet release only she could give. His need for Makena caused a physical ache.

Sleeping together at this point would only complicate the relationship. She was beginning to open up to him more and more. He sensed she was beginning to lean on him, and he liked the fact her trust in him was growing.

She needed to be sure how he felt about her before taking this to the next level. And since he was just now trying to figure that out himself, he pulled back and touched his forehead to hers. Their breathing was raspy. A smile formed on his lips.

Having twin sons had sure made one helluva grown-up out of him. Not that he'd taken sex lightly in the past. He preferred serial dating before he married Rebecca, and always made certain that his partners knew one hundred percent that the relationship would be based on mutual physical attraction. The likelihood anything emotional or permanent would come out of it was off the table.

"What is it, Colton? What's wrong? Did I do something?"

"You? Not a chance. It's me. And before you think I'm giving you the whole 'it's not you, it's me' speech, it really is me. I think whatever we have brewing between us could turn out to be something special. But the timing is off. I think we both realize that." He almost couldn't believe those words had just come out of his mouth. They were true. They needed to be said. But, damn.

He felt the need to explain further, because he didn't want her to be embarrassed or have any regrets. "For the record, I think that was probably up there with the best kisses of my life."

He could feel her smiling.

"Okay, I lied. That was the best kiss of my life. And it gets me in trouble because I don't want to stop there. I want more. And when I say more, I don't just mean physical." He could almost hear the wheels spinning in her brain and could sense she was about to do some major backpedaling.

"I hear what you're saying, Colton. I feel whatever this is happening between us, too. I don't exactly have anything to give right now." Ouch. Those words hurt more than he was expecting them to.

"You don't have to explain any of that to me. I feel the same."

"I'm sorry. This is the second time I've put you in this position. I promise not to do it again." She pulled back and put her hands up in the surrender position, palms out.

"Well, that's disappointing to hear." Colton laughed, a rumble from deep in his chest rolling up and out.

She looked at him with those clear blue eyes, so honest and still glittering with desire. The way his heart reacted, he thought he might've made a huge mistake in pulling back. Logic said that he had done the right thing in preparing her. His life didn't have room for anyone else, and she was just about to figure out what her new life was going to be. She didn't need him inserting himself right in the middle and possibly confusing her.

A sneaky little voice in the back of his mind said his defense mechanisms were kicking into high gear. He hushed that because it was time to think about something else.

"We could watch a movie to take our minds off things. We could talk." Normally, that last option would've felt like pulling teeth with no Novocain. But he actually liked talking to Makena. Go figure.

"I think what I would like more than anything is to curl up on the sofa with you and turn the fireplace on low. And maybe have something warm to drink. Maybe something without caffeine."

"Sounds like a plan. As far as the hot beverage without caffeine, I'm kind of at a loss on that one."

It was her turn to laugh. She reached up and grabbed a fistful of his shirt and tugged him toward her. She stopped him just before their lips met. "Thank you, Colton. You've brought alive parts of me that I honestly didn't know existed anymore. You've shown me what a strong, independent man can be."

This time she didn't push forward and press a kiss to his lips, and disappointment nearly swallowed him.

He smiled at her compliment and squeezed her hand, needing to refocus before he headed down that emotional path again.

"Good luck if you want something warm in this house that doesn't have caffeine."

"If you have water, a stove and maybe a lemon or honey, I can get by just fine."

"I definitely have honey. It's in the cupboard. Gert makes a point of bringing some back for everyone in the office when she visits honeybee farms. She's made a goal to visit every one in the state before the end of the year. I should have a few bottles in there to choose from. As far as lemons go, I actually might have a few of those in the bin inside the fridge. I'll just make a call and check on my boys. I really want to hear their voices before they go to sleep. So if you'll excuse me, I'll take the call in the other room while you make up your warm batch of honey-lemon water."

His smile was genuine, and when she beamed back at him his heart squeezed. His traitorous heart would have to get on board with the whole "he needed to slow the train down" plan. It was on a track of its own, running full steam ahead.

Makena pushed him back a little bit in a playful motion. He hesitated for just a second, holding her gaze just a little too long, and his heart detonated when he turned to walk away. He exhaled a sigh and grabbed his phone off the granite island before heading into the bedroom.

He gave himself a few moments to shake off the haze in his mind from kissing Makena. He was still in a little bit of shock that one kiss could ignite that level of passion in him. He chalked it up to going too long without sex. That had to be the reason. He hadn't felt a flame burning like that in far too long.

After a few more deep breaths, he was at a ready point to hear his sons' little babbling voices. He pulled up his mother's contact and let his thumb hover over her number.

He dropped his thumb onto the screen and put the phone to his ear. It took a couple of rings for his mother to pick up. When she did, he could hear the sounds of his little angels in the background, laughing. He'd recognize those voices anywhere.

"Hi, son. I was just drying off the boys after their

baths. How are you doing?" she asked. He listened for any signs of distress in her voice that meant taking care of the boys was too much for her right now.

"All is well here. We're moving forward with the investigation and I'll be up and out early tomorrow morning to go interview a potential witness. Making progress." Hearing his sons' laughter in the background warmed his heart.

"Colton, what's really wrong?" His mom could read him and his brothers better than a psychic.

"The case. I know the intended target from college. We go way back and she's a good person. She definitely doesn't deserve what's being handed to her." It would do no good to lie to his mother. She'd be able to hear it in his tone and he wouldn't feel good about it anyway. He'd been honest with her since seventh grade, after he'd hidden his phone in his room so he could call Rebecca when they were supposed to be asleep.

A young Colton hadn't slept a wink that night. He'd come clean about the deception in the morning and his mother said he'd punished himself enough. She expected him to leave his phone downstairs before he went up to bed just like the others did. Garrett had always sneaked back down to get his, but that was Garrett and beside the point.

Lying had taught Colton that he was an honest person.

Plus, his mother had been around him and his

brothers who worked in law enforcement long enough to realize they wouldn't be allowed to divulge details about an ongoing investigation. She wouldn't dig around.

And she wouldn't ask. There were lines families in law enforcement never crossed.

"I'm sorry to hear such a nice-sounding person is having a rough go of it." He could hear more of that innocent laughter come across the line and he figured his mother knew exactly the distraction he needed. "The boys have had a wonderful day. They've been angels with just enough spunk in them for me to know they're O'Connor boys through and through."

"That's good to hear."

"Do you want me to put them on the line? I can put the phone in between them. They're here on the bed. Well, mostly here on the bed. Renee is here helping me and they keep trying to move to get away from the lotion." His mom laughed. It sounded genuine, and there'd been too much of that missing in her life over the past few months. It made him feel a lot less guilty about having the boys stay over with her for a few days. They might be just the distraction she needed.

"I would love it. Put them on." He could hear shuffling noises, which he assumed was her putting the phone down.

Her mouth was away from the receiver when she

said, "Hey, boys. Guess who is calling you? It's your Dada."

It warmed his heart the way his family had accepted Silas and Sebastian despite the circumstances of their birth.

"Hey, buddies. I hope you are behaving for your Mimi and Aunt Renee." In truth, there wasn't a whole lot to say to one-year-olds. All he really wanted to hear was the sound of their giggles. Knowing how well they were being cared for and how much his mother loved them. It was kind of Renee to help.

One of the twins shrieked, "Dada!"

The other one got excited and started chanting the same word. Colton didn't care how or why his boys had come into his life. He was a better man for having them. He kept the phone to his ear and just listened.

A few minutes later, his mother came back on the line.

"Well, these two are ready for a little snack before bedtime," she said.

"Sounds good, Mom." He wanted to ask how she was really doing but figured this wasn't the time. Instead, he settled on, "They really love you."

"Well, that's a good thing because I love them more. And I love you." There was a genuine happiness to her tone that made Colton feel good.

They said their goodbyes and ended the call.

Colton glanced at the clock. It was after eight. He needed to grab a shower and get some shut eye soon. Four o'clock in the morning would come early and he wanted to be at the motel the minute the clerk started work.

Colton took a quick shower, toweled off and then threw on some sweatpants and a T-shirt. By the time he joined Makena in the other room, she was curled up on the couch. She'd figured out how to flip the switch to turn on the fireplace. He didn't want to dwell on how right it felt to see her sitting there in his home, on his sofa, looking comfortable and relaxed.

If it was just the two of them and she was in a different mental space, letting this relationship play out would be a no-brainer. But he had his children to think about and how the loss of their mother at such a young age would affect their lives. He also had to consider how bringing someone into their lives who could leave again might impact them. He couldn't see himself getting into a temporary relationship or introducing them to someone who might not stick around for the long haul.

"Shower's free. I left a fresh towel out for you and a washcloth. It's folded on the sink," he said, trying to ignore his body's reaction to her. His heart—traitor that it was—started beating faster against his rib cage.

Sitting there, smiling up at him, Makena was pure temptation. A temptation he had to ignore—for his own sanity.

Chapter Twelve

The shower was amazing and quick. Makena couldn't help but think about the case, despite trying to force it from her thoughts. It was impossible for questions not to pop into her mind after the update they'd received from Gert.

It was probably odd to appreciate the fact that she knew River. He had a physical description and a job. She couldn't imagine being targeted by someone without any idea who it could be or why.

Granted, in her case, the why was still a question mark. It could be his jealous nature. Or it could be that he believed she'd overheard something.

At least she wouldn't walk down the street next to the person targeting her without realizing it. Even Red and Mustache were on her radar.

And then there was Colton. She couldn't imagine having a better investigator or a better human being on her side. He'd grown into quite an incredible person, not that she was surprised. His cobalt blue eyes had always been just a little too serious and a little too intense even in college. He saw things most people would never notice. After hearing more about his family, she was starting to get a better understanding of him and what made him tick.

To say her feelings for him were complicated barely scratched the surface. She got dressed and brushed her teeth before venturing into the living room.

Colton sat in front of the fire, studying his laptop. Her heart free-fell at the sight of him looking relaxed and at ease. Butterflies flew in her stomach and she was suddenly transported back to biology lab at the time they had first met. Those feelings were very much alive today and sent rockets of need firing through her.

"Hey, I thought we agreed. No more working on the case tonight." She moved to the kitchen and heated more water. The lemon and honey water had done the trick earlier.

"I was just mapping out our route to the motel tomorrow morning. I wanted to be ready to go so that we're there the moment Gloria Beecham checks in for work."

"That sounds like a plan." The buzzer on the microwave dinged and she poured the warm water into the mug she'd used earlier.

"It's about a half hour's drive, so we should probably get on the road at five thirty at the latest."

"In the morning?" She gripped the mug and added a slice of lemon along with another teaspoon of honey. After stirring the mixture, she made her way back to the sofa, noticing how badly her attempt at humor had missed the mark.

Colton continued to study the screen without looking up. She hoped she hadn't offended him earlier before the showers but the air in the room had definitely shifted. A wall had come up.

Makena pulled her legs up and tucked her feet underneath her bottom. She sat a couple of feet from Colton and angled herself toward him. From this distance, she'd be less likely to reach out and touch him. The feel of his silk-over-steel muscles was too much temptation. It would be so easy to get lost with him.

But then what?

There was no way she wanted to do anything that might drive a wedge between her and Colton. He was her best and only friend right then. She had no plans to cut off her lifeline. An annoying voice in the back of her head called her out on the excuses.

"So, the way I understand it, there's a story behind why everyone in law enforcement got there. What's yours?" She wanted to know why he'd chosen this profession versus taking up ranching.

He chuckled, a low rumble in his chest. "Do you mean more than the fact that I grew up with five brothers, all of whom were close in age?"

"That would challenge anyone's sense of justice," she laughed.

"I think it was always just inside me." He closed the laptop and shifted it off his lap and onto the sofa. Then he turned to face her. "We all used to play Cops and Robbers. Growing up on a ranch, we had plenty of room to roam and enough time to use our imagination. I was always drawn to the cop. For a while, I tried to tell myself that I was a rancher. Don't get me wrong, ranching is in my blood and it's something I think I've always known I'd do at some point. We all pitch in, especially me before the boys came. I think I always knew it was just a matter of time. I want to take my place at the ranch. Later. I'm just not ready. So in college, when my parents tried to get me to go to the best agricultural school in the state, I rebelled. Our university had a pretty decent business school, and that's how I convinced my parents it was right for me. They weren't really trying to force me into anything so much as trying to guide me based on what they thought I wanted."

"They sound like amazing parents."

"They were…my mom still is," he said.

"I'm guessing by that answer there's no news about who is responsible for your father's death. I'm really sorry about that, Colton. About *all* of it."

"Before I checked the map, I was digging around in the case file. I couldn't find anything else to go on."

"Maybe no one was supposed to find him," she offered.

"It's possible. There are just so many unanswered questions. When I really focus on it, it just about drives me insane."

She could only imagine someone in his shoes, someone who was used to giving answers to others in their darkest moments, would be extremely frustrated not to be able to give those answers to his own family. She figured that between him and his brothers who worked for the US Marshal Service, they wouldn't stop until they found out why their father was killed. Their sister's kidnapping must have influenced their decisions to go into law enforcement in the first place. "How long has it been?"

"A couple of months now. He was digging around in my sister's case."

"You mentioned that she was kidnapped as a baby. Thirty-plus years is a long time. Wouldn't any leads be cold?"

"Yes. The trail was almost instantly cold and has remained so to this day. We're missing something. That's what keeps me up at night. It's the thing that I don't know yet but know is out there, which gives me nightmares. It's the one piece that, when you find it, will make the whole puzzle click together. That's been missing in my sister's case for decades."

This was the first time she'd ever heard a hint of hopelessness in Colton's voice. Despite knowing just how dangerous this path could be, she reached over and took his hand in hers. He'd done so much for her and she wanted to offer whatever reassurance she could. The electricity vibrating up her arm from their touch was something she could ignore. She needed to ignore it. Because it wasn't going to lead her down a productive path.

She couldn't agree more with Colton about timing.

"I wish there was something I could say or do to help."

"Believe it or not, just being able to talk about it for a change is nice. We never talk about Caroline's case at home. Our mother has a little gathering every year on Caroline's birthday and we have cake. She talks about what little she remembers about her daughter. It isn't much and it feels like Caroline is frozen in time. Always six months old. I've already had more time with my sons than my mother did with my sister. And I can't imagine anything happening to either one of my boys."

"It hardly seems fair," she agreed.

Colton rocked his head and twined their fingers together.

"We better get some sleep if we intend to be out the door by five thirty." He squeezed her fingers in a move that she figured was meant to be reassuring. He got up and turned off the fireplace. From the other room, he grabbed a pillow and some blankets. "For tonight, I'll take the couch."

"I thought we already talked about this." The last thing she wanted to do was steal the man's bed. It was actually a bad idea for her to think about Colton and a bed because a sensual shiver skittered across her skin.

"We did. I said I'd take the couch tonight and you'll take the bed. If I have to, I'll walk over there, pick you up and carry you to bed." At least there was a hint of lightness and playfulness in his tone now that had been missing earlier. There was also something else…something raspy in his voice when he'd mentioned his bed. And since she knew better than to tempt fate twice in one night, she pushed up to standing, walked over and gave him a peck on the cheek…and then went to bed.

COLTON SLEPT IN fifteen-minute intervals. By the time the alarm on his watch went off he'd maybe patched together an hour of sleep in seven. It was fine. He rolled off the couch and fired off a dozen pushups to get the blood pumping. He hopped to his feet and did a quick set of fifty jumping jacks. He'd been sitting way more than usual in the past thirty-six hours and his body was reminding him that it liked to be on the move.

He followed jumping jacks with sit-ups and rounded out his morning wake-up routine with squats. As quietly as he could manage, he slipped down the hall past his master bedroom, past the boys' room, where he lingered for just a second in the doorway of the open door. And then he made his way to the master bath where he washed his face, shaved and brushed his teeth.

Makena didn't need to be up for another hour. There was something right about her being curled up in his bed. He didn't need the visual, not this early in the morning. So he didn't stop off at the master bedroom on his way to the coffee machine.

The supplies were all near the machine, so he had a cup in hand and a piece of dry toast in less than three minutes. It didn't take long for the caffeine to kick in or for questions to swirl in the back of his mind.

At first, he thought about his father's case. Colton had a dedicated deputy to untangle Mrs. Hubert's financials and the contact information that had been found in her computer. Her files were all coded and his deputy was presently on full-time duty trying to crack the code. The older woman who was murdered a few months ago had ties to a kidnapping ring. Had she been involved in Caroline's case?

As a professional courtesy, and also considering the fact they were brothers, he was sharing information with Cash and Dawson. Those two were working the case in their spare time, as well. Even with a crack team of investigators, it would take time to unravel Mrs. Hubert's dealings. Time to get justice for Finn O'Connor was running out. A cold trail often led to a cold case. It occurred to Colton that his mother could be in danger, too.

There could be something hidden around the house, a file or piece of evidence their father had been hiding that could lead a perp to her door.

Colton tapped his fingers on his mug. He thought about time. And how short it could be. How unfair it could be and how quickly it could be robbed from loved ones.

It was too early in the morning to go down a path of frustration that his boys would never know their mother. Besides, as long as he had air in his lungs, he would do his best to ensure they knew what a wonderful a person she was.

Colton booted up his laptop and checked his email. Several needed attention, so he went ahead and answered those. Others could wait. A couple he forwarded on to Gert. She'd been awfully quiet since the phone call last night, which didn't mean she wasn't working. It just meant she hadn't found anything worth sharing.

He pinched the bridge of his nose to stem the headache threatening. Then he picked up the pencil from on top of his notepad. He squeezed the pencil so tight while thinking about the past that it cracked in half. Frustration that he wasn't getting anywhere in the two most important cases of his life got the best of him and he chucked the pencil pieces against the wall.

Colton cursed. He looked up in time to see a feminine figure emerge from his bedroom. Makena had on pajama bottoms and a T-shirt. The bottoms were pink plaid. Pink was his new favorite color.

"Morning." She walked into the room and right past the broken pieces of pencil.

"Back atcha." He liked that she knew where everything was and went straight to the cabinet for the coffee. She had a fresh cup in her hands and a package of vanilla yogurt by the time he moved to the spot to clean up the broken pencil.

"How'd you sleep?" he asked her as he tossed the bits into the trash.

"Like a baby." She stretched her arms out and yawned before digging into the yogurt. The movement pressed her ample breasts against the cotton of her T-shirt.

Colton forced his gaze away from her soft curves. "How's your hip today?" He'd noticed that she was walking better and barely limped.

"So far, so good," she said. "I don't think I'm ready to run a marathon anytime soon, but I can make it across the room without too much pain. The bruise is already starting to heal." She motioned toward her hip, a place his eyes didn't need to follow.

Colton made a second cup of coffee, which he polished off by the time she finished her first.

"I can be dressed and ready in five minutes. Is that okay?" she asked.

"Works for me." He gathered up a few supplies like his notebook and laptop and tucked them into a bag.

Makena emerged from the bedroom as quickly as she'd promised, looking a little too good. He liked the fact that she could sleep when she was around him, because she'd confessed that she hadn't done a whole lot of that in recent months.

He smiled as he passed by her, taking his turn in the bedroom. He dressed in his usual jeans, dark button-down shirt and windbreaker. He retrieved his belt from the safe and then clipped it on his hip.

He returned to the kitchen where Makena stood, ready to go.

The drive to the motel took exactly twenty-nine minutes with no traffic. The place was just as Gert had described. A nondescript motel off the highway that fit the information Gert had passed along—that it rented rooms by the hour. There was an orange neon sign that had M-O-T-E-L written out along with a massive arrow pointing toward the building. Colton had always driven by those places and wondered why people needed the arrow to find it. He could chew on that another day.

"It's best if you stick to my side in case anything unexpected goes down. I'm not expecting anything, but should River still be in the area or pop in to rent another room, I want you to get behind me as a first option or anything that could put the most mass between you and him. Okay?"

She nodded and he could see that she was clear on his request. She'd been silent on the ride over, staring out the window, alone in her thoughts. Colton hadn't felt the need to fill the space between them with words. It had been a comfortable silence. One that erased the years they'd been apart.

The office of the motel was a small brick building that had a screen door in front of a white wooden one. The second door was cracked open enough to see dim lighting. He opened the screen door as he tucked Makena behind him.

With his hand on her arm, he could feel her trembling. River's connection to this place seemed to be taking a toll on her. A renewed anger filled Colton as he bit back the frustration. Of course, she'd be nervous and scared. She'd been running from this guy for literally months and here she was walking inside a building where he'd recently stayed.

Inside, they were greeted by a clerk whose head could barely be seen above the four-and-a-half-foot counter. The walls were made of dark wood paneling. The worn carpet was hunter green, and the yellow laminate countertop gave the place a leftover-from-another-era look.

"How can I help you, Sheriff?" The woman didn't seem at all surprised to see him, and he figured his deputy might've let her know someone would most likely swing by to speak to her.

"Are you Gloria?" he asked. Aside from the long bar-height counter that the little old lady could barely see over, there were a pair of chairs with a small table nestled in the right-hand side of the room. To his left, in the other corner, a flat-screen TV had been mounted.

"In the flesh." She smiled.

"I understand you spoke to one of my deputies yesterday. My name is Sheriff Colton O'Connor." He walked to the counter and extended his right hand. "Pleased to meet you."

The little old lady took his hand. Her fingers might be bony and frail but she had a solid handshake and a formidable attitude.

"Pleased to make your acquaintance, Sheriff. You're in here to talk to me about one of my clients." She had the greenest eyes he'd ever seen. He didn't get the impression she'd had an easy life. The sparkle in her eyes said she'd given it hell, though.

"Yes, ma'am. This is a friend of mine and she's familiar with the case." He purposely left out Makena's name.

Gloria nodded and smiled toward Makena. "My name might be Gloria but everyone around here calls me Peach on account of the fact I was born in Georgia. I've lived in Texas for nearly sixty years but picked up the name in second grade and it stuck."

Peach's gaze shifted back to Colton. She nodded and smiled after shaking hands with Makena.

"Can you tell me everything you remember about the visitor in room 11?" Colton asked, directing the conversation.

"The name he used to check in was Ryan Reynolds. I can get the ledger for you if you'd like to see it."

"I would." Ryan Reynolds was a famous actor, so it was obviously a fake name. Colton figured that Makena could confirm whether or not the handwriting belonged to River.

Peach opened a drawer and then produced a black book before finding a page with the date from five days ago.

"I get folks' information on the computer usually, but my cash customers like to sign in by hand the old-fashioned way." He bet they did.

She hoisted the book onto the counter and, using two fingers on each hand, nudged it toward Colton. He looked at the name she pointed at. Ryan Reynolds. The movie star. Somehow, Colton seriously doubted the real Ryan Reynolds would have come all the way to this small town to rent a motel room. Last he'd checked, there were no movies being made in the area. But this wasn't the kind of place where a person would use his or her real name, and Peach clearly hadn't asked for ID.

Colton leaned into Makena and said in a low voice, "Does that handwriting look like his?"

"Yes. He always makes that weird loop on his Rs. I mean, wrong name, obviously. But that's his handwriting."

"Do you mind if I take a picture of this?" Colton glanced up at Peach, who nodded.

Colton pulled out his phone and snapped a shot.

"I'd also like to keep this book as evidence. Did Mr. Reynolds touch the book or use a pen that you gave him?"

"Now that I really think about it, I don't think he did touch the book. I can't be sure. But the pen he used would be right there." She reached for a decorated soup can that had a bunch of pens in it.

"If you don't mind, I'd like to admit that as evidence." Colton's words stopped her mid-reach.

"Yes, sir. I'm happy to cooperate in any way that I can."

"Thank you, ma'am." Colton tipped his chin. "Has anyone else who looked suspicious been here over the last week or two?"

"You'll have to clarify what suspicious means, sheriff. I get all kinds coming through here," she quipped with a twinkle in her eye.

Chapter Thirteen

Okay, bad question on Colton's part. "Let me ask another way. Did you have anyone new show up?"

"I have a couple of regulars who come in once a month or every other week. This is a good stop for my truckers who are on the road."

"Anyone here you haven't seen before other than Mr. Reynolds?" he clarified.

"I've had a couple of people come through. I'd say in the last week or so there've been four or five, but we've been slower than usual."

"Has anyone say around six feet tall with light red hair, maybe could be described as strawberry blond, been in?"

She was already shaking her head before he could finish his sentence. "No. I would remember someone like that."

"How about anyone with black hair and a mustache?" he asked.

"No, sir." Her gaze shifted up and to the left, signaling she was trying to recall information. So far, she'd passed his honesty meters.

"I can't really recall anyone who looked like that coming through recently."

"Is it possible for me to view the footage from the occupant of room 11 as he came and went?" Colton asked.

"I can pull it up on the screen behind you now that I have here one of those digital files." She smiled and her eyes lit up as she waited for his response.

"That would be a big help." Colton turned his head and shifted slightly to the left. He put his right elbow on the counter, careful not to disturb the cash ledger.

The next few sounds were the click-click-clicks of fingers on a keyboard.

"Here we go," she said with an even bigger smile. "It should come up in just a second."

Colton's left hand was at his side. He felt Makena reach for him and figured she must need reassurance considering she was about to see a video of the man she'd been in a traumatic relationship with. He twined their fingers together and squeezed her hand in a show of support.

She closed what little distance was between them, her warm body against his. He ignored the frissons of heat from the contact. He'd never get used to them, but he had come to expect the reaction that always came and the warmth that flooded him while she was this close.

The TV set came to life and the sound of static filled the room. The next thing he knew, the volume was being turned down on the set. There was a large picture window just to the left of the TV screen and Colton surveyed the parking lot of the small diner across the street. There were five vehicles: two pickup trucks, a small SUV and a sedan. He figured at least one of those had to belong to an employee, possibly two.

"Here it is. Here's the day he checked in." Peach practically beamed with her accomplishment of finding his file.

Just as Gert had explained, the video was grainy as all get-out. The man in the video wore a Rangers baseball cap and kept his chin tucked to his chest. Out of the side of his mouth, Colton asked, "Is that about his height and weight?"

"Yes." There was a lot of emotion packed in that one word and a helluva lot of fight on the ready. He couldn't help being anything but proud of her. When some would cower, she dug deep and found strength.

"I don't have a whole lot of video of him, just his coming and going." Peach fast-forwarded, pausing each time his image came into view. The time stamps revealed dates from five days ago, four days ago and three days ago. Then it was down to two days and the same thing happened every time. He'd walk in or out of the room with his chin-to-chest posture. He didn't receive any visitors during that time except for daily visits from housekeeping. He didn't come and go often, mostly staying inside. He didn't have food delivered, which meant he either packed some or went out for food once a day. His eating habits would definitely classify as strange.

And then on the last day, the morning he checked out, he did something out of character and strange. He took off his hat as he left the room and glanced up at the camera, giving the recording device a full view of his face.

Makena's body tensed and she gripped Colton's hand even tighter.

River, she'd said, was a solid six-foot-tall man with a build that made it seem like he spent serious time at the gym. He had black hair and brown eyes. And was every bit the person who'd looked straight at the camera.

From the corner of Colton's eye, he now saw a man matching the description of River exit the diner and come running at full speed toward the motel office. He put his hands in the air, palms up, in the surrender position to show that he had no gun in his hands and he was surveying the area like he expected someone to jump out at him.

MAKENA HAD NOTICED the moment she and Colton had exited the vehicle earlier that he'd rested his right hand on the butt of his gun. Having been married to someone in law enforcement, she knew exactly the reason why. It was to have instant access to his weapon. The seconds it took for his hand to reach for his gun, pull it out of the holster and shoot could mean life or death for an officer. It also reminded her of the risks they were taking by visiting the place River had been in twenty-four hours ago.

As she followed Colton's gaze, she saw her ex-husband, to the shock of her life. Her body tensed. River was running straight toward them, hands high in the air, no doubt to show that he wasn't carrying a weapon.

Colton drew his, like anyone in law enforcement would.

"Get down and stay below the counter, Ms. Peach," he directed the clerk.

He tucked Makena behind him and repositioned himself so they were behind the counter. She wanted to face River and ask him why in hell he'd tried to blow her up yesterday morning, but she wasn't stupid. She wanted to make sure she did it safely. Colton had told her to either hide behind him or put some serious mass between her and River.

She dropped Colton's hand as it went up to cup the butt of the weapon she recognized as a Glock. She glanced around, looking for some kind of weapon. There was a letter opener. She grabbed it and tightened her fist around it.

If River somehow made it past Colton to get to her, she'd be ready.

Her left hand was fisted so tightly that her knuckles went white. Anger and resentment for the way she'd had to live in the past six months bubbled up again, burning her throat.

Colton crouched so only a small portion of his head and his weapon were visible as River opened the door.

Her ex was out of breath, and the expression on his face would probably haunt her for months to come. She expected to find hurt and anger and jealousy, emotions that had been all too common during their marriage. Instead, she found panic. His eyes were wide, and he kept blinking. He was nervous.

"I swear I'm not here to hurt anyone. You have to believe me," he said. He still had that authoritative cop voice but there was a hint of fear present that was completely foreign coming from him.

"Give me one good reason we should listen to you." Colton didn't budge. "And keep your hands up where I can see them.

Colton had that same authoritative law enforcement voice that demanded attention. Hearing it from River had always caused icy fingers to grip her spine, but her body's reaction was so different when she heard it come from Colton.

All the angry words that Makena wanted to spew at River died on her tongue. It was easy to see the man was in a panic. Whatever he'd done was catching up to him. That was her first thought.

"I swear on my mother's life that I'm not here to hurt anyone." His face was still frozen on the TV that was positioned behind him. He'd taken a couple of steps inside the room and then stopped in his tracks.

"How'd you know I was here?" Makena asked.

"I saw you come in, and they will, too," came the chilling response.

"Who are *they*?" Colton asked.

"I can't tell you and you don't want to know. Believe me. The only thing you need to be aware of is that your life is in danger." River's voice shook with dread and probably a shot of adrenaline.

A half-mirthful, half-frustrated sigh shot from Makena's throat. He wasn't telling her anything she didn't already know.

Makena locked eyes with the terrified older woman at the other end of the counter. Peach kept eye contact with Makena when she pointed at something inside a shelf. It was hidden from view and Makena had a feeling it was some kind of weapon, like a bat or a shotgun.

Makena shook her head. Peach nodded and tilted her head toward it.

"Talk to me, River. Tell me why they would be after me. Is it because of you?" As much as Makena didn't believe that anymore, she had to ask. She needed to hear from him that wasn't the case, and she needed to get him talking so she could understand why it seemed like the world was crumbling around her.

"It's not important *what* you know. It's what they *think* you know. Even more important right now is that you get the hell out of here. Stay low. Stick with this guy." He motioned toward Colton. "He can probably protect you if you stay out of sight. Just give me time. I need time to straighten everything out."

"Time? To what? Plant another bomb?" she said.

She'd never seen River look this rattled before. And also…something else…helpless? His eyes darted around the room and he looked like he'd jump out of his skin if a cat hopped up on the counter.

This close, she could see his bloodshot eyes and the dark circles underneath. They always got that way when he went days without sleep. He was almost in a manic state and part of her wondered if deep down he actually did care about her well-being or if this was all some type of self-preservation act. To make it seem like he was a victim. But to what end?

"I knew they were planning something, but I had no idea…" River brought his hands on top of his head. His face distorted. "Everything's a mess now. I made everything a mess. I never meant for you to get caught up in this. Bad timing. But just do what

I say and lie low. Trust me, you don't want to get anywhere near these guys."

His words sent another cold chill racing down her spine.

"You're not getting off that easy, River," Colton said. "Start talking now. I can work with the DA. I can talk with your chief if you give me something to take to him."

River's emotions were escalating, based on the increasing intensity of his expression.

This was not good. This was so not good.

"Are you kidding me right now? It's too late for me. It's too late to go back and fix what's wrong. I messed up big-time. There's not going to be any coming back from this for me but there's still time for me to fix it for you."

"Hold on. Just do me a favor and slow down." Colton's deep voice was a study in calm. "This doesn't have to end badly. Whatever you've done… I can't promise any miracles, but I can say that I'll do everything in my power if you talk. You need to tell us what's going on. You need to tell us who those men are and exactly why they're after Makena. It's the only way that I can help you."

River seemed more agitated. "You just don't understand. You don't get this and you don't realize what I'm going through or what I've done. It's too late. It's too late for me. I can accept that. But not her. She didn't do anything wrong."

The fact that River was concerned about her when it appeared his own life was on the line told her that she hadn't married a 100 percent jerk all those years ago. There had been something good inside him then and maybe she could work with that now.

Makena stood up taller so that she could look River in the eye, hoping that would make a difference. "I don't know what happened, River. But I do know there was a decent person in there at one time. The person I first met—"

"Is gone. That guy is long gone. Forget about the past and forget that you ever knew me. Just lie low and give me some time to get this straightened out."

"I've been in hiding for half a year, River. How much more of my life do I need to give up for whatever you did?" she asked.

Instead of calming him, that seemed to rile him up even more. She'd been truthful and her words seemed to have the effect of punching him.

"I know, Makena. I realize that none of this makes sense to you, and it's best for everyone else if it doesn't. If I could go back and change things, I would. Time doesn't work like that and our past mistakes do come back to haunt us."

Makena remembered that he was on leave for some pretty hefty charges. Maybe if she pretended like she already knew, he would come clean. "The men who are after me, who tried to blow me up… are they related to your administrative leave?"

River issued a sharp sigh and then started lowering his hands.

"Keep 'em up, high and where I can see them." Colton's voice left no room for doubt that he was not playing around. He could place River under arrest, she knew, but he seemed to be holding off long enough to get answers. She took it as a sign he believed River might give them useful information.

River's hands shot up in the air. Being in law enforcement, he would be very aware just how serious Colton was about those words. Colton's department-issued Glock was still aimed directly at River. All it would take was one squeeze of the trigger to end River's life.

Considering the man was standing not ten feet away, Colton wouldn't need a crackerjack shot to take him out.

"What did you do, River?" Makena asked again, hoping to wear him down and get answers. "You can help me the most if you tell Colton what you're involved in."

Hands in the air, River started pacing. He appeared more agitated with every forward step. His mood was dangerous and volatile. Deadly?

She scanned his body for signs of a weapon, knowing full well there had to be one there somewhere. On duty, he'd worn an ankle holster. It wasn't uncommon for him to hide his Glock in another holster tucked in the waistband of his jeans.

He mumbled and she couldn't make out what he was saying. And then he spun around to face them. "Did you say his name is Colton?"

"Yes, but I don't see how that has any bearing on anything."

"Really? Isn't that your ex-boyfriend from college? I used to read your journals, Makena."

Her face burned with a mix of embarrassment and outrage. She hadn't kept a journal since their early years of marriage. And yes, she had probably written something in it about Colton. But it had been so long ago she couldn't remember what she'd written.

"Colton was never my boyfriend. He wasn't then and he isn't now. But even if he was, that's none of your business anymore. In case you forgot, we're divorced. And this is my life, a life that I want back." She'd allowed him to take so much time of hers. No more.

Makena took in a deep breath because the current assertiveness, although she deserved to stand up for herself, wasn't exactly having a calming effect on River.

In fact, she feared she might be making it worse. She willed her nerves to calm down and her stress levels to relax.

"I won't pretend to know what you're going through right now." Colton's voice was a welcome calm in the eye of the storm. "I know you're facing some charges at work but if you help in this case it'll be noted in your jacket. It won't hurt and might convince a jury to go easier on you."

River looked at Colton. His gaze bounced back to Makena.

"Man, it's too late for me now."

And then the sound of a bullet split the air, followed by glass breaking on the front door.

The next few minutes happened in slow motion. Out of the corner of her eye, Makena saw Peach reach into the shelf. The older woman came up with a shotgun in a movement that was swift and efficient. It became pretty obvious this wasn't the woman's first rodeo.

She aimed the barrel of the gun right at River. But it was River who caught and held Makena's attention. As she ducked for cover, the look on his face would be etched in her brain forever.

At first his eyes bulged, and he took a step forward. She could've sworn she heard something whiz past her ear and was certain it was a second bullet. Before she realized, Colton positioned his body in between her and River.

River's arms dropped straight out. His chest flew toward her as he puffed it out. It was then she saw the red dot flowering in the center of his white cotton T-shirt. His mouth flew open, forming a word that never came out.

Shock stamped his features. He looked down at the center of his chest and said, "I've been shot."

He looked up at Makena and then Colton before repeating the words.

Colton was already on the radio clipped to his shoulder, saying words that would stick in her mind for a long time. She heard phrases like "officer down" and "ambulance required." This was all a little too real as she saw a pair of men, side by side and weapons at the ready, making their way across the street and toward the motel.

"I have to get you out of here," Colton said to Makena. The truck was parked behind the motel and she saw the brilliance of his plan now.

"Okay." It was pretty much the only word she could form or manage to get out under the circumstances. And then more came. "What about River?"

"There's nothing we can do to help him right now. The best thing we can do is lead those men away from the motel." Colton turned to Peach. "Is the back door locked?"

"Yes, sir." She ran a hand along the shelf and produced a set of keys. She tossed them to Colton, who snatched them with one hand. "You need to come with us. It's not safe here."

Peach lowered her face to the eyepiece of the shotgun. "I'll hold 'em off. You two get out of here while you can. I'll hold down the fort."

"I'm not kidding, Peach. You need to come with us now."

The woman shook her head and that was as much as she said.

"Help is on the way," Colton shouted to River, who'd taken a few steps back and dropped against the door, closing it. He sat with a dumbfounded look on his face.

"Reach up and lock that," Peach shouted to him.

Surprisingly, he obliged.

"We have to go." Colton, with keys in one hand and a Glock in the other, offered an arm, which Makena took as they ran toward the back.

He unlocked a key-only dead bolt and then tossed the keys into the hallway before fishing his own keys out of his pocket. The two of them ran toward the truck, which was thankfully only a few spaces from the door.

Once inside, he cranked on the ignition and backed out of the parking spot. "Stay low. Keep your head down. It's best if you get down on the floorboard."

Makena did as he requested. She noticed he'd scooted down, making himself as small as possible and less visible, therefore less of a target. He put the vehicle into Drive and floored the gas pedal.

In a ball on the floorboard as directed, Makena took in a sharp breath as Colton jerked the truck forward. It was a big vehicle and not exactly nimble. Size was its best asset.

"They have no idea who they're dealing with," Colton commented, and she realized it was because they were in his personal vehicle and not one marked as law enforcement.

A crack of a bullet split the air. It was then that Makena heard the third shot being fired.

Chapter Fourteen

Colton tilted his chin toward his left shoulder where his radio was clipped on his jacket. His weapon was in the hand that he also used to steer the wheel after they'd bolted from around the back of the motel.

Peach would be safe as he drew the perps away from the building and onto the highway. River had been shot and it looked bad for him, but he was still talking and alert, and that was a good sign.

Getting Makena out of the building and Birchwood had been his first priority. River was right about one thing. She'd be safer if she kept a low profile.

Colton also realized the reason the perps were shooting was probably because they didn't realize they were shooting at a sheriff. Even so, it had been one of his better ideas to slip out the back of his office yesterday and take his personal vehicle, because it seemed as though the perps had zeroed in on Makena's location at the RV.

They also seemed ready and able to shoot River though he was an officer of the law. With River's professional reputation tarnished, plus the charges being lobbed against him, they must think they could get away with shooting him.

"Gert, can you read me?" He hoped like hell she could, because she was his best link to getting help for River and for him and Makena.

Birchwood was in Colton's jurisdiction. One of his deputies passed by this motel on his daily drive to work, and Colton hoped that he was nearby, possibly on his way into work.

Gert's voice came through the radio. "I read you loud and clear."

"I have two perps who have opened fire on my personal vehicle. And an officer is down at the motel. Makena is in my custody and we're heading toward the station, coming in hot."

"Do you have a vehicle or a license plate or can you give me anything on who might be behind you?"

"The shooter was on foot." Colton took a moment to glance into his rearview mirror in time to see the pair of perps running toward a Jeep.

With the weight of his truck, he didn't have a great chance of outrunning them. "It's looking like a Jeep Wrangler. White. Rubicon written in black letters on the hood. I don't have a license plate but I imagine it won't take them long to catch up to me.

If they have one on the front of their vehicle, I can relay it."

He heard Makena suck in a breath. She scrambled into the seat and practically glued her face to the back window. "What can I do?"

"Stay low. Stay hidden. I don't have a way to identify myself in the truck. My vehicle is slow. But I'm going to do my level best to outrun them."

Makena didn't respond, so he wasn't certain she bought into his request. He was kicking up gravel on the service road to the four-lane highway. He took the first entrance ramp, and despite it being past seven o'clock in the morning on a Friday, there were more cars than he liked.

"Where are they now?" Makena asked.

"They're making their way toward us on the service road." Colton swerved in and out of the light traffic, pressing his dual cab truck to its limits. What it lacked in get-up-and-go, it made up for in size. If nothing else, he'd use its heft to block the Jeep from pulling alongside them.

Of course, the passenger could easily get off a shot from behind.

Colton leaned his mouth to his shoulder. "Where's the nearest marked vehicle?"

"Not close enough. I'm checking on DPS now to see if I can get a trooper in your direction. How are you doing? Can you hold them off until I can get backup to you?"

"I don't have a choice." Colton meant those words.

The Jeep had taken the on-ramp onto the highway and it wouldn't be long before it was on his bumper. He glanced around at the traffic and figured he'd better take this fight off the highway rather than endanger innocent citizens.

River was in trouble at work. Colton knew that for certain. What he wasn't sure of was his partners.

Colton relayed the description of the perps to Gert. "Call Chief Shelton at Dallas PD and see if any of his officers matching those descriptions have been connected in any way to River Myers. I want to know who River's friends were. Who he hung out with in the department and if any of them had visited the shooting range lately."

Most beat cops couldn't pull off the shot Red had at that distance and through a glass door. Whoever made the shot would get high scores in marksmanship at the range. Other officers would take note. Someone would know.

Between that and the physical descriptions, maybe River's supervising officer could narrow the search.

"Hold on, I'm going to swerve off the highway," he said, noting his chance.

At the last minute, he cranked the steering wheel right and made the exit ramp. It was probably too much to hope the perps lost him in traffic. There were plenty of black trucks on these roads.

He cursed when the Jeep took the exit.

"Gert, talk to me. Do you have someone at the motel?" Colton's only sense of relief so far was that he'd drawn the perps away from Peach and River. He also had a sneaky suspicion that Peach could take care of herself and could keep River there at gunpoint. Colton had no doubt the woman could hold her own until River received medical attention.

He could only hope that River would come clean with names.

Again, all they needed was a puzzle piece. At least now they knew that River had some connection to Red and Mustache. There was something the three of them had concocted or were doing they believed would land them in jail if someone found out. That someone, unfortunately, ended up being Makena. And again, he was reminded of how timing was everything.

If Makena had gone out to that garage five minutes before, maybe the men wouldn't have been there yet. Maybe River could've convinced her to go back to bed and she could be living out a peaceful life by now after the divorce.

His mind stretched way back to college. He'd wanted to ask her out but hadn't. Again, the ripple effect of that decision caused him to wonder about his timing. Now was not the time to dredge up the past. Besides, the Jeep was gaining on him. At this pace, it would catch him.

There were fields everywhere. One was a pasture for grazing. The other was corn stalks. The truck could handle either one and so could the Jeep. Colton couldn't get any advantage by veering off road. Except that in the corn, considering it was already tall, maybe he could lose them.

The meadow on the other side of the street was useless. The last thing he needed was more flat land. And while he didn't like the idea of damaging someone's crop and potential livelihood, he knew that he could circle back and make restitution. What was the point of having a trust fund he'd never touched if not for a circumstance like this one?

"Hang on tight, okay?" he said to Makena.

When she confirmed, he nailed a hard right. The truck bounded so hard he thought he might've cracked the chassis but stabilized once he got onto the field. The last thing he saw was the Jeep following.

Colton's best chance to confuse them was to maybe do a couple of figure eights and then zigzag through the cornfield. It would at the very least keep the perps from getting off a good shot. He was running out of options.

So far, the Jeep hadn't gotten close enough to them for him to be able to read a license plate if there was one on the front. Law required it to be there. However, many folks ignored it.

Considering these guys had good reason to hide

any identifying marks, they most certainly wouldn't have a plate up front.

Gert's voice cut through his thoughts. "I got you pulled up on GPS using your cell phone. I have a location on you, sir. Can you hold tight in the area until I can get someone to you?"

"That's affirmative. I can stick around as long as I keep moving." He tried to come off as flippant so Gert wouldn't worry about him any more than she already was.

Makena was getting bounced around in the floorboard. At this point, it would be safer for her to climb into the seat and strap in. So that was exactly what he told her to do.

She managed, without being thrown around too much.

The crops had the truck bouncing and slowed his speed considerably. He cut a few sharp turns, left and then right…right and then left. A couple of figure eights.

There was a time in his life when a ride like this might've felt exciting. His adrenaline was pumping and he'd be all in for the thrill. Even having a couple of idiots with guns behind him would've seemed like a good challenge. A lot had changed in him after he'd become a dad last year.

He took life more seriously and especially his own. Because he knew without a shadow of a doubt those boys needed their father to come home every night. And he would, today, too.

He checked his mirrors and was feeling pretty good about where he stood with regard to the perps. Until he almost slammed into the Jeep that had cut an angle right in front of him.

Slamming the brake and narrowly avoiding a collision, Colton bit out a few choice words.

Gert's voice came across the radio again. "Sir, I have names. Officer Randol Bic and Officer Jimmy Stitch were known associates of River Myers and fit the descriptions you gave. Bic is a sharpshooter. They're partners in East Dallas and both of their records are clean."

A picture was emerging. Was River taking the fall for Bic and Stitch?

Had they threatened him? Were they holding something over his head?

"I've heard those names before," Makena said. Gert's voice came across the radio. "Sir, I think the GPS is messing up. It looks like you're driving back and forth on the highway."

Colton couldn't help himself; he laughed. "Well, that's because I'm presently driving in a cornfield near the highway. GPS probably can't register that location."

"I feel like I should have known it would be something like that." Now Gert laughed. It was good to break up some of the tension. A sense of humor helped with keeping a calm head, which could be the difference between making a mistake or a good decision.

The Jeep circled back, and Colton could hear its engine gunning toward him. He cut left, trying to outrun the perps.

"Gert, how are you doing over there?" Colton needed an update. Actually, what he needed was a miracle. But he'd stopped believing in those after losing Rebecca, and he figured it was best to keep his feet firmly planted on the ground and his head out of the clouds.

"Sir, I have good news for you. Do you hear anything?"

Colton strained to listen. He didn't hear anything other than the sound of his front bumper hacking through the cornfield. He hated to think what he was doing to this farmer's crops. But again, he would pay restitution.

"I don't hear much more than the noise I'm making and the sound of an engine barreling toward me." He was barely cutting around.

The Jeep was close, he could hear and feel it, if not see it.

"Well, sir, the cavalry is arriving. If you roll your window down, I think you'll be happy with what you hear. DPS got back to me and a trooper should be on top of you right now."

Well, maybe Colton had been too quick to write off the likelihood of miracles happening.

"That's the best news I've heard all day." When he really listened and got past the sounds of corn husks slapping against his front bumper, he heard the familiar wails of sirens in the distance.

Makena was practically glued to her seat, with her hands gripping the strap of her seat belt.

"If you like that news, I've got more. An ambulance is en route to the motel. Help is on the way, sir."

"Gert, remind me the next time I see you that you deserve a raise."

"Sir, I'm going to hold you to that when it's time for my review." Again, lightening the tension with teasing kept his mind at ease and his brain able to focus. The minute he thought a situation was the end of the world was the minute it would be true.

Colton circled around a few more times, ensuring that he was on the move and as far away from the Jeep as possible. He figured the perps had probably given up once they'd heard sirens.

Since they were cops with clean records, they would want to keep them that way. When he really thought about it, they'd concocted the perfect scenario. The puzzle pieces clicked together in one moment.

They had some type of hold over River. That was obvious and a given. They believed that Makena could possibly link them to River and so they would get rid of her. All the while implicating River, who was already known to have a temper and a bad relationship with his wife.

When the different parts of their plan made sense like that, he realized the genius of their plot. However, he had seen them. He knew who they were. That was where they'd messed up. Now they'd gone and left a trail.

"Are they gone?" Makena looked around as Colton slowed down.

"I believe so."

Makena sank back in the chair. "I hear the sirens."

Colton nodded as he tried to navigate back toward the highway.

"I can patch you through to Officer Staten," Gert said.

"Ten-four. Great work, Gert." But before Colton could speak to the highway patrolman through the radio, he saw the cruiser. Colton flashed his headlights and cut off his engine.

Hands up, he exited his truck and told Makena to do the same.

After greeting Officer Staten, Colton said, "It's a shame I didn't get a plate. A white Jeep Rubicon in Texas doesn't exactly stand out."

"The two of you are safe. That's the most important thing to me right now," Officer Staten said.

There was no arguing with that point.

"Do you need assistance getting back to your office?" Staten was tall and darker-skinned, with black hair, brown eyes and a deceptively lean frame. Every state trooper could pull his own weight and more in a fight. These officers traveled long distances with no backup in sight. To say they were tough was a lot like saying Dwayne Johnson had a few muscles.

Colton looked to Makena. "Any chance I can convince you to take a ride back to my office with the officer?"

Makena was already vigorously shaking her head before he could finish his sentence. He figured as much. It was worth a try. He wanted her to be safely tucked away while he circled back and checked on River and Peach.

She seemed to read his mind when she said, "I'm going with you."

There was so much determination in her voice he knew better than to argue. No use wasting precious time.

Colton turned to Officer Staten and said, "Can I get an assist to the motel where an officer was fired on? I'd like to go back and investigate the scene. And considering I have a witness with me, I think it might be best if I have backup."

Staten seemed to catch on, because he was already nodding. "I'm happy to help in any way I can."

Professional courtesy went a long way and Colton

had gone to great lengths to build a cooperative relationship with other law enforcement agencies.

Once their destination was agreed upon, Colton retreated to his truck with Makena by his side.

The drive back to the motel surprisingly took half an hour. Colton didn't realize they'd gotten so far from the motel, but then he was driving back at normal speed limits, whereas he'd flown to get away from there.

There was a BOLO out on the Jeep. If they were as smart as they appeared to be, they would ditch the vehicle. The new problem was that they'd been made and now they had nothing to lose. Dangerous.

They couldn't possibly realize that Colton had figured out who they were. So Colton had that on his side.

By the time they reached the motel, it looked like a proper crime scene. An ambulance was there. The back had been closed up and it looked as though they were about to pull away.

"Hold on a sec," Colton said to Makena.

He hopped out of his pickup, knowing that Makena would want to know River's status.

He jogged up to the driver's side of the ambulance and the driver rolled down the window. Fortunately for him, he still had on his windbreaker that had the word SHERIFF in big bold letters running down his left sleeve, so it was easy to identify that he was in law enforcement.

"How is your patient in the back?" Colton asked. "I was here at the time of the shooting. I had to get a witness out of the building. What is the status of your patient?"

"GSW to the back, exit wounds in his chest. We need to rock and roll, sir. No guarantees on this one. Still breathing, but a lot of blood loss by the time we got here."

Colton took a step back and waved them on. "Go."

It wasn't good news, but River was still alive and Colton had learned that even a tiny bit of hope was better than none. As done as Makena was with the relationship, and he had no doubt in his mind the marriage had been over for a very long time, she was the type of person to be concerned for someone she'd once cared about.

He wished he could give her better news.

Glancing toward the truck, he expected to see her waiting there. A moment of shock jolted him when he saw that she was gone. Then, he knew immediately where she would go. He raced inside to see her standing next to Peach, who was sitting in one of the chairs on the right-hand side.

Makena was offering reassurances to the older woman while rubbing her shoulders. Peach had blood all over her flowery dress.

"I did everything I could to help him, but there was so much blood. He was already pale by the time we got help. His lips were turning blue." The anguish in the older woman's voice was palpable.

"Peach, what you did was admirable. If he has any chance at all, it's because of you," Colton said.

Peach glanced up at him, those emerald green eyes sparkling with gratitude for his comments.

"I mean it. You very well could've saved his life here and I know you saved ours. I would work beside you in law enforcement any day." He meant every word.

Her chin lifted with his praise.

"I appreciate your saying so, Sheriff. It means a lot."

Colton crouched down to eye level with her before taking her statement. And then Makena took Peach into a back room where she washed up.

Makena stayed by the elderly woman's side long after the blood had been rinsed off and Peach had changed clothes.

The highway patrolman stayed outside, guarding the front door in case the perps returned. The front door was cordoned off with crime scene tape.

"My deputy here is going to process the scene. Can one of us give you a ride home?" Colton asked Peach.

"I'll be all right in a few minutes," Peach said. Her hands had steadied. "I have my car out back and I don't want to leave it here overnight."

"What's the owner's name? I'll give 'em a call and ask for someone to cover your shift."

Whatever he said seemed to tickle Peach.

"You're looking at the owner. I owned this place with my husband, God rest his soul."

"Can I call someone? It's not a good idea for you to be alone right now." The shock of what had happened would wear off and her emotions could sneak up on her. Colton didn't want her to suffer. She'd shown incredible bravery today.

"I have a daughter in town," she said. "I'll see if she'll make up the guest bedroom for me tonight."

"Any chance you could get her on the phone now?" Colton asked.

"My purse is underneath the counter where Rapture was hiding." She motioned toward her shotgun that was sitting on top of the counter. It had been opened and the shells looked to have been removed.

As he waited for Peach to call her daughter, Colton took stock of the situation. He now had names. He had motive. All he needed was opportunity to seal Bic and Stitch's fate.

Chapter Fifteen

Makena heard Colton's voice as she sat with Peach. He was talking about shock and the need to keep an eye on her. The concern in his voice brought out all kinds of emotions in Makena. She could tell that he genuinely cared about Peach and it was just about the kindest thing Makena thought she'd ever witnessed. But that was just Colton. He was genuine, kind and considerate wrapped in a devastatingly handsome and masculine package. There was nothing self-centered about him. In fact, there was a sad quality in his eyes that made him so real.

"Bernard and I spent our whole lives here at this motel. He never would take a vacation. I used to tease him about what he'd turn into with all work and no play." A wistful and loving look overtook Peach's face when she spoke about her husband.

"He sounds like an honest, hard-working man," Makena said.

"That he was. He was good to me and I was good

to him. We had two daughters. One who succumbed to illness as a child, and the other who your boyfriend is on the phone with now. She looks after me. She's been on me to sell the business for years." Peach exhaled. "It's difficult to let go. Here is where I feel Bernard's presence the most. I always thought I'd start a little restaurant. Even had a name picked out, but I never did find the time. I always would rather be feeding people. The motel was Bernard's baby."

The fact that Peach had referred to Colton as Makena's boyfriend didn't get past her. She didn't see this as the time to correct the elderly woman.

She glanced up, and it was then that the flatscreen TV caught her attention. She remembered the date stamp and the time stamp on the screen when River had looked up. He'd looked up at exactly 6:12 a.m., which meant he was at the motel and not anywhere near Katy Gulch and he must have known something was going to happen even if he didn't know what because he'd given himself an alibi. Birchwood was a solid half hour from town. He'd been inside his room the entire night, based on the camera footage. The only window was in front, next to the door. If he'd tried to climb out, the camera would've picked it up.

As far as she knew there were no other exits in the room, which pretty much ensured that he was innocent.

A flood of relief washed over her that he hadn't been involved in the bombing attempt. Bic and Stitch's whereabouts had yet to be known, and she had plenty of questions for the pair.

Makena sat with her hands folded in her lap. She refocused on the story Peach was telling her about how her beloved Bernard had singlehandedly patched up a roof after a tornado. Peach was rambling and Makena didn't mind. The woman's smooth, steady voice had a calming effect, and she figured Peach needed to keep her mind busy by talking.

Colton stepped back into the room and then handed the phone to Peach, who took it and spoke to her daughter.

While Peach was occupied, Makena motioned for Colton to come closer. He bent down and took a knee beside her. She liked that he immediately reached for her hand. She leaned toward his ear and relayed her discovery.

He rocked his head. "That's a really good point. If he was here all night, he couldn't have been the one to set the bomb. We have two names, and their department will want to be involved. I promise you here and now justice will be served."

Makena hoped he could deliver on that promise before they could get to her. Bic and Stitch had proven they'd go to any length to quiet her.

"I already figured out they were setting River up.

It's a pretty perfect setup and that's the reason we found the black key chain at the scene." After everything she'd been through with River, she probably shouldn't care one way or the other about it. She just wasn't built that way. She did care. Not just about him but about anyone who'd taken a wrong turn.

"Any chance we can stop by the hospital when we leave here?" Makena asked.

"I think that can be arranged."

She really hoped so, because she wanted to see with her own eyes that River was okay.

"Since we know he's a target, will there be security? How will that work?" she asked.

"I just called in a report that he's a material witness in an attempted murder case. One of my deputies is with him and we'll make sure he's not left unattended in the hospital while he fights for his life." Colton's words were reassuring.

"Excuse me, sir." Trooper Staten stepped inside the room.

"How can I help you?"

"Since you have a deputy here, I'd like to offer backup to one of my buddies who has a trucker pulled over not far from here. If you think you'll be good without me, I'd like to assist."

"We're good. Thank you for everything. Your help is much appreciated." Colton stood up, crossed the room and shook the state trooper's hand.

Deputy Fletcher worked to process the scene

while Colton and Makena waited for Peach's daughter to show. She did, about twenty minutes later. The young woman, who looked to be in her late twenties, had a baby on her hip and a distressed look on her face as she approached the motel.

Rather than let her step into the bloody scene before it could be cleaned up, Colton met her at the door. He turned back in time to say, "Makena, do you want to bring Peach outside?"

"Sure. No problem." She helped Peach to her feet.

The older woman gripped Makena's arm tightly and it gave her the impression Peach was holding on for dear life. It was good that her daughter was picking her up. She needed someone to take care of her.

Seeing the look on her daughter's face as soon as they stepped outside sent warmth spreading through Makena. The mother-daughter bond hit her square in the chest, and for the first time, Makena thought she was missing out on something by not having a child of her own.

When Peach was settled in her daughter's small SUV and the baby had been strapped in the back seat, the older woman looked up with weary eyes.

"Maybe it is a good idea for me to sell. My handyman, Ralph, can keep things running until the sale. He can see to it if anyone needs a rental. You were right to have me call my daughter," she said to Colton. "Good luck with everything. Take care of yourselves." Peach glanced from Makena to Colton and back. "And take care of each other. If you don't mind my saying, the two of you have something special. That's probably the most important thing you can have in life."

"Thank you, ma'am," Colton said.

Again, Makena didn't see the need to correct Peach despite the thrill of hope she felt at hearing those words. Peach had been through a traumatic experience and Makena wasn't going to ruin her romantic notions by clarifying her relationship with Colton. He had become her lifeline and that was most likely the reason the thought of being separated from him at some point gave her heart palpitations, not that she'd reactivated real feelings for him. The kind of feelings that could go the distance.

COLTON CHECKED HIS WATCH. He surveyed the area, well aware that it had only been a short while ago that two perps had been walking across that same street.

A second deputy pulled up. Colton motioned for him to go on inside. He didn't want anyone working alone on this scene or this case.

He turned to Makena. "River is probably still in surgery. Do you think you could eat something?"

Peach wasn't the only one in shock. Makena was handling hers well, but she'd had months of being on the run and hiding to practice dealing with extreme emotions.

Makena closed the distance between them and leaned against him.

Colton looped his arms around her waist and pulled her body flush with his. This time, he was the one who dipped his head and pressed a kiss to her lips. He told himself he did it to root them both in reality again, but there was so much more to it, to being with her.

The thought of how close he'd come to losing her sent a shiver rocketing down his back. He'd lost enough with Rebecca and he didn't want to lose another friend.

Makena took in a deep breath. "How do you think he knew?"

Colton knew exactly what she was talking about. She was picking up their conversational thread from a few minutes ago.

"It's possible he didn't. It's likely he assumed that something could happen. He might have followed them here. Maybe they disappeared for a couple of days, and he realized they were searching for you and had found you. So he must've decided following them was his best chance at finding you. You were the wild card. They had no idea when you were going to show up and what evidence you might bring with you. They've probably been looking for you this entire time, and the fact that you disappeared when you did made it look that much more like you had something to hide or fear."

"Timing," she said on another sigh. It was a loaded word.

She blinked up at him and those crystal clear blue eyes brought out feelings he hadn't felt since college. He had no idea what to do with them. Complicated didn't begin to describe their lives. But he liked her standing right where she was, her warm body pressed against his and his arms circling her waist.

Colton glanced around, surveying the area. Even with two deputies on-site he couldn't let his guard down.

"What do you say we eat at the cafeteria in the hospital?" Makena asked.

"I need to let these guys know where we're headed and communicate with Gert so she can keep someone close to us." Traveling this way was cumbersome and frustrating. An idea sparked. He twined his and Makena's fingers before walking back inside the building. "How about one of you gentlemen lend me your service vehicle? I can leave my truck here. I don't want either one of you driving it. I'll have it towed back to my office. And then the two of you can buddy up on the way back to the office, where you can pick up another vehicle."

Both of his deputies were already nodding their agreement.

Deputy Fletcher pitched a set of keys to Colton, which he caught with one hand. He figured that he and Makena would be a helluva lot safer in a marked vehicle than his truck. Not to mention Bic and Stitch knew exactly what he drove. They may have even pulled some strings and run the plates by now, which would work in Colton's favor. He highly doubted they would've shot at a sheriff if they'd known.

Colton led Makena out to the county-issued SUV.

The drive to the hospital was forty minutes long. Colton located a parking spot as close to the ER doors as he could find. He linked his and Makena's fingers before walking into the ER bay. He was ever aware that a sharpshooter could be anywhere, waiting to strike. But what he hoped was that Bic and Stitch had gone back to Dallas to regroup.

Now that their chief was aware, they would be brought in for questioning. It would have to be handled delicately. Their plan to set up River had blown up in their faces, as had their plans to erase Makena.

The strangest part about the whole thing was that they were targeting her based on what they thought she knew, while she really knew nothing. But now Dallas P.D and the sheriff's office knew what the men were capable of.

On the annual summer barbecue night, Colton and his staff would sit around a campfire way too late and swap stories. Conversation always seemed to drift toward what everyone would do if it went down, meaning they had to disappear.

The first thing people said was obvious. Get rid of their cell phone. The next was that they'd stay the heck away from their personal vehicle. Another thing was not to go home again. That seemed obvious. Most of the deputies said they'd go to the ATM and withdraw as much money as they could before heading to Mexico. At least one said she would head toward Canada because she thought it was the opposite way anyone would look for her.

Bic and Stitch had to have a backup plan. It was just a cop's instinct to talk through worst-case scenarios. And if they thought like typical cops, like he was certain they did considering they had twenty-six years of police experience between them, he figured they had an escape plan, too.

So the thought of them going back to their homes or to Dallas was scratched. Their cover was blown.

But did they realize it?

One thing was certain: they didn't have anything to gain sticking around town. In fact, it would do them both good to hide out until this blew over. And then take off for the border.

What would their escape plan be? He wondered where they'd been hiding while River booked the motel room.

It was a lot to think about. Colton needed a jolt of caffeine and he probably needed something in his stomach besides acid from coffee. The piece of toast he'd had for breakfast wasn't holding up anymore.

He stopped off at the nurses' station in the ER.

"Can you point me to the cafeteria?" It wouldn't

do any good to ask about River yet and these women most likely wouldn't know. He would go to the information desk, which would be in the front lobby.

"Straight down this hallway, make a right and then a left. You'll find a lobby, which you'll need to cross. You'll get to a hallway on the exact opposite side and you'll want to take that. You can't miss it from there."

Colton thanked the intake nurse and then followed her directions to a T. A minute later, they were standing in front of a row of vending machines that had everything from hot chocolate to hot dogs.

"Does any of this look appetizing?" he asked Makena.

She walked slowly, skimming the contents of each vending machine. She stopped at the third one and then pointed. "I think this ham sandwich could work."

Colton bought two of them, then grabbed a couple bags of chips. She wanted a soft drink while he stuck with black coffee.

There was a small room with a few bright orange plastic tables and chairs scattered around the room. Each table had from three to six chairs surrounding it. There were two individuals sitting at different tables, each staring at their phone.

Makena took the lead and chose a table farthest away from the others. The sun was shining, and hours had passed since breakfast.

"So I noticed you didn't ask about River." Makena took a bite and chewed on her ham sandwich.

"No, the intake nurses either wouldn't have information or wouldn't share it. There's an information desk we can stop at after we eat. I know most of the people who work there and figured that would be the best place to check his status" He checked his smartwatch. "Gert would let me know if the worst had happened, if River had died."

"Have you given much thought to what your life might look like once this is all behind you?" Colton asked Makena after they'd finished eating.

"Every day for the past six months I've thought about what I would do once this was all over. To be honest, I never really had an answer that stuck. I went through phases. One of those phases was to just buy a little farmhouse somewhere away from people and live on my own and maybe get a golden retriever for company."

"There are worse ways to spend your life."

She smiled and continued. "Then, I had a phase where I wanted to move far away from Texas and live in a major metropolitan area where there would be people everywhere, but no one would bother me unless I wanted them to. If I wanted to be left alone, people would respect that. But I would be around life again. I'd be around people doing things and being busy. I wouldn't have to hide my face." She looked out the window thoughtfully. "None of those things stuck for more than a month."

"And how about now?"

"I have a few ideas." She turned to face him and looked him in the eyes. "Now I feel like I know what I want, but that maybe it's out of reach."

Before he could respond, a text came in from Gert that River was out of surgery. Gert had connections in most places and the hospital was no different. Glancing at his watch, he realized an hour had passed since they'd arrived at the hospital.

Colton made a mental note to finish this conversation later, because a very large part of him wanted to know if she saw any chance of the two of them spending time together. It was pretty much impossible for him to think about starting a new relationship while he had one-year-old twins at home, especially with what was going on with his family.

His mind came up with a dozen reasons straight out of the chute as to why it was impossible and wouldn't happen and could never go anywhere. Why he couldn't risk it.

But the heart didn't listen to logic. It wanted to get to know Makena again. To see if the fire in the kisses they'd shared—kisses he was having one helluva time trying to erase from his memory—could ignite something that might last longer than a few months.

Logic flew out the window when it came to the heart.

"River is out of surgery and I can probably get us up to his floor if not his room."

Makena looked like she wanted to say something and then thought better of it.

"Let's do it." She took in a sharp breath, like she was steadying herself for what she knew would come.

Colton cursed the timing of the text, but it was good news. He led them to the information desk where he could get details about which floor River was housed in. Trudy, a middle-aged single mother who lived on the outskirts of Katy Gulch, sat at the counter.

As sheriff, Colton liked to get to know his residents and look out for those who seemed to need it. Trudy had been widowed while her husband had been serving in the military overseas. She'd been left with four kids and not a lot of money. Colton's office led a back-to-school backpack drive every year in part to make sure her children never went without. Gert always beamed with pride when delivering those items.

Gert organized a toy drive every year for Christmas, a book drive twice a year and coats for kids before the first cold snap.

"Hey, Trudy. You have a patient who just got out of surgery, and we'd like to go up to his floor and talk to his nurse and possibly his doctor," Colton said after introducing Trudy to Makena.

"Just a second, Sheriff. I'll look that up right now," Trudy said with a smile. Her fingers danced across the keyboard.

Makena's gaze locked onto someone. Colton followed her gaze to the man in scrubs. The doctor came from the same hallway they'd entered the lobby from, and then headed straight toward a bank of elevators.

The hair on Colton's neck prickled. Trudy's fingers worked double time. Click-click-click.

As the elevators closed on the opposite side of the lobby, something in the back of Colton's mind snapped.

"The patient you're looking for is on the seventh floor. He's in critical condition. No visitors are allowed." She flashed eyes at Colton. "No normal visitors. That doesn't mean you. He's in room 717."

Colton thanked her for the courtesy and realized what had been sticking in the back of his mind. The doctor who'd crossed the lobby wore a surgical mask and regular boots. Every doctor Colton had seen had foot coverings on their shoes. They usually wore tennis shoes with coverings over them for sanitation purposes.

This guy had on a surgical mask and no boot covers?

One look at Makena said she realized something

was up. Colton looked at Trudy before jumping into action the minute he made eye contact with Makena and realized she was thinking along the same lines.

"Trudy, call security. Send backup to the seventh floor and help to room 717." Colton linked his fingers with Makena and started toward the elevator. Of course, he had a deputy on-site and the hospital had its own security. So imagine his shock when the elevator doors opened and his deputy walked out.

"Lawson, what are you doing?"

His deputy seemed dumbfounded as Colton rushed into the elevator.

"What do you mean? I'm going to get a cup of coffee. Hospital security relieved me and said you authorized a break."

"And you didn't think to check with me first?" Colton asked.

Lawson's mistake seemed to dawn on him. He muttered a few choice words as he pushed the button for the seventh floor, apologizing the whole time.

It seemed to take forever for the elevator to ding and the doors to open. At least, they knew where one of the men was; the other had to be close by. The two seemed to travel as a pair.

As soon as the doors opened, Colton shot out. He shouted back to Lawson, "Make sure no one comes down this hallway."

There were two hallways and several sets of

stairs, but Lawson could make sure no one followed Colton.

Unwilling to let Makena out of his sight, Colton held on to her hand as he banked right toward room 717. As suspected, there was no security guard at the door.

Colton cursed as he bolted toward the open door.

Inside, he interrupted a man in a security outfit standing near River's bedside. The man in uniform had a black mustache, neatly trimmed.

"Sheriff, I saw him. Someone was in here. He ran out the door."

"Put your hands where I can see them," Colton demanded.

Chapter Sixteen

From behind the curtain dividing the room, a window leading to the outside opened.

"Hands where I can see them," Colton repeated, weapon drawn, leading the way. River lay unconscious with a breathing tube in his mouth as multiple machines beeped.

The security guard dropped down on the opposite side of the bed. And then, suddenly, an alarm began to sound on one of the machines. Was it unplugged?

Another wailing noise pierced the air.

Colton kept Makena tucked behind him as he took a couple of steps inside the room. He planted his side against the wall, inching forward.

A nurse came bolting in and froze when she saw Colton with his gun drawn. The divider curtain blew toward him with a gust of wind. Colton saw a glint of Mustache as he climbed out the window.

Red must've been on the other side of the divider all along. He must've made it inside the room.

Colton assumed he'd be the one wearing the surgical gear.

"Freeze." Colton took a few more tentative steps before squatting down so he could see underneath the curtain. He saw no sign of shoes and assumed both men had climbed out the window and onto the fire escape they'd seen earlier. And since assumptions in his life of work could kill, he proceeded with extra caution. Someone could be standing on the bed or nightstand. Hell, he'd caught a perp climbing into the ceiling tiles at the bank before.

There was no more sound coming from that side of the room. He took a few more steps until he was able to reach the curtain and pull it open. He scanned the room before checking on the other side of the bed.

"Clear. Nurse, you're okay." It was all Colton could get out as he heard the sounds of feet shuffling and her scurrying to plug in the machines that were most likely the reason River was still breathing.

Colton rushed to the window and looked out in time to see someone wearing scrubs along with Security Dude climbing down the fire escape and around the side of the building.

He glanced back at Makena.

"Stay here. Someone will come back for you. Stay in this room. Nurse, lock this room and stay with her. As soon as I'm out of this window, I want you to lock it."

A moment of hesitation crossed Makena's features. She opened her mouth like she was about to protest and then clamped it shut.

Colton climbed out the window and followed the path of the perps. He climbed down to the corner, stopping before risking a glance.

The second he so much as peeked his head a shot rang out, taking a small chunk of white brick before whizzing past his face.

Colton quickly jerked back around the side of the building and pulled himself back up. His body was flat against the building, his weapon holstered.

There was no way these guys were escaping him twice.

He scaled the wall a couple more floors, refusing to look down. He wouldn't exactly say he was afraid of heights, but he wouldn't call them his friend, either.

When Colton made it to the third story, gripping the windows for dear life, he risked another glance around the side of the building, hoping they would still be looking for him on the seventh floor. This time, thankfully, Red and Mustache were too busy climbing down to realize he'd looked. They probably still thought he was up on the seventh.

Colton continued his climb down with his stomach twisted in knots, but he made it to the ground. Without a doubt, they'd made it to the ground first. There were also two of them and only one of him.

Not the best odds. One was a sharpshooter. That would be the person who would most likely wield the weapon.

And then there was the fact that they were both cops. Maybe he could find a way to use that to his advantage.

With his back against the wall and his weapon extended, Colton leaned around the building. The pair of men were making a beeline for the parking lot. He scanned the area for the Jeep but didn't see it.

They could have another vehicle stashed by now. Since it was early evening, there was a little activity. He wouldn't risk a shot. He, like every law enforcement officer on the job, was responsible for every bullet he fired. Meaning that if he accidentally struck a citizen, he was answerable, not to mention it would be horrific.

When Red and Mustache made it to the lot, one turned around.

They took cover behind a massive black SUV. One turned back, Red, and Colton figured that of the two, he was the marksman. He had his weapon aimed at the seventh floor, where he must expect Colton to be.

He figured Mustache was looking for a vehicle to hotwire, since they didn't immediately go to a car.

Colton figured his best line of defense was to get to his county-issued vehicle and try to circle around the back and come at them from a different direction. He got on his radio to Lawson and Gert as he bolted toward his SUV.

He slid into the driver's seat and blazed around the opposite side of the lot as he informed Gert of the situation. Lawson chimed in, stating that he was on his way down and heading to the spot Colton had just left.

Colton slowed his SUV down to a crawl as he made his way around the back of the parking lot. He located a spot in the back of the lot and parked. He slipped out of his windbreaker, needing to shed anything that drew attention to him. He toed off his boots as he exited the vehicle.

As the shooter's attention was directed at the building, Colton swung wide to sneak up on him. He was ever aware that Mustache was creeping around the lot, likely looking for a vehicle.

Lawson peeked his head around the building and Red fired a shot. While Red's attention was on Lawson, Colton eased through cars and trucks.

With Red distracted by Lawson, Colton came in stealth. He rounded the back of the SUV and dove at Red, tackling him at the knees. His gun went flying as Colton wrestled him around until his knee jabbed in the center of Red's back. As tall and strong as Red was, he was no match for a man of Colton's size.

Face down, Red spit out gravel as he opened his mouth to shout for help. Colton delivered a knockout punch. The man's jaw snapped.

From there, Colton was able to easily haul Red's hands behind his back and throw on zip cuffs.

It was then that Colton heard the click of a gun's hammer being cocked.

"Make one move without me telling you to, and you're dead."

Out of the corner of his eyes, Colton could see Mustache. He cursed under his breath.

"Hands in the air where I can them." Mustache was in authoritative cop mode.

Colton slowly started lifting his hands, his weapon already holstered. And at this rate, he was as good as dead. His thoughts jumped to Lawson. Where was he?

"Uncuff my friend. You're going to help me get him into my vehicle."

The retort on Colton's lips was, *like hell*. However, he knew better than to agitate a cop on the edge.

"You won't get away with this. Your superiors know what you've done and they know you're connected to Myers. But you can get a lighter sentence. You haven't dug a hole that you can't climb out of yet. No one's dead. A murder rap is not something you can ever come back from."

"Shut up. I don't need to hear any more of your crap. The system pays criminals better than it pays us. When Bic's kid needed medical care and his insurance ran out, who do you think covered his mortgage?" Stitch grunted. "It sure as hell wasn't the department."

Psychological profiles were performed on every officer candidate to ensure a cop could handle the pressures that came with the job. The tests could give a snapshot of where a candidate's head was at the time of his or her hiring. What it couldn't do 100 percent accurately was predict how someone would handle the constraints of the job over time.

The stress could compound and end up looking something like this.

"I never said it was easy being on the job. But you and I both know you didn't get into it for the money."

Mustache laughed. "Yeah, I was a kid. What did I know about having real bills and a father-in-law with dementia who lost his business and I had to support?"

"This isn't the answer. You can still make this right. You can still go back and untangle this. Make restitution."

A half laugh escaped Mustache.

"You know what? I think I'm just going to kill you instead. Not because I have to but because I can."

Colton had no doubt Mustache was trigger-happy. A man with nothing to lose was not the kind of person Colton needed to have pointing a gun at him.

"You're going to help me put my friend in my

vehicle and then I'm going to give you ten seconds to run."

Colton knew without a doubt that the minute he put Red into a vehicle, his life was going to be over. He needed to think fast. Stall for time. He glanced over to see if Lawson was on his way.

Mustache laughed again.

"Your friend isn't coming. I don't know if you noticed but he's bleeding out over there. Guess it's too late for me after all."

Colton slowly stood with his hands in the air.

"Keep high and where I can see them. I'm going to relieve you of your weapon."

The crack of a bullet split the air.

Colton flinched and dropped to his knees. When he spun around, it was Mustache taking a couple of steps back. With his finger on the trigger, all it would take was one twitch for Colton to be shot at in point-blank range.

He dove behind the sport utility and came up with his weapon. It would take Mustache's brain a few minutes to catch up with the fact that he'd been shot. Right now, he was just as dangerous as he had been, if not more so.

Using the massive sport utility for cover, Colton drew down on Mustache.

"Hands up, Stitch." All Colton could think of was securing the area and getting to Lawson.

Another shot sounded.

Colton glanced around and saw Lawson's body. As he rounded the back of the vehicle, he heard a familiar voice.

"Drop your weapon *now*." From behind a vehicle, Makena had her arms extended out with a Glock in her hands. Red's weapon? The barrel was aimed at Mustache.

Colton was proud of the fact she'd listened to his earlier advice and used the vehicle to protect her body.

Mustache seemed dumbfounded as he took a couple of steps and locked onto her position. "You."

He brought up his weapon to shoot her and she fired again. This time, the bullet pinged his arm and his shoulder drew back. His weapon discharged, firing a wild shot, and his shoulder flew back. His Glock went skittering across the black tar.

Colton dove toward it and came up with it after making eye contact with Makena. He tucked and rolled on his shoulder and then popped up in front of the vehicle Makena used as cover.

There was no way to know if Mustache had a backup weapon, which many officers carried in an ankle holster.

"You just saved my life," Colton said to Makena. He moved beside her and realized that her body was trembling.

Her eyes were wide.

"You're okay," he said to soothe her before turning to Mustache, who was slumped against the back tire of a vehicle. "Get those hands up."

Much to his surprise, Mustache did.

It was probably the shock of realizing he'd been shot multiple times. Colton immediately fished out his cell and called Gert, telling her the perps had been subdued and that Lawson was down. She reassured Colton a team of doctors was waiting at the ER bay for word.

Before Colton could end the call, he saw the doctors racing to save Lawson's life.

Mustache's once light blue shirt was now soaked in red. Colton ran over and cuffed Mustache's hands. After a pat-down, he located a backup weapon.

"If either one of these men moves, don't hesitate to shoot," he said to Makena.

Lawson was flat on his back as he was being placed on a gurney.

"I'm sorry. I let you down," Lawson said.

"No, you didn't. I'm alive. You're alive. Those bastards are going to spend the rest of their lives behind bars. You did good."

In less than a minute, Lawson was on his way to surgery. The bullet had nicked his neck.

Colton bolted back to Makena.

"It's over," Makena said. She repeated herself a couple more times as Colton took her weapon before he pulled her into an embrace, keeping a watchful eye on the perps.

"You did good," he whispered into her ear as she melted against him.

"I found the gun on the ground," she said quietly.

Red popped his head up and shook it, like he was shaking off a fog.

"What the hell happened?" His gaze locked onto his partner, who had lost a lot of blood.

"You and your partner are going away for a very long time," Colton said. He held Makena, trying to calm her tremors.

An emergency team raced toward Mustache. In another few minutes, he was strapped and cuffed to a gurney with security in tow and another deputy on the way.

Colton pulled Red to standing after patting him down. He walked the man over to his service vehicle. "You're taking a trip in the back seat for once."

Makena climbed into the passenger side and kept silent for the drive back to Katy Gulch.

Deputy Schooner met them in the parking lot and took custody of the perp.

"You would do what you had to if your kid was sick," Bic practically spat the words. "Look as sanctimonious as you want, but I had bills stacking up and a mortgage to cover. I did what was necessary to take care of my family."

"There are other ways to accomplish the same thing and stay within the law," Colton said.

"That's what you say. Don't you get tired of

watching them get away with crimes every day? Don't you get sick of seeing criminals drive better cars and wear better clothes than us?"

"Fancy clothes were never my style," Colton said. "But why River?"

"He was on to us, so we turned the tables on him. His nose wasn't clean, either. He liked to play it rough," Bic said. "She was the problem. She threatened everything we were doing. It took months to track her down but she made mistakes and River led us right to her."

Colton was done talking. He turned to Makena. "Are you ready to go home?"

She stood there, looking a little bit lost.

"I don't have a home to go to, Colton."

"Then come home with me while you figure out your next move." He brushed the backs of his fingers against the soft skin of her face. He'd missed his opportunity with her once and did not intend to do so again. "Come home with me and stay."

"And then what?" She blinked up at him, confused.

"Stay. Meet my boys. See what you think about making a life together. I know what I want and it's you. I love you, Makena. And I think I have since college. I was too young and too dumb to realize what was happening to us in college. I had no idea how rare or special it was. But I do now. I'm a grown man and I won't make that same mistake twice."

He looked into her eyes but was having trouble reading her. Maybe it was too much. Maybe he shouldn't have thrown this all at her at once.

"But if you don't think this is right, if you don't feel what I'm feeling, then just stay with me until you get your bearings. I don't care how long. You'll always have a place to stay with me."

"Did you say that you love me?"

Colton nodded. "Yes, Makena. I love you."

"I love you, too, Colton. I think I always have. Seeing you again brought me back to life. But then what? You have boys. You have a life."

"I'd like to build a life with *you*."

"Are you sure about that, Colton? Because I have no doubts."

"I've never been more certain of anything in my life other than adopting my boys," he admitted.

She blinked up at him, confused.

It dawned on him why. He'd never told her about his twins.

"Rebecca and I had been high school sweethearts. We didn't know anything but each other. We decided to take a break in college and see if this was the real deal. I loved her and she was my best friend. But then I met you and it was different. I felt things that I had never felt with Rebecca. There was a spark inside me that said you were special and then I wanted more than a best friend as a partner. I went home and told Rebecca that I didn't think I was coming back to her."

"But you ended up together?"

"Yes, but not for years. We went our separate ways as a couple but stayed close as friends. Years later, long after she and I broke up, she ended up in a bad relationship with a man who didn't treat her right. When he found out she was pregnant he accused her of cheating on him. He questioned whether or not the boys were his and that crushed her. She said she couldn't come home pregnant to her father's house without a husband or a father for her kids. We'd always promised to have each other's back, so that's what I did. Her father, who's the mayor of Katy Gulch, got over the fact she was pregnant and still not married as soon as he found out she was marrying an O'Connor. I felt like I could've done a lot worse than marry my best friend. I figured that what you and I had was a one-and-done situation. So I asked Rebecca to marry me. I loved her, but there was no spark in our marriage, not like what I'd experienced with you. But then, no one else made me feel that way. And make no mistake about it, those boys are my sons. They are O'Connors through and through, and always will be. Can you live with that?"

"Colton, you are the most selfless man I've ever met. I think I just fell in love with you even more."

"Just so you're clear, we can take a little time for

you to get to know the boys, and we can make certain this is the life you want. But I'm in this for the long haul, and I have every intention of asking you to be my bride," he said.

"If your sons are half the person you are, I already know that I'll love them. And just so you know, when you ask me to marry you, I'll be ready to say yes. I never felt like I was home around anyone until I met you and then I lost it. I've definitely been in the wrong relationship and that taught me exactly what I wanted in a person. And it's you. It's always been you."

Colton pulled Makena into his arms and kissed his future bride, his place to call home.

"I have one condition," she warned.

"Anything." He didn't hesitate. He wanted to give her the world.

"You asked me before if I had any idea what I wanted to do once I had my freedom back."

He nodded.

"I want to volunteer at the motel to help out Peach. She told me about her and her husband building that place together and that the motel made her feel closer to him. She's considering selling, but I could tell nothing in her heart wanted that to happen. It would cut her off from the man she built a life with and she deserves so much more than that. She deserves to have her memories of him surrounding her until she takes her final breath."

"It sounds like the perfect plan to me." Colton kissed his future, his soon-to-be bride, his home.

Epilogue

"I have news."

Makena sat on the kitchen floor, playing with her favorite boys in the world. She'd taken them into her heart the minute she'd looked at those round, angelic faces. Someday, she wanted to expand their family, but after living with twins 24/7 for the past month, she realized her hands were full.

"What is it?" she asked Colton as he walked into the kitchen wearing only jeans hung low on his hips. He was fresh from the shower, hair still wet. Droplets rolled down his neck and onto his muscled chest.

She practically had to fan herself.

"Myers has agreed to testify against Bic, who will be put away a very long time for attempted murder and police corruption, among other charges."

Stitch hadn't made it, but Bic was the brains of the operation.

"Good for him," she said. "I'm so ready to close that chapter of my life. I'm done with running scared and I'm done hiding. He put me through hell and I'm just ready to move on and never look back."

Colton walked over to her and sat down behind her, wrapping his arms around her. He feathered kisses along the nape of her neck, causing her arms to break out in goose bumps and a thrill of awareness to skitter across her skin.

"I can't wait to be alone after we put the boys to bed tonight," he whispered in her ear.

She smiled as she turned her head enough for him to find her lips. The kiss sent more of that awareness swirling through her. Tonight felt like a lifetime away.

One of the boys giggled, which always made the other one follow suit. Their laughs broke into the moment happening between Makena and Colton.

"What's this?" she asked as she witnessed one pick up a block and bite it before setting it down only for the other to copy him.

Laughter filled the room and her heart.

This was her family. These were her boys. This was her home.

* * * * *

Look for more books in USA TODAY *bestselling
author Barb Han's An O'Connor Family
Mystery series in 2021!*

And don't miss the previous titles in the series:

Texas Kidnapping
Texas Target

*Available now wherever
Harlequin Intrigue books are sold!*

SPECIAL EXCERPT FROM

⟨H⟩HARLEQUIN

INTRIGUE

*When Raleigh Wilde reappears in
Deputy Beckett Foster's life asking for his help clearing
her name, he's shocked—even more so when he learns
she's pregnant with his child. But a killer is willing
to do anything to keep Raleigh from discovering who
embezzled millions from the charity she runs…*

Read on for a sneak preview of
The Fugitive *by Nichole Severn.*

Raleigh Wilde.

Hell, it'd been a while since Deputy United States Marshal Beckett Foster had set sights on her, and every cell in his body responded in awareness. Four months, one week and four days to be exact. Those soul-searching light green eyes, her soft brown hair and sharp cheekbones. But all that beauty didn't take away from the sawed-off shotgun currently pointed at his chest. His hand hovered just above his firearm as the Mothers Come First foundation's former chief financial officer—now fugitive— widened her stance.

"Don't you know breaking into someone's home is illegal, Marshal?" That voice. A man could get lost in a voice like that. Sweet and rough all in the same package. Raleigh smoothed her fingers over the gun in her hand. It hadn't taken her but a few seconds after she'd come through the door to realize he'd been waiting for her at the other end of the wide room.

It hadn't taken him but a couple hours to figure out where she'd been hiding for the past four months once her file crossed his desk. What she didn't know was how long he'd been waiting, and that he'd already relieved that gun of its rounds as well as any other weapons he'd found during his search of her aunt's cabin.

"Come on now. You and I both know you haven't forgotten my name that easily." He studied her from head to toe, memorizing the fit of her oversize plaid flannel shirt, the slight loss of color in her face and the dark circles under her eyes. Yeah, living on the run did that to a person. Beckett unbuttoned his holster. He wouldn't pull. Of all the criminals the United States Marshals Service had assigned him to recover over the years, she was the only one he'd hesitated chasing down. Then again, if he hadn't accepted the assignment, another marshal would have. And there was no way Beckett would let anyone else bring her in.

Beckett ran his free hand along the exposed brick of the fireplace. "Gotta be honest, didn't think you'd ever come back here. Lot of memories tied up in this place."

"What do you want, Beckett?" The creases around her eyes deepened as she shifted her weight between both feet. She crouched slightly, searching through the single window facing East Lake, then refocused on him.

Looking for a way out? Or to see if he'd come with backup? Dried grass, changing leaves, mountains and an empty dock were all that were out there. The cabin she'd been raised in as a kid sat on the west side of the lake, away from tourists, away from the main road. Even if he gave her a head start, she wouldn't get far. There was nowhere for her to run. Not from him.

"You know that, too." He took a single step forward, the aged wood floor protesting under his weight as he closed in on her. "You skipped out on your trial, and I'm here to bring you in."

"What was I supposed to do?" Countering his approach, she moved backward toward the front door she'd dead-bolted right after coming inside but kept the gun aimed at him. Her boot hit the go bag she stored near the kitchen counter beside the door. "I didn't steal that money. Someone at the charity did and faked the evidence so I'd take the fall."

"That's the best you got? A frame job?" Fifty and a half million dollars. Gone. The only one with continuous access to the funds stood right in front of him. Not to mention the brand-new offshore bank account, the thousands of wire transfers to that account in increments small enough they wouldn't register for the feds and Raleigh's signatures on every single one of them. "You had a choice, Raleigh. You just chose wrong."

Don't miss
The Fugitive *by Nichole Severn,*
available January 2021 wherever
Harlequin Intrigue books and ebooks are sold.

Harlequin.com

HIEXP1220

Get 4 FREE REWARDS!

We'll send you 2 FREE Books
plus 2 FREE Mystery Gifts.

Harlequin Intrigue books are action-packed stories that will keep you on the edge of your seat. Solve the crime and deliver justice at all costs.

FREE
Value Over
$20

Love Harlequin romance?

DISCOVER.

Be the first to find out about promotions, news and exclusive content!

 Facebook.com/HarlequinBooks

Twitter.com/HarlequinBooks

 Instagram.com/HarlequinBooks

Pinterest.com/HarlequinBooks

ReaderService.com

EXPLORE.

Sign up for the Harlequin e-newsletter and download a free book from any series at **TryHarlequin.com**

CONNECT.

Join our Harlequin community to share your thoughts and connect with other romance readers!
Facebook.com/groups/HarlequinConnection

HSOCIAL2020

PRAISE FOR THE NOVELS OF
TONY HILLERMAN

❖ ❖ ❖ THE FALLEN MAN ❖ ❖ ❖

"Another gripping chapter in the evocative series [Hillerman] sets on the vast Indian reservation that sprawls across Arizona and New Mexico . . . In dealing with the pragmatic older cop and his dreamy young protegé, Mr. Hillerman has always kept the frictions carefully contained. Here he gives his heroes more room to rub each other the wrong way. The personal tensions add another facet to the story, which continues the author's fascination with the savagery that men do to themselves and to the land they claim to hold sacred."
                    —*The New York Times Book Review*

"For fans of Hillerman, [*The Fallen Man*] is a welcome new chapter."
                    —*Boston Sunday Globe*

"*The Fallen Man* finds Hillerman back in top form. . . . Richly imagined, atmospheric and briskly paced . . . [reuniting] two of the most anticipated characters in crime fiction."
                    —*Chicago Tribune*

"Another of Mr. Hillerman's elegantly plotted puzzles. As usual, the tale includes evocations of splendid scenery and sympathetic respect for the Navajo nation."
                    —*Atlantic Monthly*

❖ ❖ ❖

"Hillerman has constructed one of his more intricate plots and one of his more satisfying novels."

—*Los Angeles Times*

"Hillerman's haunting new whodunit . . . burnished with descriptions of copper sunsets, trout streams, and the chirp of cedar waxwings, is a scenic ride through a land where police are more worried about cattle rustling than dope dealing, the men are 'built of sun-scorched leather, bone, and gristle,' and a cop who's been shot doesn't crave revenge—he wants harmony."

—*Entertainment Weekly*

"It's clear from page one that Hillerman has lost none of his touch. All the elements that have made the previous novels so successful are here: the flawless plot, the deeply drawn major characters, the dead-on minor ones, the picture of reservation life at the Four Corners."

—*Cleveland Plain Dealer*

"There is only one Hillerman. . . . There is no second-best at recreating the feel and the sights and sounds of the Navajo country as backdrop to crackling-good mysteries. . . . *The Fallen Man*, like Hillerman's other novels, is more than just a mystery, and tells us more than merely whodunit."

—*Fort Worth Star-Telegram*

❖ ❖ ❖

"Tony Hillerman fans can relax—Jim Chee and Joe Leaphorn are back. . . . Hillerman has brought off another splendid yarn."
—*Denver Post*

"At the top of his form, Sherlock Holmes couldn't solve more intelligently or slickly the puzzle of *The Fallen Man* than do Navajo tribal policemen Joe Leaphorn and Jim Chee. . . . As usual, the chief virtue Hillerman brings to this tangled narrative is that of pristine clarity, a quality so often needed, but rarely present in a literary work that strives for success on several levels—and achieves it magnificently."
—*Buffalo News*

"A triumphant return for Hillerman and his incomparable pair of Leaphorn and Chee."
—*St. Louis Post-Dispatch*

"Tony Hillerman is back in fine style. . . . *The Fallen Man* has everything: a plot with just the right amount of intricacy; well-developed characters, including those with minor roles; sensitive but never condescending portrayals of Navajo beliefs and life on the reservation; moving descriptions of the starkly beautiful Four Corners landscapes, mixed with insights into threats to the wilderness; danger; romance."
—*Winston-Salem Journal*

Books by TONY HILLERMAN

❖ ❖ ❖ *FICTION* ❖ ❖ ❖

The Fallen Man
Finding Moon
Sacred Clowns
Coyote Waits
Talking God
A Thief of Time
Skinwalkers
The Dark Wind
People of Darkness
Listening Woman
Dance Hall of the Dead
The Fly on the Wall
The Blessing Way
The Boy Who Made Dragonfly *(for children)*

❖ ❖ ❖ *NONFICTION* ❖ ❖ ❖

Hillerman Country
The Great Taos Bank Robbery
Rio Grande
New Mexico
The Spell of New Mexico
Indian Country

TONY HILLERMAN

THE FALLEN MAN

HarperPaperbacks
A Division of HarperCollinsPublishers

HarperPaperbacks
A Division of HarperCollins*Publishers*
10 East 53rd Street, New York, N.Y. 10022-5299

This is a work of fiction. The characters, incidents, and
dialogues are products of the author's imagination and are not to
be construed as real. Any resemblance to actual events or
persons, living or dead, is entirely coincidental.

A hardcover edition of this book was
published in 1996 by HarperCollins*Publishers*.

ISBN: 0-06-109288-6

HarperCollins®, ■ ®, and HarperPaperbacks™
are trademarks of HarperCollins*Publishers*.

Cover illustrations by Peter Thorpe

First HarperPaperbacks printing: October 1997

Printed in the United States of America

Visit HarperPaperbacks on the World Wide Web at
http://www.harpercollins.com

❖ 10 9 8 7 6 5 4 3 2 1

This book is dedicated to members of the Dick Pfaff Philosophical Group, which for the past quarter-century has gathered each Tuesday evening to test the laws of probability and sometimes, alas, the Chaos Theory.

ACKNOWLEDGMENTS

IN WRITING FICTION INVOLVING Navajo Tribal Police, I lean upon the professionals for help. In this book, it was provided by personnel of both the N.T.P. and the Navajo Rangers, and especially by old friend Captain Bill Hillgartner. My thanks also to Chief Leonard G. Butler, Lieutenants Raymond Smith and Clarence Hawthorne, and Sergeants McConnel Wood and Wilfred Tahy. If any technical details are wrong, it wasn't because they didn't try to teach me. Robert Rosebrough, author of *The San Juan Mountains*, loaned me his journal of a Ship Rock climb and gave me other help.

THE FALLEN MAN

1

FROM WHERE BILL BUCHANAN SAT with his back resting against the rough breccia, he could see the side of Whiteside's head, about three feet away. When John leaned back, Buchanan could see the snowcapped top of Mount Taylor looming over Grants, New Mexico, about eighty miles to the east. Now John was leaning forward, talking.

"This climbing down to climb back up, and climbing up so you can climb back down again," Whiteside said. "That seems like a poor way to get the job done. Maybe it's the only way to get to the summit, but I'll bet we could find a faster way down."

"Relax," Buchanan said. "Be calm. We're supposed to be resting."

They were perched on one of the few relatively flat outcrops of basalt in what climbers of Ship Rock call Rappel Gully. On the way up, it was the launching point for the final hard climb to the summit, a slightly tilted but flat surface of basalt about the size of a desktop and 1,721 feet above the prairie below. If you were going down, it was where you began a shorter but even harder almost vertical climb to reach the slope that led you downward with a fair chance of not killing yourself.

Buchanan, Whiteside, and Jim Stapp had just been to the summit. They had opened the army surplus ammo box that held the Ship Rock climbers' register and signed it, certifying their conquest of one of North America's hard ones. Buchanan was tired. He was thinking that he was getting too old for this.

Whiteside was removing his climbing harness, laying aside the nylon belt and the assortment of pitons, jumars, etriers, and carabiners that make reaching such mountaintops possible.

He did a deep knee bend, touched his toes, and stretched. Buchanan watched, uneasy.

"What are you doing?"

"Nothing," Whiteside said. "Actually, I'm following the instructions of that rock climber's guide you're always threatening to write. I am getting rid of all nonessential weight before making an unprotected traverse."

Buchanan sat up. He played in a poker game in which Whiteside was called "Two-Dollar John" because of his unshakable faith that the dealer would give him the fifth heart if he needed one. Whiteside enjoyed taking risks.

"Traversing what?" Buchanan asked.

"I'm just going to ease over there and take a look." He pointed along the face of the cliff. "Get out there maybe a hundred feet and you can see down under the overhang and into the honeycomb formations. I can't believe there's not some way to rappel right on down."

"You're looking for some way to kill yourself," Buchanan said. "If you're in such a damn hurry to get down, get yourself a parachute."

"Rappelling down is easier than up," Whiteside said. He pointed across the little basin to where Stapp was preparing to begin hauling himself up the basalt wall behind them. "I'll just be a few minutes." He began moving with gingerly care out onto the cliff face.

Buchanan was on his feet. "Come on, John! That's too damn risky."

"Not really," Whiteside said. "I'm just going out far enough to see past the overhang. Just a peek at what it looks like. Is it all this broken-up breccia or is there, maybe, a big old finger of basalt sticking up that we could scramble right on down?"

Buchanan slid along the wall, getting closer, admiring Whiteside's technique if not his judgment. The man was moving slowly along the cliff, body almost perfectly vertical, his toes holding his weight on perhaps an inch of sloping stone, his fingers finding the cracks, crevices, and rough spots that would help him keep his balance if the wind gusted. He was doing the traverse perfectly. Beautiful to watch. Even the body was perfect for the purpose. A little smaller and slimmer than Buchanan's. Just bone, sinew, and muscle, without an ounce of surplus weight, moving like an insect against the cracked basalt wall.

And a thousand feet below him—no, a quarter of a mile below him lay what Stapp liked to call "the surface of the world." Buchanan looked out at it. Almost directly below, two Navajos on horseback were riding along the base of the monolith—tiny figures that put the risk of what Whiteside was doing into terrifying perspective. If he slipped, Whiteside would die, but not for a while. It would take time for a body to drop six hundred feet, then to bounce from an outcrop, and fall again, and bounce and fall, until it finally rested among the boulders at the bottom of this strange old volcanic core.

Buchanan looked away from the riders and from the thought. It was early afternoon, but the autumn sun was far to the north and the shadow of Ship Rock already stretched southeastward for miles across the tan prairie. Winter would soon end the climbing season. The sun was already so low that it reflected only from the very tip of Mount Taylor. Eighty miles to the north early snows had already packed the higher peaks in Colorado's San Juans. Not a cloud anywhere. The sky was a deep dry-country blue; the air was cool and, a rarity at this altitude, utterly still.

The silence was so absolute that Buchanan could hear the faint sibilance of Whiteside's soft rubber shoe sole as he shifted a foot along the stone. A couple of hundred feet below him, a red-tailed hawk drifted along, riding an updraft of air along the cliff face. From behind him came the click of Stapp fastening his rappelling gear.

This is why I climb, Buchanan thought. To get

so far away from Stapp's "surface of the earth" that I can't even hear it. But Whiteside climbs for the thrill of challenging death. And now he's out about thirty yards. It's just too damn risky.

"That's far enough, John," Buchanan said. "Don't press your luck."

"Two more feet to a handhold," Whiteside said. "Then I can take a look."

He moved. And stopped. And looked down.

"There's more of that honeycomb breccia under the overhang," he said, and shifted his weight to allow a better head position. "Lot of those little erosion cavities, and it looks like some pretty good cracking where you can see the basalt." He shifted again. "And a pretty good shelf down about—"

Silence. Then Whiteside said, "I think I see a helmet."

"What?"

"My God!" Whiteside said. "There's a skull in it."

2

THE WHITE PORSCHE LOOMING in the rearview mirror of his pickup distracted Jim Chee from his gloomy thoughts. Chee had been rolling southward down Highway 666 toward Salt Creek Wash at about sixty-five miles per hour, which was somewhat more than the law he was paid to uphold allowed. But Navajo Tribal Police protocol this season was permitting speeders about that much margin of error. Besides, traffic was very light, it was past quitting time (the mid-November sunset was turning the clouds over the Carrizo Mountains a gaudy pink), and he saved both gasoline and wear on the pickup's tired old engine by letting it accelerate downhill, thereby gathering momentum for the long climb over the hump between the wash and Shiprock.

But the driver of the Porsche was making a lot more than a tolerable mistake. He was doing about ninety-five. Chee picked the portable blinker light off the passenger-side floorboard, switched it on, rolled down the window, and slapped its magnets against the pickup roof. Just as the Porsche whipped past.

He was instantly engulfed in cold air and road dust. He rolled up the window and jammed his foot down on the accelerator. The speedometer needle reached 70 as he crossed Salt Creek Wash, crept up to almost 75, and then wavered back to 72 as the upslope gravity and engine fatigue took their toll. The Porsche was almost a mile up the hill by now. Chee reached for the mike, clicked it on, and got the Shiprock dispatcher.

"Shiprock," the voice said. "Go ahead, Jim."

This would be Alice Notabah, the veteran. The other dispatcher, who was young and almost as new on the job as was Chee, always called him Lieutenant.

"Go ahead," Alice repeated, sounding slightly impatient.

"Just a speeder," Chee said. "White Porsche Targa, Utah tags, south on triple six into Shiprock. No big deal." The driver probably hadn't seen his blinker. No reason to look in your rearview when you pass a rusty pickup. Still, it added another minor frustration to the day's harvest. Trying to chase the sports car would have been simply humiliating.

"Ten four," Alice said. "You coming in?"

"Going home," Chee said.

"Lieutenant Leaphorn was in looking for you," Alice said.

"What'd he want?" It was actually former lieutenant Leaphorn now. The old man had retired last summer. Finally. After about a century. Still, retired or not, hearing that Leaphorn was looking for him made Chee feel uneasy and begin examining his conscience. He'd spent too many years working for the man.

"He just said he'd catch you later," Alice said. "You sound like you had a bad day."

"Just a total blank," Chee agreed. But that wasn't accurate. It was worse than blank. First there had been the episode with the kid in the Ute Mountain Tribal Police uniform (Chee balked at thinking of him as a policeman), and then there was Mrs. Twosalt.

Cocky kid. Chee had been parked high on the slope below Popping Rock where his truck was screened from view by brush and he had a long view of the oil field roads below. He'd been watching a mud-spattered blue two-ton GMC pickup parked at a cattle guard about a mile below him. Chee had dug out his binoculars and focused them, and was trying to determine why the driver had parked there and if anyone was sitting on the passenger's side. All he was seeing was dirt on the windshield.

About then the kid had said *"Hey!"* in a loud voice, and when Chee had turned, there he was, about six feet away, staring at him through dark and shiny sunglasses.

"What's you doing?" the kid had asked, and Chee had recognized that he was wearing what looked like a brand-new Ute Mountain Tribal Police uniform.

"I'm watching birds," Chee said, and tapped the binoculars.

Which the kid hadn't found amusing.

"Let's see some identification," he'd said. That was all right with Chee. It was proper procedure when you run across something that maybe looks suspicious. He'd fished out his Navajo Tribal Police identification folder, wishing he hadn't made the smart-aleck remark about bird-watching. It was just the sort of wisecrack cops heard every day and resented. He wouldn't have done it, he thought, if the kid hadn't sneaked up on him so efficiently. That was embarrassing.

The kid looked at the folder, from Chee's photograph to Chee's face. Neither seemed to please him.

"Navajo police?" he'd said. "What's you doing out here on the Ute reservation?"

And then Chee politely explained to the kid that they weren't on the Ute reservation. They were on Navajo land, the border being maybe a half mile or so east of them. And the kid had sort of smirked and said Chee was lost, the border was at least a mile the other way, and he'd pointed down the slope. The argument that might have started would have been totally pointless, so Chee had said good-bye and climbed back into his truck. He had driven away, thoroughly pissed off, remembering that the Utes were the enemy in a lot of Navajo mythology and understanding why. He was also thinking he had handled that encounter very poorly for an acting lieutenant, which he had been now for almost three weeks. And that led him to think of Janet Pete, who was why he'd worked for this promotion. Thinking of Janet always cheered him up a little. The day would surely get better.

It didn't. Next came Old Lady Twosalt.

Just like the Ute cop, she'd walked right up behind him without him hearing a thing. She caught him standing in the door of the school bus parked beside the Twosalt hogan, and there wasn't a damn thing he could do but continue standing there, stammering and stuttering, explaining that he'd honked his horn, and waited around and hollered, and did all the polite things one does to protect another's privacy when one visits a house in mostly empty country. And then he'd finally decided that nobody was home. Finally, too, he stopped talking.

Mrs. Twosalt had just stood there, looking politely away from him while he talked instead of looking into his eyes—which is the traditional Navajo way of suggesting disbelief. And when he'd finally finished, she went right to the heart of it.

"I was out looking after the goats," she said. "But what are you looking for in my school bus? You think you lost something in there, or what?"

What Chee was looking for in the school bus was some trace of cow manure, or cow hair, or wool, or any other evidence that the vehicle had been used to haul animals other than schoolkids. It involved the same problem that had him peering through his binoculars at the big pickup over by Popping Rock. Cattle were disappearing from grazing land in the jurisdiction of the Shiprock agency, and Captain Largo had made stopping this thievery the first priority of Chee's criminal investigation division. He put it ahead of dope dealing at the junior college, a gang shooting, bootlegging, and other crimes that Chee felt were more interesting.

He'd rolled out of the cot in his trailer house in the cold dawn this morning, put on his jeans and work jacket, and fired up the old truck intending to spend the day incognito, just prowling around looking for the kind of vehicles into which those cattle might be disappearing.

The GMC pickup was a natural. It was a fifth-wheel model designed to pull heavy trailers and known to be favored by serious rustlers who like to do their stealing in wholesale, trailer-load lots. But he'd just happened to notice the school bus while jolting down the trail from Popping Rock, and just happened to remember the Two-salt outfit not only raised cattle but had a shaky reputation, and just happened to wonder what they would want with an old school bus anyway. None of that helped him come up with the answer for which Mrs. Twosalt had stood there waiting.

"I was just curious," Chee said. "I used to ride one of these things to school when I was a kid. I was wondering if they'd changed them any." He produced a weak laugh.

Mrs. Twosalt hadn't seemed to share his amusement. She waited, looked at him, waited some more—giving him a chance to change his story and to offer a more plausible explanation for this visit.

In default of a better idea, Chee had fished out his identification folder. He'd said he'd come by to learn if the Twosalts were missing any cattle or sheep or had seen anything suspicious. Mrs. Twosalt said she kept good track of all their animals. Nothing was missing. And that had been the end of that except for the lingering embarrassment.

It was almost dark as he topped the hill and looked down at the scattering of lights of Shiprock town. No sign of the Porsche. Chee yawned. What a day! He turned off the pavement onto the gravel road, which led to the dirt road, which led to the weedy track down to his trailer under the cottonwoods beside the San Juan River. He rubbed his eyes, yawned again. He'd warm up what was left of his breakfast coffee, open a can of chili, and hit the sack early. A bad day, but now it was over.

No, it wasn't. His headlights reflected off a windshield, off a dusty car parked just past his trailer. Chee recognized it. Former lieutenant Joe Leaphorn, as promised, had caught him later.

3

CHEE'S TRAILER HAD BEEN CHILLY when he left it at dawn. Now it was frigid, having leaked what little warmth it had retained into the chill that settled along the San Juan River. Chee lit the propane heater and started the coffee.

Joe Leaphorn was sitting stiff and straight on the bench behind the table. He put his hat on the Formica tabletop and rubbed his hand through his old-fashioned crew cut, which had become appropriately gray. Then he replaced the hat, looked uneasy, and took it off again. To Chee the hat looked as weatherworn as its owner.

"I hate to bother you like this," Leaphorn said, and paused. "By the way, congratulations on the promotion."

"Thanks," Chee said. He glanced around from the coffeepot, where the hot water was still dripping through the grounds, and hesitated.

But what the hell. It had not seemed plausible when he'd heard it, but why not find out?

"People tell me you recommended me for it."

If Leaphorn heard that, it didn't show on his face. He was watching his folded hands, the thumbs of which he had engaged in circling each other.

"It gets you lots of work and worry," Leaphorn said, "and not much pay goes with the job."

Chee extracted two mugs from the cabinet, put the one advertising the *Farmington Times* in front of Leaphorn, and looked for the sugar bowl.

"How you enjoying your retirement?" Chee asked. Which was a sort of oblique way of getting the man to the point of this visit. This wouldn't be a social call. No way. Leaphorn had always been the boss and Chee had been the gofer. One way or another this visit would involve law enforcement and something Leaphorn wanted Chee to do about it.

"Well, being retired there's a lot less aggravation," Leaphorn said. "You don't have to put up with—" He shrugged and chuckled.

Chee laughed, but it was forced. He wasn't used to this strange new version of Leaphorn. This Leaphorn, come to ask him for something, hesitant and diffident, wasn't the Lieutenant Leaphorn he remembered with a mixture of puzzlement, irritation, and admiration. Seeing the man as a supplicant made him uneasy. He'd put a stop to that.

"I remember when you told me you were retiring, you said if I ever needed to pick your brains for anything, to feel free to ask," Chee said. "So I'm going to ask you what you know about the cattle-rustling business."

Leaphorn considered, thumbs still circling. "Well," he said, "I know there's always some of it going on. And I know your boss and his family have been in the cow business for about three generations. So he probably doesn't care much for cow thieves." He stopped watching his thumbs and looked up at Chee. "You having a run of it up here? Anything big?"

"Nothing very big. The Conroy ranch lost eight heifers last month. That was the worst. Had six or seven other complaints in the past two months. Mostly one or two missing, and some of them probably just strayed off. But Captain Largo tells me it's worse than usual."

"Enough to get Largo stirred up," Leaphorn said. "His family has grazing leases scattered around over on the Checkerboard."

Chee grinned.

"I'll bet you already knew that," Leaphorn said, and chuckled.

"I did," Chee said, and poured the coffee.

Leaphorn sipped.

"I don't think I know anything about catching rustlers that Captain Largo hasn't already told you," Leaphorn said. "Now we have the Navajo Rangers, and since cattle are a tribal resource and their job is protecting tribal resources, it's really their worry. But the rangers are a real small group and they tend to be tied up with game poachers and people vandalizing the parks, or stealing timber, or draining off drip gasoline. That sort of thing. Not enough rangers to go around, so you work with whoever the New Mexico Cattle Sanitary Board has covering this district, and the Arizona Brand Inspection Office, and the Colorado people. And you keep an eye out for strange trucks and horse trailers." Leaphorn looked up and shrugged. "Not much you can do. I never had much luck catching 'em, and the few times I did, we could never get a conviction."

"I don't think I'm going to get much return on the time I've been investing in it either," Chee said.

"I bet you're already doing everything I suggested." Leaphorn added sugar to his coffee, sipped, looked at Chee over the rim. "And then, of course, you're getting into the ceremonial season, and you know how that works. Somebody's having a sing. They need to feed all those kinfolks and friends who come to help with the cure. Lots of hungry people and maybe you have them for a whole week if it's a full-fledged ceremony. You know what they say in New Mexico: nobody eats his own beef."

"Yeah," Chee said. "Looking through the reports for the past years I noticed the little one or two animal thefts go up when the thunderstorms stop and the sings begin."

"I used to just snoop around a little. Maybe I'd find some fresh hides with the wrong brands on 'em. But you know there's not much use arresting anybody for that. I'd just say a word or two to let 'em know we'd caught 'em, and then I'd tell the owner. And if he was Navajo, he'd figure that he should have known they needed a little help and butchered something for them and saved 'em the trouble of stealing it."

Leaphorn stopped, knowing he was wasting time.

"Good ideas," Chee said, knowing he wasn't fooling Leaphorn. "Anything I can do for you?"

"It's nothing important," Leaphorn said. "Just something that's been sort of sticking in my mind for years. Just curiosity really."

Chee tried his own coffee and found it absolutely delicious. He waited for Leaphorn to decide how he wanted to ask this favor.

"It was eleven years this fall," Leaphorn said. "I was assigned to the Chinle office then and we had a young man disappear from the lodge at Canyon de Chelly. Fellow named Harold Breedlove. He and his wife were there celebrating their fifth wedding anniversary. His birthday, too. The way his wife told it, he got a telephone call. He tells her he has to meet someone about a business deal. He says he'll be right back and he drives off in their car. He doesn't come back. Next morning she calls the Arizona Highway Patrol. They call us."

Leaphorn paused, understanding that such a strong reaction to what seemed like nothing more sinister than a man taking a vacation from his wife needed an explanation. "They're a big ranching family. The Breedloves. The Lazy B ranch up in Colorado, leases in New Mexico and Arizona, all sorts of mining interests, and so forth. The old man ran for Congress once. Anyway, we put out a description of the car. It was a new green Land Rover. Easy to spot out here. And about a week later an officer spots it. It had been left up an arroyo beside that road that runs from 191 over to the Sweetwater chapter house."

"I'm sort of remembering that case now," Chee said. "But very dimly. I was new then, working way over at Crownpoint." And, Chee thought, having absolutely nothing to do with the Breedlove case. So where could this conversation possibly be leading?

"No sign of violence at the car, that right?" Chee asked. "No blood. No weapon. No note. No nothing."

"Not even tracks," Leaphorn said. "A week of wind took care of that."

"And nothing stolen out of the car, if I remember it right," Chee said. "Seems like I remember somebody saying it still had an expensive audio system in it, spare tire, everything still there."

Leaphorn sipped his coffee, thinking. Then he said, "So it seemed then. Now I don't know. Maybe some mountain climbing equipment was stolen."

"Ah," Chee said. He put down the coffee cup. Now he understood where Leaphorn was heading.

"That skeleton up on Ship Rock," Leaphorn said. "All I know about it is what I read in the *Gallup Independent*. Do you have any identification yet?"

"Not that I know of," Chee said. "There's no evidence of foul play, but Captain Largo got the FBI laboratory people to take a look at everything. Last I heard, they hadn't come up with anything."

"Nothing much but bare bones to work with, I heard," Leaphorn said. "And what was left of the clothing. I guess people who climb mountains don't take along their billfolds."

"Or engraved jewelry," Chee added. "Or anything else they're not using. At least this guy didn't."

"You get an estimate on his age?"

"The pathologist said between thirty and thirty-five. No sign of any health problems which affected bone development. I guess you don't expect health problems in people who climb mountains. And he probably grew up someplace with lots of fluoride in the drinking water."

Leaphorn chuckled. "Which means no fillings in his teeth and no help from any dental charts."

"We had lots of that kind of luck on this one," Chee said.

Leaphorn drained his cup, put it down. "How was he dressed?"

Chee frowned. It was an odd question. "Like a mountain climber," he said. "You know. Special boots with those soft rubber soles, all the gear hanging off of him."

"I was thinking about the season," Leaphorn said. "Black as that Ship Rock is, the sun gets it hot in the summer—even up there a mile and a half above sea level. And in the winter, it gets coated with ice. The snow packs in where it's shaded. Layers of ice form."

"Yeah," Chee said. "Well, this guy wasn't wearing cold-weather gear. Just pants and a long-sleeved shirt. Maybe some sort of thermal underwear, though. He was on a sort of shelf a couple of hundred feet below the peak. Way too high for the coyotes to get to him, but the buzzards and ravens had been there."

"Did the rescue team bring everything down? Was there anything that you'd expect to find that wasn't there? I mean, you'd expect to find if you knew anything about the gear climbers carry."

"As far as I know nothing was missing," Chee said. "Of course, stuff may have fallen down into cracks. The birds would have scattered things around."

"A lot of rope, I guess," Leaphorn said.

"Quite a bit," Chee said. "I don't know how much would be normal. I know climbing rope stretches a lot. Largo sent it to the FBI lab to see if they could tell if a knot slipped, or it broke, or what."

"Did they bring down the other end?"

"Other end?"

Leaphorn nodded. "If it broke, there'd be the other end. He would have had it secured someplace. A piton driven in or tied to something secure. In case he slipped."

"Oh," Chee said. "The climbers who went up for the bones didn't find it. I doubt if they looked. Largo asked them to go up and bring down the body. And I remember they thought there'd have to be two bodies. Nobody would be crazy enough to climb Ship Rock alone. But they didn't find another one. I guess our fallen man was that crazy."

"Sounds like it," Leaphorn said.

Chee poured them both some more coffee, looked at Leaphorn and said, "I guess this Harold Breedlove was a mountain climber. Am I right?"

"He was," Leaphorn said. "But if he's your fallen man, he wasn't a very smart one."

"You mean climbing up there alone."

"Yeah," Leaphorn said. "Or if he wasn't alone, climbing with someone who'd go off and leave him."

"I've thought about that," Chee said. "The rescue crew said he'd either climbed up to the ledge, which they didn't think would be possible without help, or tried to rappel down from above. But the skeleton was intact. Nothing broken." Chee shook his head.

"If someone was with him, why didn't they report it? Get help? Bring down the body? You have any thoughts about that?"

"Yeah," Chee said. "Makes no sense either way."

Leaphorn sipped coffee. Considered.

"I'd like to know more about this climbing gear you said was stolen out of Breedlove's car," Chee said.

"I said it might have been stolen, and maybe from the car," Leaphorn said.

Chee waited.

"About a month after the guy vanished, we caught a kid from Many Farms breaking into a tourist's car parked at one of the Canyon de Chelly overlooks. He had a bunch of other stolen stuff at his place, car radios, mobile phones, tape decks, so forth, including some mountain climbing gear. Rope, pitons, whatever they call those gadgets. By then we'd been looking for Breedlove long enough to know he was a climber. The boy claimed he found the stuff where runoff had uncovered it in an arroyo bottom. We had him take us out and show us. It was about five hundred yards upstream from where we'd found Breedlove's car."

Chee considered this.

"Did you say the car hadn't been broken into?"

"It wasn't locked when we found it. The stuff kids usually take was still there."

Chee made a wry face. "You have any idea why he'd just take the climbing gear?"

"And leave the stuff he could sell? I don't know," Leaphorn said. He picked up his cup, noticed it was empty, put it down again.

"I heard you're getting married," he said. "Congratulations."

"Thanks. You want a refill?"

"A very pretty lady," Leaphorn said. "And smart. A good lawyer." He held out his cup.

Chee laughed. "I never heard you use that adjective talking about a lawyer before. Anyway, not about a defense lawyer." Janet Pete worked for Dinebeiina Nahiilna be Agaditahe, which translates more or less literally as "People who talk fast and help people" and was more likely to be called DNA, or public defenders, or with less polite language by Navajo Police.

"Has to be a first time for everything," Leaphorn said. "And Miss Pete—" Leaphorn couldn't think of a way to finish that sentence.

Chee took his cup and refilled it.

"I hope you'll let me know if anything interesting turns up on your fallen man."

That surprised Chee. Wasn't it finished now? Leaphorn had found his missing man. Largo's fallen man was identified. Case closed. What else interesting would there be?

"You mean if we check out the Breedlove identification and the skeleton turns out to be the wrong size, or wrong race, or Breedlove had false teeth? Or what?"

"Yeah," Leaphorn said. But he still sat there, holding his replenished coffee cup. This conversation wasn't finished. Chee waited, trying to deduce the way it would be going.

"Did you have a suspect? I guess the widow would be one?"

"There seemed to be a good reason for it in this case. But that didn't pan out. Then there was a cousin. A Washington lawyer named George Shaw. Who just happened to also be a mountain climber, and just happened to be out here and looked just perfect as the odd man in a love triangle if you wanted one. He said he'd come out to talk to Breedlove about some sort of mineral lease proposal on the Lazy B ranch. That seemed to be true from what I could find out. Shaw was representing the family's business interests and a mining company was dickering for a lease."

"With Harold? Did he own the place?"

Leaphorn laughed. "He'd just inherited it. Three days before he disappeared."

"Well, now," Chee said, and thought about it while Leaphorn sipped his coffee.

"Did you see the report on the shooting over at Canyon de Chelly the other day?" Leaphorn asked. "An old man named Amos Nez shot apparently by somebody up on the rim?"

"I saw it," Chee said. It was an odd piece of business. Nez had been hit in the side. He'd fallen off his horse still holding the reins. The next shot hit the horse in the head. It had fallen partly across Nez and then four more shots had been fired. One hit Nez in the forearm and then he had pulled himself into cover behind the animal. The last Chee'd seen on it, six empty 30.06 cartridges had been recovered among the boulders up on the rim. As far as Chee knew that's where the trail in this case ended. No suspects. No motive. Nez was listed in fair condition at the Chinle hospital—well enough to say he had no idea why anyone would want to shoot him.

"That's what stirred me up," Leaphorn said. "Old Hosteen Nez was one of the last people to see this Hal Breedlove before he disappeared."

"Quite a coincidence," Chee said. When he'd worked for Leaphorn at Window Rock, Leaphorn had told him never to believe in coincidences. Told him that often. It was one of the man's cardinal rules. Every effect had its cause. If it seemed to be connected and you couldn't find the link it just meant you weren't trying hard enough. But this sounded like an awfully strained coincidence.

"Nez was their guide in the canyon," Leaphorn said. "When the Breedloves were staying at the lodge he was one of the crew there. The Breedloves hired him to take them all the way up Canyon del

Muerto one day, and the main canyon the next. I talked to him three times."

That seemed to Leaphorn to require some explanation.

"You know," he said. "Rich guy with a pretty young wife disappears for no reason. You ask questions. But Nez told me they seemed to like each other a lot. Having lots of fun. He said one time he'd been up one of the side canyons to relieve himself and when he came back it looked like she was crying and Breedlove was comforting her. So he waited a little before showing up and then everything was all right."

Chee considered. "What do you think? It could have been anything?"

"Yep," Leaphorn said, and sipped coffee. "Did I mention they were celebrating Breedlove's birthday? We found out that he'd turned thirty just the previous week, and when he turned thirty he inherited. His daddy left him the ranch but he put it into a family trust. It had a provision that the trustee controlled it until Breedlove got to be thirty years old. Then it was all his."

Chee considered again. "And the widow inherited from him?"

"That's what we found out. So she had a motive and we had the logical suspect."

"But no evidence," Chee guessed.

"None. Not only that. Just before Breedlove drove away, our Mr. Nez arrived to take them on another junket up the canyon. He remembered Breedlove apologized for missing out, paid him in advance, and gave him a fifty-dollar tip. Then

Mrs. Breedlove and Nez took off. They spent the day sight-seeing. Nez remembered she was in a hurry when it was getting dark because she was supposed to meet Breedlove and another couple for dinner. But when they got back to the lodge, no car. That's the last Nez saw of her."

Leaphorn paused, looked at Chee, and added, "Or so he says."

"Oh?" Chee said.

"Well, I didn't mean he'd seen her again. It's just that I always had a feeling that Nez knew something he wasn't telling me. That's one reason I kept going back to talk to him."

"You think he had something to do with the disappearance. Maybe the two of them weren't up the canyon when Breedlove was supposed to be driving away?"

"Well, no," Leaphorn said. "People staying at the lodge saw them coming out of the canyon in Nez's truck about seven P.M. Then a little after seven, she went over to the lodge and asked if Breedlove had called in. About seven-thirty she's having dinner with the other couple. They remembered her being irritated about him being so late, mixed with a little bit of worry."

"I guess that's what they call an airtight alibi," Chee said. "So how long did it take her to get old Hal declared legally dead so she could marry her coconspirator? And would I be wrong if I guessed that would be George Shaw?"

"She's still a widow, last I heard," Leaphorn said. "She offered a ten-thousand-dollar reward and after a while upped it to twenty thousand and didn't petition to get her husband declared legally dead until five years later. She lives up near Mancos, Colorado. She and her brother run the Lazy B now."

"You know what?" Chee said. "I think I know those people. Is the brother Eldon Demott?"

"That's him."

"He's one of our customers," Chee said. "The ranch still has those public land leases you mentioned on the Checkerboard Reservation and they've been losing Angus calves. He thinks maybe some of us Navajos might be stealing them."

"Eldon is Elisa Breedlove's older brother," Leaphorn said. "Their daddy was old man Breedlove's foreman, and when their daddy died, I think Eldon just sort of inherited the job. Anyway, the Demott family lived on the ranch. I guess that's how Elisa and the Breedlove boy got together."

Chee stifled a yawn. It had been a long and tiring day and this session with Leaphorn, helpful as it had been, didn't qualify as relaxation. He had accumulated too many memories of tense times trying to live up to the man's high expectations. It would be a while before he could relax in Leaphorn's presence. Maybe another twenty years would do it.

"Well," Chee said. "I guess that takes care of the fallen man. I've got a probable identification of our skeleton. You've located your missing Hal Breedlove. I'll call you when we get it confirmed."

Leaphorn drained his cup, got up, adjusted his hat.

"I thank you for the help," he said.

"And you for yours."

Leaphorn opened the door, admitting a rush of cold air, the rich perfume of autumn, and a reminder that winter was out there somewhere, like the coyote, just waiting.

"All we need to do now—" he said, and stopped, looking embarrassed. "All that needs to be done," he amended, "is find out if your bones really are my Breedlove, and then find out how the hell he got from that abandoned Land Rover about a hundred fifty miles west, and way up there to where he could fall off of Ship Rock."

"And why," Chee said. "And how he did it all by himself."

"If he did," Leaphorn said.

4

THE STRANGE TRUCK PARKED in one of the Official Visitor slots at the Shiprock headquarters of the Navajo Tribal Police wore a New Jersey license and looked to Jim Chee anything but official. It had dual back wheels and carried a cumbersome camper, its windows covered by decals that certified visitation at tourist traps from Key West to Vancouver Island. Other stickers plastered across the rear announced that A BAD DAY FISHING IS BETTER THAN A GOOD DAY AT WORK, and declared the camper-truck to be OUR CHILDREN'S INHERITANCE. Bumper decals exhorted viewers to VISUALIZE WHIRLED PEAS and to TRY RANDOM ACTS OF KINDNESS, and endorsed the National Rifle Association. A broad band of silver duct tape circled the camper's rear panel, sealing the dust out of the joint and giving the camper a ramshackle, homemade look.

Chee stuck his head into Alice Notabah's

dispatcher office and indicated the truck with a nod: "Who's the Official Visitor?"

Notabah nodded toward Largo's office. "In with the captain," she said. "And he wants to see you."

The man who drove the truck was sitting in the comfortable chair Captain Largo kept for important visitors. He held a battered black hat with a silver concha band in his lap and looked relaxed and comfortable.

"I'll catch you later," Chee said, but Largo waved him in.

"I want you to meet Dick Finch," Largo said. "He's the New Mexico brand inspector working the Four Corners, and he's been getting some complaints."

Chee and Finch shook hands. "Complaints?" Chee said. "Like what?"

"'Bout what you'd expect for a brand inspector to get," Finch said. "People missing their cattle. Thinking maybe somebody's stealing 'em."

Finch grinned when he said it, eliminating some of the sting from the sarcasm.

"Yeah," Chee said, "we've been hearing some of that, too."

Finch shrugged. "Folks always say that nobody likes to eat his own beef. But it's got a little beyond that, I think. With bred heifers going at sixty dollars a hundred pounds, it just takes three of 'em to make you a grand larceny."

Captain Largo was looking sour. "Sixty dollars a hundred, like hell," he said. "More like a thousand dollars a head for me. I've been trying to raise purebred stock." He nodded in Chee's direction. "Jim here is running our criminal investigation division. He's been working on it."

Largo waited. So did Finch.

"I'm here on something else now," Chee said finally. "I think we may have an identification on that skeleton that was found up on Ship Rock."

"Well, now," Largo said. "Where'd that come from?"

"Joe Leaphorn remembered a missing person case he had eleven years ago. The man disappeared from Canyon de Chelly but he was a mountain climber."

"Leaphorn," Largo said. "I thought old Joe was supposed to be retired."

"He is," Chee said.

"Eleven years is a hell of a long time to remember a missing person case," Largo said. "How many of those do we get in an average month?"

"Several," Chee said. "But most of 'em don't stay missing long."

Largo nodded. "So who's the man?"

"Harold Breedlove was the missing man. He used to own the Lazy B ranch south of Mancos. Or his family owned it."

"Fella named Eldon Demott owns it now," Finch said. "Runs a lot of Herefords down in San Juan County. Has some deeded land and some BLM leases and a big home place up in Colorado."

"What have you got beyond this Breedlove fella's been missing long enough to become a skeleton and him being a climber?" Largo asked.

Chee explained what Leaphorn had told him.

"Just that?" Largo asked, and thought a moment. "Well, it could be right. It sounds like it is and Joe Leaphorn never was much for being wrong. Did Joe have any notion why this guy left his wife at the canyon? Or why he'd be climbing Ship Rock all by himself?"

"He didn't say, but I think he figures maybe Breedlove wasn't alone up there. And maybe the widow knew more than she was telling him at the time."

"And what's that about Amos Nez getting shot last week down at Canyon de Chelly? You lost me on that connection."

"It was sort of thin," Chee said. "Nez happened to be one of the witnesses in the disappearance case. Leaphorn said he was the last person known to have seen Breedlove alive. Except for the widow."

Largo considered. Grinned. "And she was Joe's suspect, of course," he said. And shook his head. "Joe never could believe in coincidences."

"They still had that mountain climbing gear in the evidence room at Window Rock and I had them send it up," Chee said. "It looks to me a lot like the gear they found on our Fallen Man, so I called Mrs. Breedlove up at Mancos."

"What'd she say?"

"She'd gone into town for something. The housekeeper said she'd be back in a couple of hours. I left word that I was coming up this afternoon to show her some stuff that might bear on her missing husband."

Finch cleared his throat, glanced up at Chee. "While you're there why not just kind of keep your eyes open? Tell 'em you've heard good things about the way they run their place. Look around. You know?"

Finch looked to Chee to be about fifty. He had a hollowed scar high on his right cheek (resulting, Chee guessed, from some sort of surgery), small, bright blue eyes, and a complexion burned and cracked by the Four Corners weather. He was waiting now for Chee's response to this suggestion.

"You think Demott's sort of augmenting his herd with some strangers?" Chee asked.

"Well, not exactly," Finch said, and shrugged. "But who knows? People losing their cattle. Maybe the coyotes are getting 'em. Maybe Demott's got fifteen or twenty head he's shipping off to the feedlot and he thinks it would be nice to round it off at twenty or twenty-five. No harm in looking. Seeing what you can see."

"I'll do that," Chee said. "But were you telling me you don't have anything specific against Demott?"

Finch was studying Chee, looking quizzical. He's trying to decide, Chee thought, how stupid I am.

"Nothing I could take in to a judge and get a search warrant with. But you hear things." With that, Finch broke into a chuckle. "Hell, you hear things about everybody." He jerked a thumb at Largo. "I've even been told that your captain here has some peculiar-looking brands on some of his stock. That right, Captain?"

"I've heard that myself," Largo said, grinning. "We have a barbecue over at the place, all the neighbors want to go out and take a look at the cowhides."

"Well, it's a lot cheaper than buying beef at the butcher shop. So maybe somebody's eating Demott's sirloin and the Demotts are eating theirs."

"Or mutton," added Largo, who was missing some ewes as well as a calf or two.

"How about me going along for the ride?" Finch said. "I mean up to the Lazy B?"

"Why not?" Chee said.

"You wouldn't have to introduce me, you know. I'll just sort of get out and stretch my legs. Look around a little bit. You never know what you might see."

5

THEY CAME INTO VIEW OF THE HEADQUARTERS of the Lazy B with the autumn sun low over Mesa Verde, producing shadow patterns on Bridge Timber Mountain. Chee had been thinking more of home sites lately and he thought now that this little valley would be a beautiful place for Janet and him. The house in the cluster of cottonwoods below them would be far, far too large for him to feel comfortable in. But Janet would love it.

Finch had been doing the talking on the drive up from Shiprock. After the first fifty miles of that, Chee began listening just enough to nod or grunt at the proper intervals. Mostly he was thinking about Janet Pete and the differences between what they liked and what they didn't. This house, for example. Women usually had most to say about living places, but if he retained veto power, theirs certainly wouldn't be anything as huge as the fieldstone, timber, and slate mansion the Breedlove family had built for itself. Even if they could afford it, which they certainly never would.

That reminded Chee of the white Porsche that had zipped past him yesterday. Why did he connect it to Janet? Because it had class, as did she. And was beautiful. And, sure, she'd like it. Who wouldn't? So why did he resent it? Was it because it was a part of the world she came from in which he would never be comfortable? Or understand? Maybe.

But now he was about to walk in and see if he could get a widow to identify a bunch of stuff that would tell her that her husband was truly dead. Tell her, that is, unless she already knew—having killed him herself. Or arranged it. He'd worry about the Porsche later. The Breedlove mansion was now just across the fence.

According to Finch, old Edgar Breedlove had built it as a second home—his first one being in Denver, from which he ran his mining operations. But he'd never lived in it. He'd bought the ranch because his prospectors had found a molybdenum deposit on the high end of the property. But the ore price fell after the war and somehow or other the place got left to a grandson, Harold. Hal had adopted his granddad's policy of overgrazing it and letting it run down.

"That ain't happening now," Finch had told him. "This place ain't going to go to hell while Demott's running it. He's sort of a tree-hugger. That's what people say. Say he never got married 'cause he's in love with this place."

Chee parked under a tree a polite distance

from the front entrance, turned off the ignition, and sat, killing the time needed by hosts to get decent before welcoming guests. Finch, another empty-country man, seemed to understand that. He yawned, stretched, and examined the half dozen cows in the feedlot beside the barn with a professional eye.

"How do you know all this about the Breedlove ranch, and Demott and everything?" Chee asked. "This is Colorado. It's not your territory."

"Ranching—and stealing cows off of ranches—don't pay much attention to state lines," Finch said, not taking his eyes off the cows. "The Lazy B has leases in New Mexico. Makes 'em my business."

Finch extracted a twenty-stick pack of chewing gum from his jacket pocket, offered it to Chee, extracted two sticks for himself, and started chewing them. "Besides," he said, "you got to have something going to make the job interesting. I got one particular guy I keep looking for. Most of these cow thieves are 'hungries.' Folks run out of eating money, or got a payment due, and they go out and get themselves a cow or two to sell. Or, on the reservation, maybe they got somebody sick in the family, and they're having a sing for the patient, and they need a steer to feed all the kinfolks coming in. I never worried too much about them. If they keep doing it, they get careless and they get caught and the neighbors talk to them about it. Get it straightened out. But then there's some others who are in it for business. It's easy money and it beats working."

"Who's this one you're specially after?"

Finch laughed. "If I knew that, we wouldn't be talking about it, now would we?"

"I guess not," Chee said, impressed with how insulting Finch could be even when he was acting friendly.

"We'd just go out and get him then, wouldn't we?" Finch concluded. "But all I know about him is the way he operates. Modus operandi, if you know your Latin. He always picks the spread-out ranches where a few head won't be missed for a while. He always takes something that he can sell quick. No little calves that you have to wean, no big, expensive, easy-to-trace breeding bulls. Never messes with horses, 'cause some people get attached to a nag and go out looking for it. Has some other tricks, too. Like he finds a good place beside a back road where there wouldn't be any traffic to bother him and he'll put out feed. Usually good alfalfa hay. Do it several times so the cattle get in the habit of coming up and looking for it when they see his truck parking."

Finch stopped, looked at Chee, waited for a comment.

"Pretty smart," Chee said.

"Yes, sir," Finch agreed. "So far, he's been smarter than me."

Chee had no comment on that. He glanced at his watch. Another three minutes and he'd go ring the doorbell and get this job over with.

"Then I've found a place or two where he fixed up the fence so he could get 'em through it fast." He paused again, seeing if Chee understood this. Chee did, but to hell with Finch.

"You could cut the wire, of course," Finch explained, "but then the herd gets out on the road and somebody notices it right away and they do a head count and know some are missing."

Chee said, "Really?"

"Yeah," Finch said. "Anyway, I've been after this son of a bitch for years now. Every time I take off from home to come out this way, he's the one I'm thinking of."

Chee didn't comment.

"Zorro," Finch said. "That's what I call him. And this time I think I'll finally get him."

"How?"

Silence, unusual for Finch, followed. Then he said, "Well, now, that's sort of complicated."

"You think it might be Demott?"

"Why you say that?"

"Well, you wanted to come up here. And you've collected all that information about him."

"If you're a brand inspector you learn to pick up on all the gossip you can hear if you want to get your job done. And there was some talk that Demott paid off a mortgage by selling a bunch of calves nobody knew he owned."

"So what's the gossip about the widow Breedlove?" Chee asked. "Who was the lover who helped her kill her husband? What do the neighbors say about that?"

Finch was wearing a broad smile. "People I know up in Mancos have her down as the broken-hearted, wronged, abandoned bride. The majority of them, that is. They figured Hal ran off with some bimbo."

"How about the minority?"

"They think she had herself a local boyfriend. Somebody to keep her happy when Hal was off in New York, or climbing his mountains or playing his games."

"They have a name for him?"

"Not that I ever heard," Finch said.

"Which bunch you think is right?"

"About her? I never thought about it," Finch said. "None of my business, that part of it wasn't. Talk like that just means that folks around here didn't like Hal."

"What'd he do?"

"Well, for starters he got born in the East," Finch said. "That's two strikes on you right there. And he was raised there. Citified. Preppy type. Papa's boy. Ivy Leaguer. He didn't get any bones broke falling off horses, lose a finger in a hay baler. Didn't pay his dues, you know. You don't have to actually do anything to have folks down on you."

"How about the widow? You hear anything specific about her?"

"Don't hear nothing about her, except some fellas guessing. And she's a real pretty woman, so that was probably just them wishing," Finch said. He was grinning at Chee. "You know how it works. If you're behaving yourself it's not interesting."

The front door of the Breedlove house opened and Chee could see someone standing behind the screen looking out at them. He picked up his evidence satchel and stepped out of the vehicle.

"I'll wait here for you," Finch said, "and maybe scout around a little if I get too stiff from sitting."

Mrs. Elisa Breedlove was indeed a real pretty woman. She seemed excited and nervous, which was what Chee had expected. Her handshake grip was hard, and so was the hand. She led him into a huge living room, dark and cluttered with heavy, old-fashioned furniture. She motioned him into a chair, explaining that she'd had to run into Mancos "to get some stuff."

"I got back just before you drove up and Ramona told me you'd called and were coming."

"I hope I'm not—" Chee began, but she cut him off.

"No. No," she said. "I appreciate this. Ramona said you'd found Hal. Or think so. But she didn't know anything else."

"Well," Chee said, and paused. "What we found was merely bones. We thought they might be Mr. Breedlove."

He sat on the edge of the sofa, watching her.

"Bones," she said. "Just a skeleton? Was that the skeleton they found about Halloween up on Ship Rock?"

"Yes, ma'am. We wanted to ask you to look at the clothing and equipment he was wearing and see if—tell us if it was the right size, and if you thought it was your husband's stuff."

"Equipment?" She was standing beside a table, her hand on it. The light slanting through windows on each side of the fireplace illuminated her face. It was a small, narrow face framed by light brown hair, the jaw muscles tight, the expression tense. Middle thirties, Chee guessed. Slender, perfectly built, luminous green eyes, the sort of classic beauty that survived sun, wind, and hard winters and didn't seem to require the disguise of makeup. But today she looked tired. He thought of a description Finch had applied to a woman they both knew: "Been rode hard and put up wet."

Mrs. Breedlove was waiting for an answer, her green eyes fixed on his face.

"Mountain climbing equipment," Chee said. "I understand the skeleton was in a cleft down the face of a cliff. Presumably, the man had fallen."

Mrs. Breedlove closed her eyes and bent slightly forward with her hips against the table.

Chee rose. "Are you all right?"

"All right," she said, but she put a hand against the table to support herself.

"Would you like to sit down? A drink of water?"

"Why do you think it's Hal?" Her eyes were still closed.

"He's been missing for eleven years. And we're told he was a mountain climber. Is that correct?"

"He was. He loved the mountains."

"This man was about five feet nine inches tall," Chee said. "The coroner estimated he would have weighed about one hundred and fifty pounds. He had perfect teeth. He had rather long fingers and—"

"Hal was about five eight, I'd say. He was slender, muscular. An athlete. I think he weighed about a hundred and sixty. He was worried about gaining weight." She produced a weak smile. "Around the belt line. Before we went on that trip, I let out his suit pants to give him another inch."

"He'd had a broken nose," Chee continued. "Healed. The doctor said it probably happened when he was an adolescent. And a broken wrist. He said that was more recent."

Mrs. Breedlove sighed. "The nose was from playing fraternity football, or whatever the boys play at Dartmouth. And the wrist when a horse threw him after we were married."

Chee opened the satchel, extracted the climbing equipment, and stacked it on the coffee table. There wasn't much: a nylon belt harness, the ragged remains of a nylon jacket, even more fragmentary remains of trousers and shirt, a pair of narrow shoes with soles of soft, smooth rubber, a little rock hammer, three pitons, and a couple of steel gadgets that Chee presumed were used somehow for controlling rope slippage.

When he glanced up, Mrs. Breedlove was staring at them, her face white. She turned away, facing the window but looking at nothing except some memory.

"I thought about Hal when I saw the piece the paper had on the skeleton," she said. "Eldon and I talked about it at supper that night. He thought the same thing I did. We decided it couldn't be Hal." She attempted a smile. "He was always into derring-do stuff. But he wouldn't try to climb Ship Rock alone. Nobody would. That would be insane. Two great rock men were

killed on it, and they were climbing with teams
of experienced experts."

She paused. Listening. The sound of a car
engine came through the window. "That was
before the Navajos banned climbing," she added.

"Are you a climber?"

"When I was younger," she said. "When Hal
used to come out, Eldon started teaching him to
climb. Hal and his cousin George. Sometimes I
would go along and they taught me."

"How about Ship Rock?" Chee asked. "Did
you ever climb it?"

She studied him. "The tribe prohibited that a
long time ago. Before I was big enough to climb
anything."

Chee smiled. "But some people still climbed
it. Quite a few, from what I hear. And there's not
actually a tribal ordinance against it. It's just
that the tribe stopped issuing those 'back country' permits. You know, to allow non-Navajos the
right to trespass."

Mrs. Breedlove looked thoughtful. Through
the window came the sound of a car door slamming.

"To make it perfectly legal, you'd go see one
of the local people who had a grazing permit
running up to the base and get him to give you
permission to be on the land," Chee added. "But
most people even don't bother to do that."

Mrs. Breedlove considered this. Nodded.
"We always got permission. I climbed it once. It
was terrifying. With Eldon, Hal, and George. I
still have nightmares."

"About falling?"

She shuddered. "I'm up there looking all around. Looking at Ute Mountain up in Colorado, and seeing the shape of Case del Eco Mesa in Utah, and the Carrizos in Arizona, and Mount Taylor, and I have this dreadful feeling that Ship Rock is getting higher and higher and then I know I can never get down." She laughed. "Fear of falling, I guess. Or fear of flying away and being lost forever."

"I guess you've heard our name for it," Chee said. "Tse´ Bit´ a´i̇—the Rock with Wings. According to the legend it flew here from the north bringing the first Navajos on its back. Maybe it was flying again in your dream."

A voice from somewhere back in the house shouted: "Hey, Sis! Where are you? What's that Navajo police car doing parked out there?"

"We've got company," Mrs. Breedlove said, barely raising her voice. "In here."

Chee stood. A man wearing dusty jeans, a faded jean jacket with a torn sleeve, and well-worn boots walked into the room. He held a battered gray felt hat in his right hand.

"Mr. Chee," said Mrs. Breedlove, "this is my brother Eldon. Eldon Demott."

"Oh," Demott said. "Hello." He shifted his hat to his left hand and offered Chee the right one. His grip was like his sister's and his expression was a mixture of curiosity, worry, and fatigue.

"They think they've found Hal," Elisa Breedlove said. "You remember talking about that skeleton on Ship Rock. The Navajo police think it must be him."

Demott was eyeing the little stack of climbing

equipment on the table. He sighed, slapped the hat against his leg. "I was wrong then, if it really is Hal," he said. "That makes him a better climber than I gave him credit for, climbing that sucker by himself and getting that high." He snorted. "And a hell of a lot crazier, too."

"Do you recognize any of this?" Chee asked, indicating the equipment.

Demott picked up the nylon belt and examined it. He was a small man. Wiry. A man built of sun-scorched leather, bone, and gristle, with a strong jaw and a receding hairline that made him look older than he probably was.

"It's pretty faded out but it used to be red," he said, and tossed it back to the tabletop. He looked at his sister, his face full of concern and sympathy. "Hal's was red, wasn't it?"

"It was," she said.

"You all right?"

"I'm fine," she said. "And how about this jumar? Didn't you fix one for Hal once?"

"By God," Demott said, and picked it up. It reminded Chee of an oversized steel pretzel with a sort of ratchet device connected. Chee had wondered about it and concluded that the ratchet would allow a rope to slip in one direction and not the other. Thus, it must be used to allow a climber to pull himself up a cliff. Demott obviously knew what it was for. He was examining the place where the ratchet had been welded to the steel.

"I remember I couldn't fix it. Hal and you took it into Mancos and had Gus weld it," Demott said to Elisa. "It sure looks like the same one."

"I guess we can close this up then," Chee said. "I don't see any reason for you going down to Shiprock to look at the bones. Unless you want to."

Demott was inspecting one of the climbing shoes. "The soles must be all the same," he said. "At least all I ever saw was just soft, smooth rubber like this. And his were white. And he had little feet, too." He glanced at Elisa. "How about the clothing? That look like Hal's?"

"The jacket, yes," she said. "I think that's Hal's jacket."

Something in her tone caused Chee to glance back at her. She held her lips pressed together, face tense, determined somehow not to cry. Her brother didn't see that. He was studying the artifacts on the table.

"It's pretty tore up," Demott said, poking the clothing with a finger. "You think coyotes? But from what the paper said, it would be too high for them."

"Way too high," Chee said.

"Birds, then," Demott said. "Ravens. Vultures and—" He cut that off, with a repentant glance at Elisa.

Chee picked up the evidence valise and stuffed the tattered clothing into it, getting it out of Elisa's sight.

"I think I should go to Shiprock," Elisa said. She looked away from Chee and out the window. "To take care of things. Hal would have wanted to be cremated, I think. And his ashes scattered in the San Juan Mountains."

"Yeah," Demott said. "Over in the La Plata

range. On Mount Hesperus. That was his very favorite."

"We call it Dibe Nitsaa," Chee said. He thought of a dead man's ashes drifting down on serene slopes that the spirit called First Man had built to protect the Navajos from evil. First Man had decorated the mountain with jet-black jewelry to fend off all bad things. But what could protect it from the invincible ignorance of this white culture? These were good, kind people, he thought, who wouldn't knowingly use corpse powder, the Navajo symbol for the ultimate evil, to desecrate a holy place. But then climbing Ship Rock to prove that man was the dominating master of the universe was also a desecration.

"It's our Sacred Mountain of the North," Chee said. "Was that what Mr. Breedlove was trying to do? Put his feet on top of all our sacred places?" Having said it, Chee instantly regretted it. This was not the time or place to show his resentment.

He glanced at Demott, who was looking at him, surprised. But Elisa Breedlove was still staring out the window.

"Hal wasn't like that," she said. "He was just trying to find some happiness," she said. "Nobody had ever taught him anything about sacred things. The only god the Breedloves ever worshiped was cast out of gold."

"I don't think Hal knew anything about your mythology," Demott agreed. "It's just that Hesperus is over thirteen thousand feet and an easy climb. I like them high and easy and I guess Hal did, too."

Chee considered that. "Why Ship Rock, then? I know it's killed some people. I've heard it's one of the hardest climbs."

"Yeah," Demott said. "Why Ship Rock? And why by himself? And if he wasn't by himself, how come his friends just left him there? Didn't even report it."

Chee didn't comment on that. Elisa was still staring blindly out the window.

"How high did he get?" Demott asked.

Chee shrugged. "Close to the top, I think. I think the rescue party said the skeleton was just a couple hundred feet down from the crest."

"I knew he was good, but if he got that high all by himself he was even better than I thought," Demott said. "He'd gotten past the hardest parts."

"He'd always wanted to climb Ship Rock," Elisa said. "Remember?"

"I guess so," Demott said thoughtfully. "I remember him talking about climbing El Diente and Lizard's Head. I thought they were next on his agenda." He turned to Chee, frowning. "Have you fellows looked into who else he might have climbed with? I have trouble believing he did that alone. I guess he could have and he was reckless enough to try it. But it damn sure wouldn't be easy. Not getting that high."

"It's not a criminal case," Chee said. "We're just trying to close up an old missing person file."

"But who the hell would go off and leave a fallen man like that? Not even report so the rescue people could go get him? You think they was afraid you Navajos would arrest 'em for trespassing?" He shook his head. "Or the way things are now, maybe they thought they'd get sued." He laughed, put on his hat. "But I got to get moving. Good to meet you, Mr. Chee," he said, and was gone.

"I've got to be going, too," Chee said. He dumped the rest of the equipment in the valise.

She walked with him to the door, opened it for him. He pulled at the valise zipper, then stopped. He should really leave this stuff with her. She was the widow. It was her property.

"Mr. Chee," she said. "The skeleton. Were the bones all broken up?"

"No," Chee said. "Nothing broken. And all the joints were still articulated."

From Elisa's expression he first thought she didn't understand that anthropology jargon. "I mean, the skeleton was all together in one piece. And nothing was broken."

"Nothing was broken?" she repeated. "Nothing." And then he realized the expression reflected disbelief. And shock.

Why shock? Had Mrs. Breedlove expected her husband's body to be broken apart? Why would she? If he asked her why, she'd say it must have been a long fall.

He zipped the valise closed. He'd keep these artifacts from the Fallen Man, at least for a while.

6

HE MET JANET AT THE CARRIAGE INN in Farmington,
halfway between his trailer at Shiprock and the
San Juan County courthouse at Aztec where she
had been defending a Checkerboard Reservation
Navajo on a grand theft charge. He arrived late—
but not very late—and her kidding about his
watch being on Navajo time lacked its usual
vigor. She looked absolutely used up, he thought.
Beautiful but tired, and maybe the fatigue
explained the diminution of the usual spark, of
the delight he usually sensed in her when she
first saw him. Or maybe it was because he was
weary himself. Anyway, just being with her, seeing her across the table, cheered him. He took
her hand.

"Janet, you work too hard," Chee said. "You
should marry me and let me take you away from
all this."

"I intend to marry you," she said, rewarding

him with a weary smile. "You keep forgetting that. But all you do is keep making more work for me. Arresting these poor innocent people."

"That sounds to me like you won today," Chee said. "Charmed the jury again?"

"It didn't take any charm. This time it wouldn't have been reasonable to have even a reasonable doubt. His brother-in-law did it and the state cops totally screwed up the investigation."

"Do you have to go right back to Window Rock tomorrow? Why not take a day off? Tell 'em you are doing the post-trial paperwork. Maybe preparing a false arrest suit or something."

"Ah, Jim," she said. "I have to drive down there tonight."

"Tonight! That's crazy. That's more than two hours on a dangerous road," he said. "You're tired. Get some sleep. What's the hurry?"

She looked apologetic. Shrugged. "No choice, Jim. I'd love to stay over. Can't do it. Duty calls."

"Ah, come on," Chee said. "Duty can wait."

Janet squeezed his hand. "Really," she said. "I have to go to Washington. On a bunch of legal stuff with Justice and the Bureau of Indian Affairs. I have to be there day after tomorrow ready to argue." She shrugged, made a wry face. "So I have to pack tonight and drive to Albuquerque tomorrow to catch my plane."

Chee picked up the menu, said, "Like I've been telling you, you work way too hard." He tried to keep it out, but the disappointment again showed in his voice.

"And as I told you, it's the fault of you police-men," she said, smiling her tired smile. "Arresting too many innocent people."

"I haven't had much luck at arresting people lately," he said. "I can't even catch any guilty ones."

The Carriage Inn had printed a handsome menu on which nothing changed but the prices. Variety was provided by the cooks, who came and went. Chee decided to presume that the current one was adept at preparing Mexican foods.

"Why not try the chile relleños?"

Janet grimaced. "That's what you said last time. This time I'm trying the fish."

"Too far from the ocean for fish," Chee said. But now he remembered that his last time here the cook had converted the relleños to some-thing like leather. Maybe he'd order the chicken-fried steak.

"It's trout," Janet said. "A local fish. The waiter told me they steal 'em out of the fish hatchery ponds."

"Okay then," Chee said. "Trout for me, too."

"You look totally worn-out," she said. "Is Captain Largo getting to be too much for you?"

"I spent the day with a redneck New Mexico brand inspector," Chee said. "We drove all the way up to Mancos with him talking every inch of the way. Then back again, him still talking."

"About what? Cows?"

"People. Mr. Finch works on the theory that you catch cattle rustlers by knowing everything about everybody who owns cattle. I guess it's a

pretty good system, but then he passed all that
information along to me. You want to know anything about anybody who raises cows in the Four
Corners area? Or hauls them? Or runs feedlots?
Just ask me."

"Finch?" she said. "I've run into him twice in
court." She shook her head, smiling.

"Who won?"

"He did. Both times."

"Oh, well," Chee said. "It's too bad, but sometimes justice triumphs over you public defenders. Were your clients guilty?"

"Probably. They said they weren't. But this
Finch guy is smart."

Chee did not want to talk about Finch.

"You know, Janet," he said. "Sometime we
need to talk about . . . "

She put down the menu and looked at him
over her glasses. "Sometime, but not tonight.
What took you and Mr. Finch to Mancos?"

No. Not tonight, Chee thought. They would
just go over the same ground. She'd say that if
the police were doing their jobs properly there
really wasn't a conflict of interest if a public
defender was the wife of a cop. And he'd say,
yeah, but what if the cop had arrested the very
guy she was defending and was a witness? What
if she were cross-examining her own husband
as a hostile witness? And she'd fall back on her
Stanford Law School lecture notes and tell him
that all she wanted to extract from anyone was
the exact truth. And he'd say, but sometimes the
lawyer isn't after quite 100 percent of the truth,
and she'd say that some evidence can't be

admitted, and he'd say, as an attorney it would be easy for her to get a job with a private firm, and she'd remind him he'd turned down an offer from the Arizona Department of Public Safety and was a cinch for a job with the Bureau of Indian Affairs law-and-order division if he would take it. And he'd say, that would mean leaving the reservation, and she'd say, why not? Did he want to spend his life here? And that would open a new can of worms. No. Tonight he'd let her change the subject.

The waiter came. Janet ordered a glass of white wine. Chee had coffee.

"I went to Mancos to tell a widow that we'd found her husband's skeleton," Chee said. "Mr. Finch went along because it gave him an excuse to contemplate the cows in the lady's feedlot."

"All you found were dry bones? Her husband must have been away a lot. I'll bet he was a policeman," she said, and laughed.

Chee let that pass.

"Was it the skeleton they spotted up on Ship Rock about Halloween?" she asked, sounding mildly repentant.

Chee nodded. "He turned out to be a guy named Harold Breedlove. He owned a big ranch near Mancos."

"Breedlove," Janet said. "That sounds familiar." The waiter came—a lanky, rawboned Navajo who listened attentively to Janet's questions about the wine and seemed to understand them no better than did Chee. He would ask the cook. About the trout he was on familiar ground. "Very fresh," he said, and hurried off.

Janet was looking thoughtful. "Breedlove," she said, and shook her head. "I remember the paper said there was no identification on him. So how'd you get him identified? Dental chart?"

"Joe Leaphorn had a hunch," Chee said.

"The legend-in-his-own-time lieutenant? I thought he'd retired."

"He did," Chee said. "But he remembered a missing person case he'd worked on way back. This guy who disappeared was a mountain climber and an inheritance was involved, and—"

"Hey," Janet said. "Breedlove. I remember now."

Remember what? Chee thought. And why? This had happened long before Janet had joined the DNA, and become a resident reservation Navajo instead of one in name only, and entered his life, and made him happy. His expression had a question in it.

"From when I was with Granger-hyphen-Smith in Albuquerque. Just out of law school," she said. "The firm represented the Breedlove family. They had public land grazing leases, some mineral rights deals with the Jicarilla Apaches, some water rights arrangements with the Utes." She threw out her hands to signify an endless variety of concerns. "There were some dealings with the Navajo Nation, too. Anyway, I remember the widow was having the husband declared legally dead so she could inherit from him. The family wanted that looked into."

She stopped, looking slightly abashed. Picked up the menu again. "I'll definitely have the trout," she said.

"Were they suspicious?" Chee asked.

"I presume so," she said, still looking at the menu. "I remember it did look funny. The guy inherits a trust and two or three days later he vanishes. Vanishes under what you'd have to consider unusual circumstances."

The waiter came. Chee watched Janet order trout, watched the waiter admire her. A classy lady, Janet. From what Chee had learned about law firms as a cop, lawyers didn't chat about their clients' business to rookie interns. It was unethical. Or at least unprofessional.

He knew the answer but he asked it anyway. "Did you work on it? The looking into it?"

"Not directly," Janet said. She sipped her water.

Chee looked at her.

She flushed slightly. "The Breedlove Corporation was John McDermott's client. His job," she said. "I guess because he handled all things Indian for the firm. And the Breedlove family had all these tribal connections."

"Did you find anything?"

"I guess not," Janet said. "I don't remember the family having us intervene in the case."

"The family?" Chee said. "Do you remember who, specifically?"

"I don't," she said. "John was dealing with an attorney in New York. I guess he was representing the rest of the Breedloves. Or maybe the family corporation. Or whatever." She shrugged. "What did you think of Finch, aside from him being so talkative?"

John, Chee thought. John. Professor John

McDermott. Her old mentor at Stanford. The man who had hired her at Albuquerque when he went into private practice there, and took her to Washington when he transferred, and made her his mistress, used her, and broke her heart.

"I wonder what made them suspicious?" Chee said. "Aside from the circumstances."

"I don't know," Janet said.

Their trout arrived. Rainbows, neatly split, neatly placed on a bed of wild rice. Flanked by small carrots and boiled new potatoes. Janet broke off a tiny piece of trout and ate it.

Beautiful, Chee thought. The perfect skin, the oval face, the dark eyes that expressed so much. He found himself wishing he was a poet, a singer of ballads. Chee knew a lot of songs but they were the chants the shaman sings at the curing ceremonials, recounting the deeds of the spirits. No one had taught him how to sing to someone as beautiful as this.

He ate a bite of trout.

"If I had been driving a patrol car yesterday instead of my old pickup," he said, "I could have given a speeding ticket to a guy driving a white Porsche convertible. Really flying. But I was driving my truck."

"Wow," Janet said, looking delighted. "My favorite car. I have a fantasy about tooling around Paris in one of those. With the top down."

Maybe she looked happy because he was changing the subject. Moving away from unhappy ground. But to Chee the trout now seemed to have no taste at all.

7

JOE LEAPHORN, UNEASILY CONSCIOUS that he was now a mere civilian, had given himself three excuses for calling on Hosteen Nez and thereby butting into police business.

First, he'd come to like the old man way back when he was picking his brain in the Breedlove missing person case. Thus going to see him while Nez was recuperating from being shot was a friendly thing to do. Second, Canyon de Chelly wasn't much out of his way, since he was going to Flagstaff anyway. Third, a trip into the canyon never failed to lift Joe Leaphorn's spirits.

Lately they had needed a lift. Most of the things he'd yearned to do when retirement allowed it had now been done—at least once. He was bored. He was lonely. The little house he and Emma had shared so many years had never recovered from the emptiness her death had left in every room. That was worse now without the job to distract him. Maybe he was oversensitive, but he felt like an intruder down at the police headquarters. When he dropped in to chat with old friends he often found them busy. Just as he had always been. And he was a mere civilian now, no longer one of the little band of brothers.

Good excuses or not, Leaphorn had been a policeman too long to go unprepared. He took his GMC Jimmy with the four-wheel drive required in the canyon both by National Park Service rules and by the uncertain bottom up Chinle Wash. He had stopped at the grocery in Ganado and bought a case of assorted soda pop flavors, two pounds of bacon, a pound of coffee, a large can of peaches, and a loaf of bread. Only then did he head for Chinle.

Once there, he made another stop at the district Tribal Police office to make sure his visit wouldn't tread on the toes of the investigating officer. He found Sergeant Addison Deke at his desk. They chatted about family matters and mutual friends and finally got around to the shooting of Amos Nez.

Deke shook his head, produced a wry grin. "The people around here have that one all solved for us," he said. "They say old Nez was tipping us off about who was breaking into tourists' cars up on the canyon lookout points. So the burglars got mad at him and shot him."

"That makes sense," Leaphorn said. Which it did, even though he could tell from Deke's face that it wasn't true.

"Nez hadn't told us a damn thing, of course," Deke said. "And when we asked him about the rumor, it pissed him off. He was insulted that his neighbors would even think such a thing."

Leaphorn chuckled. Car break-ins at several of the Navajo Nation's more popular tourist attractions were a chronic headache for the Tribal Police. They usually involved one or two hard-up families whose boys considered the salable items left in tourist cars a legitimate harvest—like wild asparagus, rabbits, and sand plums. Their neighbors disapproved, but it wasn't the sort of thing one would get a boy in trouble over.

Leaphorn's next stop was seven-tenths of a mile up the rim road from the White House Ruins overlook—the point from which the sniper had shot Nez. Leaphorn pulled his Jimmy off into the grass at the spot where Deke had told him they'd found six newly fired 30.06 cartridges. Here the layer of tough igneous rock had broken into a jumble of room-sized boulders, giving the sniper a place to watch and wait out of sight from the road. He looked directly down and across the canyon floor. Nez would have been riding his horse along the track across the sandy bottom of the wash. Not a difficult shot in terms of distance for one who knew how to use a rifle, but shooting down at that angle would require some careful adjustment of the sights to avoid an overshot. Whoever shot Nez knew what he was doing.

The next stop was at the Canyon de Chelly park office on the way in. He chatted with the rangers there and picked up the local gossip. Relative to Hosteen Nez, the speculation was exactly what Leaphorn had heard from Deke. The old man had been shot because he was tipping the cops on the car break-ins. How about enemies? No one could imagine that, and they knew him well. Nez was a kindly man, a traditional who helped his family and was generous with his neighbors. He loved jokes. Always in good humor. Everybody liked him. He'd guided in the canyon for years and he could even handle the tourists who wanted to get drunk without making them angry. Always contributed something to help out with the ceremonials when somebody was having a curing sing.

How about eccentricities? Gambling? Grazing rights problems? Any odd behavior? Well, yes. Nez's mother-in-law lived with him, which was a direct violation of the taboo against such conduct. But Nez rationalized that. He said he and old lady Benally had been good friends for years before he'd met her daughter. They'd talked it over and decided that when the Holy People taught that a son-in-law seeing his mother-in-law caused insanity, blindness, and other maladies, they meant that this happened when the two didn't like each other. Anyway, old lady Benally was still going strong in her nineties and Nez was not blind and didn't seem to be any crazier than anyone else.

Indeed, Nez seemed to be feeling pretty good when Leaphorn found him.

"Pretty good," he said, "considering the shape I'm in." And when Leaphorn laughed at that, he added, "But if I'd known I was going to live so damn long, I'd have taken better care of myself."

Nez was sprawled in a wired-together over-stuffed recliner, his head almost against the red sandstone wall of a cul-de-sac behind his hogan. The early afternoon sun beat down upon him. Warmth radiated from the cliff behind him, the sky overhead was almost navy blue, and the air was cool and fresh, and smelled of autumn's last cutting of alfalfa hay from a field up the canyon. Nothing in the scene, except for the cast on the Nez legs and the bandages on his neck and chest, reminded Leaphorn of a hospital room.

Leaphorn had introduced himself in the traditional Navajo fashion, identifying his parents and their clans. "I wonder if you remember me," he said. "I'm the policeman who talked to you three times a long time ago when the man you'd been guiding disappeared."

"Sure," Nez said. "You kept coming back. Acting like you'd forgot something to ask me, and then asking me everything all over again."

"Well, I was pretty forgetful."

"Glad to hear that," Nez said. "I thought you figured I was maybe lying to you a little bit and if you asked me often enough I'd forget and tell the truth."

This notion didn't seem to bother Nez. He motioned Leaphorn to sit on the boulder beside his chair.

"Now you want to talk to me about who'd want to shoot me. I tell you one thing right now. It wasn't no car burglars. That's a lot of lies they're saying about me."

Leaphorn nodded. "That's right," he said.

"The police at Chinle told me you weren't help-ing them catch those people."

Nez seemed pleased at that. He nodded.

"But you know, maybe the car burglars don't know that," Leaphorn said. "Maybe they think you're telling on 'em."

Nez shook his head. "No," he said. "They know better. They're my kinfolks."

"You picked a good place to get some sun-shine here," Leaphorn said. "Lots of heat off the cliff. Out of the wind. And—"

Nez laughed. "And nobody can get a shot at me here. Not from the rim anyway."

"I noticed that," Leaphorn said.

"I figured you had."

"I read the police report," Leaphorn said, and recited it to Nez. "That about right?"

"That's it," Nez said. "The son of a bitch just kept shooting. After I sort of crawled under the horse, he hit the horse twice more." Nez whacked his hand against the cast. "Thump. Thump."

"Sounds like he wanted to kill you," Leaphorn said.

"I thought maybe he just didn't like my horse," Nez said. "He was a pretty sorry horse. Liked to bite people."

"The last time I came to see you it was also bad news," Leaphorn said. "You think there could be any connection?"

"Connection?" Nez said. He looked gen-uinely surprised. "No. I didn't think of that." But he thought now, staring at Leaphorn, frowning. "Connection," he repeated. "How could there be? What for?"

Leaphorn shrugged. "I don't know. It was just a thought. Did anybody tell you our missing man from way back then has turned up?"

"No," Nez said, looking delighted. "I didn't know that. After a month or so I figured he must be dead. Didn't make any sense to leave that pretty woman that way."

"You were right. He was dead. We just found his bones," Leaphorn said, and watched Nez, waiting for the question. But no question came.

"I thought so," Nez said. "Been dead a long time, too, I bet."

"Probably more than ten years," Leaphorn said.

"Yeah," Nez said. He shook his head, said, "Crazy bastard," and looked sad.

Leaphorn waited.

"I liked him," Nez said. "He was a good man. Funny. Lots of jokes."

"Are you going to play games with me like you did eleven years ago, or you going to tell me what you know about this? Like why you think he was crazy and why you thought he'd been dead all this time."

"I don't tell on people," Nez said. "There's already plenty of trouble without that."

"There won't be any more trouble for Harold Breedlove," Leaphorn said. "But from the look of all those bandages, there's been some trouble for you."

Nez considered that. Then he considered Leaphorn.

"Tell me if you found him on Ship Rock," Nez said. "Was he climbing Tse´ Bit´ a´i´?"

Absolutely nothing Amos Nez could have said would have surprised Leaphorn more than that. He spent a few moments re-collecting his wits.

"That's right," he said finally. "Somebody spotted his skeleton down below the peak. How the hell did you know?"

Nez shrugged.

"Did Breedlove tell you he was going there?"

"He told me."

"When?"

Nez hesitated again. "He's dead?"

"Dead."

"When I was guiding them," Nez said. "We were way up Canyon del Muerto. His woman, Mrs. Breedlove, she'd gone up a little ways around the corner. To urinate, I guess it was. Breedlove, he'd been talking about climbing the cliff there." He gestured upward. "You been up there. It's straight up. Worse than that. Some places the top hangs over. I said nobody could do it. He said he could. He told me some places he'd climbed up in Colorado. He started talking then about all the things he wanted to do while he was still young and now he was already thirty years old and he hadn't done them. And then he said—" Nez cut it off, looking at Leaphorn.

"I'm not a policeman anymore," he said. "I'm retired, like you. I just want to know what the hell happened to the man."

"Maybe I should have told you then," Nez said.

"Yeah. Maybe you should have," Leaphorn said. "Why didn't you?"

"Wasn't any reason to," Nez said. "He said he wasn't going to do it until spring came. Said now it was too close to winter. He said not to talk about it because his wife wanted him to stop climbing."

"Did Mrs. Breedlove hear him?"

"She was off taking a leak," Nez said. "He said he thought maybe he'd do it all by himself. Said nobody had ever done that."

"Did you think he meant it? Did he sound serious?"

"Sounded serious, yes. But I thought he was just bragging. White men do that a lot."

"He didn't say where he was going?"

"His wife came back then. He shut up about it."

"No, I mean did he say anything about where he was going to go that evening? After you came in out of the canyon."

"I remember they had some friends coming to see them. They were going to eat together."

"Not drinking, was he?"

"Not drinking," Nez said. "I don't let my tourists drink. It's against the law."

"So he said he was going to climb Tse´ Bit´ a´i´ the following spring," Leaphorn said. "Is that the way you remember it?"

"That's what he said."

They sat a while, engulfed by sunlight, cool air, and silence. A raven planed down from the rim, circled around a cottonwood, landed on a Russian olive across the canyon floor, and perched, waiting for them to die.

Nez extracted a pack of cigarettes from his shirt, offered one to Leaphorn, and lit one for himself.

"Like to smoke while I'm thinking," he said.

"I used to do that, too," Leaphorn said. "But my wife talked me into quitting."

"They'll do that if you're not careful," Nez said.

"Thinking about what?"

"Thinking about why he told me that. You know, maybe he figured I'd say something and his woman would hear it and stop him." Nez exhaled a cloud of blue smoke. "And he wanted somebody to stop him. Or when spring came and he slipped off to climb it by himself, he thought maybe he'd fall off and get killed and if nobody knew where he was nobody would find his body. And he didn't want to be up there dead and all alone."

"And you think he figured you'd hear about him disappearing and you'd tell people where to find him?" Leaphorn asked.

"Maybe," Nez said, and shrugged.

"It didn't work."

"Because he was already missing," Nez said. "Where was he all those months between when he goes away from his wife here, and when he climbed our Rock with Wings?"

Leaphorn grinned. "That's what I was hoping you'd know something about. Did he say anything that gave you ideas about where he was going after he left here? Who he was meeting?"

Nez shook his head. "That's a long time to stay away from that good woman," Nez said. "Way too long, I think. I guess you policemen haven't found out where he was?"

"No," Leaphorn said. "We don't have the slightest idea."

8

A MILD PRELUDE TO WINTER had come quietly during
the night, slipping across the Arizona border,
covering Chee's house trailer with about five
inches of wet whiteness. It caused him to shift his
pickup into four-wheel drive to make the climb
from his site under the San Juan River cottonwoods up the slope to the highway. But the first
snow of winter is a cheering sight for natives of
the high, dry Four Corners country. It's especially cheering for those doing Chee's criminal
investigation division's job. The snow was making extra work for the troopers out on the highways, but for the detectives it dampened down
the crime rate.

Lieutenant Jim Chee's good humor even survived the sight of the stack of folders Jenifer had
dumped on his desk. The note atop them said:
"Cap. Largo wants to talk to you right away
about the one on top but I don't think he'll be in

before noon because with this snow he'll have to get some feed out to his cows."

On the table of organization, Jenifer was Chee's employee, the secretary of his criminal investigation unit. But Jenifer had been hired by Captain Largo a long time ago and had seen lieutenants come and go. Chee understood that as far as Jenifer was concerned he was still on probation. But the friendly tone of the note suggested she was thinking he might meet her standards.

"Hah!" he said, grinning. But that faded away before he finished working through the folders. The top one concerned the theft of two more Angus calves from a woman named Roanhorse who had a grazing lease west of Red Rock. The ones in the middle involved a drunken brawl at a girl dance at the Lukachukai chapter house, in which shots were fired and the shooter fled in a pickup, not his own; a request for a transfer from this office by Officer Bernadette (Bernie) Manuelito, the rookie trainee Chee had inherited with the job; a report of drug use and purported gang activity around Hogback, and so forth. Plus, of course, forms to be filled out on mileage, maintenance, and gasoline usage by patrol vehicles, and a reminder that he hadn't submitted vacation schedules for his office.

The final folder held a citizen's complaint that he was being harassed by Officer Manuelito. What remained of Chee's high spirits evaporated as he read it.

The form was signed by Roderick Diamonte. Mr. Diamonte alleged that Officer Manuelito was

parking her Tribal Police car at the access road
to his place of business at Hogback, stopping his
customers on trumped-up traffic violations, and
using what Diamonte called "various sneaky
tricks" in an effort to violate their constitutional
protection against illegal searches. He asked
that Officer Manuelito be ordered to desist from
this harassment and be reprimanded.

Diamonte? Yes, indeed. Chee remembered
the name from the days when he had been a
patrolman assigned here. Diamonte operated a
bar on the margin of reservation land and was
one of the first people to come to mind when
something lucrative and illegal was going on.
Still, he had his rights.

Chee buzzed Jenifer and asked if Manuelito
was in. She was out on patrol.

"Would you call her? Tell her I want to talk to
her when she comes in. Please." Chee had
learned early on that Jenifer's response time
shortened when an order became a request.

"Right," Jenifer said. "I thought you'd want to
talk to her. I guess you know who that Diamonte
is, don't you?"

"I remember him," Chee said.

"And you had a call," Jenifer said. "From
Janet Pete in Washington. She left a number."

Someday when he was better established
Chee intended to talk to his secretary about her
practice of deciding which calls to tell him about
when. Calls from Janet tended to get low priority. Maybe that was because Jenifer had the typical cop attitude about defense lawyers. Or
maybe not.

He called the number.

"Jim," she said. "Ah, Jim. It's good to hear your voice."

"And yours," he said. "You called to tell me you're headed out to National Airport. Flying home. You want me to pick you up at the Farmington Airport?"

"Don't I wish," she said. "But I'm stuck here a little longer. How about you? The job getting any easier? And did you get a snowstorm? The weather girl always stands in front of the Four Corners when she's giving us the news, but it looked like a front was pushing across from the west."

They talked about the weather for a moment, talked about love, talked about wedding plans. Chee didn't ask her about the Justice Department and Bureau of Indian Affairs business that had called her away. It was one of several little zones of silence that develop when a cop and a defense lawyer are dating.

And then Janet said: "Anything new developing on the Fallen Man business?"

"Fallen Man?" Chee hadn't been giving that any thought. It was a closed case. A missing person found. A corpse identified. Officially an accidental death. Officially none of his business. A curious affair, true, but the world of a police lieutenant was full of such oddities and he had too much pressing stuff on his desk to give it any time.

"No. Nothing new." Chee wanted to say, "He's in the dead file," but he was a little too traditional for that. Death is not a subject for Navajo humor.

"Do you know if anyone ever climbed up there—I mean after the rescue party brought the bones down—to see if they could find any evidence of funny stuff?"

Chee thought about that. And about Janet's interest in it.

"You know," she continued, talking into his silence. "Was there any suggestion that it might not have been an accident? Or that somebody was up there with him and just didn't report it?"

"No," Chee said. "Anyway, we didn't send anyone up." He found himself feeling defensive. "The only apparent motive would be the widow wanting his money, and she waited five years before getting him declared legally dead. And had an ironclad alibi. And—" But Chee stopped. Irked. Why explain all this? She already knew it. They'd talked about it the last time he'd seen her. At dinner in Farmington.

"Why—" he began, but she was already talking. A new subject. She'd gone to a dinner concert at the Library of Congress last night, some fifteenth-century music played on the fifteenth-century instruments. Very interesting. The French ambassador was there—and his wife. You should have seen her dress. Wow. And so it went.

When the call was over, Chee picked up the Manuelito file again. But he held it unopened while he thought about Janet's interest in the Fallen Man. And about how a dinner concert at the Library of Congress must have been by invitation only. Or restricted to major donors to some fund or other. Super exclusive. In fact he had no idea the Library of Congress even produced such events, no idea how he could wangle an invitation if he'd wanted to go, no idea how Janet had come to be there.

Well, yes, he did have an idea about that. Of course. Janet had friends in Washington. From those days when she had worked there as what she called "the House Indian" of Dalman, MacArthur, White and Hertzog, Attorneys at Law. One of those friends had been John McDermott. Her ex-lover and exploiter. From whom Janet had fled.

Chee escaped from that unhappy thought into the problem presented by Officer Bernadette Manuelito.

The Navajo culture that had produced Acting Lieutenant Jim Chee had taught him the power of words and of thought. Western metaphysicians might argue that language and imagination are products of reality. But in their own migrations out of Mongolia and over the icy Bering Strait, the Navajos brought with them a much older Asian philosophy. Thoughts, and words that spring from them, bend the individual's reality. To speak of death is to invite it. To think of sorrow is to produce it. He would think of his duties instead of his love.

Chee flipped open the Manuelito folder. He read through it, wondering why he could have ever believed he wanted an administrative post. That brought him back to Janet. He'd wanted the promotion to impress her, to make himself eligible, to narrow the gap between the child of the urban privileged class and the child of the isolated sheep camp. Thus he had made a thor-

oughly non-Navajo decision based on an utterly
non-Navajo way of thinking. He put down the
Manuelito file and buzzed Jenifer.

Officer Manuelito, it seemed, had come in
early, and called in about nine saying she was
working on the cattle-rustling problem. Chee
allowed himself a rare expletive. What the hell
was she doing about cattle theft? She was supposed to be finding witnesses to a homicide at a
wild party.

"Would you ask the dispatcher to contact
her, please, and ask her to come in?" Chee said.

"Want 'em to tell her why?" Jenifer asked.

"Just tell her I want to talk to her," Chee
said, forgetting to say please.

But what would he say to Officer Manuelito?
He'd have time to decide that by the time she got
to the office. It would keep him from thinking
about what might have provoked Janet's curiosity about Harold Breedlove, late of the Breedlove
family that had been a client of John McDermott.

9

As it happened, Officer Manuelito didn't get to the office.

"She says she's stuck," Jenifer reported. "She went out Route 5010 south of Rattlesnake and turned off on that dirt track that skirts around the west side of Ship Rock. Then she slid off into a ditch." This amused Jenifer, who chuckled. "I'll see if I can get somebody to go pull her out."

"I think I'll just take care of it myself," Chee said. "But thanks anyway."

He pulled on his jacket. What the devil was Manuelito doing out in that empty landscape by the Rock with Wings? He'd told her to work her way down a list of people who might be willing to talk about gang membership at Shiprock High School, not practicing her skill at driving in mud.

Just getting out of the parking lot demonstrated to Chee how Manuelito could manage to get stuck. The overnight storm had drifted eastward, leaving the town of Shiprock under a cloudless sky. The temperature was already well above freezing and the sun was making short work of the snow. But even after he shifted into four-wheel drive, Chee's truck did some wheel-spinning. The ditches beside the highway were already carrying runoff water and a cloud of white steam swirled over the asphalt where the moisture was evaporating.

Navajo Route 5010, according to the road map, was "improved." Which meant it was graded now and then and in theory at least had a gravel surface. On a busy day, probably six or eight vehicles would use it. This morning, Officer Manuelito's patrol car had been the first to leave its tracks in the snow and Chee's pickup was number two. Chee noted approvingly that she had made a slow and careful left turn off of 5010 onto an unnumbered access road that led toward Ship Rock—thereby leaving no skid marks. He made the same turn, felt his rear wheels slipping, corrected, and eased the truck gingerly down the road.

All muscles were tense, all senses alert. He was enjoying testing his skill against the slick road surface. Enjoying the clean, cold air in his lungs, the gray-and-white patterns of soft snow on sage and salt bush and chamisa, enjoying the beauty, the vast emptiness, and a silence broken only by the sound of his truck's engine and its tires in the mud. The immense basalt monolith of Ship Rock towered beside him, its west face still untouched by the warming sun and thus still coated with its whitewash of snow. The Fallen

Man must have prayed for that sort of moisture before his thirst killed him on that lonely ledge.

Then the truck topped a hillock, and there was Officer Bernadette Manuelito, a tiny figure standing beside her stuck patrol car, representing an unsolved administrative problem, the end of joy, and a reminder of how good life had been when he was just a patrolman. Ah, well, there was a bright side. Even from here he could see that Manuelito had stuck her car so thoroughly that there would be no hope of towing it out with his vehicle. He'd simply give her a ride back to the office and send out a tow truck.

Officer Manuelito had seemed to Lieutenant Jim Chee to be both unusually pretty and unusually young to be wearing a Navajo Tribal Police uniform. This morning she wouldn't have made that impression. She looked tired and disheveled and at least her age, which Chee knew from her personnel records was twenty-six years. She also looked surly. He leaned across the pickup seat and opened the door for her.

"Tough luck," he said. "Get your stuff out of it, and the weapons, and lock it up. We'll send out a tow truck to get it when the mud dries."

Officer Manuelito had prepared an explanation of how this happened and would not be deterred.

"The snow covered up a little wash, there. Drifted it full so you couldn't see it. And . . ."

"It could happen to anybody," Chee said. "Let's go."

"You didn't bring a tow chain?"

"I did bring a tow chain," Chee said. "But

look at it. There's no traction now. It's clay and it's too soft."

"You have four-wheel drive," she said.

"I know," Chee said, feeling in no mood to debate this. "But that just means you dig yourself in by spinning four wheels instead of two. I couldn't budge it. Get your stuff and get in."

Officer Manuelito brushed a lock of hair off her forehead, leaving a streak of gray mud. Her lips parted with a response, then closed. "Yes, sir," she said.

That was all she said. Chee backed the pickup to a rocky place, turned it, and slipped and slid his way back to 5010 in leaden silence. Back on the gravel, he said:

"Did you know that Diamonte filed a complaint against you? Charged you with harassment."

Officer Manuelito was staring out the windshield. "No," she said. "But I knew he said he was going to."

"Yep," Chee said. "He did. Said you were hanging around. Bothering his customers."

"His dope buyers."

"Some of them, probably," Chee said.

Manuelito stared relentlessly out of the windshield.

"What were you doing?" Chee asked.

"You mean besides harassing his customers?"

"Besides that," Chee said, thinking that the very first thing he would do when they got back to the office was approve this woman's transfer to anywhere. Preferably to Tuba City, which was about as far as he could get her from Shiprock. He glanced at her, waiting for a reply. She was still focused on the windshield.

"You know what he runs out there?" she said.

"I know what he used to do when I was assigned here before," Chee said. "In those days he wholesaled booze to the reservation bootleggers, fenced stolen property, handled some marijuana. Things like that. Now I understand he's branched out into more serious dope."

"That's right," she said. "He still supplies the creeps who push pot and now he's selling the worse stuff, too."

"That's what I always heard," Chee said. "And most recently from Teddy Begayaye. The kid Begayaye picked up at the community college last week named Diamonte as his source for coke. But then he changed his mind and decided he just couldn't remember where he got it."

"I know Diamonte's selling it."

"So you bring in your evidence. We take it to the captain, he takes it to the federal prosecutors, or maybe the San Juan County cops, and we put the bastard in jail."

"Sure," Manuelito said.

"But we don't go out there, with no evidence, and harass his customers. There's a law against it."

Chee sensed that she was no longer staring at the windshield. She was looking at him.

"I heard that you did," she said. "When you were a cop here before."

Chee felt his face flushing. "Who told you that?"

"Captain Largo told us when we were in recruit training."

The son of a bitch, Chee thought.

"Largo was using me as a bad example?"

"He didn't say who did it. But I asked around. People said it was you."

"It just about got me kicked out of the police," Chee said. "The same thing could happen to you."

"I heard it got the place shut down, too," Manuelito said.

"Yeah, and about the time I got off suspension, he was going full blast again."

"Still . . ." Manuelito said. And let the thought trail off.

"Don't say 'still.' You stay away from there. It's Begayaye's job, looking into the dope situation. If you run across anything useful, tell Teddy. Or tell me. Don't go freelancing around."

"Yes, sir," Manuelito said, sounding very formal.

"I mean it," Chee said. "I'll put a letter in your file reporting these instructions."

"Yes, sir," Manuelito said.

"Now. What's this transfer request about? What's wrong with Shiprock? And where do you want to go?"

"I don't care. Anywhere."

That surprised Chee. He'd guessed Manuelito wanted to be closer to a boyfriend somewhere. Or that her mother was sick. Something like that. But now he remembered that she was from Red Rock. By Big Rez standards, Shiprock was conveniently close to her family.

"Is there something about Shiprock you don't like?"

That question produced a long silence, and finally:

"I just want to get away from here."

"Why?"

"It's a personal reason," she said. "I don't have to say why, do I? It's not in the personnel rules."

"I guess not," Chee said. "Anyway, I'll approve it."

"Thank you," Manuelito said.

"That's no guarantee you'll get it, though. You know how it works. Largo may kill it. And there has to be the right kind of opening somewhere. You'll have to be patient."

Officer Manuelito was pointing out the window. "Did you notice that?" she asked.

All Chee saw was the grassland rolling away toward the great dark shape of Ship Rock.

"I mean the fence," she said. "There where that wash runs down into the borrow ditch. Notice the posts."

Chee noticed the posts, two of which were leaning sharply. He stopped the pickup.

"Somebody dug at the base of the posts," she said. "Loosened them so you could pull them up."

"And lay the fence down?"

"More likely raise it up," she said. "Then you could drive cows down the wash and right under it."

"Do you know whose grazing lease this is?"

"Yes, sir," she said. "A man named Maryboy has it."

"Has he lost any cattle?"

"I don't know. Not lately, anyway. At least I haven't seen a report on it."

Chee climbed out of the truck, plodded through the snow, and tried the posts. They lifted easily but the snow made it impossible to determine exactly why. He thought about Zorro, Mr. Finch's favorite cow thief.

Manuelito was standing beside him.

"See?" she said.

"When did you notice this?"

"I don't know," Officer Manuelito said. "Just a few days ago."

"If I remember right, just a few days ago— and today, too—you were supposed to be running down that list of people at that dance. Looking for anyone willing to tell us about gang membership. About what they saw. Who'd tell us who had the gun. Who shot it. That sort of thing. Is that right? That was number one on the list you were handed after the staff meeting."

"Yes, sir," Officer Manuelito said, proving she could sound meek if she wanted to. She was looking down at her hands.

"Do any of those possible witnesses live out here?"

"Well, not exactly. The Roanhorse couple is on the list. They live over near Burnham."

"Near Burnham?" The Burnham trading post was way to hell south of here. Down Highway 666.

"I sort of detoured over this way," Manuelito explained uneasily. "We had that report that Lucy Sam had lost some cattle, and I knew the captain was after you about catching somebody and putting a stop to that and—"

"How did you know that?"

Now Manuelito's face was a little flushed. "Well," she said. "You know how people talk about things."

Yes, Chee knew about that.

"Are you telling me you just drove out here blind? What were you looking for?"

"Well," she said. "I was just sort of looking."

Chee waited. "Just sort of looking?"

"Well," she said. "I remembered my grandfather telling me about Hosteen Sam. That was Lucy's father. About him hating it when white people came out here to climb Ship Rock. They would park out there, over that little rise there by the foot of the cliff. He would write down their license number or what the car looked like and when he went into town he would go by the police station and try to get the police to arrest them for trespassing. So when I was assigned here, and one of the problems worrying the captain was people stealing cattle, I came out here to ask Hosteen Sam if he would keep track of strange pickups and trucks for us."

"Pretty good idea," Chee said. "What did he say?"

"He was dead. Died last year. But his daughter said she would do it for me and I gave her a little notebook for it, but she said she had the one her father had used. So, anyway, I thought I would just make a little detour by there and see if she had written down anything for us."

"Quite a little detour," Chee said. "I'd say about sixty miles or so. Had she?"

"I don't know. I noticed some other posts leaning over and I decided to pull off and see if they had been cut off or dug up or anything else funny. And then I got stuck."

It was a clever idea, Chee was thinking. He should have thought of it himself. He'd see if he could find some people to keep a similar eye on things up near the Ute reservation, and over on the Checkerboard. Wherever people were losing cattle. Who could he get? But he was distracted from that thought. His feet, buried to the ankles in the melting snow, were complaining about the cold. And the sun had now risen far enough to illuminate a different set of snowfields high above them on Ship Rock. They reflected a dazzling white light.

Officer Manuelito was watching him. "Beautiful, isn't it?" she said. "Tse´ Bit´ a´i´. It never seems to look the same."

"I remember noticing that when I was a little boy and I was staying for a while with an aunt over near Toadlena," Chee said. "I thought it was alive."

Officer Manuelito was staring at it. "Beautiful," she said, and shuddered. "I wonder what he was doing up there. All alone."

"The Fallen Man?"

"Deejay doesn't think he fell. He said no bones were broken and if you'd fallen down that cliff it would break something. Deejay thinks he was climbing with somebody and they just stranded him there."

"Who knows?" Chee said. "Anyway, it's not in the books as anything but an accidental death. No evidence of foul play. We don't have to worry about it." Chee's feet were telling him that his boots were leaking. Leaking ice water. "Let's go," he said, heading back for his truck.

Officer Manuelito was still standing there, staring up at the cliffs towering above her.

"They say Monster Slayer couldn't get down either. When he climbed up to the top and killed the Winged Monster he couldn't get down."

"Come on," Chee said. He climbed into the truck and started the engine, thinking that you'd have a better chance if you were a spirit like Monster Slayer. When spirits scream for help other spirits hear them. Spider Woman had heard and came to the rescue. But Harold Breedlove could have called forever with nothing but the ravens to hear him. The stuff of bad dreams.

They drove in silence.

Then Officer Manuelito said, "To be trapped up there. I try not to even think about it. It would give me nightmares."

"What?" Chee said, who hadn't been listening because by then he was working his way around a nightmare of his own. He was trying to think of another reason Janet Pete might have asked him about the Fallen Man affair. He wanted to find a reason that didn't involve John McDermott and his law firm representing the Breedlove family. Maybe it was the oddity of the skeleton on the mountain that provoked her question. He always came back to that. But then he'd find himself speculating on who had taken Janet to that concert and he'd think of John McDermott again.

10

THE FIRST THING JOE LEAPHORN NOTICED when he
came through the door was his breakfast dishes
awaiting attention in the sink. It was a bad habit
and it demanded correction. No more of this sink-
ing into slipshod widower ways. Then he noticed
the red light blinking atop his telephone answering machine. The indicator declared he'd received
two calls today—pretty close to a post-retirement
record. He took a step toward the telephone.

But no. First things first. He detoured into
the kitchen, washed his cereal bowl, saucer, and
spoon, dried them, and put them in their place
on the dish rack. Then he sat in his recliner, put
his boots on the footstool, picked up the telephone, and pushed the button.

The first call was from his auto insurance
dealer, informing him that if he'd take a defensive driving course he could get a discount on his
liability rates. He punched the button again.

"Mr. Leaphorn," the voice said. "This is John McDermott. I am an attorney and our firm has represented the interests of the Edgar Breedlove family for many years. I remember that you investigated the disappearance of Harold Breedlove several years ago when you were a member of the Navajo Tribal Police. Would you be kind enough to call me, collect, and discuss whether you might be willing to help the family complete its own investigation of his death?"

McDermott had left an Albuquerque number. Leaphorn dialed it.

"Oh, yes," the secretary said. "He was hoping you'd call."

After the "thank you for calling," McDermott didn't linger long over formalities.

"We would like you to get right onto this for us," he said. "If you're available, our usual rate is twenty-five dollars an hour, plus your expenses."

"You mentioned completing the investigation," Leaphorn said. "Does that mean you have some question about the identification of the skeleton?"

"There is a question concerning just about everything," McDermott said. "It is a very peculiar case."

"Could you be more specific? I need a better idea of what you'd like to find out."

"This isn't the sort of thing we can discuss over the telephone," McDermott said. "Nor is it the sort of thing I can talk about until I know whether you will accept a retainer." He produced a chuckle. "Family business, you know."

Leaphorn discovered he was allowing himself to be irritated by the tone of this—not a weakness he tolerated. And he was curious. He produced a chuckle of his own.

"From what I remember of the Breedlove disappearance, I don't see how I could help you. Would you like me to recommend someone?"

"No. No," McDermott said. "We'd like to use you."

"But what sort of information would I be looking for?" Leaphorn asked. "I was trying to find out what happened to the man. Why he didn't come back to Canyon de Chelly that evening. Where he went. What happened to him. And of course the important thing was what happened to him. We know that now, if the identification of the skeleton is correct. The rest of it doesn't seem to matter."

McDermott spent a few moments deciding how to respond.

"The family would like to establish who was up there with him," he said.

Now this was getting a bit more interesting. "They've learned someone was up there when he fell? How did they learn that?"

"A mere physical fact. We've talked to rock climbers who know that mountain. They say you couldn't do it alone, not to the point where they found the skeleton. They say Harold Breedlove didn't have the skills, the experience, to have done it."

Leaphorn waited but McDermott had nothing to add.

"The implication, then, is that someone went up with him. When he fell, they abandoned him and didn't report it. Is that what you're suggesting?"

"And why would they do that?" McDermott asked.

Leaphorn found himself grinning. Lawyers! The man didn't want to say it himself. Let the witness say it.

"Well, let's see then. They might do it if, for example, they had pushed him over. Given him a fatal shove. Watched him fall. Then they might forget to report it."

"Well, yes."

"And you're suggesting the family has some lead to who this forgetful person might be."

"No, I'm not suggesting anything."

"The only lead, then, is the list of those who might be motivated. If I can rely on my memory, the only one I knew of was the widow. The lady who would inherit. I presume she did inherit, didn't she? But perhaps there's a lot I didn't know. We didn't have a criminal case to work on, you know. We didn't—and still don't—have a felony to interest the Navajo Police or the Federal Bureau of Investigation. Just a missing person then. Now we have what is presumed to be an accidental death. There was never any proof that he hadn't simply—" Leaphorn paused, looked for a better way to phrase it, found none, and concluded, "Simply run away from wife and home."

"Greed is often the motivation in murder," McDermott said.

Murder, Leaphorn thought. It was the first time that word had been used.

"That's true. But if I am remembering what I was told at the time, there wasn't much to inherit except the ranch, and it was losing money. Unless there was some sort of nuptial agreement, she would have owned half of it anyway. Colorado law. The wife's community property. And if I remember what I learned then, Breedlove had already mortgaged it. Was there a motive beyond greed?"

McDermott let the question hang. "If you'll work with this, I'll discuss it with you in person."

"I always wondered if there was a nuptial agreement. But now I've heard that she owns the ranch."

"No nuptial agreement," McDermott said, reluctantly. "What do you think? If you don't like the hourly arrangement, we could make it a weekly rate. Multiply the twenty-five dollars by forty hours and make it a thousand a week."

A thousand a week, Leaphorn thought. A lot of money for a retired cop. And what would McDermott be charging his client?

"I tell you what I'll do," Leaphorn said. "I'll give it some thought. But I'll have to have some more specific information."

"Sleep on it, then," McDermott said. "I'm coming to Window Rock tomorrow anyway. Why don't we meet for lunch?"

Joe Leaphorn couldn't think of any reason not to do that. He wasn't doing anything else tomorrow. Or for the rest of the week, for that matter.

They set the date for one P.M. at the Navajo Inn. That allowed time for the lunch-hour crowd to thin and for McDermott to make the two-hundred-mile drive from Albuquerque. It also gave Leaphorn the morning hours to collect information on the telephone, talking to friends in the ranching business, a Denver banker, a cattle broker, learning all he could about the Lazy B ranch and the past history of the Breedloves.

That done, he drove down to the Inn and waited in the office lobby. A white Lexus pulled into the parking area and two men emerged: one tall and slender with graying blond hair, the other six inches shorter, dark-haired, sun-browned, with the heavy-shouldered, slim-waisted build of one who lifts weights and plays handball. Ten minutes early, but it was probably McDermott and who? An assistant, perhaps.

Leaphorn met them at the entrance, went through the introductions, and ushered them in to the quiet corner table he'd arranged to hold.

"Shaw," Leaphorn said. "George Shaw? Is that correct?"

"Right," the dark man said. "Hal Breedlove was my cousin. My best friend, too, for that matter. I was the executor of the estate when Elisa had him declared legally dead."

"A sad situation," Leaphorn said.

"Yes," Shaw said. "And strange."

"Why do you say that?" Leaphorn could think of a dozen ways Breedlove's death was strange. But which one would Mr. Shaw pick?

"Well," Shaw said. "Why wasn't the fall reported, for one thing?"

"You don't think he made the climb alone?"

"Of course not. He couldn't have," Shaw said.

"I couldn't do it, and I was a grade or two better at rock climbing than Hal. Nobody could."

Leaphorn recommended the chicken enchilada, and they all ordered it. McDermott inquired whether Leaphorn had considered their offer. Leaphorn said he had. Would he accept, then? They'd like to get moving on it right away. Leaphorn said he needed some more information. Their orders arrived. Delicious, thought Leaphorn, who had been dining mostly on his own cooking. McDermott ate thoughtfully. Shaw took a large bite, rich with green chile, and frowned at his fork.

"What sort of information?" McDermott asked.

"What am I looking for?" Leaphorn said.

"As I told you," McDermott said, "we can't be too specific. We just want to know that we have every bit of information that's available. We'd like to know why Harold Breedlove left Canyon de Chelly, and precisely when, and who he met and where they went. Anything that might concern his widow and her affairs at that time. We want to know everything that might cast light on this business." McDermott gave Leaphorn a small, deprecatory smile. "Everything," he said.

"My first question was what I would be looking for," Leaphorn said. "My second one is why? This must be expensive. If Mr. Shaw here is willing to pay me a thousand a week through your law firm, you will be charging him, what? The rate for an Albuquerque lawyer I know about used to be a hundred and ten dollars an hour. But that was long ago, and that was Albuquerque. Double it for a Washington firm? Would that be about right?"

"It isn't cheap," McDermott said.

"And maybe I find nothing useful at all. Probably you learn nothing. Tracks are cold after eleven years. But let us say that you learn the widow conspired to do away with her husband. I don't know for sure but I'd guess then she couldn't inherit. So the family gets the ranch back. What's it worth? Wonderful house, I hear, if someone rich wants to live in it way out there. Maybe a hundred head of cattle. I'm told there's still an old mortgage Harold's widow took out six years ago to pay off her husband's debts. How much could you get for that ranch?"

"It's a matter of justice," McDermott said. "I am not privy to the family's motives, but I presume they want some equity for Harold's death."

Leaphorn smiled.

Shaw had been sipping his coffee. He drained the cup and slammed it into the saucer with a clatter.

"We want to see Harold's killer hanged," he said. "Isn't that what they do out here? Hang 'em?"

"Not lately," Leaphorn said. "The mountain is on the New Mexico side of the reservation and New Mexico uses the gas chamber. But it would probably be federal jurisdiction. We Navajos don't have a death penalty and the federal government doesn't hang people." He signaled the waiter, had their coffee replenished, sipped his own, and put down the cup.

"If I take this job I don't want to be wasting

my time," he said. "I would look for motives. An obvious one is inheritance of the ranch. That gives you two obvious suspects—the widow and her brother. But neither of them could have done it—at least not in the period right after Harold disappeared. The next possibility would be the widow's boyfriend, if she had one. So I would examine all that. Premeditated murder usually involves a lot of trouble and risk. I never knew of one that didn't grow out of a strong motivation."

Neither Shaw nor Breedlove responded to that.

"Usually greed," Leaphorn said.

"Love," said Shaw. "Or lust."

"Which does not seem to have been consummated, from what I know now," Leaphorn said. "The widow remained single. When I was investigating the disappearance years ago I snooped around a little looking for a boyfriend. I couldn't pick up any gossip that suggested a love triangle was involved."

"Easy enough to keep that quiet," Shaw said.

"Not out here it isn't," Leaphorn said. "I would be more interested in an economic motive." He looked at Shaw. "If this is a crime it's a white man's crime. No Navajo would kill anyone on that sacred mountain. I doubt if a Navajo would be disrespectful enough even to climb it. Among my people, murder tends to be motivated by whiskey or sexual jealousy. Among white people, I've noticed crime is more likely to be motivated by money. So if I take the job, I'd be turning on my computer and tapping into the metal market statistics and price trends."

Shaw gave McDermott a sidewise glance, which McDermott didn't notice. He was staring at Leaphorn.

"Why?"

"Because the gossipers around Mancos say Edgar Breedlove bought the ranch more because his prospectors had found molybdenum deposits on it than for its grazing. They say the price of moly ore rose enough about ten or fifteen years ago to make development profitable. They say Harold, or the Breedlove family, or somebody, was negotiating for a mineral lease and the Mancos Chamber of Commerce had high hopes of a big mining payroll. But then Harold disappeared and before you know it the price was down again. I'd want to find out if any of that was true."

"I see," McDermott said. "Yes, it would have made the ranch more valuable and made the motive stronger."

"What the hell," Shaw said. "We were keeping quiet about it because news like that leaks out, it causes problems. With local politicians, with the tree-huggers, with everybody else."

"Okay," Leaphorn said. "I guess if I take this job, then I'm safe in figuring the ranch is worth a lot more than the grass growing on it."

"What do you say?" Shaw said, his voice impatient. "Can we count on you to do some digging for us?"

"I'll think about it," Leaphorn said. "I'll call your office."

"We'll be here a day or two," Shaw said. "And we're in a hurry. Why not a decision right now?"

A hurry, Leaphorn thought. After all these years. "I'll let you know tomorrow," he said. "But you haven't answered my question about the value of the ranch."

McDermott looked grim. "You'd be safe to assume it was worth killing for."

11

"TWISTING THE TAIL OF A COW will encourage her to move forward," the text declared. "If the tail is held up over the back, it serves as a mild restraint. In both cases, the handler should hold the tail close to the base to avoid breaking it, and stand to the side to avoid being kicked."

The paragraph was at the top of the fourth-from-final page of a training manual supplied by the Navajo Nation for training brand inspectors of its Resource Enforcement Agency. Acting Lieutenant Jim Chee read it, put down the manual, and rubbed his eyes. He was not on the payroll of the tribe's REA. But since Captain Largo was forcing him to do its job he'd borrowed an REA brand inspector manual and was plowing his way through it. He'd covered the legal sections relating to grazing rights, trespass, brand registration, bills of sale, when and how livestock could be moved over the reservation boundary, and disease quarantine rules, and was now into advice about handling livestock without getting hurt. To Chee, who had been kicked by several horses but never by a cow, the advice seemed sound. Besides, it diverted him from the paper-work—vacation schedules, justifications for overtime pay, patrol car mileage reports, and so forth—that was awaiting action on his cluttered desk. He picked up the manual.

"The ear twitch can be used to divert atten-tion from other parts of the body," the next para-graph began. "It should be used with care to avoid damage to the ear cartilage. To make the twitch, fasten a loop of cord or rope around the base of the horns. The rope is then carried around the ear and a half-hitch formed. The end of the rope is pulled to apply restraint."

Chee studied the adjoining illustration of a sleepy-looking cow wearing an ear twitch. Chee's childhood experience had been with sheep, on which an ear twitch wouldn't be needed. Still, he figured he could make one easily enough.

The next paragraph concerned a "rope cast-ing harness" with which a person working alone could tie up a mature cow or bull without the risk of strangulation that was involved with usual bulldogging techniques. It looked easy, too, but required a lot of rope. Two pages to go and he'd be finished with this.

Then the telephone rang.

The voice on the telephone belonged to Officer Manuelito.

"Lieutenant," she said, "I've found something I think you should know about."

"Tell me," Chee said.

"Out near Ship Rock, that place where the fence posts had been dug out. You remember?"

"I remember."

"Well, the snow is gone now and you can see where before it snowed somebody had thrown out a bunch of hay."

"Ah," Chee said.

"Like they wanted to attract the cattle. Make them easy to get a rope on. To get 'em into a chute. Into your trailer."

"Manuelito," Chee said. "Have you finished interviewing that list of possible witnesses in that shooting business?"

Silence. Finally, "Most of them. Some of them I'm still looking for."

"Do they live out near Ship Rock?"

"Well, no. But—"

"Don't say but," Chee said. He shifted his weight in his chair, aware that his back hurt from too much sitting, aware that out in the natural world the sun was bright, the sky a dark blue, the chamisa had turned gold and the snakeweed a brilliant yellow. He sighed.

"Manuelito," he said. "Have you gone out to talk to the Sam woman about whether she's seen anything suspicious?"

"No, sir," Officer Manuelito said, sounding surprised. "You told me to—"

"Where are you calling from?"

"The Burnham trading post," she said. "The people there said they hadn't seen anything at the girl dance. But I think they did."

"Probably," Chee said. "They just didn't want

to get the shooter into trouble. So come on in now, and buzz me when you get here, and we'll go out and see if Lucy Sam has seen anything interesting."

"Yes, sir," Officer Manuelito said, and she sounded like she thought that was a good idea. It seemed like a good idea to Chee, too. The tossing hay over the fence business sounded like Zorro's trademark as described by Finch, and that sounded like an opportunity to beat that arrogant bastard at his own game.

Officer Manuelito looked better today. Her uniform was tidy, hair black as a raven's wing and neatly combed, and no mud on her face. But she still displayed a slight tendency toward bossiness.

"Turn up there," she ordered, pointing to the road that led toward Ship Rock, "and I'll show you the hay."

Chee remembered very well the location of the loosened fence posts, but the beauty of the morning had turned him amiable. With Manuelito, he would work on correcting one fault at a time, leaving this one for a rainy day. He turned as ordered, parked when told to park, and followed her over to the fence. With the snow cover now evaporated, it was easy to see that the dirt had been dug away from the posts. It was also easy to see, scattered among the sage, juniper, and rabbit brush, what was left of several bales of alfalfa after the cattle had dined.

"Did you tell Delmar Yazzie about this?" Chee asked.

Officer Manuelito looked puzzled. "Yazzie?"

"Yazzie," Chee said. "The resource-enforcement ranger who works out of Shiprock. Mr. Yazzie is the man responsible for keeping people from stealing cattle."

Officer Manuelito looked flustered. "No, sir," she said. "I thought we could sort of stake this place out. Keep an eye on it, you know. Whoever is putting out this hay bait will be back and once he gets the cows used to coming here, he'll—"

"He'll rig himself up a sort of chute," Chee said, "and back his trailer in here, and drive a few of 'em on it, and . . ."

Chee paused. Her flustered look had been replaced by the smile of youthful enthusiasm. But now Chee's impatient tone had caused the smile to go away.

Acting Lieutenant Chee had intended to tell Officer Manuelito some of what he'd learned in digesting the brand inspector training manual. If they did indeed catch the cattle thief and managed to get a conviction, the absolute maximum penalty for his crime would be a fine "not to exceed $100" and a jail term "not to exceed six months." That's what it said in section 1356 of subchapter six of chapter seven of the Livestock Inspection and Control Manual. Reading that section just after Manuelito's call had fueled Chee's urge to get out of the office and into the sunlight. But why was he venting his bad mood on this rookie cop? Even interrupting her to do it—an inexcusable rudeness for any Navajo. It wasn't her fault, it was Captain Largo's. And besides, Finch had hurt his pride. He wanted to deflate that pompous jerk by catching Finch's

Zorro before Finch got him. Manuelito looked like a valuable help in that project.

Chee swallowed, cleared his throat. ". . . and then we'd have an easy conviction," he concluded.

Officer Manuelito's expression had become unreadable. A hard lady to mislead.

"And put a stop to one cow thief," he added, conscious of how lame it sounded. "Well, let's go. Let's see if anyone's at home at the Sam place."

The Rural Electrification Administration had run a power line across the empty landscape off in the direction of the Chuska Mountains, which took it within a few miles of the Sam place, and the Navajo Communication Company had followed by linking such inhabited spots as Rattlesnake and Red Rock to the world with its own telephone lines. But the Sam outfit had either been too far off the route to make a connection feasible, or the Sam family had opted to preserve its privacy. Thus the fence posts that lined the dirt track leading to the Sam hogan were not draped with telephone wire, and thus there had been no way for Jim Chee to warn Ms. Sam of the impending visit.

But as he geared down into low to creep over the cattle guard and onto the track leading into the Sam grazing lease, he noticed the old boot hanging on the gate post was right side up. Someone must be home.

"I hope someone's here," Officer Manuelito said.

"They are," Chee said. He nodded toward the boot.

Officer Manuelito frowned, not understanding.

"The boot's turned up," Chee said. "When you're leaving, and nobody's going to be home, you turn the boot upside down. Empty. Nobody home. That saves your visitor from driving all the way up to the hogan."

"Oh," Manuelito said. "I didn't know that. We lived over near Keams Canyon before Mom moved to Red Rock."

She sounded impressed. Chee became aware that he was showing off. And enjoying it. He nodded, said: "Yep. You probably had a different signal over there." And thought it would be embarrassing now if nobody was home. The trouble with cattle guard signaling was that people forgot to stop and change the boot.

But Lucy Sam's pickup was resting in front of her double-wide mobile home and Lucy Sam was peering out of the screen door at them. Chee let the patrol car roll to a stop amid a flock of startled chickens. They waited, giving Ms. Sam the time required to prepare herself for receiving visitors. It also gave Chee time to inspect the place.

The mobile home was one of the flimsier models but it had been placed solidly on a base of concrete blocks to keep the wind from blowing under it. A small satellite dish sat on its roof, helping a row of old tires hold down the aluminum panels as well as bringing in a television signal. Beside this insubstantial residence stood the Sam hogan, solidly built of sandstone slabs with its door facing properly eastward. Chee's practiced eyes could tell that it had been built to the specifications prescribed for the People by Changing Woman, their giver of laws. Beyond the hogan was a hay shed with a plank holding pen for cattle, a windmill with attendant water tank, and, on top of the shed, a small wind generator, its fan blades spinning in the morning breeze. Down the slope a rusty and long-deceased Ford F100 pickup rested on blocks with its wheels missing. Farther down stood an outhouse. Beyond this untidy clutter of rural living, the view stretched away forever.

It reminded Chee of a professor he'd had once at the University of New Mexico who had done a research project on how Navajos place their hogans. The answer seemed to Chee glaringly obvious. A Navajo, like a rancher anywhere, would need access to water, to grazing, to a road, and above all a soul-healing view of— in the words of one of the curing chants—"beauty all around you."

The Sam family had put beauty first. They had picked the very crest of the high grassy ridge between Red Wash and Little Ship Rock Wash. To the west the morning sun lit the pink and orange wilderness of erosion that gave the Red Rock community its name. Beyond that the blue-green mass of the Carrizo Mountains rose. Far to the north in Colorado, the Roman nose shape of Sleeping Ute Mountain dominated, and west of that was the always-changing pattern of lights and shadows that marked the edge of Utah's canyon country. But look eastward, and all of this was overpowered by the dark monolith of the Rock with Wings towering over the rolling grassland. Only five or six million years old, the geologists said, but in Chee's mythology it had been there since God created time or, depending on the version one preferred, had flown in fairly recently carrying the first Navajo clans down from the north.

Lucy Sam reappeared at her doorway, the signal that she was ready to receive her visitors. She had started a coffeepot brewing on her propane stove, put on a blouse of dark blue velveteen, and donned her silver and turquoise jewelry in their honor. Now they went through the polite formalities of traditional Navajo greetings, seated themselves beside the Sam table, and waited while Ms. Sam extracted what she called her "rustler book" from a cabinet stacked with magazines and papers.

Chee considered himself fairly adept at guessing the ages of males and fairly poor with females. Ms. Sam he thought must be in her late sixties—give or take five or ten years. She did her hair bound up in the traditional style, wore the voluminous long skirt demanded by traditional modesty, and had a television set on a corner table tuned to a morning talk show. It was one of the sleazier ones—a handsome young woman named Ricki something or other probing into the sexual misconduct, misfortune, hatreds, and misery of a row of retarded-looking guests, to the amusement of the studio audience. But Chee was distracted from this spectacle by what was sharing table space with the television set.

It was a telescope mounted on a short tripod

and aimed through the window at the world outside. Chee recognized it as a spotting scope—the sort the marksmanship instructor had peered through on the police recruit firing range to tell him how far he'd missed the bull's-eye. This one looked like an older, bulkier model, probably an artillery observer's range-finding scope and probably bought in an army surplus store.

Ms. Sam had placed her book, a black ledger that looked even older than the scope, on the table. She settled a pair of bifocals on her nose and opened it.

"I haven't seen much since you asked me to be watching," she said to Officer Manuelito. "I mean I haven't seen much that you'd want to arrest somebody for." She looked over the bifocals at Chee, grinning. "Not unless you want to arrest that lady that used to work at the Red Rock trading post for fooling with somebody else's husband."

Officer Manuelito was grinning, too. Chee apparently looked blank, because Ms. Sam pointed past the telescope and out the window.

"Way over there toward Rock with Wings," she explained. "There's a nice little place down there. Live spring there and cottonwood trees. I was sort of looking around through the telescope to see if any trucks were parked anywhere and I see the lady's little red car just driving up toward the trees. And then in a minute, here comes Bennie Smiley's pickup truck. Then, quite a little bit later, the truck comes out over the hill again, and then four or five minutes, here comes the little red car."

She nodded to Chee, decided he was hopeless, and looked at Manuelito. "It was about an hour," she added, which caused Officer Manuelito's smile to widen.

"Bennie," she said. "I'll be darned."

"Yes," Ms. Sam said.

"I know Bennie," Officer Manuelito said. "He used to be my oldest sister's boyfriend. She liked him but then she found out he was born to the Streams Come Together clan. That's too close to our 'born to' clan for us."

Ms. Sam shook her head, made a disapproving sound. But she was still smiling.

"That lady with the red car," Manuelito said. "I wonder if I know her, too. Is that Mrs.—"

Chee cleared his throat.

"I wonder if you noticed any pickups, anything you could haul a load of hay in, stopped over there on the road past the Rattlesnake pumping station. Probably a day or so before the snow." He glanced at Officer Manuelito, tried to read her expression, decided she was either slightly abashed for gossiping instead of tending to police business, or irritated because he'd interrupted her. Probably the latter.

Ms. Sam was thumbing through the ledger, saying, "Let's see now. Wasn't it Monday night it started snowing?" She thumbed past another page, tapped the paper with a finger. "Big fifth-wheel truck parked there beside Route 33. Dark blue, and the trailer he was pulling was partly red and partly white, like somebody was painting it and didn't get it finished. Had Arizona plates. But that was eight days before it snowed."

"That sounds like my uncle's truck," Manuelito said. "He lives over there at Sanostee."

Ms. Sam said she thought it had looked familiar. And, no, she hadn't noticed any strange trucks the days just before the storm, but then she'd gone into Farmington to buy groceries and was gone one day. She read off the four other entries she'd made since getting Manuelito's request. One sounded like Dick Finch's truck with its bulky camper. None of the others would mean anything unless and until some sort of pattern developed. Pattern! That made him think of the days he'd worked for Leaphorn. Leaphorn was always looking for patterns.

"How did you know it was an Arizona license?" Chee asked. "The telescope?"

"Take a look," Ms. Sam said, and waved at the scope.

Chee did, twiddling the adjustment dial. The mountain jumped at him. Huge. He focused on a slab of basalt fringed with mountain oak. "Wow," Chee said. "Quite a scope."

He turned it, brought in the point where Navajo Route 33 cuts through the Chinese Wall of stone that wanders southward from the volcano. A school bus was rolling down the asphalt, heading for Red Rock after taking kids on their fifty-mile ride into high school at Shiprock.

"We bought it for him, long time ago when he started getting sick," Ms. Sam said—using the Navajo words that avoided alluding directly to the name of the dead. "I saw it in that big pawnshop on Railroad Avenue in Gallup. Then he could sit there and watch the world and keep track of his mountain."

She produced a deprecatory chuckle, as if Chee might think this odd. "Every day he'd write down what he saw. You know. Like which pairs of kestrels were coming back to the same nests. And where the red-tailed hawks were hunting. Which kids were spray-painting stuff on that old water tank down there, or climbing the windmill. That sort of thing."

She sighed, gestured at the talk show. "Better than this stuff. He loved his mountain. Watching it kept him happy."

"I heard he used to come down to Shiprock, to the police station, and report people trespassing and climbing Tse´ Bit´ a´i´," Chee said. "Is that right?"

"He wanted them arrested," she said. "He said it was wrong, those white people climbing a mountain that was sacred. He said if he was younger and had some money he would go back East and climb up the front of that big cathedral in New York." Ms. Sam laughed. "See how they liked that."

"What sort of things did he write in the book?" Chee asked, thinking of Lieutenant Leaphorn and feeling a twinge of excitement. "Could I see it?"

"All sorts of things," she said, and handed it to him. "He was in the marines. One of the code talkers, and he liked to do things the way they did in the marines."

The entries were dated with the numbers of day, month, and year, and the first one was

25/7/89. After the date Hosteen Sam had written in a tiny, neat missionary-school hand that he had gone into Farmington that day and bought this book to replace the old one, which was full. The next entry was dated 26/7/89. After that Sam had written: "Redtail hawks nesting. Sold two rams to D. Nez."

Chee closed the book. What was the date Breedlove had vanished? Oh, yes.

He handed Ms. Sam the ledger.

"Do you have an earlier book?"

"Two of them," she said. "He started writing more after he got really sick. Had more time then." She took two ledgers down from the top of the cabinet where she stored canned goods and handed them to Chee. "It was something that kills the nerves. Sometimes he would feel pretty good but he was getting paralyzed."

"I've heard of it," Manuelito said. "They say there's no cure."

"We had a sing for him," Ms. Sam said. "A Yeibichai. He got better for a little while."

Chee found the page with the day of Hal Breedlove's disappearance and scanned the dates that followed. He found crows migrating, news of a coyote family, mention of an oil field service truck, but absolutely nothing to indicate that Breedlove or anyone else had come to climb Hosteen Sam's sacred mountain.

Disappointing. Well, anyway, he would think about this. And he'd tell Lieutenant Leaphorn about the book. That thought surprised him. Why tell Leaphorn? The man was a civilian now. It was none of his business. He didn't exactly like

Leaphorn. Or he hadn't thought he did. Was it respect? The man was smarter than anybody Chee had ever met. Damn sure smarter than Acting Lieutenant Jim Chee. And maybe that was why he didn't exactly like him.

12

FOR THE FIRST TIME IN HIS LIFE that metaphor whites use about money burning a hole in your pocket had taken on meaning for Joe Leaphorn. The heat had been caused by a check for twenty thousand dollars made out to him against an account of the Breedlove Corporation. Leaphorn had endorsed it and exchanged it for a deposit slip to an account in his name in the Mancos Security Bank. Now the deposit slip resided uneasily in his wallet as he waited for Mrs. Cecilia Rivera to finish dealing with a customer and talk to him. Which she did, right now.

Leaphorn rose, pulled back a chair for her at the lobby table where she had deposited him earlier. "Sorry," she said. "I don't like to keep a new customer waiting." She sat, examined him briefly, and got right to the point. "What did you want to ask me about?"

"First," Leaphorn said, "I want to tell you

what I'm doing here. Opening this account and all."

"I wondered about that," Mrs. Rivera said. "I noticed your address was Window Rock, Arizona. I thought maybe you were going into some line of business up here." That came out as a question.

"Did you notice who the check was drawn against?" Leaphorn asked. Of course she would have. It was a very small bank in a very small town. The Breedlove name would be famous here, and Leaphorn had seen the teller discussing the deposit with Mrs. Rivera. But he wanted to make sure.

"The Breedloves," Mrs. Rivera said, studying his face. "It's been a few years since we've seen a Breedlove check but I never heard of one bouncing. Hal's widow banked here for a little while after he—after he disappeared. But then she quit us."

Mrs. Rivera was in her mid-seventies, Leaphorn guessed, thin and sun-wrinkled. Her bright black eyes examined him through the top half of her bifocals with frank curiosity.

"I'm working for them now," Leaphorn said. "For the Breedloves." He waited.

Mrs. Rivera drew in a long breath. "Doing what?" she asked. "Would it be something to do with that moly mine project?"

"It may be that," Leaphorn said. "To tell the truth, I don't know. I'm a retired policeman." He extracted his identification case and showed it to her. "Years ago when Hal Breedlove disappeared, I was the detective working that case." He produced a deprecatory expression. "Obviously I didn't have much success with it, because it took about eleven years to find him, and then it was by accident. But anyway, the family seems to have remembered."

"Yes," Mrs. Rivera said. "Young Hal did like to climb up onto the mountains." A dim smile appeared. "From what I read in the *Farmington Times*, I guess he needed more studying on how to climb down off of them."

Leaphorn rewarded this with a chuckle.

"In my experience," he said, "bankers are like doctors and lawyers and ministers. Their business depends a lot on keeping confidences." He looked at her, awaiting confirmation of this bit of misinformation. Leaphorn had always found bankers wonderful sources of information.

"Well, yes," she said. "Lot of business secrets come floating around when you're negotiating loans."

"Are you willing to handle another one?"

"Another secret?" Mrs. Rivera's expression became avid. She nodded.

And so Lieutenant Joe Leaphorn, retired, laid his cards on the table. More or less. It was a tactic he'd used for years—based on his theory that most humans prefer exchanging information to giving it away. He'd tried to teach Jim Chee that rule, which was: Tell somebody something interesting and they'll try to top it. So now he was going to tell Mrs. Rivera everything he knew about the affair of Hal Breedlove, who had been by Four Corners standards her former neighbor and was her onetime customer. In return he expected Mrs. Rivera to tell him something she knew about Hal Breedlove, and his ranch, and his business. Which was why he had opened this account here. Which was what he had decided to do yesterday when, after long seconds of hesitation, he had accepted the check he had never expected to receive.

They had met again yesterday at the Navajo Inn—Leaphorn, McDermott, and George Shaw.

"If I take this job," Leaphorn had said, "I will require a substantial retainer." He kept his eyes on Shaw's face.

"Substantial?" said McDermott. "How sub—"

"How much?" asked Shaw.

How much, indeed, Leaphorn thought. He had decided he would mention a price too large for them to pay, but not ludicrously overdone. Twenty thousand dollars, he had decided. They would make a counteroffer. Perhaps two thousand. Two weeks pay in advance. He would drop finally to, say, ten thousand. They would counter. And finally he would establish how important this affair was to Shaw.

"Twenty thousand dollars," Leaphorn said.

McDermott had snorted, said, "Be serious. We can't—"

But George Shaw had reached into his inside coat pocket and extracted a checkbook and a pen.

"From what I've heard about you we won't need to lawyer this," he said. "The twenty thousand will be payment in full, including any expenses you incur, for twenty weeks of your time or until you develop the information we need to settle this business. Is that acceptable?"

Leaphorn hadn't intended to accept anything—certainly not to associate himself with
these two men. He didn't need money. Or want
it. But Shaw was writing the check now, face
grim and intent. Which told Leaphorn there was
much more involved here than he'd expected.

Shaw had torn out the check, handed it to
him. A little piece of the puzzle that had stuck in
Leaphorn's mind for eleven years—that had
been revived by the shooting of Hosteen Nez—
had clicked into place. Unreadable yet, but it
shed a dim light on the effort to kill Nez. If
twenty thousand dollars could be tossed away
like this, millions more than that must be somehow involved. That told him hardly anything.
Just a hint that Nez might still be, to use that
white expression, "worth killing." Or for Shaw,
perhaps worth keeping alive.

He had held the check a moment, a little
embarrassed, trying to think of what to say as he
returned it. He knew now that he would try
again to find a way to solve this old puzzle, but
for himself and not for these men. He extended
the check to Shaw, said, "I'm sorry. I don't
think—"

Then he had seen how useful that check
could be. It would give him a Breedlove connection. He wasn't a policeman any longer. This
would give him the key he'd need to unlock
doors.

And this morning, in this small, old-fashioned
bank lobby, Leaphorn was using it.

"This is sort of hard to explain," he told Mrs.
Rivera. "What I'm trying to do for the Breedlove

family is vague. They want me to find out everything about the disappearance of Hal Breedlove
and about his death on Ship Rock."

Mrs. Rivera leaned forward. "They don't
think it was an accident?"

"They don't exactly say that. But it was a
pretty peculiar business. You remember it?"

"I remember it very well," Mrs. Rivera said,
with a wry laugh. "The Breedlove boy did his
banking here—like the ranch always had. He
was my customer and he was four payments
behind on a note. We'd sent him notices. Twice, I
believe it was. And the next thing you know, he's
vanished."

Mrs. Rivera laughed. "That's the sort of thing
a banker remembers a long, long time."

"How was it secured? I understand he didn't
get title to the ranch until his birthday—just
before he disappeared."

Mrs. Rivera leaned back now and folded her
arms. "Well, now," she said. "I don't think we
want to get into that. That's private business."

"No harm me asking, though," Leaphorn
said. "It's a habit policemen get into. Let me tell
you what I know, and then you decide if you
know anything you would be free to add that
might be helpful."

"That sounds fair enough," she said. "You
talk. I'll listen."

And she did. Nodding now and then, sometimes indicating surprise, enjoying being an
insider on an investigation. Sometimes indicating agreement as Leaphorn explained a theory,
shaking her head in disapproval when he told

her how little information Shaw and McDermott had given him to work on. As Leaphorn had hoped, Mrs. Rivera had become a partner.

"But you know how lawyers are," he said. "And Shaw's a lawyer, too. I checked on it. He specializes in corporate tax cases. Anyway, they sure didn't give me much to work with."

"I don't know what I can add," she said. "Hal was a spendthrift, I know that. Always buying expensive toys. Snowmobiles, fancy cars. He'd bought himself a—can't think of the name—one of those handmade Italian cars, for example. A Ferrari, however you pronounce that. Cost a fortune and then he drove it over these old back roads and tore it up. He'd worked out some sort of deal with the trust and got a mortgage on the ranch. But then when they sold cattle in the fall and the money went into the ranch account he'd spend it right out of there instead of paying his debts."

She paused, searching for something to add. "Hal always had Sally get him first-class tickets when he flew—Sally has Mancos Travel—and first class costs an arm and a leg."

"And coach class gets there almost as quick," Leaphorn said.

Mrs. Rivera nodded. "Even when they went places together Sally had her instructions to put Hal into first class and Demott in coach. Now what do you think of that?"

Leaphorn shook his head.

"Well, I think it's insulting," Mrs. Rivera said.

"Could have been Demott's idea," Leaphorn said.

"I don't think so," Mrs. Rivera said. "Sally told—" She cut that off.

"I talked to Demott when I was investigating Breedlove's disappearance," Leaphorn said. "He seemed like a solid citizen."

"Well, yes. I guess so. But he's a strange one, too." She chuckled. "I guess maybe we all get a little odd. Living up here with mountains all around us, you know."

"Strange," Leaphorn said. "How?"

Mrs. Rivera looked slightly embarrassed. She shrugged. "Well, he's a bachelor for one thing. But I guess there's a lot of bachelors around here. And he's sort of a halfway tree-hugger. Or so people say. We have some of those around here, too, but they're mostly move-ins from California or back East. Not the kind of people who ever had to worry about feeding kids or working for a living."

"Tree-hugger? How'd he get that reputation?" Leaphorn was thinking of a favorite nephew, a tree-hugger who'd gotten himself arrested leading a noisy protest at a tribal council meeting, trying to stop a logging operation in the Chuskas. In Leaphorn's opinion his nephew had been on the right side of that controversy.

"Well, I don't know," Mrs. Rivera said. "But they say Eldon was why they didn't do that moly operation. Up there in the edge of the San Juan National Forest."

Leaphorn said, "Oh. What happened?"

"It was years ago. I think the spring after Hal went missing. We weren't in on the deal, of course. This bank is way too little for the multi-

million-dollar things like that. A bank up in
Denver was involved I think. And I think the
mining company was MCA, the Moly Corp.
Anyway, the way it was told around here, there
was some sort of contract drawn up, a mineral
lease involving Breedlove land up the canyon,
and then at first the widow was going to handle
it, but Hal legally was still alive and she didn't
want to file the necessary papers to have the
courts say he was dead. So that tied it up. People
say she stalled on that because Demott was
against it. Demott's her brother, you know. But
to tell the truth, I think it was her own idea.
She's loved that place since she was a tot. Grew
up on it, you know."

"I don't know much about their background,"
Leaphorn said.

"Well, it used to be the Double D ranch.
Demott's daddy owned it. The price of beef was
way down in the thirties. Lot of ranches around
here went at sheriff's auction, including that one.
Old Edgar Breedlove bought it, and he kept the
old man on as foreman. Old Breedlove didn't
care a thing about ranching. One of his prospectors had found the moly deposit up the head-
waters of Cache Creek and that's what he
wanted. But anyway, Eldon and Elisa grew up on
the place."

"Why didn't he mine the molybdenum?"
Leaphorn asked.

"War broke out and I guess he couldn't get
the right kind of priority to get the manpower or
the equipment." She laughed. "Then when the
war ended, the price of the ore fell. Stayed down

for years and then went shooting up. Then Hal got himself lost and that tied it all up once again."

"And by the time she had Breedlove declared dead, the price of ore had gone down. Is that right?"

"Right," Mrs. Rivera said. And looked thoughtful.

"And now it's up again," Leaphorn said.

"That's just what I was thinking."

"You think that might be why the Breedlove Corporation would pay me the twenty thousand?"

She looked over her glasses at him. "That's an unkind thought," she said, "but I confess it occurred to me."

"Even though Hal's widow owns the place now?"

"She owns it, unless they can prove she had something to do with killing him. We had our lawyer look into that. She wanted to extend a mortgage on the place." She looked mildly apologetic. "Can't take chances, you know, with your investors' money."

"Did you extend the mortgage?"

Mrs. Rivera folded her arms again. But finally she said, "Well, yes, we did."

Leaphorn grinned. "Could I guess then that you don't think she had anything to do with killing Breedlove? Or anyway, nobody is ever going to prove it?"

"I just own a piece of this bank," Mrs. Rivera said. "There's people I'm responsible to. So I'd have to agree with you. I thought the loan was safe enough."

"Still do?"

She nodded, remembering. Then shook her head.

"When it happened, I mean when he just disappeared like that, I had my doubts. I always thought Elisa was a fine young lady. Good family. Raised right. She used to help take care of her grandmother when the old lady had the cancer. But you know, it sure did look suspicious. Hal inherits the Lazy B and then the very same week—or pretty close to that, anyway—he's gone. So you start thinking she might of had herself another man somewhere and—well, you know."

"That's what I thought, too," Leaphorn said. "What do you think now?"

"I was wrong," she said.

"You sound certain," Leaphorn said.

"You live in Window Rock," she said. "That's a little town like Mancos. You think some widow woman there with a rich husband lost somewhere could have something going with a boyfriend and everybody wouldn't know about it?"

Leaphorn laughed. "I'm a widower," he said. "And I met this nice lady from Flagstaff on some police work I was doing. The very first time I had lunch with her, when I got back to the office they were planning my wedding."

"It's the same way out here," Mrs. Rivera said. "About the time everybody around here decided that Hal was gone for good, they started marrying Elisa off to the Castro boy."

Leaphorn smiled. "You know," he said, "we

cops tend to get too high an opinion of ourselves. When I was up here asking around after Hal disappeared I went away thinking there wasn't a boyfriend in the background."

"You got here too quick," Mrs. Rivera said. "Here at Mancos we let the body get cold before the talking starts."

"I guess nothing came of that romance," Leaphorn said. "At least she's still a widow."

"From what I heard, it wasn't from lack of Tommy Castro's trying. About the time she got out of high school everybody took for granted they were a pair. Then Hal showed up." Mrs. Rivera shrugged, expression rueful. "They made a kind of foursome for a while."

"Four?"

"Well, sometimes it was five of 'em. This George Shaw, he'd come out with Hal sometimes and Eldon would go. He and Castro were the old heads, the coaches. They'd go elk hunting together. Camping. Rock climbing. Growing up with her dad raising her, and then her big brother, Elisa was quite a tomboy."

"What broke up the group? Was it the country boy couldn't compete with the big-city glamour?"

"Oh, I guess that was some of it," she said. "But Eldon had a falling-out with Tommy. They're too much alike. Both bull-headed."

Leaphorn digested that. Emma's big brother hadn't liked him, either, but that hadn't bothered Emma. "Do you know what happened?"

"I heard Eldon thought Tommy was out of line making a play for his little sister. She was just out of high school. Eight or ten years between 'em, I guess."

"So Elisa was willing to let big brother monitor her love life," Leaphorn said. "I don't hear about that happening much these days."

"Me neither," Mrs. Rivera said, and laughed. "But you know," she said, suddenly dead serious, "Elisa is an unusual person. Her mother died when she was about in the second grade, but Elisa takes after her. Has a heart big as a pumpkin and a cast-iron backbone, just like her mother. When old man Demott was losing the ranch it was Elisa's mama who held everything together. Got her husband out of the bars, and out of jail a time or two. One of those people who are aways there in the background looking out for other people. You know?"

Mrs. Rivera paused at this to see what Leaphorn thought of it. Leaphorn, not sure of where this was leading, just nodded.

"So there Elisa was after Hal was out of the picture. Tommy was beginning to court her again, and Eldon wanted to run him off. They even got into a yelling match down at the High Country Inn. So there's Elisa with two men to take care of—and knowing how she is I have a theory about that." She paused again. "It's just a theory."

"I'd like to hear it," Leaphorn said.

"I think she loved them both," Mrs. Rivera said. "But if she married the Castro boy, what in the wide world was Eldon going to do? It was her ranch now. Eldon loved it but he wouldn't stay around and work for Tommy, and Tommy wouldn't want him to." She sighed. "If we had a Shakespeare around here, they could have made a tragedy out of it."

"So this Castro was a rock climber, too," Leaphorn said. "Does he still live here?"

"If you got gas down at the Texaco station you might have seen him. That's his garage."

"What do you think? Did this affection for Castro linger on after she married Hal?"

"If it did, she didn't let it show." She thought about that awhile, looked sad, shook her head. "Far as you could tell being an outsider, she was the loyal wife. I couldn't see much to love in Hal myself but every woman's different about that and Elisa was the sort who—the more that was wrong with a man, the more she'd stand behind him. She mourned for him. Matter of fact, I think she still does. You hardly ever see her looking happy."

"How about her brother, then? You said he was sort of strange."

She shrugged. "Well, he liked to climb up cliffs. To me, that's strange."

"Somebody said he taught Hal the sport."

"That's not quite the way it was. After old Edgar got the place away from Demott's daddy, Hal and Shaw would come out in the summers. Shaw had been climbing already. So he didn't need much teaching. And Demott and Castro were already into climbing some when they had time. Eldon was about six or eight years older than Hal and more of an athlete. From what I heard he was the best of the bunch."

A customer came in and the cool smell of autumn and the sound of laughter followed him through the doorway from the street. Leaphorn could think of just one more pertinent question.

"You mentioned Hal Breedlove had overdue note payments when he disappeared. How'd that get paid off?"

It was the sort of bank business question he wasn't sure she would answer. Neither was she. But finally she shook her head and laughed.

"Well, you sort of guessed right about not having it secured the way we should have. Old family, and all. So we weren't pressing. But we'd sold off another loan to a Denver bank. Made it to a feedlot operator who liked to go off to Vegas and try to beat the blackjack tables. With people like that you make sure you have it secured. Wrote it on sixty-two head of bred heifers he had grazing up in a Forest Service lease. The Denver people foreclosed on it and they called us for help on claiming the property."

She laughed. "Those Denver people had sixty-two head of cows out in the mountains grazing on a Forest Service lease and not an idea in the world about what to do with them. So I told 'em Eldon Demott might round them up for 'em and truck them over to Durango to the auction barn. And he did."

"He got paid enough for that to pay off Breedlove's note?"

She laughed again. "Not directly. But I mentioned we made the loan on bred heifers. So we sold the Denver bank a mortgage on sixty-two head, but when Demott went to get 'em, they weren't pregnant anymore. They were mama cows."

She paused, wanting to see if Leaphorn understood the implications of this. Leaphorn said: "Ah, yes. He didn't get back from Las Vegas to brand 'em."

"Ah, yes, is right," Mrs. Rivera said. "In fact he didn't get back at all. The sheriff has a warrant out for him. So there was Eldon with sixty-two cows loaded up and all those calves left over. They were all still slicks. Not any of 'em branded yet. Nobody in the world had title to 'em. Nobody owned 'em but the Lord in heaven."

"Enough to pay off the note?"

"He might've had a little bit left over," she said, and looked at Leaphorn over her glasses. "Wait a minute now," she said. "Don't you get any wrong ideas. I don't actually know what in the world happened to those calves. And I've been talking way too much and it's time to get some work done."

Back at his car, Leaphorn fished his cellular telephone from the glove compartment, dialed his Window Rock number, and punched in the proper code to retrieve any messages accumulated by his answering machine. The first call was from George Shaw, asking if he had anything to report and saying he could be reached at room 23, Navajo Inn. The second call was from Sergeant Addison Deke at the Chinle police station.

"Better give me a call, Joe," Deke said. "It probably doesn't amount to anything but you asked me to sort of keep an eye on Amos Nez and you might like to hear about this."

Leaphorn didn't check on whether there was

a third call. He dialed the Arizona area code and Chinle police department number. Yes, Sergeant Deke was in.

He sounded apologetic. "Probably nothing, Joe," he said. "Probably wasting your time. But after we talked, I told the boys to keep it in their minds that whoever shot Nez might try it again. You know, keep an eye out. Be looking." Deke hesitated.

Leaphorn, who almost never allowed impatience to show, said, "What did they see?"

"Nothing, actually. But Tazbah Lovejoy came in this morning—I don't think you know him. He's a young fellow out of recruit training two years ago. Anyway Tazbah told me he'd run into one of those Resource Enforcement Agency rangers having coffee, and this guy was telling him about seeing a poacher up on the rim of Canyon del Muerto yesterday."

Sergeant Deke hesitated again. This time Leaphorn gave him a moment to organize his thoughts.

"The ranger told Tazbah he was checking on some illegal firewood cutting, and he stopped at that turnout overlook down into del Muerto. Wanted to take a leak. He was getting that done, standing there, looking out across the canyon, and he kept seeing reflections off something or other across the canyon. No road over there, you know, and he wondered about it. So he went to his truck and got his binoculars to see what he could see. There was a fellow over there with binoculars. The reflections turned out to be coming off the lenses, I guess. Anyway, he had a rifle, too."

"Deer hunter, maybe," Leaphorn said.

Deke laughed. "Joe," he said. "How long's it been since you've been deer hunting? That'd be out on that tongue of the plateau between del Muerto and Black Rock Canyon. Nobody's seen a deer over there since God knows when."

"Maybe it was an Anglo deer hunter then. Did he get a good look at him?"

"I don't think so. The ranger thought it was funny. Hunter over there and nothing to hunt. But I guess he was going to call it attempted poaching, or conspiracy to poach. So he drove back up to Wheatfields campground and tried to get back in there as far as he could on that old washed-out track. But he gave up on it."

"Did he get a good enough look to say man or woman?"

"I asked Tazbah and he said the ranger didn't know for sure. He said they were thinking man, on grounds a woman wouldn't be stupid enough to go hunting where there wasn't anything to shoot at. I thought you'd like to know about it because it was just up the canyon a half mile or so from where that sniper shot old Amos."

"Which would put it just about right over the Nez place," Leaphorn said.

"Exactly," Deke said. "You could jump right down on his roof."

ACTING LIEUTENANT JIM CHEE was parked at sunrise on the access road to Beclabito Day School because he wanted to talk to Officer Teddy Begayaye at a private place. Officer Begayaye would be driving to the office from his home at Tec Nos Pos. Chee wanted to tell him that vacation schedules were being posted today, that he was getting the Thanksgiving week vacation time he had asked for. He wanted Begayaye to provide him some sort of justification (beyond his twelve years of seniority) for approving it. Another member of Chee's criminal investigation squad wanted the same days off, namely, Officer Manuelito. She had applied for them first, and Chee wanted to give her some reason (beyond her total lack of seniority) why she didn't get it—thereby avoiding friction in the department. Thus Chee had parked where Begayaye could see him instead of hiding his patrol car behind the day school sign in hope of nabbing a speeder.

But now Chee wasn't thinking of vacation schedules. He was thinking of the date he had tonight with Janet Pete, back from whatever law business had taken her to Washington. Janet shared an apartment at Gallup with Louise Guard, another of the DNA lawyers. Chee had hopes that Louise, as much as he liked her, would be away somewhere for the evening (or, better, had found herself another apartment). He wanted to show Janet a videotape he'd borrowed of a traditional Navajo wedding. She had more or less agreed, with qualifications, that they would do the ceremony the Navajo way and that he could pick the haatalii to perform it. But she clearly had her doubts about it. Janet's mother had something more socially correct in mind. However, if he lucked out and Ms. Guard actually had shoved off for somewhere, he would hold the videotape for another evening. He and Janet hadn't seen each other for a week and there were better ways to occupy the evening.

The vehicle rolling down U.S. 64 toward him was a camper truck, dirty and plastered with tourist stickers. Dick Finch's vehicle. It slowed to a crawl, with Finch making a series of hand signals. Most of them were meaningless to Chee, but one of them said "follow me."

Chee started his engine and followed, driving eastward on 64 with Finch speeding. Chee topped the ridge. Finch's truck had already disappeared, but a plume of dust hanging over the dirt road that led past the Rattlesnake pump station betrayed it. Chee made the left turn into the dust—thinking how quickly this arid climate could replace wet snow with blowable dirt. Just out of sight of the highway the camper was parked, with Finch standing beside it.

Finch walked over, smiling that smile of his. Lots of white teeth.

"Good morning," Chee said.

"Captain Largo wants us to work together," Finch said. "So do my people. Get along with the Navajos, they tell me. And the Utes and the Zunis, Arizona State Police, the county mounties, and everybody. Good policy, don't you think?"

"Why not?" Chee said.

"Well, there might be a reason why not," Finch said, still smiling, waiting for Chee to say, "Like what?" Chee just looked at him until Finch tired of the game.

"For example, somebody's been taking a little load of heifers now and then off that grazing lease west of your Ship Rock mountain. They're owned by an old codger who lives over near Toadlena. He rents grass from a fella named Maryboy, and his livestock is all mixed up with Maryboy's and nobody keeps track of the cattle."

Finch waited again. So did Chee. What Finch was telling him so far was common enough. People who had grazing leases let other people use them for a fee. One of the problems of catching cattle thieves was the animals might be gone a month before anyone noticed. Finally Chee said: "What's your point?"

"Point is, as we say, I've got reason to believe

that the fella picking up these animals is this
fella I've been trying to nail. He comes back to
the mountain about every six months or so and
picks up a load. Does the same thing over
around Bloomfield, and Whitehorse Lake, and
Burnham, and other places. When I catch him, a
lot of this stealing stops. My job gets easier. So a
couple of months ago, I found where he got the
last ones he took from that Ship Rock pasture.
The son of a bitch was throwing hay over a fence
at a place where he could back his truck in.
Chumming them up like he was a fisherman. I
imagine he'd blow his horn when he threw the
hay over. Cows are curious. Worse than cats.
They'd come to see about it. And they've got
good memories. Do it about twice, and when
they hear a horn they think of good alfalfa hay.
Come running."

Finch laughed. Chee knew exactly where
this was leading.

"Manuelito spotted that hay, too," Chee said.
"She noticed how the fence posts had been dug
up there, loosened so they can be pulled up. She
took me out to show me."

"I saw you," Finch said. "Watched you
through my binoculars from about two miles
away. Trouble is, our cow thief was probably
watching, too. He's baited that place three times
now. No use wasting any more hay. It's time to
collect his cows."

Finch stared at Chee, his smile still genial.
Chee felt his face flushing, which seemed to be
the reaction Finch was awaiting.

"But he ain't going to do it now, is he? You

can bet your ass he's got a set of binoculars every bit as good as mine, and he's careful. He sees a police car parked there. Sees a couple of cops tromping around. He's gone and he won't be back and a lot of my hard work is down the goddamn tube."

"This suggests something to me," Chee said.

"I hoped it would. I hoped it would make you want to learn a little more about this business before you start practicing it."

"Actually it suggests that you screwed up. You had about four hours of talking to me on that ride up to Mancos, with me listening all the way. You told me about this Zorro you're trying to catch—and I guess this is him. But you totally forgot to tell me about this trap you were going to spring so we could coordinate. How could you forget something like that?"

Finch's face had also become a little redder through its windburn. The smile had gone away. He stared at Chee. Looked down at his boots. When he looked up he was grinning.

"Touché! I got a bad habit of underestimating folks. You say that woman cop with you noticed the fence posts had been dug loose. I missed that. Good-looking lady, too. You give her my congratulations, will you. Tell her any old time she wants to work alongside of me, or under me either, she's more than welcome."

Chee nodded, started his engine.

"Hold it just a minute," Finch said, his smile looking slightly more genuine. "I didn't stop you just to start an argument. Wondered if I could get you to be a witness for something."

Chee left the motor running. "For what?"

"There's five Angus calves at a feedlot over by Kirtland. Looks like they were branded through a wet gunnysack, like the wise guys do it, but they're still so fresh they haven't even scabbed over yet. And the fellow that signed the bill of sale hasn't got any mother cows. He claimed he sold 'em off—which we can check on. On the other hand, a fellow named Bramlett is short five Angus calves off some leased pasture. I'm going over and see if there's five wet cows there. If there is I call the feedlot and they bring the calves over and I turn on my video camera and get a tape of the mama cows saying hello to their missing calves. Letting 'em nurse, all that."

"So what do you need me for?"

"It'd be a mostly Navajo jury, and the cow thief—he's a Navajo," Finch said. "Be good to have a Navajo cop on the witness stand."

Chee looked at his watch. By now Teddy Begayaye would be at the office celebrating getting his requested vacation time, and Manuelito would be sore about it. Too late for any preventive medicine there. But he had, after all, ruined Finch's trap. Besides, it would give him another hour away from the office and something positive for a change to report to Captain Largo on the cow-theft front.

"I'll follow you," Chee said, "and if you speed, you get a ticket."

Finch sped, but kept it within the Navajo Tribal Police tolerance zone. He parked beside the fence at the holding pasture at just about nine A.M. It was bottomland here, a pasture irrigated by a ditch from the San Juan River, and it held maybe two hundred head of Angus—young cows and their calves—last spring's crop but still nursing. Chee parked as Finch was climbing the fence, snagging his jeans on the barbed wire.

"I think I saw a wet one already," he shouted, pointing into the herd, which now was moving uneasily away. "You stay back by your car."

Wet one? Chee thought. He'd been raised with sheep, not cows. But "wet" must be what you called a cow with a painfully full udder. A cow whose nursing calf was missing. Finch had been right about cow memories. Their memory connected men on foot with being roped, bull-dogged, and branded. They were scattering away from Finch. So the question was, how was Finch going to locate five such cows in that milling herd and know he hadn't just counted the same cow five times?

Finch picked himself a spot free of cow manure, dropped to his knees, and rolled over on his back. He folded his arms under his head and lay motionless. The cows, which had shied fearfully away from him, stopped their nervous milling. They stared at Finch. He yawned, squirmed into a more comfortable position. A heifer, head and ears stretched forward, moved a cautious step toward him. Others followed, noses pointed, ears forward. The calves, with no memory of branding to inhibit them, were first. By eleven minutes after nine, Finch was surrounded by a ring of Angus cattle, sniffing and staring.

As for Finch, only his head was moving, and

he made an udder inspection. He arose, creating a panic, and walked through the scattering herd, already dialing his portable telephone, talking into it as he climbed the fence. He closed it, walked up to Chee's window.

"Five wet ones," he said. "They're going to bring the calves right out. I'm going to videotape it, but it'd help if you'd stick around so you can testify. You know, tell the jury that the calves ran right up to their mamas and started nursing, and their mamas let 'em do it."

"That was pretty damn clever," Chee said.

"I told you about cows being curious," Finch said. "They're scared of a man standing up. Lay down and they say, 'What the hell's going on here?' and come on over to take a look." He brushed off his jeans. "Drawback is you're likely to get manure all over yourself."

"Well, it's a lot quicker than chasing them all over the pasture, trying to get a look."

Finch was enjoying this approval.

"You know where I learned that trick? I was in the dentist's office at Farmington waiting to get a root canal. Picked up a *New Yorker* magazine and there was an article in there about a Nevada brand inspector name of Chris Collis. It was a trick he used. I called him and asked him if it really worked. He said sure."

Finch fished his video camera out of the truck cab, fiddled with it. Chee radioed his office, reported his location, collected his messages. One was from Joe Leaphorn. It was brief.

A truck from the feedlot arrived bearing two men and five terrified Angus calves. Each was ear-tagged with its number and released into the pasture. Each ran, bawling, in search of its mother, found her, underwent a maternal inspection, was approved and allowed to nurse while Finch videotaped the happy reunions.

But Chee wasn't paying as much attention as he might have been. While Finch was counting turgid udders, Chee had checked with his office. Leaphorn wanted to talk to him again about the Fallen Man. He said he was working for the Breedlove family now.

14

THE QUESTION NAGGING AT JIM CHEE wasn't the sort
he wanted to explore on the Tribal Police radio
band. He stopped at the Hogback trading post,
dropped a quarter in the pay phone, and called
the number Leaphorn had left. It proved to be
the Anasazi Inn in Farmington, but the front
desk said Leaphorn had checked out. Chee
dropped in another quarter and called his own
office. Jenifer answered. Yes, Leaphorn had
called again. He said he was on his way back
from Farmington to Window Rock and he would
drop by and try to catch Chee at his office.

Chee got there about five minutes faster
than the speed limit allowed. Leaphorn's car was
in the parking lot. The man himself was perched,
ramrod straight, on a chair in the waiting room,
reading yesterday's copy of *Navajo Times*.

"If you have a couple of minutes, I want to
pass on some information," Leaphorn said.

"Otherwise, I can catch you when you have some time."

"I have time," Chee said, and ushered him into his office.

Leaphorn sat. "I'll be brief. I've taken a retainer from the Breedlove Corporation. Actually, it's really the family, I guess. They want me to sort of reinvestigate the disappearance of Hal Breedlove." He paused, awaited a reaction. If he was reading Chee's studiously blank expression properly, the young man didn't like the arrangement.

"So it's official business for you now," Chee said. "At least unofficially official."

"Right," Leaphorn said. "I wanted you to know that because I may be bothering you now and then. With questions." He paused again.

"Is that it?" Chee asked. If it was, he had some questions of his own.

"There's something else I wanted to tell you. I think it's pretty clear the family thinks Hal was murdered. If they have any evidence of that they're not telling me. Maybe it's just that they want it to be murder. And they want to be able to prove it. They want to regain title to the ranch."

"Oh," Chee said. "Did they tell you that?"

Leaphorn hesitated, his expression quizzical. What the devil was bothering Chee? "I was thinking that would be the most likely motive," he said. "What do you think?"

Chee nodded noncommittally.

"Can you tell me who you made the deal with?" he asked.

"You mean the individual?" Leaphorn said. "I

think private detectives are supposed to have a thing about client confidentiality, but I haven't learned to think like a private eye. Never will. This is my one and only venture. George Shaw handed me my check." He laughed, and told Chee how he'd outsmarted himself, trying to learn how big a deal this was for the Breedlove Corporation.

"So Hal's cousin signed the check, but the lawyer with him, you remember his name?"

"McDermott," Leaphorn said. "John McDermott. He's the lawyer handling it. He called me and arranged the meeting. Works for a Washington firm, but I think he used to have an office in Albuquerque. And—" He stopped, aware of Chee's expression. "You know this guy?"

"Indirectly," Chee said. "He was sort of an Indian affairs specialist for an Albuquerque firm. I think he represented Peabody Coal when they were negotiating one of the coal contracts with us, and a couple of pipeline companies dealing with the Jicarillas. Then he moved to Washington and is doing the same thing on that level. I think it's with the same law firm."

Leaphorn looked surprised. "You know a lot more about him than I do," he said. "How's his reputation? It okay?"

"As a lawyer? I guess so. He used to be a professor."

"He struck me as arrogant. Is that your impression?"

Chee shrugged. "I don't know him. I just know a little about him."

"Well, he didn't make a good first impression."

"Could you tell me when he called you? I mean made the first contact."

The question obviously surprised Leaphorn. "Let's see," he said. "Two or three days ago."

"Was it last Tuesday?"

"Tuesday? Let's see. Yeah. It was a call on my answering machine. I returned it."

"Morning or afternoon?"

"I don't know. It could have been either one. But it's still on the recording. I think I could find out."

"I'd appreciate that," Chee said.

"Will do," Leaphorn said, and paused. "I'm trying to place the date. That would have been about the day after you got the skeleton identified. Right?"

Chee sighed. "Lieutenant Leaphorn," he said, "you already know just what I'm thinking, don't you?"

"Well, I'd guess you're wondering how that lawyer found out so quickly that the skeleton had turned out to be somebody so important to his client. No announcement had been made. Nothing in the papers until a day or so later and I don't think it ever made the national news. Just a little story around here, and about three paragraphs in the *Albuquerque Journal*, and a little bit more in the *Rocky Mountain News*."

"That's what I'm thinking," Chee said.

"But you're ahead of me on something else. I don't know why it's important."

"You couldn't guess," Chee said. "It's something personal."

"Oh," Leaphorn said. He ducked his head,

shook it, and said, "Oh," again. Sad, now. And
then he looked up. "You know, they could have
had this thing staked out, though. An important
client. Maybe they had some law firm out here
retained to tip them off if anything turned up
that would bear in any way at all on this son-and-
heir being missing. They knew he was a mountain climber. So when an unidentified body turns
up . . ." He shrugged. "Who knows how law firms
operate?" he said, not believing it himself.

"Sure," Chee said. "Anything's possible."

Leaphorn was leaving, hat in hand, but he
stopped in the doorway and turned.

"One other thing that might bear on all this,"
he said. He told Chee of Sergeant Deke's
account of the man with the binoculars and the
rifle on the canyon rim. "Deke said he's going up
the canyon and warn Nez that somebody may
still be trying to kill him. I hope we can figure
this out before they do it."

Chee sat for a moment looking at the closed
door, thinking of Leaphorn, thinking of Janet
Pete, of John McDermott back in New Mexico.
Was he back in her life? Apparently he was. For
the first time, the Fallen Man became more than
an abstract tragedy in Chee's mind. He buzzed
Jenifer.

"I'm taking off now for Gallup," he said. "If
Largo needs me—if anybody calls—tell them I'll
be back tomorrow."

"Hey," Jenifer said, "you have two meetings
on the calendar for this afternoon. The security
man from the community college and Captain
Largo was—"

"Call them and tell them I had to cancel," Chee said, forgetting to say please, and forgetting to say thanks when he hung up. Captain Largo wouldn't like this. But then he didn't particularly like Captain Largo and he sure as hell didn't like being an acting lieutenant.

15

LOUISE GUARD'S FORD ESCORT was not in the driveway of the little house she shared with Janet Pete in Gallup. Good news, but not as good as it would have seemed when Jim Chee was feeling better about life. This evening his mood had been swinging back and forth between a sort of grim anger at the world that Janet occupied and self-contempt for his own immature attitude. It hadn't taken long for Chee, who was good at self-analysis, to determine that his problem was mostly jealousy. Maybe it was 90 percent jealousy. But even so, that left 10 percent or so that seemed legitimate.

He gave the door of his pickup the hard slam required to shut it and walked up the pathway with the videotape of the traditional wedding clutched in one hand and the other holding a pot of some sort of autumn-blooming flowers he'd bought for her at Gallup Best Blossoms. It wasn't a very impressive floral display, but what could you expect in November?

"Ah, Jim," Janet said, and greeted him with such a huge and enthusiastic hug that it left him helpless—tape in one hand and flowerpot in the other. It also left him feeling guilty. What the devil was wrong with him? Janet was beautiful. Janet was sweet. She loved him. She was wearing a set of designer jeans that fit her perfectly and a blouse of something that shimmered. Her black hair was done in a new fashion he'd been observing on the nighttime soap opera shows. It made her look young and jaunty and like someone the muscular actor in the tank top would be laughing with at the fancy party in a Coca-Cola commercial.

"I'd almost forgotten how beautiful you are," Chee said. "Just back from Washington, you should be looking tired."

Janet was in the kitchen by then, watering whatever it was he'd brought her, opening the refrigerator and fixing something for them.

"It wasn't tiresome," she shouted. "It was lots of fun. The people in the BIA were on their very best behavior, and the people over at Justice were reasonable for a change. And there was time to see a show some German artist had going in the National Gallery. It was really interesting stuff. Partly sculpture and partly drawings. And then there was the concert I told you about. The one in the Library of Congress hall. It was partly Mozart. Really great."

Yes. The concert. He'd thought about that before. Maybe too much. In Washington and at the Library of Congress it wouldn't be a public event. It would be exclusive. Some sort of high-society fund-raiser. Shaking down the social set for some worthy literacy cause, probably. Almost certainly it would be by invitation only. Or just members and guests for the big-money patrons of library projects. She'd mentioned some ambassador being there. He had thought, once, that John McDermott might have taken her. But that was crazy. She detested the man. He had taken advantage of the leverage a distinguished professor has over his students. He'd seduced Janet. He'd taken her to Albuquerque as his live-in intern, had taken her to Washington as his token Indian. She had come back to New Mexico ashamed and brokenhearted when she realized what he was doing. There were a dozen ways McDermott could have learned the Fallen Man had been identified. Leaphorn, as usual, was right. McDermott's firm probably had connections with lawyers in New Mexico. Of course they would. They would be working with Arizona and New Mexico law firms on Indian business. Anyway, he damn sure wasn't going to bring it up. It would be insulting.

From the kitchen the sound of something clattering, the smell of coffee. Chee inspected the room around him. Nothing different that he could see except for something or other on the mantle over the gas-log fireplace. It was made of thin stainless steel tubing combined with shaped Plexiglas in three or four colors held together by what seemed to be a mixture of aluminum wiring and thread. Most peculiar. In fact, weird.

Chee grinned at it. Something Louise had found somewhere. A conversation piece. Louise haunted garage sales, and in Gallup, garage sales were always offering odd harvests.

Janet emerged with a cup of coffee for him—fragile china on a thin-as-paper saucer—and a crystal goblet of wine for herself. She snuggled onto the sofa beside him, clicked glass against cup, smiled at him, and said, "To your capture of a whole squadron of cattle rustlers, your promotion to commander in chief of the Navajo police, chief honcho of the Federal Bureau of Ineptitude, and international boss of Interpol."

"You forgot my busting up the Shiprock graffiti vandals and election as sheriff of San Juan County and bureaucrat in chief of the Drug Enforcement Agency."

"All that, too," Janet said, raised her glass again, and sipped. She picked up the videocassette and inspected it. "What's this?"

"Remember?" Chee said. "My paternal uncle's niece was having a traditional wedding at their place north of Little Water. I got him to get me a copy of the videotape they had made."

Janet turned it over and inspected the back, which was just as black and blank as the other side. "You want me to look at it?"

"Sure," Chee said, his good feelings fading fast. "Remember? We talked about that." They had argued a little, actually. About cultures, and traditions, and all that. It wasn't that Janet was opposed, but her mother wanted a huge ceremony in an Episcopal cathedral in Baltimore. And Janet had agreed, or so he thought, that they would do both. "You said you had never been to a regular Navajo wedding with a shaman and the entire ceremony. I thought you'd be interested."

"Louise described it to me," Janet said, and put the videotape on the coffee table in a way that made Chee want to change the subject. Suddenly Louise's peculiar purchase seemed useful.

"I see Louise has been sailing the garage sales again. Quite an acquisition there," he said, nodding toward the thing. He laughed. "Louise is a wonderful lady, but I wonder about her taste sometimes."

Janet had no comment.

Chee said: "What's it for?" And waited, and belatedly understood that he should have kept his stupid mouth shut.

"It's called 'Technic Inversion Number Three, Side View,'" Janet said.

"Remarkable," Chee said. "Very interesting."

"I found it in the Kremont Gallery," Janet said, glum. "The artist is a man named Egon Kuzluzski. The critic at the *Washington Post* called him the most innovative sculptor of the decade. An artist who finds beauty and meaning in the technology which is submerging modern culture."

"Very complex," Chee said. "And the colors . . ." He couldn't think of a way to finish the sentence.

"I really thought you would like it," Janet said. "I'm sorry you don't."

"I do," Chee said, but he knew it was too late

for that. "Well, not really. But I think it takes time to understand something that's so innovative. And then tastes vary, of course."

Janet didn't respond to that.

"It's the reason they have horse races," Chee said, and attempted a chuckle. "Differences of opinion, you know."

"I ran into something interesting in Washington," Janet said, in a fairly obvious effort to cut off this discussion. "I think it was why everybody was so cooperative with our proposals. Crime on Indian reservations has become very chic inside the Beltway. Everybody had read up on narcotics invading Indian territory, and Indian gang problems, Indian graffiti, Indian homicides, child abuse, the whole schmear. All very popular with the Beltway intelligentsia. We have finally made it into the halls of the mighty."

"I guess that would fall into the bad news, good news category," Chee said, grinning with relief at being let off the hook.

"Whatever you call it, it means everybody is looking for our expertise these days."

Chee's grin faded. "You got a job offer?"

"I didn't mean me. But one of the top assistants in BIA Law and Order wanted to let me know they're recruiting experienced reservation cops with the right kind of credentials for Civil Service, and I heard the same thing over at Justice." She smiled at him. "At Justice they actually asked me to be a talent scout for them, and when they told me what they wanted it sounded like they were describing you." She patted him on the leg. "I told 'em I'd already signed you up."

"Thank God for that," Chee said. "I did time in Washington a couple of times, remember? At the FBI academy for their training course, and once on an investigation." He shuddered, remembering. At the academy he had been the tolerated rube, one of "them." But they would, naturally, look on Janet as one of "us." It was a fact he'd have to find a way to deal with.

Janet removed her hand.

"Really, Jim, Washington's a nice place. It's cleaner than most cities, and something beautiful every place you look and there's always—"

"Beautiful what? Buildings? Monuments? There's too much smog, too much noise, too much traffic, too damn many people everywhere. You can't see the stars at night. Too cloudy to see the sunset." He shook his head.

"There's the breeze coming in off the Potomac," Janet said. "And the clean salty smell of the bay, and seafood fresh from the ocean and good wine. In April, the cherry blossoms, and the green, green hills, and the great art galleries, and theater, and music." She paused, waved her hands, overcome by the enormous glories of Washington's culture. "And the pay scales are about double what either one of us can make here—especially in the Justice Department."

"Working in the J. Edgar Hoover Building," Chee said. "That'd be a real kick. That old blackmailer should have been doing about twenty years for misuse of public records, but they named the building after him. At least it's an appropriately ugly building."

Janet let that one lie, sipped her wine, reminded Chee his coffee was getting cold. He tested it. She was right.

"Jim," she said, "that concert was absolutely thrilling. It was the Philadelphia Orchestra. The annual Founders Society affair. The First Lady was there, and all sorts of diplomats—all white tie and the best jewels dug out of the safety-deposit boxes. And Mozart. You like Mozart."

"I like a lot of Mozart," Chee said.

He took a deep breath. "It was one of those members-only things, I guess," he said. "Members and guests."

"Right," she said, smiling at him. "I was mingling with the *crème de la crème*."

"I'll bet your old law firm is a member," Chee said. "Probably a big donor."

"You betcha," Janet said, still smiling. Then she realized where Chee was headed. The smile went away.

"You're going to ask me who took me," she said.

"No, I'm not."

"I was a guest of John McDermott," she said.

Chee sat silent and motionless. He had known it, but he still didn't want to believe it.

"Does that bother you?"

"No," Chee said. "I guess not. Should it?"

"It shouldn't," she said. "After all, we go way back. He was my teacher. And then I worked with him."

He was looking at her. Wondering what to

say. She flushed. "What are you thinking?" she said.

"I'm thinking I had it all wrong. I thought you detested the man for the way he treated you. The way he used you."

She looked away. "I did for a while. I was angry."

"But not now? No longer angry?"

"The Navajo way," she said. "You're supposed to get yourself back into harmony with the way the world is."

"Did you know he's out here again?"

She nodded.

"Did you know he's hired Joe Leaphorn to look into that Fallen Man business?"

"He told me he was going to try," she said.

"I wondered how he learned about the skeleton being identified as Harold Breedlove," Chee said. "It wasn't the sort of story that would have hit the *Washington Post*."

"No," she said.

"Did you tell him?"

"Why not?" she said, staring at him. "Why the hell not?"

"Well, I don't know. The man you're going to marry is on the telephone reminding you he loves you. And you ask him about a case he's working on, and so he sort of violates police protocol and tells you the skeleton has been identified." He stopped. This wasn't fair. He'd held this anger in for too many hours. He had heard his voice, thick with emotion.

She was still staring at him, face grim, waiting for him to continue.

"So?" she said. "Go on."

"So I'm not exactly sure what happened next. Did you call him right away and tell him what you'd learned?"

She didn't respond to that. But she edged a bit away from him on the sofa.

"One more question and then I'll drop it. Did that son of a bitch ask you to get that information out of me? In other words, I want to know whether he—"

Janet was on her feet.

"I think you'd better go now," she said.

He got up. His anger had drained away now. He simply felt tired and sick.

"Just one more thing I'd like to know," he said. "It would tell me something about just how important this business is to the Breedlove Corporation. In other words if you'd told him about the skeleton being found up there when you first got to Washington, it might naturally have reminded McDermott of Hal Breedlove disappearing. And he'd want to know who the skeleton belonged to. But if it was already on his mind even before that, if he brought it up instead of you, then it would mean a higher level of—it would mean they already—"

"Go away," Janet said. She handed him the videotape. "And take this with you."

He took the tape.

"Janet," he said. "Did you recommend that he hire Leaphorn to work for him?"

He asked that before he noticed the angry tears in Janet's eyes. She didn't answer and he didn't expect her to.

DECEMBER CAME TO THE FOUR CORNERS but winter lingered up in the Utah mountains. It had buried the Wasatch Range under three feet and ventured far enough south to give Colorado's San Juans a snowcap. But the brief post-Halloween storm that had whitened the slopes of Ship Rock and the Chuskas proved to be a false threat. It was dry again across the Navajo Nation—skies dark blue, mornings cool, sun dazzling. The south end of the Colorado Plateau was enjoying that typically beautiful autumn weather that makes the inevitable first blizzard such a dangerous surprise.

Beautiful or not, Jim Chee was keeping himself far too busy to enjoy it—even if his glum mood would have allowed it. He had learned that he could handle administrative duties if he tried hard enough, and that he would never, ever enjoy them. For the first time in his life, he felt no sense of pleasure as he went to work. But the work got done. He made progress. The vacation schedules were established in a way that produced no serious discontent among the officers who worked with him. A system had been devised whereby whatever policemen who happened to be in the Hogback neighborhood would drop in on Diamonte's establishment for a friendly chat. This happened several times a week, thus keeping Diamonte careful and his customers uneasy without giving him any solid grounds for complaint. As a by-product, it had also produced a couple of arrests of young fellows who had been ignoring fugitive warrants.

On top of that, his budget for next year was about half finished and a plan had been drafted for keeping better track of gasoline usage and patrol car maintenance. This had produced an unusual (indeed, unprecedented in the experience of Acting Lieutenant Jim Chee) smile on the face of Captain Largo. Even Officer Bernadette Manuelito seemed to be responding to this new efficiency in Chee's criminal investigation domain.

This came about after the word reached the ear of Captain Largo (and very shortly thereafter the ear of Acting Lieutenant Chee) that Mr. Finch had nailed a pair of cattle-stealing brothers so thoroughly that they had actually admitted not just rustling five unweaned calves but also about six or seven other such larcenies from the New Mexico side of Chee's jurisdiction. So overwhelming was the evidence, the captain said, that they had plea-bargained themselves into jail at Aztec.

"Well, good," Chee had said.

"Well, goddammit," Largo replied, "why can't we nail some of those bastards ourselves?"

Largo's imperial "we" had actually meant him, Chee realized. He also realized, before this uncomfortable conversation ended, that Finch had revealed to Largo not only Chee's ignorance of heifer curiosity but how he and Officer Manuelito had screwed up Finch's trap out by Ship Rock. Chee had walked down the hall away from this meeting with several resolutions strongly formed. He would catch Finch's favorite cow thief before Finch could get his hands on him. Having beaten Finch at Finch's game, he would resign his role as acting lieutenant and go back to being a real policeman. There would be no more trying to be a bureaucrat to impress Janet. And to accomplish the first phase of this program he would shift Manuelito over to work on rustler cases—she and Largo being the only ones in the Shiprock District who took it seriously.

Officer Bernadette Manuelito responded to this shift in duties by withdrawing her request for a transfer. At least, that was Jim Chee's presumption. Jenifer had another notion. She had noticed that the frequent calls between the lady lawyer in Window Rock and the acting lieutenant in Shiprock had abruptly ceased. Jenifer was very good at keeping the Shiprock District criminal investigation office running smoothly because she made it her business to know what the hell was going on. She made a couple of calls to old friends in the small world of law enforcement down at Window Rock. Yes, indeed. The pretty lawyer had been observed shedding tears while in conversation with a lady friend in her car. She had also been seen having dinner at the Navajo Inn with that good-looking lawyer from Washington. Things, it seemed, were in flux. Having learned this, it was Jenifer's theory that Officer Manuelito would learn of it, too—not as directly perhaps, or as fast, but she would learn of it.

Whatever her motives, Manuelito seemed to like her new duties. She stood in front of Chee's desk, looking excited, but not about rustling.

"That's what I said," she said. "They showed up at old Mr. Maryboy's place last night. They told him they wanted trespass permission on his grazing lease. They wanted to climb Ship Rock."

"And it was George Shaw and John McDermott?" Chee said.

"Yes, sir," Officer Manuelito said. "That's what they told him. They paid him a hundred dollars and said if they did any damage they'd pay him for that."

"My God," Chee said. "You mean those two lawyers are going to climb Ship Rock?"

"Old man Maryboy said the little one had climbed it before. Years ago. He said most of the white people just sneaked in and climbed it, but George Shaw had come to his house to get permission. He remembered that. How polite Shaw had been. But this time Shaw said they were bringing a team of climbers."

"So the tall one with the mustache probably isn't going up," Chee said, wondering if he sounded disappointed. But should he be disappointed? Would having McDermott fall off a cliff solve his problem with Janet? He didn't think so.

"They didn't say why they were going up there, I guess," Chee said.

"No, sir. I asked him about that. Mr. Maryboy said they didn't tell him why." She laughed, showing very pretty white teeth. "He said why do white men do anything? He said he knew a white fellow once who was trying to get a patent on a cordless bungee jumper."

Chee rewarded that with a chuckle. The way he'd heard it, it was a stringless yo-yo, but Maryboy had revised it to fit mountain climbers.

"But what I wanted to tell you about was business," Officer Manuelito said. "Mr. Maryboy told me he was missing four steers."

"Maryboy," Chee said. "Let's see. He has—"

"Yes, sir," she said. "That's his lease where we found the loose fence posts. Where somebody was throwing the hay over the fence. I went by his place to tell him about that. I was going to give him a notebook and ask him to keep track of strange trucks and trailers. He said I was a little late, but he took the notebook and said he'd help."

"Did he say how late?" Maryboy hadn't reported a cattle theft. Chee was sure of that. He checked on everything involving rustling every day. "Did he say why he hadn't reported the loss?"

"He said he missed 'em sometime last spring. He was selling off steers and came up short. And he said he didn't report it because he didn't think it would do any good. He said when it happened before, a couple of times, he went in and told us about it but he never did get his animals back."

That was one of the frustrations Chee had been learning to live with in dealing with rustling. People didn't keep track of their cattle. They turned them out to graze, and if they had a big grazing lease and reliable water maybe they'd only see them three or four times a year. Maybe only at calving time and branding time. And if you did see them, maybe you wouldn't notice if you were short a couple. Chee had spent his boyhood with sheep. He could tell an Angus from a Hereford but beyond that one cow looked a lot like every other cow. He could understand how you wouldn't miss a couple, and if you did, what could you do about it? Maybe the coyotes had got 'em, or maybe it was the little green men coming down in flying saucers. Whatever, you weren't going to get 'em back.

"So we put an X on our map and mark it 'unreported,'" Chee said, "which doesn't help much."

"It might," Officer Manuelito said. "Later on."

Chee was extracting their map from his desk drawer. He kept it out of sight on the theory that everyone in the office except Manuelito would think this project was silly. Or, worse, they would think he was trying to copy Joe Leaphorn's famous map. Everybody in the Tribal Police seemed to know about that and the Legendary Lieutenant's use of it to exercise his theory that everything fell into a pattern, every effect had its cause, and so forth.

The map was a U.S. Geological Survey quadrangle chart large enough in scale to show every arroyo, hogan, windmill, and culvert. Chee pushed his in basket aside, rolled it out and penned a tiny blue ? on the Maryboy grazing lease with a tiny 3 beside it. Beside that he marked in the date the loss had been discovered.

Officer Manuelito looked at it and said: "A blue three?"

"Signifies unreported possible thefts," Chee said. "Three of them." He waved his hand around the map, indicating a scattering of such designations. "I've been adding them as we learn about them."

"Good idea," Manuelito said. "And add an X there, too. Maryboy is going to be a lookout for us." She pulled up a chair, sat, leaned her elbows on the desk, and studied the chart.

Chee added the X. The map now had maybe a score of those, each marking the home of a volunteer equipped with a notebook and ballpoint pen. Chee had bought the supplies with his own money, preferring that to trying to explain this system to Largo. If it worked, which today didn't seem likely to Chee, he would decide whether to ask for a reimbursement of his twenty-seven-dollar outlay.

"Funny how this is already working out," Manuelito said. "I thought it would take months."

"What do you mean?"

"I mean the patterns you talked about," she

said. "How those single-animal thefts tend to fall around the middle of the month."

Chee looked. Indeed, most of the 1s that marked single-theft sites were followed by mid-month dates. And a high percentage of those midmonth dates were clustered along the reservation border. But what did that signify? He said: "Yeah."

"I don't think we should concentrate on those," she said, still staring thoughtfully at the map. "But if you want me to, I could check with the bars and liquor stores around Farmington and try to work up a list of guys who come in about the middle of the month with a fresh supply of money." She shook her head. "It wouldn't prove anything, but it would give us a list of people to look out for."

About halfway through this monologue, Chee's brain caught up with Manuelito's thinking. The Navajo Nation relief checks arrived about the first of the month. Every reservation cop knew that the heavy workload produced by the need to arrest drunks tended to ease off in the second week when the liquor addicts had used up their cash. He visualized a dried-out drunk driving past a pasture and seeing a five-hundred-dollar cow staring through the fence at him. How could the man resist? And why hadn't he thought of that?

He thought of it now. Weeks compiling the list, weeks spent cross-checking, sorting, coming up finally with four or five cases, getting maybe two convictions resulting in hundred-dollar fines, which would be suspended, and thirty-day sentences, which would be converted to probation. Meanwhile, serious crime would continue to flourish.

"I think instead we'll sort those out and set them aside. Let's concentrate on solving the multiple thefts," Chee said.

"There's a pattern there, too, I think," Officer Manuelito said. "Am I right?"

Chee had noticed this one himself. The multiple thefts tended to show up in empty country—from grazing leases like Maryboy's where the owner might not see his herd for a month or so. They talked about that, which led them back to their growing list of rustler-watchers, which led them back to Lucy Sam.

"You looked through her telescope," Manuelito said. "Did you notice she could see that place where the fence posts were loose?"

Chee shook his head. He had been looking at the mountain. Thinking of the Fallen Man stranded on the cliff up there, calling for help.

"You could," Manuelito said. "I looked."

"I think I should go talk to her," Chee said. But he wasn't thinking of rustling when he said it. He was wondering what Lucy Sam's father might have seen all those years ago when Hal Breedlove had huddled on that little shelf waiting to die.

17

THE SOUND OF *BANG, BANG, BANG, thud, thud* stopped Joe Leaphorn in his tracks. It came from somewhere up Cache Creek, nearby, just around the bend and beyond a stream-side stand of aspens. But it stopped him just for a moment. He smiled, thinking he'd spent too many years as a cop with a pistol on his hip, and moved up the path. The aspen trunks were wearing their winter white now, their leaves forming a yellow blanket on the ground around them. And through the barren branches Leaphorn could see Eldon Demott, bending over something, back muscles straining.

Doing what? Leaphorn stopped again and watched. Demott was stretching barbed wire over what seemed to be a section of aspen trunk. And now, with more banging, stapling the wire to the wood.

Something to do with a fence, he guessed. Here a cable had been stretched between ponderosas on opposite sides of the stream, and the fence seemed to be suspended from that. Leaphorn shouted, "Hello!"

It took Demott just a moment to recognize him but he did even before Leaphorn reminded him.

"Yeah," Demott said. "I remember. But no uniform now. Are you still with the Tribal Police?"

"They put me out to pasture," Leaphorn said. "I retired at the end of June."

"Well, what brings you all this way up the Cache? It wouldn't have something to do with finally finding Hal, would it? After all these years?"

"That's a good guess," Leaphorn said. "Breedlove's family hired me to go over the whole business again. They want me to see if I overlooked anything. See if I could find out where he went when he left your sister at Canyon de Chelly. See if anything new turned up the past ten years or so."

"That's interesting," Demott said. He retrieved his hammer. "Let me get done with this." He secured the wire with two more staples, straightened his back, and stretched.

"I'm trying to rig up something to solve a problem here," he explained. "The damned cows come to drink here, and then they move downstream a little ways—or their calves do—and they come out on the wrong side of the fence. We call it a water gap. Is that the term you use?"

"We don't get enough water down in the low

country where I was raised to need 'em much," Leaphorn said.

"In the mountains, it's the snowmelt. The creek gets up, washes the brush down, it catches on the fence and builds up until it makes a dam out of it, and the dam backs up the water until the pressure tears out the fence," Demott said. "It's the same story every spring. And then you got cattle up and down the creek, ruining the stream banks, getting erosion started and everything silted up."

It was cool up here, probably a mile and a half above sea level, but Demott was sweating. He wiped his brow on his shirtsleeve.

"The way it's supposed to work, it's kinda like a drawbridge. You make a section of fence across the creek and just hang it from that cable with a dry log holding the bottom down. When the flood comes down, the log floats. That lifts the wire, the brush sails right by under it, and when the runoff season's over, the log drops back into place and you've got a fence again."

"It sounds pretty foolproof," Leaphorn said, thinking that it might work with snowmelt, but runoff from a male rain roaring down the side of a mesa would knock it into the next county and take the cable with it, and the trees, too. "Or maybe I should say cowproof."

Demott looked skeptical. "Actually, it just works until too much stuff catches on the log," he said. "Anyway, it's worth trying." He sat on a boulder, wiped his face again.

"What can I tell you?"

"I don't know," Leaphorn said. "But we wrote

off this thing with your brother-in-law almost eleven years ago. It was just another adult missing person case. Another skip-out without a clue to where or why. So there's been a lot of time for you to get a letter, or hear some gossip, or find out that somebody who knew him had seen him playing the slots in Las Vegas. Something like that. There's no crime involved, so you wouldn't have had any reason to tell us about it."

Demott was wiping mud off the side of his hand on his pant leg. "I can tell you why they hired you," he said.

Leaphorn waited.

"They want this place back."

"I thought they might," Leaphorn said. "I couldn't think of another reason."

"The sons-a-bitches," Demott said. "They want to lease out the mineral rights. Or more likely, just sell the whole outfit to a mining company and let 'em wreck it all."

"That's the idea I got from the bank lady at Mancos."

"Did she tell the plan? They'd do an open pit operation on the molybdenum deposits up there." Demott pointed up Cache Creek, past the clusters of white-barked aspens, past the stately forest of ponderosa, into the dark green wilderness of firs. "Rip it all out," he said, "and then . . ."

The emotion in Demott's voice stopped him. He took a deep breath and sat for a moment, looking down at his hands.

Leaphorn waited. Demott had more than this to say. He wanted to hear it.

Demott gave Leaphorn a sidewise glance. "Have you seen the Red River canyon in New Mexico? Up north of Taos?"

"I've seen it," Leaphorn said.

"You seen it before and after?"

"I haven't been there for years," Leaphorn said. "I remember a beautiful trout stream, maybe a little bigger than your creek here, winding through a narrow valley. Steeper than this one. High mountains on both sides. Beautiful place."

"They ripped the top right off of one of those mountains," Demott said. "Left a great whitish heap of crushed stone miles long. And the holding ponds they built to catch the effluent spill over and that nasty stuff pours down into Red River. They use cyanide in some sort of solution to free up the metal and that kills trout and everything else."

"I haven't been up there for years," Leaphorn said.

"Cyanide," Demott repeated. "Mixed with sludge. That's what we'd have pouring down Cache Creek if the Breedlove Corporation had its way. That slimy white silt brewed with cyanide."

Leaphorn didn't comment on that. He spent a few minutes letting Demott get used to him being there, listening to the music of Cache Creek bubbling over its rocky floor, watching a puffy white cloud just barely making it over the ridge upstream. It was dragging its bottom through the tips of the fir trees, leaving rags of mist behind. A beautiful day, a beautiful place. A cedar waxwing flew by. It perched in the aspens across the creek and watched them, chirping bird comments.

Demott was watching him, too, still absently picking at the resin and dirt on his left hand. "Well, enough of that," he said. "I don't know what to tell you. I got no letters and neither did Elisa. If she had, I would have known it. We're a family that don't keep secrets, not from one another. And we didn't hear anything, either. Nothing."

"You'd think there'd be rumors," Leaphorn said. "You know how people are."

"I do," Demott said. "I thought it was strange, too. I'm sure there must have been a lot of talk about it up at Mancos and around. Hal disappearing was the most exciting thing that happened around here in years. I'm sure some people would say Elisa killed her husband so she could get the ranch, or she had a secret boyfriend do it, or I killed him so the ranch would come back into the Demott family."

"Yeah," Leaphorn said. "I'd think that would be the natural kind of speculation, considering the circumstances. But you didn't hear any of that kind of talk?"

Demott looked shocked. "Why, they wouldn't say things like that around me. Or Elisa either, of course. And you know, the funny thing was Elisa loved Hal, and I think folks around here understood that."

"How about you? What did you think of him?"

"Oh, I got pretty sick of Hal," Demott said. "I won't lie about it. He was a pain in the butt. But you know in a lot of ways I liked him. He had a good heart, and he was good for Elisa. Treated her like a quality lady, and that's what she is. And it made you feel sad, you know. I think he could have amounted to something if he'd been raised right."

Demott despaired of getting the hand suitably clean by rubbing at it. He got up, squatted by the stream, and washed it.

"I'm not sure I know what you mean," Leaphorn said. "What went wrong?"

Finished with his ablutions, Demott resumed his seat and thought about how to tell this.

"Hard to put it exactly," he said. "But when he was just a kid his folks would send him out here and we'd get him on a horse, and he'd do his share of work just like everybody else. Made a good enough hand, for a youngster. When we was baling hay, or moving the cows or anything, he'd do the twelve-hour day right along with us. And when the work was laid by, he'd go rock climbing with me and Elisa. In fact he got good at it before she did." Demott exhaled hugely, shook his head.

No mention of Tommy Castro. "Just the three of you?" Leaphorn asked.

Demott hesitated. "Pretty much."

"Tommy Castro didn't go along?"

Demott flushed. "Where'd you hear about him?"

Leaphorn shrugged.

Demott drew in a deep breath. "Castro and I were friends in high school and, yeah, he and I climbed together some. But then when Elisa got big enough to learn and she'd come along, Tommy began to make a move on her. I told him she was way too young and to knock it off. I put a stop to that."

"He still climb?"

"I have no idea," Demott said. "I stay away from him. He stays away from me."

"No problem with Hal, though."

"He was more her age and more her type, even though he was citified and born with the old silver spoon." Demott thought about that. "You know," he said, "I think he really did love this place as much as we did. He'd talk about getting his family to leave it to him as his part of the estate. Had it all figured out on paper. It wasn't worth near as much as the share he'd get otherwise, but it was what he wanted. That's what he'd say. Prettiest place on earth, and he'd make it better. Improve the stream where it was eroding. Plant out some ponderosa seedlings where we had a fire kill. Keep the herd down to where there wouldn't be any more overgrazing."

"I didn't see much sign of overgrazing now," Leaphorn said.

"Not now, you don't. But before Hal's daddy died he always wanted this place to carry a lot more livestock than the grass could stand. He was always putting the pressure on my dad, and after dad passed away, putting it on me. As a matter of fact he was threatening to fire me if I didn't get the income up to where he thought it ought to be."

"You think he would have done it?"

"We never will know," Demott said. "I wasn't

going to overgraze this place, that's for damn sure. But just in time Breedlove had his big heart attack and passed away." He chuckled. "Elisa credited it to the power of my prayers."

Leaphorn waited. And waited. But Demott was in no hurry to interrupt his memories. A breeze came down the stream, cool and fresh, rustling the leaves behind Leaphorn and humming the little song that breezes sing in the firs.

"It's a mighty pretty day," Demott said finally. "But blink your eyes twice and winter will be coming over the mountain."

"You were going to tell me what went wrong with Hal," Leaphorn said.

"I got no license to practice psychiatry," Demott said. He hesitated just a moment, but Leaphorn knew it was coming. It was something Demott wanted to talk about—and probably had for a long, long time.

"Or theology, either," he continued. "If that's the word for it. Anyway, you know how the story goes in our Genesis. God created Adam and gave him absolutely everything he could want, to see if he could handle it and still be obedient and do the right thing. He couldn't. So he fell from grace."

Demott glanced at Leaphorn to see if he was following.

"Got kicked out of paradise," Demott said.

"Sure," Leaphorn said. "I remember it." It wasn't quite the way he'd always heard it, but he could see the point Demott might make with his version.

"Old Breedlove put Hal in paradise," Demott

said. "Gave him everything. Prep school with the other rich kids, Dartmouth with the children of the ruling class—absolutely the very goddamn best that you can buy with money. If I was a preacher I'd say Hal's daddy spent a ton of money teaching his boy to worship Mammon— however you pronounce that. Anyway, it means making a god out of things you can buy." He paused, gave Leaphorn a questioning glance.

"We have some of the same philosophy in our own Genesis story," Leaphorn said. "First Man calls evil 'the way to make money.' Besides, I took a comparative religion course when I was a student at Arizona State. Made an A in it."

"Okay," Demott said. "Sorry. Anyway, when Hal was about a senior or so he flew into Mancos one summer in his own little airplane. Wanted us to grade out a landing strip for it near the house. I figured out how much it would cost, but his daddy wouldn't come up with the money. They got into a big argument over it. Hal had already been arguing with him about taking better care of this place, putting money in instead of taking it all out. I think it was about then that the old man got pissed off. He decided he'd give Hal the ranch and nothing else and let him see if he could live off it."

"Figuring he couldn't?"

"Yep," Hal said. "And of course the old man was right. Anyhow Breedlove eased up on the pressure for profits some and I got to put in a lot of fencing we needed to protect a couple of the sensitive pastures and get some equipment in there for some erosion control along the Cache.

Elisa and Hal got married after that. Everything going smooth. But that didn't last long. Hal took Elisa to Europe. Decided he just had to have himself a Ferrari. Great car for our kind of roads. But he bought it. And other stuff. Borrowed money. Before long we weren't bringing in enough from selling our surplus hay and the beef to cover his expenses. So he went to see the old man."

At this point Demott's voice was thickening. He paused, rubbed his shirtsleeve across his forehead. "Warm for this time of year," he said.

"Yeah," Leaphorn said, thinking it was a cool, dry sixty degrees or so even with the breeze gone.

"Anyway, he came back empty. Hal didn't have much to say but I believe they must have had a big family fight. I know for sure he tried to borrow from George—that's George Shaw, his cousin who used to come out and climb with us—and George must have turned him down, too. I think the family must have told him they were going ahead with the moly strip mine deal, and to hell with him."

"But they didn't," Leaphorn said. "Why not?"

"I think it was because the old man had his heart attack a little bit after that. When he passed away it hung everything up in probate court for a while. This ranch was in trust for Hal. He didn't get it until he turned thirty, but of course the family didn't control it anymore. That's sort of where it stood for a while."

Demott paused. He inspected his newly washed hand. Leaphorn was thinking, too, about this friction between Hal and his family and what it might imply.

"When I had my visit with Mrs. Rivera at the bank," Leaphorn said, "she told me things were starting to brew on the moly mine development again just before Hal disappeared. But this time she thought it was going to be a deal with a different mining company. She didn't think the family corporation was involved."

Demott lost interest in his hand.

"She tell you that?"

"That's what she said. She said a Denver bank was involved in the deal somehow. It was way too big an operation for her little bank to handle the money end of it."

"With Mrs. Rivera in business we don't really need a newspaper around here," Demott said.

"So I was thinking that if the family told Hal they were going to run right over him, maybe he decided he'd screw them instead. He'd make his own deal and cut them out."

"I think that's probably about the way it was," Demott said. "I know his lawyer told him all he had to do was slow things down in court long enough to get to his birthday. Then he'd have clear title and he could do what he wanted. That's what Elisa wanted him to do. But Hal was a fella who just could not wait. There were things he wanted to buy. Things he wanted to do. Places he hadn't seen yet. And he'd borrowed a lot of money he had to pay back."

Demott produced a bitter-sounding laugh. "Elisa didn't know about that. She didn't know he could use the ranch as collateral when he didn't own it yet. Came as quite a shock. But he had his lawyer work out some sort of deal which put up some sort of overriding interest in the place as a guarantee."

"Lot of money?"

"Quite a bit. He'd gotten rid of that little plane he had and made a down payment on a bigger one. After he disappeared we let them take the plane back but we had to pay back the loan."

With that, Demott rose and collected his tools. "Back to work," he said. "Sorry I didn't know anything that would help you."

"One more question. Or maybe two," Leaphorn said. "Are you still climbing?"

"Too old for it," he said. "What's that in the Bible about it? About when you get to be a man you put aside the ways of the boy. Something like that."

"How good was Hal?"

"He was pretty good but he was reckless. He took more chances than I like. But he had all the skills. If he'd put his mind to it he could have been a dandy."

"Could he have climbed Ship Rock alone?"

Demott looked thoughtful. "I thought about that a lot ever since Elisa identified his skeleton. I didn't think so at first, but I don't know. I wouldn't even try it myself. But Hal . . ." He shook his head. "If he wanted something, he just had to have it."

"George Shaw went out to the Maryboy place the other day and got permission for a climb," Leaphorn said. "Next day or two. Any idea what he thinks might be found up there?"

"George is going to climb it?" Demott's tone was incredulous and his expression shocked. "Where'd you hear that?"

"All I know is that he told me he paid Maryboy a hundred dollars for trespass rights. Maybe he'll get somebody to climb it but I think he meant he was going up himself."

"What the hell for?"

Leaphorn didn't answer that. He gave Demott some time to answer it himself.

"Oh," Demott said. "The son of a bitch."

"I would imagine he thinks maybe somebody gave Hal a little push."

"Yeah," Demott said. "Either he thinks I did it, and I left something behind that would prove it—and he could use that to void Elisa's inheritance—or he did it himself and he remembers that he left something up there that would nail him and he wants to go get it."

Leaphorn shrugged. "As good a guess as any."

Demott put down his tools.

"When Elisa came back from having the bones cremated she told me none of them had been broken," he said. "Some of them were disconnected, you know. That could have been done in a fall, or maybe the turkey vultures pulled 'em apart. They're strong enough to do that, I guess. Anyway, I hope it was a fall, and he didn't just get hung up there to starve to death for water. He could have been a damn good man."

"I never knew him," Leaphorn said. "To me he was just somebody to hunt for and never find."

"Well, he was a good, kind boy," Demott said. "Big-hearted." He picked up his tools again. "You know, when the cop came up to show Elisa Hal's stuff I saw that folder he had with him. He had it labeled 'Fallen Man.' I thought, Yes, that described Hal. The old man gave him paradise and it wasn't enough for him."

18

Lucy Sam had seemed glad to see Chee.

"I think they're going to be climbing up Tse´ Bit´ a´i´ again," she told Chee. "I saw a big car drive down the road toward Hosteen Maryboy's place two days ago, and it stayed a long time, and when I saw it coming back from there, I drove over there to see how he was doing and he told me about it."

"I heard about it, too," Chee said, thinking how hard it was to keep secrets in empty country.

"The man paid Hosteen Maryboy a hundred dollars," she said, and shook her head. "I don't think we should let them climb up there, even for a thousand dollars."

"I don't think so either," Chee said. "They have plenty of their own mountains to play around on."

"The one who lived here before," Lucy Sam

said, using the Navajo circumlocution to avoid saying the name of the dead, "he'd say that it would be like us Navajos climbing all over that big church in Rome, or getting up on top of the Wailing Wall, or crawling all over that place where the Islamic prophet went up to heaven."

"It's disrespectful," Chee agreed, and with that subject out of the way he shifted the conversation to cattle theft.

Had Hosteen Maryboy mentioned to her that he'd lost some more cattle? He had, and he was angry about it. There would have been enough money in those cows to make the last payments on his pickup truck.

Had Ms. Sam seen anything suspicious since the last time he'd been here? She didn't think so.

Could he look at the ledger where she kept her notes? Certainly. She would get it for him.

Lucy Sam extracted the book from its desk drawer and handed it to Chee.

"I kept it just the same way," she said, tapping the page. "I put down the date and the time right here at the edge and then I write down what I see."

As he leafed backward through the ledger, Chee saw that Lucy Sam wrote down a lot more than that. She made a sort of daily journal out of it, much as her father had done. And she had not just copied her father's system, she also followed his Franciscan padres' writing style—small, neat lettering in small, neat lines—which had become sort of a trademark of generations of those Navajos educated at St. Michael's School west of Window Rock. It was easily legible and wasted neither paper nor ink. But readable or not, Chee found nothing in it very helpful.

He skipped back to the date when he and Officer Manuelito had visited the site of the loose fence posts. They had rated an entry, right after Lucy Sam's notation that, "Yazzie came. Said he would bring some firewood" and just before, "Turkey buzzards are back." Between those Lucy had written, "Police car stuck on road under Tse´ Bit´ a´i´. Truck driver helps." Then, down the page a bit: "Tow truck gets police car." The last entry before the tow truck note reported, "That camper truck stopped. Driver looked around."

That camper truck? Chee felt his face flush with remembered embarrassment. That would have been Finch checking to see how thoroughly they had sprung his Zorro trap. He worked his way forward through the pages, learning more about kestrels, migrating grosbeaks, a local family of coyotes, and other Colorado Plateau fauna than he wanted to know. He also gained some insights into Lucy Sam's loneliness, but nothing that he could see would be useful to Acting Lieutenant Chee in his role as rustler hunter. If Zorro had come back to collect a load of Maryboy's cows from the place he'd left the hay, he'd done it when Lucy Sam wasn't looking.

But she was looking quite a lot. There was a mention of a "very muddy" white pickup towing a horse trailer on the dirt road that skirted Ship Rock, but no mention of it stopping. Chee made a mental note to check on that. About a dozen other vehicles had come in view of Lucy Sam's spotting scope, none of them potential rustlers.

They included a Federal Express delivery truck, which must have been lost, another mention of Finch's camper truck, and three pickups that she had identified with the names of local-area owners.

So what was useful about that? It told him that if Manuelito's network of watchers would pay off at all, it would require patience, and probably years, to establish suspicious-looking patterns. And it told him that Mr. Finch looked upon him as a competitor in his hunt for the so-called Zorro. Finch wanted him to write off Maryboy's loose-fence-posts location, but Finch hadn't written it off himself. He was keeping his eye on the spot. That produced another thought. Maryboy had been losing cattle before. Had either Lucy Sam or her father noticed anything interesting in the past? Specifically, had they ever previously noticed that white truck pulling its horse trailer? He would page back through the book and check on that when he had time. And he would also look through the back pages for school buses. He'd noticed a Lucy Sam mention of a school bus stuck on that same dirt road, and the road wasn't on a bus route. She had also mentioned "that camper truck" being parked almost all day at the base of the mountain the year before. Her note said "Climbing our mountain?"

Chee put down the ledger. Lucy Sam had gone out to feed her chickens and he could see her now in her sheep pen inspecting a young goat that had managed to entangle itself in her fence. He found himself imagining Janet Pete in that role and himself in old man Sam's wheelchair. It didn't scan. The white Porsche roared in and rescued her. But that wasn't fair. He was being racist. He had been thinking like a racist ever since he'd met Janet and fallen in love with her. He had been thinking that because her name was Pete, because her father was Navajo, her blood somehow would have taught her the ways of the *Dine´* and made her one of them. But only your culture taught you values, and the culture that had formed Janet was blue-blooded, white, Ivy League, chic, irreligious, old-rich Maryland. And that made it just about as opposite as it could get from the traditional values of his people, which made wealth a symbol for selfishness, and had caused a friend of his to deliberately stop winning rodeo competitions because he was getting unhealthily famous and therefore out of harmony.

Well, to hell with that. He got up, refocused the spotting scope, and found the place where the posts had been loosened. That road probably carried no more than a dozen vehicles a week—none at all when the weather was wet. It was empty today, and there was no sign of anything around Mr. Finch's Zorro trap. Beyond it in the pasture he counted eighteen cows and calves, a mixture of Herefords and Angus, and three horses. He scanned across the Maryboy grass-land to the base of Ship Rock and focused on the place where Lucy Sam had told him the climbing parties liked to launch their great adventures. Nothing there now but sage, chamisa, and a red-tailed hawk looking for her lunch.

Chee sat down again and picked up the oldest ledger. On his last visit he'd checked the entries on the days following Breedlove's disappearance but only with a casual glance. This time he'd be thorough.

Lucy Sam came in, washed her hands, and looked at him while she dried them.

"Something wrong?"

"Disappointed," Chee said. "So many details. This will take forever."

"He didn't have anything else to do," Lucy Sam said, voice apologetic. "After he got that sickness with his nerves, all he could do after that was get himself into his wheelchair. He couldn't go anyplace, he'd just sit there in the chair and sometimes he would read, or listen to the radio. And then he would watch through his telescope and keep his notes."

And he kept them very well, Chee noticed. Unfortunately they didn't seem to include what he wanted to find.

The date Hal Breedlove vanished came about midpoint in the old ledger. In Hosteen Sam's eyes it had been a windy day, cool, crows beginning to gather as they did when summer ended, flying in great, disorganized twilight flocks past Ship Rock to their roosting places in the San Juan River woods. Three oil field service trucks came down the road toward Red Rock and turned toward the Rattlesnake field. Some high clouds appeared but there had been no promise of rain.

The next day's entry was longer, devoted largely to the antics of four yearling coyotes who seemed to be trying to learn how to hunt in the prairie dog town down the slope. Interesting, but not what Chee was hoping for.

An hour and dozens of pages later, he closed the ledger, rubbed his eyes, and sighed.

"You want some lunch?" Lucy Sam asked, which was just the question Chee had been hoping to hear. Lucy had been there at the stove across the kitchen from him, cutting up onions, stirring, answering his questions about abbreviations he couldn't read or points he didn't understand, and the smell of mutton stew had gradually permeated the room and his senses—making this foolish search seem far less important than his hunger.

"Please," he said. "That smells just like the stew my mother used to make."

"Probably is the same," Lucy said. "Everybody has to use the same stuff—mutton, onions, potatoes, can of tomatoes, salt, pepper." She shrugged.

Like his mother's stew, it was delicious. He told Lucy what he was looking for—about the disappearance of Hal Breedlove and then his skeleton turning up on the mountain. He was looking for some idea of when Hal Breedlove returned to make his fatal climb.

"You find anything?"

"I think I learned that the man didn't come right back here after running away from his wife in Canyon de Chelly. At least there was no mention of anybody climbing."

"There would have been," she said. "How far did you get?"

"Just through the first eight weeks after he disappeared. It's going to take forever."

"You know, they always do it the same way. They start climbing just at dawn, maybe before. That's because they want to get down before dark, and because there's some places where that black rock gets terribly hot when the afternoon sun shines on it. So all you got to do is take a look at the first thing written down each day. He would always do the same every morning. He would get up at dawn and roll his wheelchair to the door. Then he would sing the song to Dawn Boy and bless the morning with his pollen. Next he would take a look at his mountain. If there was anything parked there where the climbers always left their cars, it would be the first thing he wrote down."

"I'll try that, then," he said.

On the page at which Chee reopened the ledger the first entry was marked 9/15/85, which was several pages and eight days too early. He glanced at the first line. Something about a kestrel catching a meadowlark. He paged forward, checking Lucy's advice by scanning down the first notes after dates.

Now he was at 9/18/85—halfway down the page. The first line read, "Climbers. Funny looking green van where climbers park. Three people going up. If Lucy gets back from Albuquerque I will get her to go into Shiprock and tell the police."

Chee checked the date again. September 18, 1985. That would be five days before Hal Breedlove disappeared from the Canyon de

Chelly. He scanned quickly down the page, looking for other mentions of the climbers. He found two more on the same day.

The first said: "They are more than half way up now, creeping along under a cliff—like bugs on a wall." And the second: "The headlights turned on on the fancy green car, and the inside lights. I see them putting away their gear. Gone now, and the police did not come. I told Maryboy he should not let anyone climb Tse´ Bit´ a´i´ but he did not listen to me."

Lucy was washing dishes in a pan of water on the table by the stove, watching him while she worked. He took the ledger to her, pointed to the entry.

"Do you remember this?" Chee asked. "It would have been about eleven years ago. Three people came to climb Ship Rock in some sort of green van. Your father wanted you to go tell the police but you had gone to Albuquerque."

Lucy Sam put on her glasses and read.

"Now why did I take the bus to Albuquerque?" she asked herself. "Yes," she answered. "Irma was having her baby there. Little Alice. Now she's eleven. And when I came home he was excited about those climbers. And angry. He wanted me to take him to see Hosteen Maryboy about it. And I took him over there, and they argued about it. I remember that."

"Did he say anything about the climbers?"

"He said they were a little bit slow. It was after dark when they got back to the car."

"Anything about the car?"

"The car?" She looked thoughtful. "I remember

he hadn't seen one like it before. He said it was ugly, clumsy looking, square like a box. It was green and it had a ski rack on top."

Chee closed the ledger and handed it to Lucy, trying to remember how Joe Leaphorn had described the car Hal Breedlove had abandoned after he had abandoned his wife. It was a recreational vehicle, green, something foreign-made. Yes. A Land-Rover. That would fit old man Sam's description of square and ugly.

"Thank you," he said to Lucy Sam. "I have to go now and see what Hosteen Maryboy can remember."

19

THE SUNSET HAD FLARED OUT behind Beautiful Mountain when Chee's patrol car bounced over Lucy Sam's cattle guard and gained the pavement. In the darkening twilight his headlights did little good and Chee almost missed the unmarked turnoff. That put him on the dirt track that led southward toward Rol Hai Rock, Table Mesa, and the infinity of empty country between these massive old buttes and the Chuska range.

Lucy Sam had told him: "Watch your odometer and in about eight miles from the turnoff place you come to the top of a ridge and you can see Maryboy's place off to the left maybe a mile."

"It'll be dark," Chee said. "Is the turnoff marked?"

"There's a little wash there, and a big cottonwood where you turn," she said. "It's the only tree out there, and Maryboy keeps a ghost light burning at his hogan. You can't miss it."

"Okay," Chee said, wishing she hadn't added that 'can't miss it' phrase. Those were the landmarks he always missed.

"There's a couple of places with deep sand where you cross arroyos. If you're going too slow, you might get stuck. But it's a pretty good road in dry weather."

Chee had been over this track a time or two when duty called, and did not consider it pretty good. It was bad. Too bad to warrant even one of those dim lines that were drawn on the official road map with an "unimproved" label and a footnoted warning. But Chee drove it a little faster than common sense dictated. He was excited. That boxy green vehicle must have been Hal Breedlove's boxy green Land-Rover—the same car he'd seen at the Lazy B. One of those three men who climbed out of it must have been Breedlove. Why not suspect that one of the other two was the man who had called Breedlove at the Thunderbird Lodge three or four days later and lured him away from his wife to oblivion? He would get a description from Maryboy if the old man could provide one. And he might be able to because those who live lonely lives where fellow humans are scarce tend to remember strangers—especially those on the strange mission of risking their lives on Ship Rock. Whatever, he would learn all he could and then he would call Leaphorn.

For a reason he didn't even try to understand, sitting across a table from the Legendary Lieutenant and telling him all this seemed extremely important to Chee. He had thought he was angry at Leaphorn for signing up with John McDermott. But Leaphorn's clear black eyes would study him with approval. Leaphorn's dour expression would soften into a smile. Leaphorn would think awhile and then Leaphorn would tell him how this bit of information had solved a terrible puzzle.

The odometer had clicked off almost exactly the eight prescribed miles from the turnoff and the track was topping the ridge. The moon was not yet up, but the ragged black shape of the Chuskas to the right and the flat-topped bulk of Table Mesa to the left were outlined against a sky a-dazzle with stars. Ahead an ocean of darkness stretched toward the horizon. Then the track curved past a hummock of Mormon tea, and there shone the Maryboy ghost light, punctuating the night with a bright yellow spot.

Chee made the left turn past the cottonwood Lucy Sam had described into two sandy ruts separated by a grassy ridge. They led him along a shallow wash toward the light. The track dipped down a slope and the bright spot became just a glow. He heard a thud from somewhere a long ways off. More like a sudden clapping sound. But he was too busy driving for the moment to wonder what caused it. The track had veered down the bank of the wash, tilting his police car. It entered a dense tangle of chaparral, converted by his headlights into a tunnel of brightness. He emerged from that.

The ghost light was gone.

Chee frowned, puzzled. He decided it must be just out of sight behind the screen of brush he was driving past. The track emerged from the brush into flat grassland where nothing grew higher than the sage. Still no ghost light. Why not? Maryboy had turned it off, what else? Or the bulb had burned out. Out here, Maryboy wouldn't be on a Rural Electrification Administration power line. He'd be running a windmill generator and battery system. Perhaps the batteries had gone dead. Nonsense. And yet the only reason one puts out a ghost light is because, for some reason, he believes he is threatened by the spirits of the dead. And if he believes that, why would he turn it off before Dawn Boy has restored harmony to the world? And why would he turn it off when he'd seen he had a visitor coming? Had Maryboy been expecting someone he would want to hide from?

Chee covered the last quarter mile slower than he would have had the light still been burning. His patrol car rolled past a plank stock pen with a loading ramp for cattle. His headlights reflected from the aluminum siding of a mobile home. Beyond it he could see the remains of a truck with its back wheels removed. Beyond that a fairly new pickup stood, and behind that, a small hogan, a small goat pen, a brush arbor, and two sheds. He parked a little further from the house than he would have normally and left the motor running a bit longer. And when he turned off the ignition he rolled down the window beside him and sat listening.

There was no light in the mobile home. Cold, dry December air poured through the truck window. It brought with it the smell of sage and dust, of dead leaves, of the goat pen. It brought the dead silence of a windless winter night. A dog emerged from one of the sheds, looking old, ragged, and tired. It limped toward his truck and stopped, the glare of his headlights reflecting from its eyes.

Chee leaned out of the window toward it. "Anybody home?" he asked. The dog turned and limped back into the shed. Chee switched off the car lights and waited, uneasy, for some sign of life from the house. Tapped his fingers on the steering wheel. Listened. From somewhere far away he heard the call of a burrowing owl hunting its prey. He thought. Someone turned off that damned ghost light. Therefore someone is here. I am absolutely not going back home and admit I came out here to talk to Maryboy and was too afraid of the dark to get out of the car.

Chee muttered an expletive, made sure that his official .38-caliber pistol was securely in its holster, took the flashlight from its rack, opened the car door, and got out—thankful for the policy that eliminated those dome lights that went on when the door opened. He stood beside the car, glad of the darkness, and shouted, "Hosteen Maryboy," and a greeting in Navajo. He identified himself by clan and family. He waited.

Only silence. But the sound of his own voice, loud and clear, had burst the bubble of his nervousness. He waited as long as politeness required, walked up to the entrance, climbed the two concrete block steps that led to the door, and tapped on the screen.

Nothing. He tapped again, harder this time.

Again, no response. He tried the screen, swung it open. Tried the door. The knob turned easily in his hand.

"Hosteen Maryboy," Chee shouted. "You've got company." He listened. Nothing. And opened the door to total darkness. Flicked on his flash.

If time is measurable in such circumstances, it might have taken a few nanoseconds for Chee's flashlight beam to traverse this tiny room from end to end and find it unoccupied. But even while this was happening, his peripheral vision was telling him otherwise. He turned the flashlight downward.

The body lay on its back, feet toward the door, as if the man had come to answer a visitor's summons and then had been knocked directly backward.

In the moment that elapsed before Chee snapped off the flash and jumped into the darkness of the house he had reached several conclusions. The man had been shot near the center of the chest. He was probably, but not certainly, Mr. Maryboy. The claplike sound he had heard had been the fatal shot. Thus the shooter must be nearby. Having shot Maryboy, and seen Chee's headlights, he had switched off the ghost light. And, more to the immediate point, Acting Lieutenant Jim Chee was likely to get shot himself. He leaned against the wall beside the door, drew the pistol, cocked it, and made sure the safety was off.

Chee spent the next few minutes listening to the silence and thinking his situation through. Among the aromas that came from Hosteen

Maryboy's kitchen he had picked up the acrid smell of burned gunpowder, confirming his guess that Maryboy had been shot only a few minutes ago. A frightening conclusion, it reinforced the evidence offered by the doused ghost light. The killer had not driven away. Chee would have met him on the access track. That he had walked away was possible but not likely. It would have meant abandoning his vehicle. Was it the pickup he'd noticed? Perhaps. But that was most likely Maryboy's. The killer, having seen him coming, would have had plenty of time to move his car but no way to drive out without meeting Chee on the track.

So what options did he have?

Chee squatted beside the body, felt for a pulse, and found none. The man was dead. That reduced the urgency a little. He could wait for daylight, which would even the odds. As it now stood the killer knew exactly where he was and he didn't have a clue. But waiting had a downside, too. It would occur to the killer sooner or later to fire a shot into the patrol car gas tank— or do something else to disable it. Then he could drive away unpursued. Or he might drain out some gasoline from any one of the vehicles, set this mobile home ablaze, and shoot Chee as he came out.

By now his eyes had adjusted to the darkness. Chee could easily see the windows. The starlight that came through them—dim as it was—allowed him to make out a chair, a couch, a table, and the door that led into the kitchen.

Could the killer be there? Or in the bedroom

beyond it? Not likely. He sat against the wall, holding his breath, focusing every instinct on listening. He heard nothing. Still, he dreaded the thought of being shot in the back.

Chee picked up the flash, held it far from his body, pointed both his pistol and the flash at the kitchen doorway, and flicked it on. Nothing moved in the part of the room visible to him. He edged to the door, keeping the flash away from him. The kitchen was empty. And so, when he repeated that process, were the bedroom and the tiny bath behind it.

Back in the living room, Chee sat on the couch and made himself as comfortable as the circumstances permitted. He weighed the options, found no new ones, imagined dawn coming, imagined the sun rising, imagined waiting and waiting, imagined finally saying to hell with it and walking out to the patrol car. Then he would either be shot, or he wouldn't be. If he wasn't shot, he would have to get on the radio and report this affair to Captain Largo.

"When did this happen?" the captain would ask, and then, "Why did you wait all night to report it?" and then, "Are you telling me that you sat in the house all night because you were afraid to come out?" And the only answer to that would be, "Yes, sir, that's what I did." And then, a little later, Janet Pete would be asking why he was being dismissed from the Navajo Tribal Police, and he would say— But would Janet care enough to ask? And did it matter anyway?

Something mattered. Chee got up, stood beside the door, looking and listening—

impressed with how bright the night now seemed outside the lightless living room. But he saw nothing, and heard nothing. He pushed open the screen and, pistol in hand, dashed to the patrol car, pulled open the door and slid in— crouched low in the seat, grabbed the mike, started the engine.

The night dispatcher responded almost instantly. "Have a homicide at the Maryboy place," Chee said, "with the perpetrator still in the area. I need—"

The dispatcher remembered hearing the sound of two shots, closely spaced, and of breaking glass, and something she described as "scratching, squeaking, and thumping." That was the end of the message from Acting Lieutenant Jim Chee.

20

AT FIRST CHEE WAS CONSCIOUS only of something uncomfortable covering much of his head and his left eye. Then the general numbness of the left side of his face registered on his consciousness and finally some fairly serious discomfort involving his left ribs. Then he heard two voices, both female, one belonging to Janet Pete. He managed to get his right eye in focus and there she was, holding his hand and saying something he couldn't understand. Thinking about it later, he thought it might have been "I told you so," or something to that effect.

When he awoke again, the only one in the room was Captain Largo, who was looking at him with a puzzled expression.

"What the hell happened out there?" Largo said. "What was going on?" And then, as if touched by some rare sentiment, he said, "How you feeling, Jim? The doctor tells us he thinks you're going to be all right."

Chee was awake enough to doubt that Largo expected an answer and gave himself a few moments to get oriented. He was in a hospital, obviously. Probably the Indian Health Service hospital at Gallup, but maybe Farmington. Obviously something bad had happened to him, but he didn't know what. Obviously again, it had something to do with his ribs, which were hurting now, and his face, which would be hurting when the numbness wore off. The captain could bring him up to date. And what day was it, anyway?

"What the hell happened?" Chee asked. "Car wreck?"

"Somebody shot you, goddammit," Largo said. "Do you know who it was?"

"Shot me? Why would somebody do that?" But even before he finished the sentence he began to remember. Hosteen Maryboy dead on the floor. Getting back into the patrol car. But it was very vague and dreamlike.

"They shot you twice through the door of the patrol car," Largo said. "It looked to Teddy Begayaye like you were driving away from the Maryboy place and the perpetrator fired two shots through the driver's-side door. Teddy found the empties. Thirty-eights by the looks of them, and of what they took out of you. But you had the window rolled down, so the slugs had to get through that shatterproof glass after they punched through the metal. The doc said that probably saved you."

Chee was more or less awake now and didn't feel like anything had saved him. He felt terrible. He said, "Oh, yeah. I remember some of it now."

"You remember enough to tell me who shot you? And what the hell you were doing out at the Maryboy place in the middle of the night? And who shot Maryboy? And why they shot him? Could you give us a description? Let us know what the hell we're looking for—man, woman, or child?"

Chee got most of the way through answering most of those questions before whatever painkillers they had shot into him in the ambulance, and the emergency room, and the operating room, and since then cut in again and he started fading away. The nurse came in and was trying to shoo Largo out. But Chee was just awake enough to interrupt their argument. "Captain," he said, hearing his voice come out soft and slurry and about a half mile away. "I think this Maryboy homicide goes all the way back to that Hal Breedlove case Joe Leaphorn was working on eleven years ago. That Fallen Man business. That skeleton up on Ship Rock. I need to talk to Leaphorn about . . ."

The next time he rejoined the world of the living he did so more or less completely. The pain was real, but tolerable. A nurse was doing something with the flexible tubing to which he was connected. A handsome, middle-aged woman whose name tag said SANCHEZ, she smiled at him, asked him how he was doing and if there was anything she could do for him.

"How about a damage assessment?" Chee

said. "A prognosis. A condition report. The captain said he thought I might live, but how about this left eye? And what's with the ribs?"

"The doctor will be in to see you pretty soon," the nurse said. "He's supposed to be the one to give the patient that sort of information."

"Why don't you do it?" Chee said. "I'm very, very interested."

"Oh, why not?" she said. She picked up the chart at the foot of his bed and scanned it. She frowned, made a disapproving clicking sound with her tongue.

"I don't like the sound of that," Chee said. "They're not going to decide I'm too banged up to be worth repairing?"

"We've got two misspelled words in this," she said. "They quit teaching doctors how to spell. But, no, I just wish I was as healthy as you are," she said. "I guess a body shop estimator would rate you as a moderately serious fender bender. Not bad enough to total you out, and just barely bad enough to cause the insurance company to send in its inspector and raise your premium rates."

"How about the eye?" Chee said. "It has a bandage over it."

"Because of"—she glanced down at the chart and read—"'multiple superficial lacerations caused by glass fragments.' But from the looks of this, no damage was done where it might affect your vision. Maybe you'll have some bumpy shaving on that cheek for a while, and need to grow yourself about an inch of new eyebrow. But apparently no sight impairment."

"That's good to hear," Chee said. "How about the rest of me?"

She looked down at him sternly. "Now when the doctor comes in, you've got to act surprised. All right? Everything he tells you is news to you. And for God's sake don't argue with him. Don't be saying: 'That ain't what Florence Nightingale told me.' You understand?"

Chee understood. He listened. Two bullets involved. One apparently had struck the thick bone at the back of the skull a glancing blow, causing a scalp wound, heavy bleeding, and concussion. The other, apparently fired after he had fallen forward, came through the door. While the left side of his face was sprayed with debris, the slug was deflected into his left side, where it penetrated the muscles and cracked two ribs.

"I'd say you were pretty lucky," the nurse said, looking at him over the chart. "Except maybe in your choice of friends."

"Yeah," Chee said, wincing. "Does that chart show who sent me those flowers?"

There were two bunches of them, one a dazzling pot of some sort of fancy chrysanthemum and the other a bouquet of mixed blossoms.

The nurse extracted the card from the bouquet. "Want me to read it to you?"

"Please," Chee said.

"It says, 'Learn to duck,' and it's signed, 'Your Shiprock Rat Terriers.'"

"Be damned," Chee said, and felt himself flushing with pleasure.

"Friends of yours?"

"Yes, indeed," Chee said. "They really are."

"And the other card reads 'Get well quick, be more careful and we have to talk,' and it's signed 'Love, Janet.'" With that Nurse Sanchez left him to think about what it might mean.

The next visitor was a well-dressed young man named Elliott Lewis, whose tidy business suit and necktie proclaimed him a special agent of the Federal Bureau of Investigation. Nevertheless, he displayed his identification to Chee. His interest was in the wrongful death of Austin Maryboy, such felonious events on a federal reservation being under the jurisdiction of the Bureau. Chee told him what he knew, but not what he guessed. Lewis, in the best FBI tradition, told Chee absolutely nothing.

"This thing must have made some sort of splash in the papers," Chee said. "Am I right about that?"

Lewis was restoring his notebook and tape recorder to his briefcase. "Why you say that?"

"Because the FBI got here early."

Lewis looked up from the housekeeping duties in his briefcase. He suppressed a grin and nodded. "It made the front page in the *Phoenix Gazette*, and the *Albuquerque Journal*, and the *Deseret News*," he said. "And I guess you could add the *Gallup Independent*, *Navajo Times*, *Farmington Times*, and the rest of 'em."

"How long you been assigned out here?" Chee asked.

"This is week three," Lewis said. "I'm fresh out of the academy but I've heard about our reputation for chasing the headlines. And you'll notice I've already got the names of the pertinent papers memorized."

Which left Chee regretting the barb. What was Lewis but another young cop trying to get along? Maybe the Bureau would teach him its famous arrogance. But it hadn't yet, and maybe with the old J. Edgar Hoover gang fading away, it was dropping the superman pose. Chee had worked with both kinds.

Lewis was also efficient. He asked the pertinent questions, which made it apparent that the theory of the crime appealing to the Bureau was a motive involving cattle theft—of which Maryboy was known to be a victim. Chee considered introducing mountain climbing into the conversation but decided against it. His head ached. Life was already too complicated. And how the devil could he explain it anyway? Lewis closed his notebook, switched off his tape recorder, and departed.

Chee turned his thoughts to the note Janet had signed. Remembering earlier notes, it sounded cool, considering the circumstances. Or was that his imagination? And there she was now, standing in the doorway, smiling at him, looking beautiful.

"You want a visitor?" she said. "They gave the fed first priority. I had to wait."

"Come in," he said, "and sit and talk to me."

She did. But en route to the chair, she bent over, found an unbandaged place, and kissed him thoroughly.

"Now I have two reasons to be mad at you," she said.

He waited.

"You almost got yourself killed," she said. "That's the worst thing. Lieutenants are supposed to send their troops out to get shot at. They're not supposed to get shot themselves."

"I know," he said. "I've got to work on it."

"And you insulted me," she added. "Are you recovered enough to talk about that?" No more banter now. The smile was gone.

"Did I?" Chee said.

"Don't you think so? You implied that I had tricked you. You pretty well said that I had used you to get information to pass along to John."

Chee didn't respond to that. "John," he was thinking. Not "McDermott," or "Mr. McDermott," but "John."

He shrugged. "I apologize, then," he said. "I think I misunderstood things. I had the impression the son of a bitch was your enemy. Everything I know about the man is what you told me. About how he had used you, taken advantage of his position. You the student and the hired hand. Him the famous professor and the boss. That made him your enemy, and anyone who treats you like that is my enemy."

She sat very still, hands folded in her lap, while he said all that. "Jim," she began, and then stopped, her lower lip between her teeth.

"I guess it shocked me," he said. "There I was, the naive romantic, thinking of myself as Sir Galahad saving the damsel from the dragon, and I find out the damsel is out partying with the dragon."

Janet Pete's complexion had become slightly pink.

"I agree with some of that," she said. "The part about you being naive. But I think we'd better talk about this later. When you're better. I shouldn't have brought it up now. I wasn't thinking. I'm sorry. I want you to hurry up and get well, and this isn't good for you."

"Okay," Chee said. "I'm sorry I hurt your feelings."

She stopped at the door. "I hope one really good thing will come out of this," she said. "I hope this being almost killed will cure you of being a policeman."

"What do you mean?" Chee said, knowing full well what she meant.

"I mean you could stay in law enforcement without carrying that damned gun, and doing that sort of work. You could take your pick of half a dozen jobs in—"

"In Washington," Chee said.

"Or elsewhere. There are dozens of offices. Dozens of agencies. In the BIA, the Justice Department. I heard of a wonderful opening in Miami. Something involving the Seminole agency."

Chee's head ached. He didn't feel well. He said, "Thanks for coming, Janet. Thanks for the flowers."

And then she was gone.

Chee drifted into a shallow sleep punctuated by uneasy dreams. He was awakened to take antibiotics and to have his temperature and vital signs checked. He dozed again, and was aroused to eat a bowl of lukewarm cream of mushroom soup, a portion of cherry Jell-O, and some banana-flavored yogurt. He was reminded that he was supposed to rise from his bed now and walk around the room for a while to get everything working properly. While dutifully doing that, he sensed a presence behind him.

Joe Leaphorn was standing in the doorway, his face wearing that expression of disapproval that Chee had learned to dread when he was the Legendary Lieutenant's assistant and gofer.

21

"ARENT YOU SUPPOSED TO BE IN BED?" Leaphorn asked. He was wearing a plaid shirt and a Chicago Cubs baseball cap, but even that didn't minimize the effect. He still looked to Chee like the Legendary Lieutenant.

"I'm just doing what the doc told me to do," Chee said. "I'm getting used to walking so these ribs don't hurt." He was also getting used to looking at the image of himself in the mirror with one eye bandaged and the other one hideously black. But he wasn't admitting that to Leaphorn. In fact, he was disgusted with himself for explaining his conduct to Leaphorn. He should have told him to bug off. But he didn't. Instead he said, "Yes, sir. I'm being the model patient so they'll give me time off for good behavior."

"Well, I'm glad it's not as bad as I first heard it was," Leaphorn said, and helped himself to a chair. "I'd heard he almost killed you."

They dealt with all the facts of the incident then, quickly and efficiently—became two professionals talking about a crime. Chee eased himself back onto the bed. Leaphorn sat, holding his cap. His bristly short haircut was even grayer now than Chee had remembered.

"I'm not going to stay long," Leaphorn said. "They told me you're supposed to be resting. But I have something I wanted to tell you."

"I'm listening," Chee said, thinking, *You also have something you want to ask me*. But so what? That was the tried-and-true Leaphorn strategy. There was nothing underhanded about it.

Leaphorn cleared his throat. "You sure you don't want to get some rest?"

"To hell with resting," Chee said. "I want out of here and I think they may let me go this evening. The doc wants to change the bandages again and check everything."

"The quicker the better," Leaphorn said. "Hospitals are dangerous places."

Chee cut off his laugh just as it started. Leaphorn's wife had died in this very hospital, he remembered. A brain tumor removed. Everything went perfectly. The tumor was benign. But the staph infection that followed was lethal.

"Yes," he said. "I want to go home."

"I've done a little checking," Leaphorn said. He made an abashed gesture. "When you've been in the NTP as long as I was—and out of it just a little bit—then it seems people have trouble remembering you're just a civilian. That you're no longer official."

"Lieutenant," Chee said, and laughed. "I'm

afraid you're always going to seem official to a lot of people. Including me."

Leaphorn looked vaguely embarrassed by that. "Well, anyway, things are going about the way you'd expect. It was a slim day for news, and the papers made a pretty big thing out of it. That brings the feds hurrying right in. You've seen the newspapers, I guess?"

"No," Chee said, and pointed to his left eye. "I haven't been in very sharp focus until today. But I've seen the fed."

"Well, you can't be surprised they're on it. Big headlines. Slayer shoots policeman at the scene of the murder. No suspect. No motive. Big mystery. Big headlines. So the Bureau moves in right away without requiring the usual prodding. They found out that Maryboy had been having some livestock stolen. They found out you'd gone out there to check on rustling. So they're working that angle some . . ." Leaphorn paused, gave Chee a wry grin. "You know what I mean?"

Chee laughed. "Unless they've reformed since day before yesterday it means they're having my friends in the NTP at Shiprock working on it, and the Arizona Highway Patrol, and the New Mexico State Police, and the San Juan and McKinley County sheriff's deputies."

Leaphorn didn't object to that analysis. "And then they think maybe there might be a drug angle, or a gang angle. All those good things," he added.

"No other theories?"

"Not from what I'm hearing."

"You're telling me something right now," Chee said, unable to suppress a grin, even though it hurt. "I think you're telling me that neither the feds nor anyone else has shown any interest in trying to tie an eleven-year-old runaway-husband case into this felony homicide. Am I right?"

Leaphorn was never very much a man for laughing, but his amusement showed. "That is correct," he said.

"I've been trying to visualize that," Chee said. "You've known Captain Largo longer than I have. But can you visualize him trying to explain to some special agent that I had actually gone out to interview Maryboy to see if he could identify who had climbed Ship Rock eleven years ago, because we were still working on a 1985 missing person case? Can you imagine Largo doing it? Trying to get the guy's attention, especially when Largo doesn't understand it himself."

The amusement had left Leaphorn's face.

"I guessed that's why you were out there," he said. "What'd you find out?"

Chee couldn't pass up this opportunity to needle the Legendary Lieutenant. Besides, Leaphorn was working for McDermott. So Chee said, "Nothing. Maryboy was dead when I got there."

"No. No." Leaphorn let his impatience show. "I meant what had you learned that caused you to go out there? In the night?"

The moment had come:

"I learned that on the morning of September 18, 1985, a dark green, square, ugly recreational vehicle with a ski rack on its roof was driven to the usual climbers' launch site on Maryboy's grazing lease. Three men got out and climbed Ship Rock. Maryboy had given them trespass permission. Now, to bring things up to date, I learned yesterday that John McDermott hands this same Hosteen Maryboy one hundred dollars for trespass rights for another climb. I presume that George Shaw and others intend to climb the mountain, probably just as quickly as they can get a party organized. So, I went out to learn if Hosteen Maryboy remembered who had paid him for climbing trespass rights back in 1985."

Chee recited this slowly, watching Leaphorn's face. It became absolutely still. Breathing stopped. The green vehicle was instantly translated into Breedlove's status truck, the date into a week before Hal had begun his vanishing act, and two days before his all-important thirtieth birthday. All that, and all the complex implications suggested, had been processed by the time Chee finished his speech. Leaphorn's first question, Chee knew, would be how he had learned this. Whether the source of this information was reliable. Well, let him ask it. Chee was ready.

Leaphorn sighed.

"I wonder how many people knew that George Shaw was looking for a team to climb that mountain with him," Leaphorn said.

Chee looked at the ceiling, clicked his tongue against his teeth, and said, "I have no idea." Why did he continue trying to guess how the Legendary Lieutenant's mind worked? It was miles and miles beyond him.

Leaphorn abruptly clapped his hands together.

"Now you've given us the link that can fit the pattern together," Leaphorn said, with rare exuberance. "Finally something to work with. I spent most of my time for months trying to think this case through and I didn't come up with this. Emma was still healthy then, and she thought about it, too. And I've spent a lot of thought on it since then, even though we officially gave up. And in—how many days was it?—less than ten, you come up with the link."

Chee found himself baffled. But Leaphorn was beaming at him, full of pride. That made it both better and worse.

"But we still don't know who killed Hosteen Maryboy," Chee said, thinking at least he didn't know.

"But now we have something to work on," Leaphorn said. "Another part of the pattern takes shape."

Chee said, "Umm," and tried to look thoughtful instead of confused.

"Breedlove's skeleton is found on Ship Rock," Leaphorn said, holding up a blunt trigger finger. "Amos Nez is promptly shot." Leaphorn added a second finger. "Now, shortly thereafter, just as arrangements are being made for another climb of Ship Rock, one of the last people to see Breedlove is shot." He added a third finger.

"Yes," Chee said. "If we have all the pertinent facts it makes for a short list of suspects."

"I can add a little light to that," Leaphorn said. "Actually, it's what I came in to tell you. Eldon Demott told me some interesting things about Hal. The key one was that he'd quarreled with his father, and his family. He had decided to cut the family corporation out of the mining lease as soon as he inherited the ranch."

"Did the family know that?"

"Demott presumed they did. So do I. He probably told them himself. Demott understood Hal had tried to get money out of his father, and got turned down, and came home defiant. But even if he tried to keep it secret, the money people seemed to have known about it. Hal was in debt. Borrowing money. And if the money people knew, I'm sure the word got back to the Breedlove Corporation."

"Ah," Chee said. "So we add George Shaw to the list of people who would be happy if Hal Breedlove died before he celebrated the pertinent birthday."

"Or even happier to prove that Hal Breedlove was murdered by his wife, which would mean she couldn't inherit. I would guess that would put the ranch back into probate. And the Breedlove family would be the heir."

They sat for a while, thinking about it.

"If you want a little bit more confusion, I turned up a possible boyfriend for Elisa," Leaphorn said. "It turns out their climbing team was once a foursome." He explained to Chee what Mrs. Rivera had told him of Tommy Castro and what Demott had added to it.

"Another rock climber," Chee said. "You think he killed Hal to gain access to the widow? Or the widow and Castro conspired to get Hal out of the way?"

"If so, they didn't do much about it. As far as we know, that is."

"How about Shaw as the man who left Breedlove dying on the ledge? Or maybe gave him a shove?"

Leaphorn shrugged. "I think I like one of the Demotts a little better."

"How about the shootings?"

"About the same," Leaphorn said.

They thought about it some more, and Chee felt himself being engulfed with nostalgia. Remembering the days he'd worked for Leaphorn, sat across the desk in the lieutenant's cramped second-floor office in Window Rock trying to put the pieces of something or other together in order to understand a crime. Stressful as it had been, demanding as Leaphorn tended to be, it had been a joyful time. And damn little paperwork.

"Do you still have your map?" Chee asked.

If Leaphorn heard the question he didn't show it. He said, "The problem here is time."

Lost again, Chee said, "Time?"

"Think how different things would be if Hal Breedlove's thirtieth birthday had been a week after he disappeared, instead of a week before," Leaphorn said.

"Yeah," Chee said. "Wouldn't that have simplified things?"

"Then the presumption that went with his

disappearance would have been foul play. A homicide to prevent the inheritance."

"Right," Chee said.

Leaphorn rose, recovered his Cubs cap from Chee's table.

"Do you think you can get Largo to make Ship Rock off limits to climbers for a few days?"

"Do I tell him why?" Chee asked.

"Tell him that mountain climbers have this tradition of leaving a record behind when they reach a difficult peak. Ship Rock is one of those. On top of it, there's a metal box—one of those canisters the army uses to hold belted machine gun ammunition. It's waterproof, of course, and there's a book in it that climbers sign. They jot down the time and the date and any note they'd like to leave to those who come later."

"Shaw told you that?"

"No. I've been asking around. But Shaw would certainly know it."

"You want to keep Shaw from going up and getting it," Chee said. "Didn't you tell me you were working for him?"

"He retained me to find out everything I could about what happened to Hal Breedlove," Leaphorn said. "How can I learn anything I can depend on from that book if Mr. Shaw gets it first?"

"Oh," Chee said.

"I want to know who was in that party of three who made the climb before Hal disappeared. Was one of them Hal, or Shaw, or Demott, or maybe even Castro? Three men, Hosteen Sam said. But how could he be sure of gender through a spotting scope miles away? Climbers wear helmets and they don't wear skirts. Was one of the three Mrs. Breedlove? If Hal was one of them and he got to the top, his name will be in the book. If it isn't, that might help explain why he went back after he vanished from Canyon de Chelly: to try again. If he got to the top that time, his name and the date will be there. I want to know when he made the climb that killed him."

"It wasn't in the first forty-three days after he disappeared," Chee said.

"What?" Leaphorn said, startled. "How do you know that?"

Chee described Hosteen Sam's ledger, his habit of rolling his wheelchair to the window each day after his dawn prayers and looking at the mountain. He described Sam's meticulous entry system. "But there was no mention of a climbing party from September eighteenth, when he watched the three climb it and then complained to Maryboy about it, through the first week of November. So if Hal climbed it in that period he had to somehow sneak in without old Sam seeing him. I doubt if that's possible, even if he knew Sam would be watching—which he wouldn't—or had some reason to be sneaky. I'm told that that's the starting point for the only way up."

"I think we need to keep that ledger somewhere safe," Leaphorn said. "It seems to be telling us that Breedlove was alive a lot longer than I'd been thinking."

"I'll call Largo and get him to stall off climbing for a while," Chee said. "And I'll call my office. Manuelito knows Lucy Sam. She can go out and take custody of that ledger for a little while."

"You take care of yourself," Leaphorn said, and headed for the door.

"Wait a second. If we get the climbing stopped, how are you going to get someone up there to look at the register?"

"I'm going to rent a helicopter," Leaphorn said. "I know a lawyer in Gallup. A rock climber who's been up Ship Rock himself. I think he'd be willing to go up with me and the pilot, and we put him down on the top, and he takes a look."

"And brings down the book."

"I didn't want to do that. I'm a civilian now. I don't want to tamper with evidence. We'll take along a camera."

"And make some photocopies?"

"Exactly."

"That's going to cost a lot of money, isn't it?"

"The Breedlove Corporation is paying for it," Leaphorn said. "I've got their twenty thousand dollars in the bank."

22

THE KOAT-TV WEATHER MAP the previous night had shown a massive curve of bitterly cold air bulging down the Rocky Mountains out of Canada, sliding southward. The morning news reported snow across Idaho and northern Utah, with livestock warnings out. The weather lady called it a "blue norther" and told the Four Corners to brace for it tomorrow. But at the moment it was a beautiful morning for a helicopter ride, if you enjoyed such things, which Leaphorn didn't.

The last time he'd ridden in one of these ugly beasts he was being rushed to a hospital to have a variety of injuries treated. It was better to go when one was healthy, he thought, but not much.

However, Bob Rosebrough seemed to be enjoying it, which was good because Rosebrough had volunteered to climb down the copter's ladder to the tip of Ship Rock, photograph the documents in the box there, and climb back up.

"No problem, Joe," he'd said. "Climbing down a cliff can be harder than climbing up it, but ladders are different. And I sort of like the idea of being the first guy to climb down onto the top of Ship Rock." Liking the idea meant he wouldn't accept any payment for taking the day off from his Gallup law practice. That appealed to Leaphorn. The copter rental was taking eight hundred dollars out of the Breedlove Corporation's twenty thousand retainer, and Leaphorn was beginning to have some ethical qualms about how he was using that fee.

The view now was spectacular. They were flying south from the Farmington Airport and if Leaphorn had cared to look straight down, which he didn't, he would have been staring into row after row of dragon's teeth that erosion had formed on the east side of the uplift known as the Hogback. The rising sun outlined the teeth with shadows, making them look like a grotesquely oversized tank trap—even less hospitable than they appeared from the ground. The slanting light was also creating a silver mirror of the surface of Morgan Lake to the north and converting the long plume of steam from the stacks of the Four Corners Power Plant into a great white feather. The scale of it made even Leaphorn, a desert rat raised in the vastness of the Four Corners, conscious of its immensity.

The pilot was pointing down.

"How about having to land in those shark's teeth?" he asked. "Or worse, parachuting down into it. Just think about that. It makes your crotch hurt."

Leaphorn preferred to think of something else, which in its way was equally unpleasant. He thought about the oddity of murder in general, and of this murder in particular. Hal Breedlove disappears. Ten quiet years follow. Then, rapidly, in a matter of days, an unidentified skeleton is found on the mountain, apparently a man who has fallen to his death in a climbing accident. Then Amos Nez is shot. Next the bones are identified as the remains of Hal Breedlove. Then Hosteen Maryboy is murdered. Cause and effect, cause and effect. The pattern was there if he could find the missing part—the part that would bring it into focus. At the center of it, he was certain, was the great dark volcanic monolith that was now looming ahead of them like the ruins of a Gothic cathedral built for giants. On top of it a metal box was cached. In the box would be another piece to fit into the puzzle of Hal Breedlove.

"The spire on the left is it," Rosebrough said, his voice sounding metallic through the earphones they were wearing. "They look about the same height from this vantage, but the one on the left is the one you have to stand on top of if you want to say you've climbed Ship Rock."

"I'm going to circle around it a little first," the pilot said. "I want to get a feeling for wind, updrafts, downdrafts, that sort of thing. Air currents can be tricky around something like this. Even on a calm, cool morning."

They circled. Leaphorn had been warned

about what looking down while a copter is spiraling does to one's stomach. He folded his hands across his safety belt and studied his knuckles.

"Okay," Rosebrough said. "That's it just below us."

"It doesn't look very flat," the pilot said, sounding doubtful. "And how big is it?"

"Not very," Rosebrough said. "About the size of a desktop. The box is on that larger flattish area just below. I'll have to climb down to get it."

"You have twenty feet of ladder, but I guess I could get close enough for you to just jump down," the pilot said.

Rosebrough laughed. "I'll take the ladder," he said.

And he did.

Leaphorn looked. Rosebrough was on the mountain, standing on the tiny sloping slab that formed the summit, then climbing down to the flatter area. He removed an olive drab U.S. Army ammunition box from the crack, opened it, removed the ledger, and tried to protect it from the wind produced by the copter blades. He waved them away. Leaphorn, stomach churning, resumed the study of his knuckles.

"You all right?" the pilot asked.

"Fine," Leaphorn said, and swallowed.

"There's a barf bag there if you need it."

"Fine," Leaphorn said.

"He's taking the pictures now," the pilot said. "Photographing one of the pages."

"Okay," Leaphorn said.

"It'll just be a minute."

Leaphorn, busy now with the bag, didn't respond. But by the time the rhetorical minute had dragged itself past and Rosebrough was climbing back into the copter, he was feeling a little better.

"I took a bunch of different exposures so we'll have some good ones," he said, settling himself in his seat and fastening his safety belt. "And I shot the five or six pages before and after. That what you wanted?"

"Fine," Leaphorn said, his mind working again, buzzing with the questions that had brought them up here. "Did you find Breedlove's name? And who else—" He stopped. He was breaking his own rule. Much better to let Rosebrough tell what he had found without intervention.

"He signed it," Rosebrough said, "and wrote 'vita brevis.'"

He didn't explain to Leaphorn that the inscription was Latin and provide the translation—which was one of the reasons Leaphorn liked the man. Why would Breedlove have bothered to leave that epigram? "Life is short." Was it to explain why he'd taken the dangerous way down in case he didn't make it? He'd worry about that later.

"Funny thing," Rosebrough said. "No one else signed it on that date. I told you I didn't think he could possibly climb it alone. But it looks like maybe I was wrong."

"Maybe the people with him had climbed it before," Leaphorn said.

"That wouldn't matter. You'd still want to

have it on the record that you'd done it again. It's a hell of a hard climb."

"Anything else?"

"He said he made it up at eleven twenty-seven A.M. and under that he wrote, 'Four hours, twenty-nine minutes up. Now, I'm going down the fast way.'"

"Looks like he tried," the pilot said. "But it took him about eleven years to make it all the way to the bottom."

"Could he have climbed it that fast alone?" Leaphorn asked. "Is that time reasonable?"

Rosebrough nodded. "These days the route is so well mapped, a good, experienced crew figures about four hours up and three hours down."

"How about the fast way down?" Leaphorn asked. To him it sounded a little like a suicide note. "What do you think he meant by that?"

Rosebrough shook his head. "It took teams of good climbers years to find the way you can get from the bottom to the top. Even that's no cinch. It involves doing a lot of exposed climbing, with a rope to save you if you slip. Then you have to climb down a declivity to reach the face where you can go up again. That's the way everybody who's ever got to the top of Ship Rock got there. And as far as I know, that's the way everybody always got down."

"So there isn't any 'fast way down'?"

Rosebrough gave that some thought. "There has been some speculation of a shortcut. But it would involve a lot of rappelling, and I never heard of anyone actually trying it. I think it's way too dangerous."

They were moving away from Ship Rock now, making the long slide down toward the Farmington Airport. Leaphorn was feeling better. He was thinking that whatever Breedlove had meant by the fast way down, he had certainly done something dangerous.

"I'm thinking about that rappel route," Rosebrough said. "If he tried that by himself, that would help explain where they found the skeleton." He was looking at Leaphorn quizzically. "You're awfully quiet, Joe. Are you okay? You're looking pale."

"I'm feeling pale," Leaphorn said, "but I'm quiet because I'm thinking about the other two people who made the climb with him that day. Didn't they get all the way up? Or what?"

"Who were they?" Rosebrough asked. "I know most of the serious rock climbers in this part of the world."

"We don't know," Leaphorn said. "All we have are the notes of an old mountain watcher. Sort of shorthand, too. He just jotted down nine slash eighteen slash eighty-five and said three men had parked at the jump-off site and were climbing the—"

"Wait a minute," Rosebrough said. "You said nine eighteen eighty-five? That's not the date Breedlove wrote. He put down nine thirty eighty-five."

Leaphorn digested that. No thought of nausea now. "You're sure?" he asked. "Breedlove dated his climb September thirty. Not September eighteen."

"I'm dead certain," Rosebrough said. "That's

what the photo is going to show. Was I confused or something?"

"No," Leaphorn said. "I was the one who was confused."

"You sure you feel all right?"

"I feel fine," Leaphorn said. Actually he was feeling embarrassed. He had been conned, and it had taken him eleven years to get his first solid inkling of how they had fooled him.

23

CHEE HAD DECIDED THE GREASE in the frying pan was hot enough and was pulling the easy-open lid off the can of Vienna sausages when the headlight beam flashed across his window. He flicked off his house trailer's overhead light—something he wouldn't have considered doing a few days ago. But his cracked ribs still ached, and the person who had caused that was still out there somewhere. Possibly in the car that was now rolling to a stop under the cottonwood outside.

Whoever had driven it got out and walked into the headlights where Chee could see him. It was Joe Leaphorn, the Legendary Lieutenant, again. Chee groaned, said, "Oh, shit!" and switched on the light.

Leaphorn entered hat in hand. "It's getting cold," he said. "The TV forecaster said there's a snow warning out for the Four Corners. Livestock warning. All that."

"It's just about time for that first bad one," Chee said. "Can I take your hat?"

Which got Leaphorn's mind off the weather. "No. No," he said, looking apologetic. He regretted the intrusion, the lateness of the hour, the interruption of Chee's supper. He would only take a moment. He wanted Chee to see what they'd found in the ammunition box on top of Ship Rock. He extracted a sheaf of photographs from the big folder he'd been carrying and handed them to Chee.

Chee spread them on the table.

"Note the date of the signature," Leaphorn said. "It's the week after Breedlove disappeared from Canyon de Chelly."

Chee considered that. "Wow," he said. And considered it again. He studied the photograph. "Is this it? No one else signed the book that day?"

"Only Breedlove," Leaphorn said. "And I'm told that it's traditional for everyone in the climbing party to sign if they get to the top."

"Well, now," Chee said. He tapped the inscription. "It looks like Latin. Do you know what it means?"

Leaphorn told him the translation. "But what did he mean by it? Your guess is as good as mine." He explained to Chee what Rosebrough had told him about the 'fast way down' remark— that if Hal had tried this dangerous rappelling route it might explain how his body came to be on the ledge where it was found.

They stood at the table, Chee staring at the photograph and Leaphorn watching Chee. The aroma of extremely hot grease forced itself into Leaphorn's consciousness, along with the haze of blue smoke that accompanied it. He cleared his throat.

"Jim," he said. "I think I interrupted your cooking."

"Oh," Chee said. He dropped the photograph, snatched the smoking pan off the propane burner, and deposited it outside on the doorstep. "I was going to scramble some eggs and mix in these sausages," he said. "If you haven't eaten I can dump in a few more."

"Fine," said Leaphorn, who had deposited his breakfast in the barf bag, had been suffering too much residual queasiness for lunch, and had been too busy since to stop for dinner. In his current condition, even the smell of burning grease aroused his hunger.

They replaced the photos with plates, retrieved the frying pan, replenished the incinerated grease with a chunk of margarine, put on the coffeepot, performed those other duties required to prepare dinner in a very restricted space, and dined. Leaphorn had always tried to avoid Vienna sausages even as emergency rations but now he found the mixture remarkably palatable. While he attacked his second helping, Chee picked up the crucial photograph and resumed his study.

"I hesitate to mention it," Chee said, "but what do you think of the date?"

"You mean being a date when the keen eye of Hosteen Sam saw no one climbing Ship Rock?"

"Exactly," Chee said.

"I've reached no precise conclusion," Leaphorn said. "What do you think?"

"About the same," Chee said. "And how about nobody at all signing the book twelve days earlier? What do you think about that? I'm thinking that the three people who old man Sam saw climbing up there must not have made it to the top. Either that, or they were too modest to take credit for it. Or, if his ledger hadn't told me how exactly precise Sam was, I'd think he got his dates wrong."

Leaphorn was studying him. "You think there's no chance of that, then?"

"I'd say none. Zero. You should see the way he kept that ledger. That's not the explanation. Forget it."

Leaphorn nodded. "Okay, I will."

The entry signed by Breedlove was near the center of the page. Above it the register had been signed by four men, none with names familiar to Chee, and dated April 4, 1983. Below it, a three-climber party—two with Japanese names—had registered their conquest of the Rock with Wings on April 28, 1988.

"Skip back to September eighteenth," Leaphorn said. "Let's say that Hal was one of the three Hosteen Sam saw climbing. It sounds like the car they climbed out of was that silly British recreation vehicle he drove. And then let's say they didn't make it to the top because Hal screwed up. So Hal broods about it. He gets the call at Canyon de Chelly from one of his climbing buddies. He decides to go back and try again."

"All right," Chee said. "Then we'll suppose the climbing buddy went with him, they tried the dangerous way down. This time the climbing buddy—and let's call him George Shaw—well, George screws up and drops Hal down the cliff. He feels guilty and he figures Hal's dead anyway, so slips away and tells no one."

"Yeah," Leaphorn said. "I thought about that. Trouble is, why hadn't the climbing buddy signed the register before they started down?"

Chee shook his head, dealt Leaphorn some more of the Vienna-and-eggs mixture, and put down the pan.

"Modesty, you think?" Leaphorn said. "He didn't want to take the credit?"

"The only reason I can think of involves first-degree murder," Chee said. "The premeditated kind."

"Right," Leaphorn said. "Now, how about a motive?"

"Easy," Chee said. "It would have something to do with the ranch, and with that moly mine deal."

Leaphorn nodded.

"Now Hal has inherited. It's his. So let's say George Shaw figures Hal's going to keep his threat and do his own deal on the mineral lease, cutting out Shaw and the rest of the family. So Shaw drops him."

"Maybe," Leaphorn said. "One problem with that, though."

"Or maybe Demott's the climbing buddy. He knows Hal's going for the open strip mine, so he knocks him off to save his ranch. But what's the problem with the first idea?"

"Elisa inherits from Hal. Shaw would have to deal with her."

"Maybe he thought he could?"

"He says he couldn't. He told me this afternoon that Elisa was just as fanatical about the ranch as her brother. Said she told him there wouldn't be any strip-mining on it as long as she was alive."

"You saw Shaw today?" Chee sounded as much shocked as surprised.

"Sure," Leaphorn said. "I showed him the photographs. After all, I spent his money getting them."

"What'd he think?"

"He acted disappointed. Probably was. He'd like to be able to prove that Hal was dead about a week or so before he signed that register."

Chee nodded.

"There's a problem with your second theory, too."

"What?"

"I was talking with Demott on the telephone September twenty-fourth. Twice, in fact."

"You remember that? After eleven years?"

"No. I keep a case diary. I looked it up."

"Mobile phone, maybe?"

"No. I called him at the ranch. Elisa didn't remember the license number on the Land-Rover. I called him about the middle of the morning and he gave me the number. Then I called him again in the afternoon to make sure Breedlove hadn't checked in. And to find out if he'd had any other calls. Anything worthwhile."

"Well, hell," Chee said. "Then I guess we're

left with Breedlove climbing up there alone, or with Shaw, and then taking the suicidal shortcut down."

Leaphorn's expression suggested he didn't agree with that conclusion, but he didn't comment on it directly.

"It also means I'm going to have to run down all these people who climbed up there in the next ten years and find out if any of them got off with a long piece of that climbing rope."

"Not necessarily," Leaphorn said. "You're forgetting our Fallen Man business is still not a crime. It's a missing person case solved by the discovery of an accidental death."

"Yeah," Chee said, doubtful.

"It makes me glad I'm a civilian these days."

The wind gusted, rattling sand against the aluminum side of Chee's home, whistling around its aluminum cracks and corners.

"So does the weather," Leaphorn said. "Everybody in uniform is going to be working overtime and getting frostbite this week."

Chee pointed to Leaphorn's plate. "Want some more?"

"I'm full. Probably ate too much. And I took too much of your time." He got up, retrieved his hat.

"I'm going to leave you these pictures," he said. "Rosebrough has the negatives. He's a lawyer. An agent of the court. They'll stand up as evidence if it comes to that."

"You mean if anyone gets up there and steals the ledger?"

"It's a thought," Leaphorn said. "What are you going to do tomorrow?"

Chee had worked for Leaphorn long enough for this question to produce a familiar uneasy feeling. "Why?"

"If I go up to the ranch tomorrow and show Demott and Elisa these pictures and ask her what she thinks about them, and ask her who was trying to climb that mountain on that September eighteenth date, then I think I could be accused of tampering with a witness."

"Witness to what? Officially there's no crime yet," Chee reminded him.

"Don't you think there will be one? Presuming we're smart enough to get this sorted out."

"You mean not counting Maryboy and me? Yeah. I guess so. But you could probably get away with talking to Elisa until the official connection is made. Now you're just a representative of the family lawyer. Perfectly legit."

"But why would Demott or the widow want to talk to a representative of the family's lawyer?"

Chee nodded, conceding the point.

"And I think there's something else I should be doing."

Chee let his stare ask the question.

"Old Amos Nez trusts me," Leaphorn said, and paused to consider it. "Well, more or less. I want to show him this evidence that Hal climbed Ship Rock just one week after he left the canyon and tell him about Maryboy being murdered, and ask him if Hal said anything about trying to climb Ship Rock just before he came to the canyon. Things like that."

"That could wait," Chee said, thinking of his

aching ribs and the long painful drive up into Colorado.

"Maybe it could wait," Leaphorn said. "But you know the other afternoon you decided Hosteen Maryboy couldn't wait and you rushed right out there to see if he could identify those climbers for you. And you were right. Turned out it couldn't wait."

"Ah," Chee said. "But I'm not clear on what makes Amos Nez so important. You think Breedlove might have told him something?"

"Let's try another theory," Leaphorn said. "Let's say that Hal Breedlove didn't live until his thirtieth birthday. Let's say those people Hosteen Sam saw climbing on September eighteenth got to the top, or at least two of them did. One of the two was Hal. The other one—or maybe two—push him off. Or, more likely he just falls. Now he's dead and he's dead two days too soon. He's still twenty-nine years old. So the climber's register is falsified to show he was alive after his birthday."

Chee held up his hand, grinning. "Huge hole in that one," he said. "Remember Hal was prowling around the canyon with his wife and Amos Nez until the twenty-third of . . ." Chee's voice trailed off into silence. And then he said, "Oh!" and stared at Leaphorn.

Leaphorn was making a wry face, shaking his head. "It sure took me long enough to see that possibility," he said. "I never could have if you hadn't got into old man Sam's register."

"My God," Chee said. "If that's the way it worked, I can see why they have to kill Nez. And if they're smart, the sooner the better."

"I'm going to ask you to call the Lazy B and find out if Demott and the widow are there and then arrange to drive up tomorrow and talk to them about what we found on top of the mountain."

"What if they're not at home?"

"Then I think we ought to be doing a little more to keep Amos Nez safe," Leaphorn said. And he opened the door and stepped out into the icy wind.

24

ELISA BREEDLOVE HAD ANSWERED the telephone. And, yes, Eldon was home and they'd be glad to talk to him. How about sometime tomorrow afternoon?

So Acting Lieutenant Chee showed up at his office in Shiprock early to get his desk cleared and make the needed arrangements. He arrived with tape plastered over the stitches around his left eye and a noticeable shiner visible behind them. He lowered himself carefully into the chair behind the desk to avoid jarring his ribs and gave Officers Teddy Begayaye, Deejay Hondo, Edison Bai, and Bernadette Manuelito a few moments to inspect the damage. In Begayaye and Bai it seemed to provoke a mixture of admiration and amusement, well suppressed. Hondo didn't seem interested and Officer Bernie Manuelito's face reflected a sort of shocked sympathy.

With that out of the way, he satisfied their curiosity with a personal briefing of what actually happened at the Maryboy place, supplementing the official one they would have already received. Then down to business.

He instructed Bai to try to find out where a .38-caliber pistol confiscated from a Shiprock High School boy had come from. He suggested to Officer Manuelito that she continue her efforts to locate a fellow named Adolph Deer, who had jumped bond after a robbery conviction but was reportedly "frequently being seen around the Two Gray Hills trading post." He told Hondo to finish the paperwork on a burglary case that was about to go to the grand jury. Then it was Teddy Begayaye's turn.

"I hate to tell you, Teddy, but you're going to have to be taxi driver today," Chee said. "I have to go up to the Lazy B ranch on this Maryboy shooting thing. I thought I could handle it myself, but"—he lifted his left arm, flinched, and grimaced—"the old ribs aren't quite as good as I thought they were."

"You shouldn't be riding around in a car," Officer Manuelito said. "You should be in bed, healing up. They shouldn't have let you out of the hospital."

"Hospitals are dangerous," Chee said. "People die in them."

Edison Bai grinned at that, but Officer Manuelito didn't think it was funny.

"Something goes wrong with broken ribs and you have a punctured lung," she said.

"They're just cracked," Chee said. "Just a

bruise." With that subject closed, he kept Bai
behind for a fill-in about the pistol-carrying student. Typically, Bai provided far more details
than Chee needed. The boy had been involved in
a joyride car theft during the summer. He was
born to the Streams Come Together people, his
mother's clan, and for the Salt clan, for his paternal people, but his father was also part Hopi. He
was believed to be involved in the smaller and
rougher of Shiprock's juvenile gangs. He was
meanness on the hoof. People weren't raising
their kids the way they used to. Chee agreed, put
on his hat and hurried stiffly out the door into
the parking lot. It had been chilly and clouding
up when he came to work. Now there was solid
overcast and an icy northwest wind swept dust
and leaves past his ankles.

The gale was blowing Begayaye back toward
him.

"Jim," he said. "I forgot. The wife made a
dental appointment for me today. How about me
switching assignments with Bernie? That Deer
kid isn't going anywhere."

"Well," Chee said. Across the parking lot he
saw Bernie Manuelito standing on the sheltered
side of his patrol car, watching them. "Is it okay
with Manuelito?"

"Yes, sir," Begayaye said. "She don't mind."

"By the way," Chee said, "I forgot to thank
you guys for sending me those flowers."

Begayaye looked puzzled. "Flowers? What
flowers?"

Thus it was that Acting Lieutenant Jim Chee
headed north toward the Colorado border leaning

his good shoulder against the passenger-side door with Officer Bernadette Manuelito behind the wheel. Chee, being a detective, had figured out who had sent him the flowers. Begayaye hadn't done it, and Bai would never think of doing such a thing even if he was fond of Chee—which Chee was pretty sure he wasn't. That left Deejay Hondo and Bernie. Which clearly meant Bernie had sent them and made it look like everybody did it so he wouldn't think she was buttering him up. That probably meant she liked him. Thinking back, he could remember a couple of other signs that pointed to that conclusion.

All things considered, he liked her, too. She was really smart, she was sweet to everybody around the office, and she was always using her days off to take care of an apparently inexhaustible supply of ailing and indigent kinfolks, which gave her a high score on the Navajo value scale. When the time came he would have to give her a good efficiency rating. He gave her a sidewise glance, saw her staring unblinkingly through the windshield at the worn pavement of infamous U.S. Highway 666. A very slight smile curved the corner of her lip, making her look happy, as she usually was. No doubt about it, she really was an awfully pretty young woman.

That wasn't the way he should be thinking about Officer Bernadette Manuelito. Not only was he her superior officer and supervisor, he was more or less engaged to marry another woman. And he was thinking that way, most likely, because he was having a very confusing problem with that other woman. He was beginning to suspect that she didn't really want to marry him. Or, at least, he wasn't sure she was willing to marry Jim Chee as he currently existed—a just-plain cop and a genuine sheep-camp Navajo as opposed to the more romantic and politically correct Indigenous Person. Making it worse, he didn't know what the hell to do about it. Or whether he should do anything. It was a sad, sad situation.

Chee sighed, decided the ribs would feel better if he shifted his weight. He did it, sucked in his breath, and grimaced.

"You all right?" Bernie asked, giving him a worried look.

"Okay," Chee said.

"I have some aspirin in my stuff."

"No problem," Chee said.

Bernie drove in silence for a while.

"Lieutenant," she said. "Do you remember telling us how Lieutenant Leaphorn was always trying to get you to look for patterns? I mean when you had something going on that was hard to figure out."

"Yeah," Chee said.

"And that's what you wanted me to try to find in this cattle-stealing business?"

Chee grunted, trying to remember if he had made any such suggestion.

"Well, I got Lucy Sam to let me take that ledger to that Quik-Copy place in Farmington and I got copies made of the pages back for several years so I'd have them. And then I went through our complaint records and copied down the dates of all the cattle-theft reports for the same years."

"Good Lord," Chee said, visualizing the time that would take. "Who was doing your regular work for you?"

"Just the multiple-head thefts," Officer Manuelito said, defensively. "The ones which look sort of professional. And I did it in the evenings."

"Oh," Chee said, embarrassed.

"Anyway, I started comparing the dates. You know, when Mr. Sam would write down something about a certain sort of truck, and when there would be a cattle theft reported in our part of the reservation."

Officer Manuelito had been reciting this very carefully, as if she had rehearsed it. Now she stopped.

"What'd you notice?"

She produced a deprecatory laugh. "I think this is probably really silly," she said.

"I doubt it," Chee said, thinking he would like to get his mind off of Janet Pete and quit trying to find a way to turn back the clock and make things the way they used to be. "Why don't you just go ahead and tell me about it."

"There was a correlation between multiple-theft reports and Mr. Sam seeing a big banged-up dirty white camper truck in the neighborhood," Manuelito said, looking fixedly at the highway center stripe. "Not all the time," she added. "But often enough so it made you begin to wonder about it."

Chee digested this. "The trailer like Mr.

Finch's rig?" he said. "The New Mexico brand inspector's camper?"

"Yes, sir." She laughed again. "I said it was probably silly."

"Well, I guess our theft reports would be passed along to him. Then he'd come out here to see about it."

Officer Manuelito kept her eyes on the road, her lips opened as if she were about to say something. But she didn't. She simply looked disappointed.

"Wait a minute," Chee said, as understanding belatedly dawned. "Was Hosteen Sam seeing Finch's trailer after the thefts were reported? Or—"

"Usually before," Bernie said. "Sometimes both, but usually before. But you know how that is. Sometimes the cattle are gone for a while before the owner notices they're missing."

Bernie drove, looking very tense. Chee digested what she'd told him. Suddenly he slammed his right hand against his leg. "How about that?" he said. "That wily old devil."

Officer Manuelito relaxed, grinned. "You think so? You think that might be right?"

"I'd bet on it," Chee said. "He'd have everything going for him. All the proper legal forms for moving cattle. All the brand information. All the reasons for being where the cattle are. And all cops would know him as one of them. Perfect."

Bernie was grinning even wider, delighted. "Yes," she said. "That's sort of what I was thinking."

"Now we need to find out how he markets them. And how he gets them from the pasture to the feedlots."

"I think it's in the trailer," Bernie said.

"The trailer? You mean he hauls cattle in his house trailer?"

Chee's incredulous tone caused Bernie to flush slightly. "I think so," she said. "I couldn't prove it."

A few moments ago Acting Lieutenant Chee might have scoffed at this remarkable idea. But not now. "Tell me," he said. "How does he get them through the door?"

"It took me a long time to get the idea," she said. "I think it was noticing that now and then I'd see that trailer parked at the Anasazi Inn at Farmington, and I'd think it was funny that you'd drive that big clumsy camper trailer around if you didn't want to sleep in it. I thought, you know, well, maybe he just wants a hot bath, or something like that. But it stuck in my mind."

She laughed. "I'm always trying to understand white people."

"Yeah," Chee said. "Me too."

"So the other day when he parked the trailer in the lot at the station, when I walked past it I noticed how it smelled."

"A little whiff of cow manure," said Chee, who had walked behind it, too. "I just thought, you know, he's around feedlots all the time. Stepping in the stuff. Probably gets used to it. Doesn't clean his boots."

"That occurred to me, too," Bernie said. "But

it was pretty strong. Maybe women are more sensitive to smells."

Or smarter, Chee thought. "Did you look inside?"

"He's got all the windows all stuck full of those tourist stickers, and they're high windows. I tried to take a peek but I didn't want him to see me snooping."

"I guess we could get a search warrant," Chee said. "What would you put on the petition? Something about the brand inspector's camper smelling like cow manure, to which the judge would say 'Naturally,' and about Finch not liking to sleep in it, which would cause the judge to say 'Not if it smells like cow manure.'"

"I thought about the search warrant," Bernie said. "Of course there's no law against hauling cows in your camper if you want to."

"True," Chee said. "Might be able to get him committed for being crazy."

"Anyway," Bernie said. "I called his office and I—"

"You *what*!"

"I just wanted to know where he was. If he answered I was going to hang up. If he didn't, I'd ask 'em where I could find him. He wasn't there, and the secretary said he'd called in from the Davis and Sons cattle-auction place over by Iyanbito. So I drove over there and his camper truck was parked by the barn and he was out in back with some people loading up steers. So I got a closer look."

"You didn't break in?" Chee asked, thinking

she'd probably say she had. Nothing this woman did was going to surprise him anymore.

She glanced at him, looking hurt, and ignored the question.

"Maybe you noticed that camper has just a straight-up flat back. There's no door in it and no window. Well, all around that back panel it's sealed up with silvery duct tape. Like you'd maybe put on to keep the dust out. But when you get down and look under you can see a row of big, heavy-duty hinges."

Chee was into this now. "So you back your trailer up to the fence, pull off the duct tape, lower the back down, and that makes a loading ramp out of it. He probably has it rigged up with stalls to keep 'em from moving around."

"I guessed it would handle about six," Bernie said. "Two rows of cows, three abreast."

"Bernie," Chee said. "If my ribs weren't so sore, and it wasn't going to get me charged with sexual harassment and cause us to run off the road, I would reach over there and give you a huge congratulatory hug."

Bernie looked both pleased and embarrassed.

"You put a lot of work into this," he said. "And a lot of thought, too. Way beyond the call of duty."

"Well, I'm trying to learn to be a detective. And it got sort of personal, too," she said. "I don't like that man."

"I don't much either," Chee said. "He's arrogant."

"He sort of made a move on me," she said. "Maybe not. Not exactly."

"Like what?"

"Well, he gives you that 'doll' and 'cute' stuff, you know. Then he said how would I like to get assigned to work with him. But of course he said 'under' him. He said I could be Tonto to his Lone Ranger."

"Tonto?" Chee said. "Well, now. Here's what we do. We keep an eye on him. And when he's on the road with a load, we nail him. And when we do, you're the one who gets to put the handcuffs on him."

25

When Officer Bernadette Manuelito parked Chee's patrol car at the Lazy B ranch Elisa Breedlove was standing in the doorway awaiting them—hugging herself against the cold wind. Or was it, Chee thought, against the news he might be bringing?

"Four Corners weather," she said. "Yesterday it was sunny, mild autumn. Today it's winter." She ushered them into the living room, exchanged introductions gracefully with Bernie, expressed the proper dismay at Chee's condition, wished him a quick recovery, and invited them to be seated.

"I saw the story about you being shot on television," she said. "Bad as you look, they made it sound even worse."

"Just some cracked ribs," Chee said.

"And old Mr. Maryboy being killed. I only met him once, but he was very nice to us. He invited us in and offered to make coffee."

"When was that?"

"Way back in the dark ages," she said. "When Hal and George would come out for the summer and Eldon and I would go climbing with them."

"Is your brother here now?" Chee asked. "I was hoping to talk to you both."

"He was here earlier, but one of the mares got herself tangled up in a fence. He went out to see about her. There's supposed to be a snowstorm moving in and he wanted to get her into the barn."

"Do you expect him back soon?"

"She's up in the north pasture," Elisa said. "But he shouldn't be long unless she's cut so badly he had to go into Mancos and get the vet. Would you two care for something to drink? It's a long drive up here from Shiprock."

She served them both coffee but poured none for herself. Chee sipped and watched her over the rim, twisting her hands. If she had been one of the three climbers that day, if she had reached the top, she should know what was coming now. He took out the folder of photographs and handed Elisa the one signed with her husband's name.

"Thanks," she said, and looked at it. Officer Manuelito was watching her, sitting primly on the edge of her chair, cup in saucer, uncharacteristically quiet. It occurred to Chee that she looked like a pretty girl pretending to be a cop.

Elisa was frowning at the photograph. "It's a picture of the page from the climbers' ledger," she said slowly. "But where—"

She dropped the picture on the coffee table, said, "Oh, God," in a strangled voice, and covered her face with her hands.

Officer Manuelito leaned forward, lips apart. Chee shook his head, signaled silence.

Elisa picked up the picture again, stared at it, dropped it to the floor and sat rigid, her face white.

"Mrs. Breedlove," Chee said. "Are you all right?"

She shook her head. Shuddered. Composed herself, looked at Chee.

"This photograph. That's all there was on the page?"

"Just what you saw."

She bent, picked up the print, looked at it again. "And the date. The date. That's what was written?"

"Just as you see it," Chee said.

"But of course it was." She produced a laugh on the razor edge of hysteria. "A silly question. But it's wrong, you know. It should have been— but why—" She put her hand over her mouth, dropped her head.

The noise the wind was making—rattles, whistles, and howls—filtered through windows and walls and filled the dark room with the sounds of winter.

"I know the date's wrong," Chee said. "The entry is dated September thirty. That's a week after your husband disappeared from Canyon de Chelly. What should—" He stopped. Elisa wasn't listening to him. She was lost in her own memory. And that, combined with what the picture had told her, was drawing her to some ghastly conclusion.

"The handwriting," she said. "Have you—" But she cut that off, too, pressed her lips together as if to keep them from completing the question.

But not soon enough, of course. So she hadn't known what had happened on the summit of Ship Rock. Not until moments ago when the forgery of her husband's signature told her. Told her exactly what? That her husband had died before he'd had a chance to sign. That her husband's death, therefore, must have been preplanned as well as postdated. The pattern Leaphorn had taught him to look for took its almost final dismal shape. And filled Jim Chee with pity.

Officer Manuelito was on her feet.

"Mrs. Breedlove, you need to lie down," she said. "You're sick. Let me get you something. Some water."

Elisa sagged forward, leaned her forehead against the table. Officer Manuelito hurried into the kitchen.

"We haven't checked the handwriting yet," Chee said. "Can you tell us what that will show?"

Elisa was sobbing now. Bernie emerged from the kitchen, glass of water in one hand, cloth in the other. She gave Chee a "How could you do this?" look and sat next to Elisa, patting her shoulder.

"Take a sip of water," Bernie said. "And you should lie down until you feel better. We can finish this later."

Ramona appeared in the doorway, wrapped

in a padded coat, her face red with cold. She watched them anxiously. "What are you doing to her?" she said. "Go away now and let her rest."

"Oh, God," Elisa said, her voice muffled by the table. "Why did he think he had to do it?"

"Where can I find Eldon?" Chee asked.

Elisa shook her head.

"Does he have a rifle?" But of course he would have a rifle. Every male over about twelve in the Rocky Mountain West had a rifle. "Where does he keep it?"

Elisa didn't respond. Chee motioned to Bernie. She left in search of it.

Elisa raised her head, wiped her eyes, looked at Chee. "It was an accident, you know. Hal was always reckless. He wanted to rappel down the cliff. I thought I had talked him out of it. But I guess I hadn't."

"Did you see it happen?"

"I didn't get all the way to the top. I was below. Waiting for them to come down."

Chee hesitated. The next question would be crucial, but should he ask it now, with this woman overcome by shock and grief? Any lawyer would tell her not to talk about any of this. But she wouldn't be the one on trial.

Bernie reappeared at the doorway, Ramona behind her. "There's a triple gun rack in the office," she said. "A twelve-gauge pump shotgun in the bottom rack and the top two empty."

"Okay," Chee said.

"And in the wastebasket beside the desk, there's a thirty-ought-six ammunition box. The top's torn off and it's empty."

Chee nodded and came to his decision.

"Mrs. Breedlove. No one climbed the mountain on the date by your husband's name. But on September eighteenth three people were seen climbing it. Hal was one of them. You were one. Who was the third?"

"I don't want to talk to you anymore," Elisa said. "I want you to go."

"You don't have to tell us anything," Chee said. "You have the right to remain silent, and to call your lawyer if you think you need one. I don't think you've done anything you could be charged with, but you never really know what a prosecuting attorney will decide."

Officer Manuelito cleared her throat. "And anything you say can be used against you. Remember that."

"I don't want to say any more."

"That's okay," Chee said. "But I should tell you this. Eldon isn't here and neither is his rifle and it looks like he just reloaded it. If we have this figured out right, Eldon is going to know there is just one man left alive who could ruin this for him."

Chee paused, waiting for a response. It didn't come. Elisa sat as if frozen, staring at him.

"It's a man named Amos Nez. Remember him? He was your guide in Canyon de Chelly. Right after Hal's skeleton was found on Ship Rock last Halloween, Mr. Nez was riding his horse up the canyon. Someone up on the rim shot him. He wasn't killed, just badly hurt."

Elisa sagged a little with that, looked down at her hands, and said, "I didn't know that."

"With a thirty-ought-six rifle," Chee added.

"What day was it?"

Chee told her.

She thought a moment. Remembering. Slumped a little more.

"If anyone kills Mr. Nez the charge will be the premeditated murder of a witness. That carries the death penalty."

"He's my brother," Elisa said. "Hal's death was an accident. Sometimes he acted almost like he wanted to die. No thrills, he said, if you didn't take a chance. He fell. When Eldon climbed down to where I was waiting, he looked like he was almost dead himself. He was devastated. He was so shaken he could hardly tell me about it." She stopped, looking at Chee, at Bernie, back at Chee.

Waiting for our reaction, Chee thought. *Waiting for us to give her absolution? No, waiting for us to say we believe what she is telling us, so that she can believe it again herself.*

"I think you were driving that Land-Rover," Chee said. "When police found it abandoned up an arroyo north of Many Farms they said there was a telephone in it."

"But what good would it have done to call for help?" Elisa asked, her voice rising. "Hal was dead. He was all broken to pieces on that little ledge. Nobody could bring him back to life again. He was dead!"

"Was he?"

"Yes," she shouted. "Yes. Yes. Yes."

And now Chee understood why Elisa had been so shocked when she learned the skeleton was intact—with not a bone broken. She didn't want to believe it. Refused to believe it still. That made the next question harder to ask. What had Eldon told her of the scene at the top? Had he explained why Hal had started his descent before he signed the book? Why he falsified the register? Had he—

Ramona rushed into the room, sat beside Elisa, hugged the woman to her. She glared at Chee. "I said go away now," she said. "Get out. No more. No more. She has suffered too much."

"It's all right," Elisa said. "Ramona, when you came in did you see the Land-Rover in the garage?"

"No," Ramona said. "Just Eldon's pickup truck."

Elisa looked at Chee, sighed, and said, "Then I guess he didn't go up to see about the mare. He would have taken his truck."

Chee picked up his hat and the photographs. He thanked Mrs. Breedlove for the cooperation, apologized for bringing her bad news, and hurried out, with Bernie trotting along behind him. The wind was bitter now, and carrying those dry-as-dust first snowflakes that were the forerunners of a storm.

"I want to get Leaphorn on the radio," he said, as Bernie started the engine, "and maybe we'll have to make a fast trip to Canyon de Chelly."

Bernie was looking back at the house. "Do you think she will be all right?"

"I think so," Chee said. "Ramona will take good care of her."

"Ramona's pretty shaken up, too," Bernie said. "She was crying when she helped me look for the rifle. She said it was always the wrong men with Elisa—always having to take care of them. That Hal was a spoiled baby and Eldon was a bully. She said if it wasn't for Eldon she'd be married to a good man who wanted to take care of her."

"She say who?"

"I think it was Tommy Castro. Or maybe Kaster. Something like that. She was crying." Bernie was staring back at the house, looking worried.

"Bernie," Chee said. "It's starting to snow. It's probably going to be a bad one. Start the car. Go. Go. Go."

"You're worried about Amos Nez," Bernie said, starting the engine. "We can just call the station at Chinle and have them stop any Land-Rover driving in. Bet Mr. Leaphorn already did that."

"He said he would," Chee said. "But I want to get a message to him about Demott taking off with his thirty-ought-six loaded. Maybe Eldon won't be driving in. If you can climb seventeen hundred feet up Ship Rock, maybe you can climb down a six-hundred-foot cliff."

26

THEY DROVE INTO THE FULL BRUNT of the storm halfway between Mancos and Cortez, the wind buffeting the car and driving a blinding sheet of tiny dry snowflakes horizontally past their windshield.

"At least it's sweeping the pavement clear," Bernie said, sounding cheerful.

Chee glanced at her. She seemed to be enjoying the adventure. He wasn't. His ribs hurt, so did the abrasions around his eye, and he was not in the mood for cheer.

"That won't last long," he said.

It didn't. In Cortez, snow was driving over the curbs and the pavement was beginning to pack, and the broadcasts on the emergency channel didn't sound promising. A last gasp of the Pacific hurricane system was pushing across Baja California into Arizona. There it met the first blast of Arctic air, pressing down the east slope of the Rockies from Canada. Interstate 40 at Flagstaff, where the two fronts had collided, was already closed by snow. So were highways through the Wasatch Range in Utah. Autumn was emphatically over on the Colorado Plateau.

They turned onto U.S. 666 to make the forty-mile run almost due south to Shiprock. With the icy wind pursuing them, the highway emptied of traffic by storm warnings, and speed limits ignored, Bernie outran the Canadian contribution to the storm. The sky lightened now. Far ahead, they could see where the Pacific half of the blizzard had reached the Chuska range. Its cold, wet air met the dry, warmer air on the New Mexico side at the ridgeline. The collision produced a towering wall of white fog, which poured down the slopes like a silent slow-motion Niagara.

"Wow," Bernie said. "I never saw anything quite like that before."

"The heavy cold air forces itself under the warmer stuff," said Chee, unable to avoid a little showing off. "I'll bet it's twenty degrees colder at Lukachukai than it is at Red Rock—and they're less than twenty miles apart."

They crossed the western corner of the Ute reservation, then roared into New Mexico and across the mesa high above Malpais Arroyo.

"Wow," Bernie said again. "Look at that."

Instead Chee glanced at the speedometer and flinched.

"You drive," he said. "I'll check the scenery for both of us." It was worth checking. They looked down into the vast San Juan River basin—dark with storm to the right, dappled with sunlight to the left. Ship Rock stood just at the edge of the shadow line, a grotesque sunlit thumb thrust into the sky, but through some quirk of wind and air pressure, the long bulge of the Hogback formation was already mostly dark with cloud shadow.

"I think we're going to get home before the snow," Bernie said.

They almost did. It caught them when Bernie pulled into the parking lot at the station—but the flakes blowing against Chee as he hurried into the building were still small and dry. The Canadian cold front was still dominating the Pacific storm.

"You look terrible," Jenifer said. "How do you feel?"

"I'd say well below average," Chee said. "Did Leaphorn call?"

"Indirectly," Jenifer said, and handed Chee three message slips and an envelope.

It was on top—a call from Sergeant Deke at the Chinle station confirming that Leaphorn had received Chee's message about Demott leaving his ranch with his rifle. Leaphorn had gone up the canyon to the Nez place and would either bring Nez out with him or stay, depending on the weather, which was terrible.

Chee glanced at the other messages. Routine business. The envelope bore the word "Jim" in Janet's hand. He tapped it against the back of his hand. Put it down. Called Deke.

"I've seen worse," Deke said. "But it's a bad one for this time of year. Still above zero but it won't be for long. Blowing snow. We have Navajo 12 closed at Upper Wheatfields, and 191 between here and Ganado, and 59 north of Red Rock, and—well, hell of a night to be driving. How about there?"

"I think we're just getting the edge of it," Chee said. "Did Leaphorn get my message?"

"Yep. He said not to worry."

"What do you think? Demott's a rock climber. Is Nez going to be safe enough?"

"Except for maybe frostbite," Deke said. "Nobody's going to be climbing those cliffs tonight."

And so Chee opened the envelope and extracted the note.

"Jim. Sorry I missed you. Going to get a bite to eat and will come by your place—Janet."

Her car wasn't there when he drove up, which was just as well, he thought. It would give him a little time to get the place a little warmer. He fired up the propane heater, put on the coffee, and gave the place a critical inspection. He rarely did. His trailer was simply where he lived. Sometimes it was hot, sometimes it was cold. But otherwise it was not something he gave any thought to. It looked cramped, crowded, slightly dirty, and altogether dismal. Ah, well, nothing to do about it now. He checked the refrigerator for something to offer her. Nothing much there in the snack line, but he extracted a slab of cheese and pulled a box of crackers and a bowl with a few Oreos in it off the shelf over the stove. Then he sat on the edge of the bunk, slumped, listening to the icy wind buffeting the trailer, too tired to think about what might be about to happen.

Chee must have dozed. He didn't hear the car coming down the slope, or see the lights. A tapping at the door awakened him, and he found her standing on the step looking up at him.

"It's freezing," she said as he ushered her in.

"Hot coffee," he said. Poured a cup, handed it to her, and offered her the folding chair beside the fold-out table. But she stood a moment, hugging herself and shivering, looking undecided.

"Janet," he said. "Sit down. Relax."

"I just need to tell you something," she said. "I can't stay. I need to get back to Gallup before the weather gets worse." But she sat.

"Drink your coffee," he said. "Warm up."

She was looking at him over the cup. "You look awful," she said. "They told me you'd gone up to Mancos. To see the Breedlove widow. You shouldn't be back at work yet. You should be in bed."

"I'm all right," he said. And waited. Would she ask him why he'd gone to Mancos? What he'd learned?

"Why couldn't somebody else do it?" she said. "Somebody without broken ribs."

"Just cracked," Chee said.

She put down her cup. He reached for it. She intercepted his hand, held it.

"Jim," she said. "I'm going away for a while. I'm taking my accrued leave time, and my vacation, and I'm going home."

"Home?" Chee said. "For a while. How long is that?"

"I don't know," she said. "I want to get my head together. Look forward and backwards." She tried to smile but it didn't come off well. She shrugged. "And just think."

It occurred to Chee that he hadn't poured himself any coffee. Oddly, he didn't want any. It occurred to him that she wasn't burning her bridges.

"Think?" he said. "About us?"

"Of course." This time the smile worked a little better.

But her hand was cold. He squeezed it. "I thought we were through that phase."

"No, you didn't," she said. "You never really stopped thinking about whether we'd be compatible. Whether we really fit."

"Don't we?"

"We did in this fantasy I had," she said, and waved her hands, mocking herself. "Big, good-looking guy. Sweet and smart and as far as I could tell you really cared about me. Fun on the Big Rez for a while, then a big job for you in someplace interesting. Washington. San Francisco. New York. Boston. And the big job for me in Justice, or maybe a law firm. You and I together. Everything perfect."

Chee said nothing to that.

"Everything perfect," she repeated. "The best of both worlds." She looked at him, trying to hold the grin and not quite making it.

"With twin Porsches in the triple garage," Chee said. "But when you got to know me, I didn't fit the fantasy."

"Almost," she said. "Maybe you do, really."

Suddenly Janet's eyes went damp. She looked away. "Or maybe I change the fantasy."

He extracted his handkerchief, frowned at it, reached into the storage drawer behind him, extracted paper napkins, and handed them to Janet. She said, "Sorry," and wiped her eyes.

He wanted to hold her, very close. But he said, "A cold wind does that."

"So I thought maybe as time goes by everything changes a little. I change and so do you."

He could think of nothing honest to say to that.

"But after the other evening in Gallup, when you were so angry with me, I began to understand," she said.

"Remember once a long time ago you asked me about a schoolteacher I used to date? Somebody told you about her. From Wisconsin. Just out of college. Blonde, blue eyes, taught second grade at Crownpoint when I was a brand-new cop and stationed there. Well, it wasn't that there was anything much wrong with me, but for her kids she wanted the good old American dream. She saw no hope for that in Navajo country. So she went away."

"Why are you telling me this?" Janet said. "She wasn't a Navajo."

"But I am," he said. "So I thought, what's the difference? I'm darker. Rarely sunburn. Small hips. Wide shoulders. That's racial, right? Does that matter? I think not much. So what makes me a Navajo?"

"You're going to say culture," Janet said. "I studied social anthropology, too."

"I grew up knowing it's wrong to have more than you need. It means you're not taking care of your people. Win three races in a row, you better slow down a little. Let somebody else win. Or somebody gets drunk and runs into your car and tears you all up, you don't sue him, you want to have a sing for him to cure him of alcoholism."

"That doesn't get you admitted into law school," Janet said. "Or pull you out of poverty."

"Depends on how you define poverty."

"It's defined in the law books," Janet said. "A family of x members with an annual income of under y."

"I met a middle-aged man at a Yeibichai sing a few years ago. He ran an accounting firm in Flagstaff and came out to Burnt Water because his mother had a stroke and they were doing the cure for her. I said something about it looking like he was doing very well. And he said, 'No, I will be a poor man all my life.' And I asked him what he meant, and he said, 'Nobody ever taught me any songs.'"

"Ah, Jim," she said. She rose, took the two steps required to reach the bunk where he was sitting, put her arms carefully around him and kissed him. Then she pressed the undamaged side of his face against her breast.

"I know having a Navajo dad didn't make me a Navajo," she said. "My culture is Stanford sorority girl, Maryland cocktail circuit, Mozart, and tickets to the Met. So maybe I have to learn not to think that being ragged, and not having indoor plumbing, and walking miles to see the dentist means poverty. I'm working on it."

Chee, engulfed in Janet's sweater, her perfume, her softness, said something like "Ummmm."

"But I'm not there yet," she added, and released him.

"I guess I should work on it from the other end, too," he said. "I could get used to being a lieutenant, trying to work my way up. Trying to put some value on things like—" He let that trail off.

"One thing I want you to know," she said. "I didn't use you."

"You mean—"

"I mean deliberately getting information out of you so I could tell John."

"I guess I always knew that," he said. "I was just being jealous. I had the wrong idea about that."

"I did tell him you'd found Breedlove's body. He invited Claire and me to the concert. Claire and I go all the way back to high school. And we were remembering old times and, you know, it just came out. It was just something interesting to tell him."

"Sure," Chee said. "I understand."

"I have to go now," she said. "Before you guys close the highway. But I wanted you to know that. Breedlove had been his project when the widow filed to get the death certified. It looked so peculiar. And finally, now, I guess it's all over."

Her tone made that a question.

She was zipping up her jacket, glancing at him.

"Lieutenant Leaphorn gave Mr. Shaw that photograph of the climber's ledger," she said.

"Yeah," Chee said. The wind buffeted the trailer, made its stormy sounds, moved a cold draft against his neck.

"She must have thought that terribly odd— for him to just leave her at the canyon, and then abandon their car, and go back to Ship Rock to climb it like that."

Chee nodded.

"Surely she must have had some sort of theory. I know I would have had if you'd done something crazy like that to me."

"She cried a lot," Chee said. "She could hardly believe it."

And in a minute Janet was gone. The goodbye kiss, the promises to write, the invitation to come and join her. Then holding the car door open for her, commenting on how it always got colder when the snowing stopped, and watching the headlights vanish at the top of the slope.

He sat on the bunk again then, felt the bandages around his eye, and decided the soreness there was abating. He probed the padding over his ribs, flinched, and decided the healing there was slower. He noticed the coffeepot was still on, got up, and unplugged it. He switched on the radio, thinking he would get some weather news. Then switched it off again and sat on the bed.

The telephone rang. Chee stared at it. It rang again. And again. He picked it up.

"Guess what?" It was Officer Bernadette Manuelito.

"What?"

"Begayaye just told me," she said. "He

detoured past Ship Rock today. The cattle were crowded around our loose-fence-post place, eating some fresh hay."

"Well," Chee said, and gave himself a moment to make the mental transition from Janet Pete to the Lone Ranger competition. "I'd say this would be a perfect time for Mr. Finch to supplement his income. The cops all away working weather problems, and everybody staying home by the fire."

"That's what I thought," she said.

"I'll meet you there a little before daylight. When's sunup these days?"

"About seven."

"I'll meet you at the office at five. Okay?"

"Hey," Bernie said. "I like it."

27

"I'M GOING TO SHOW YOU SOME PICTURES," Leaphorn said to Amos Nez, and he dug a folder out of his briefcase.

"Pretty women in bikinis," old man Nez said, grinning at his mother-in-law. Mrs. Benally, who didn't much understand English, grinned back.

"Pictures which I should have showed you eleven years ago," Leaphorn said, and put a photograph on the arm of the old sofa where Nez was sitting. The old iron stove that served for heating and cooking in the Nez hogan was glowing red from the wood fire within it. Cold was in the canyon outside; Leaphorn was sweating. But Nez had kept his sweater on and Mrs. Benally had her shawl draped over her shoulders.

Nez adjusted his glasses on his nose. Looked. He smiled at Leaphorn, handed him back the print. "That's her," he said. "Mrs. Breedlove."

"Who's the man with her?"

Nez retrieved the print, studied it again. He shook his head. "I don't know him."

"That's Harold Breedlove," Leaphorn said. "You're looking at a photograph the Breedloves had taken at a studio in Farmington on their wedding anniversary—the summer before they came out here and got you to guide them."

Nez stared at the photograph. "Well, now," he said. "It sure is funny what white people will do. Who is that man she was here with?"

"You tell me," Leaphorn said. He handed Nez two more photographs. One was a photocopy he'd obtained, by imposing on an old friend in the Indian Service's Washington office, of George Shaw's portrait from the Georgetown University School of Law alumni magazine. The others had been obtained from the photo files of the *Mancos Weekly Citizen*—mug shots of young Eldon Demott and Tommy Castro wearing Marine Corps hats.

"I don't know this fella here," Nez said, and handed Leaphorn the Shaw photo.

"I didn't think you would," Leaphorn said. "I was just making sure."

Nez studied the other photo. "Well, now," he said. "Here's my friend Hal Breedlove."

He handed Leaphorn the picture of Eldon Demott.

"Not your friend now," Leaphorn said, and tapped Nez's leg cast. "He's the guy that tried to kill you."

Nez retrieved the photo, looked at it, and shook his head. "Why did he do—" he began, and stopped, thinking about it.

Leaphorn explained about ownership of the ranch depending on the date of Breedlove's death, and now depending upon continuing the deception. "There were just two people who knew something that could screw this up. One of them knew the date Hal Breedlove and Demott climbed Ship Rock—a man named Maryboy who gave them permission to climb. Demott shot him the other day. That leaves you."

"Well, now," Nez said, and made a wry face.

"A policeman who is looking into all this sent me a message that Demott loaded up his rifle this morning and headed out. I guess he'd be coming out here to see if he could get another shot at you."

"Why don't they arrest him?"

"They have to catch him first," Leaphorn said, not wanting to get into the complicated explanation of legalities—and the total lack of any concrete evidence that there was any reason to arrest Demott. "My idea was to take you and Mrs. Benally into Chinle and check you into the motel there. The police can keep an eye on you until they get Demott locked up."

Nez gave himself some time to think this over. "No," he said. "I'll just stay here." He pointed to the shotgun in the rack on the opposite wall. "You just take old lady Benally there. Look after her."

Mrs. Benally may not have been able to translate "bikini" into Navajo, but she had no trouble with "motel."

"I'm not going into any motel," she said.

For practical purposes, that ended the argument. Nobody was moving.

Leaphorn wasn't unprepared for that. Before he'd parked at the Nez hogan, he had scouted up Canyon del Muerto, examining the south-side cliff walls below the place where the ranger had reported seeing the man with the rifle. Sergeant Deke had said it was just five or six hundred yards up-canyon from the Nez place. Leaphorn had seen no location within rifle range where the top of the south cliff offered a fair shot at the Nez hogan. But about a quarter mile up-canyon a huge slab of sandstone had given way to the erosion undercutting it.

The cliff had split here. The slab had separated from the wall. He'd studied it. Someone who knew rock climbing, had the equipment, and didn't mind risking falling off a forty-story building could get down here. This must have been what Demott had been doing here—if it was Demott. He was looking for a way in and out that avoided the bottleneck entrance.

It was certainly conveniently close for a climber. Or a bird. Being neither meant Leaphorn would have to drive about fifteen miles down Canyon del Muerto to its junction with Canyon de Chelly, then another five or six to the canyon mouth to reach the pavement of Navajo Route 64. Then he'd have to reverse directions and drive twenty-four miles northeastward along the north rim of del Muerto, turn southwestward maybe four miles toward Tsaile, then complete the circle down the brushy dirt-and-boulder track that took those foolhardy enough to use it down that finger of mesa separating the canyons. The last six or seven miles on that circuit would take about as long as the first fifty.

Leaphorn hurried. He wanted enough daylight left to check the place carefully—to either confirm or refute his suspicions. More important, if Demott was coming Leaphorn wanted to be there waiting for him.

He seemed to have managed that. He stopped across the cattle guard where the unmarked track connected with the highway, climbed out, and made a careful inspection. The last vehicle to leave its tracks here had been coming out, and that had been shortly after the snowfall began. Eight or nine jolting miles later, he pulled his car off the track and left it concealed behind a cluster of junipers. The wind was bitter now, but the snow had diminished to occasional dry flakes.

The west rim of Canyon del Muerto was less than fifty yards away over mostly bare sandstone. If he had calculated properly, he was just about above the Nez home site. In fact, he was perhaps a hundred yards below it. He stood a foot or two back from the edge looking down, confirming that the Nez hogan was too protected by the overhang to offer a shot from here. He could see the track where Nez drove in his truck, but the hogan itself and all of its outbuildings except a goat pen were hidden below the wall. But he could see from here the great split-off sandstone slab, and he walked along the rim toward it. He was almost there when he heard an engine whining in low gear.

Along the cliff here finding concealment was no problem. Leaphorn moved behind a great block of sandstone surrounded by piñons. He checked his pistol and waited.

The vehicle approaching was a dirty, battered, dark green Land-Rover. It came almost directly toward him. Stopped not fifty feet away. The engine died. The door opened. Eldon Demott stepped out. He reached behind him into the vehicle and took out a rifle, which he laid across the hood. Then he extracted a roll of thin, pale yellow rope and a cardboard box. These two also went onto the hood. From the box he took a web belt and harness, a helmet, and a pair of small black shoes. He leaned against the fender, removed a boot, replaced it with a shoe, and repeated the process. Then he put on the belt and the climbing harness. He looked at his watch, glanced at the sky, stretched, and looked around him.

He looked directly at Joe Leaphorn, sighed, and reached for the rifle.

"Leave it where it is," Leaphorn said, and showed Demott his .38 revolver.

Demott took his hand away from the rifle, dropped it to his side.

"I might want to shoot something," he said.

"Hunting season is over," Leaphorn said.

Demott sighed and leaned against the fender. "It looks like it is."

"No doubt about it. Even if I get careless and you shoot me, you can't get out of here anyway. Two police cars are on their way in after you. And if you climb down, well, that's hopeless."

"You going to arrest me? How do you do that? You're retired. Or is it a citizen's arrest?"

"Regular arrest," Leaphorn said. "I'm still deputized by the sheriff in this county. I didn't get around to turning in the commission."

"What do you charge me with—trespass?"

"Well, I think more likely it will start out being attempted homicide of Amos Nez, and then after the FBI gets its work done, the murder of Hosteen Maryboy."

Demott was staring at him, frowning. "That's it?"

"I think that would do it," Leaphorn said.

"Nothing about Hal."

"Nothing so far. Except that Amos Nez thinks you're him."

Demott considered that. "I'm getting cold," he said, and reopened the car door. "Going to get out of the wind."

"No," Leaphorn said, and shifted the pistol barrel before him.

Demott stopped, shut the door. He smiled at Leaphorn, shook his head. "Another weapon in there, you think?"

Leaphorn returned the smile. "Why take chances?" he said.

"Nothing about Hal," he said. "Well, I'm glad of that."

"Why?"

Demott shrugged. "Because of Elisa," he said. "The other cop, Jim Chee I think it was, he was coming up to see us. He said you had looked at the climber register. What did Elisa say about that?"

"I wasn't there. Chee showed her the page with Hal's name on it, and the date. He said she sort of went to pieces. Cried." Leaphorn shrugged. "About what you'd expect, I guess."

Demott slumped against the fender. "Ah, hell," he said, and slammed his fist against the hood. "Damn! Damn! Damn! Damn!"

"It made it look premeditated, of course," Leaphorn said.

"Of course," Demott said. "And it wasn't."

"An accident. If it wasn't, it may be hard to keep her out of it."

"She was still in love with the bastard. Didn't have a damn thing to do with it."

"I'm not surprised," Leaphorn said. "But considering what's involved, the Breedloves will probably hire a special prosecutor and they'll be aimed at getting the ranch back. Voiding the inheritance."

"Voiding the inheritance? What do you mean? Wouldn't that sort of be automatic? I mean, with what you said about Nez knowing . . . You know, Hal didn't inherit until he was thirty. The way the proviso read, if he didn't reach that birthday, everything was voided."

"Nez thinking you were Hal isn't the only evidence that he lived past that birthday," Leaphorn said. "There's his signature in the climbers' register. That's dated September thirty. You know of any evidence that he died before that?"

Demott was staring at Leaphorn, mouth partly open. "Wait a minute," he said. "Wait. What are you saying?"

"I guess I'm saying that I think there's sometimes a difference between the law and justice. If there's justice here, you're going to spend life in prison for the premeditated murder of Mr. Maryboy, with maybe an add-on twenty years or so for the attempted murder of Amos Nez. I think that would be about right. But it probably won't work quite like that. Your sister's probably going to be charged with accessory to murder—maybe as a conspirator and certainly as an accessory after the fact. And the Breedloves will get her ranch."

Demott inhaled a deep breath. He looked down at his hands, rubbed at his thumb.

"And Cache Creek will be running water gray with cyanide and mining effluent."

"Yeah," Demott said. "I really screwed it up. Year after year you're nervous about it. Sunny day you think you're clear. Nothing to worry about. Then you wake up with a nightmare."

"What happened up there?" Leaphorn said.

Demott gave him a questioning look. "You asking for a confession?"

"You're not under arrest. If you were, I'd have to tell you about your rights not to say anything until you get your lawyer. Elisa told Chee she didn't get all the way to the top. Is that right?"

"She didn't," Demott said. "She was getting scared." He snorted. "I should say sensible."

Leaphorn nodded.

"This birthday was a big deal for Hal," Demott said. "He'd say, Lord God Almighty, I'll be free at last, and get all excited thinking about it. And he'd invited this guy he'd known at Dartmouth to bring his girlfriend to see Canyon de Chelly and Navajo National Monument, the Grand Canyon, all that. Meet him and Elisa at the canyon for a birthday party for starters. But first he wanted to climb Ship Rock before he was thirty. That proved something to him. So we climbed it. Or almost."

Demott looked away. Deciding how much of this he wants to tell me, Leaphorn thought. Or maybe just remembering.

"We stopped in Rappel Gulch," Demott said. "Elisa had dropped out about an hour before that. Said she would just wait for us. So Hal and I were resting for that last hard climb. He had been talking about how the route up involves so much climbing up and then climbing back down to get to another up-route. He said there surely had to be a better way with all the good rappelling equipment we had now. Anyway, he edged out on the cliff. He said he wanted to see if there was a faster way down."

Demott stopped. He sat on the fender, studying Leaphorn.

"I take it there was," Leaphorn said.

Demott nodded. "Partway."

"Gust of wind caught him. Something like that?"

"Why are you doing this?"

"I like your sister," Leaphorn said. "A kind, caring woman. And besides, I don't like strip miners ruining the mountains."

The wind was blowing a little harder now, and colder. It came out of the northwest, blowing the hair away from Demott's face and dust around the tires of the Land-Rover.

"How does this come out?" Demott said. "I don't know much about the law."

"It will depend mostly on how you handle it," Leaphorn said.

"I don't understand."

"Here's where we are now. We have three felonies. The Maryboy homicide and the related shooting of a Navajo policeman. The FBI is handling that one. Then there is the assault upon Amos Nez, in which the FBI has no interest."

"Hal?"

"Officially, formally, an accident. FBI's not interested. Nobody else is, except the Breedlove Corporation."

"Now what happens?"

"Depends on you," Leaphorn said. "If I were still a Navajo Tribal Policeman and working this case, I'd take you in on suspicion of shooting Amos Nez. The police do a ballistics check on that rifle of yours and if the bullets match the one they got from Nez's horse, then they charge you with attempted murder. That gets Nez on the witness stand, which makes Elisa an accessory after the fact but probably indicted as coconspirator. That leads the Breedloves to file legal papers to void the inheritance. And what Nez says wakes up the FBI and they make the Maryboy connection. The ballistics test on whatever you shot him with, which I suspect we'll find either in your glove compartment or under the front seat, nails you on that one. I'd say you do life. Elisa? I don't know. Much shorter."

Demott had been following this intently, nodding sometimes. Sometimes frowning.

"But why Elisa?"

"If they can't make the jury believe she helped plan it, you can see how easy it is to prove she helped cover it up. Just get Nez and some of the people at the Thunderbird Lodge under oath. They saw you there with her."

"You mentioned an option. Said it depends on me. How could it?"

"We go into Gallup. You turn yourself in. Say you want to confess to the shooting of Hosteen Maryboy and Jim Chee. No mention of Nez. No mention of Hal. No mention of climbing Ship Rock."

"And what do you say? I mean about where you found me. And why and all that."

"I'm not there," Leaphorn said. "I park where I can see you walk into the police station and wait awhile and when you don't come out, I go somewhere and get something to eat."

"Just Maryboy, then, and Chee?" Demott said. "And Elisa wouldn't get dragged into it?"

"Without Nez involved, how would she?"

"Well, that other cop. The one I shot. Doesn't he have a lot of this figured out?"

"Chee?" Leaphorn chuckled. "Chee's a genuine Navajo. He isn't interested in revenge. He wants harmony."

Demott's expression was skeptical.

"What would he do?" Leaphorn asked. "It's obvious why you shot Chee. You were trying to escape. But you have to give them some plausible reason for shooting Maryboy. Chee isn't going to rush in and say the real motive was some complicated something or other to cover up not reporting that Hal Breedlove fell off the mountain eleven years ago. What's to be gained by it? Except a lot of work and frustration. Either way, you are going to do life in prison."

"Yes," Demott said, and the way he said it caused Leaphorn to lose his cool.

"And you damn sure deserve it. And worse. Killing Maryboy was cold-blooded murder. I've seen it before but it was always done by psychopaths. Emotional cripples. I want you to tell me how a normal human can decide to go shoot an old man to death."

"I didn't," Demott said. "They found the skeleton. Then they identified Hal. The nightmare was coming true. I got panicky. Nobody knew I'd climbed up there with Hal and Elisa that day but the old man. We went to ask him about trespassing, but that was eleven years ago. I didn't think he'd remember. But I had to find out. So I drove down there that evening, and knocked on the door. If he didn't recognize me, I'd go away and forget it. He opened the door and I told him I was Eldon Demott and heard he had some heifers to sell. And right away I could see he knew me. He said I was the man who'd climbed up there with Mr. Breedlove. He got all excited. He asked how I could have gone off and left a friend up there on the mountain. And now that he knew who I was, he was going to tell the police about it. I went out and got into the car and there he was coming out after me, carrying a thirty-thirty, and wanted me to go back into the house. So I got my pistol out of the glove box and put it in my coat pocket. He went into his house and put on his coat and hat, and he was going to take me right into the police station at Shiprock. And, you know . . ."

"That's how it was, then?"

"Yeah," Demott said. "But if I can just keep Nez out of it, maybe we save Elisa?"

Leaphorn nodded.

Demott reached his hand slowly toward the rifle.

"What I'd like to do is slip the bolt out of this thing so it's harmless."

"Then what?"

"Then I walk five steps over there to the cliff, and I toss it down into that deepest crack where nobody could ever find it."

"Do it," Leaphorn said. "I won't look."

Demott did it. "Now," he said. "I want just a few minutes to write Elisa a little letter. I want her to know I didn't kill Hal. I want her to know that when I climbed on up there and signed that register for him, it was just so she wouldn't lose her ranch."

"Go ahead."

"Got to get my notebook out of the glove box then."

"I'll watch," Leaphorn said. He moved around to where he could do that.

Demott dug out a little spiral notebook and a ballpoint pen, closed the box, backed out of the vehicle, and used the hood as a writing desk. He wrote rapidly, using two pages. He tore them out, folded them, and dropped them on the car seat.

"Now," he said, "let's get this over with."

"Demott," Leaphorn shouted. "Wait!"

But Eldon Demott had already taken the half dozen running steps to the rim of Canyon del Muerto and jumped, arms and legs flailing, out into empty space.

Leaphorn stood there a while listening. And heard nothing but the wind. He walked to the rim and looked. Demott had apparently hit the stone where the cliff bulged outward, down some two hundred feet. The body bounced out and landed on the stony talus slope just beside the canyon road. The first traveler to come along would see it.

Demott had left the door open on the Land-Rover. Leaphorn reached in and picked up the letter, holding it by its edges.

Dear Sister:

The first thing you do when you read this is call Harold Simmons at his law office don't tell anyone anything until you talk it over with him. I've made an awful mess of things, but I'm out of it now and you can still have a good life taking care of the ranch. But I want you to know that I didn't kill Hal. I'm ashamed to tell you a lot of this but I want you to know what happened.

About a week after Hal disappeared from the canyon I got a call from him. He was in a motel in Farmington. He wouldn't tell me where he had been, or why he was doing this, but he said he wanted to climb Ship Rock right away, before it got too cold. I said hell no. He said if I didn't I was fired. I wouldn't anyway. Then he said if I would and I didn't say anything to you, he would decide against signing that strip mining contract and put it off for another full year. He said he wanted to explain everything to you after we got down. So I said okay and I picked him up at the motel about five the next morning. He wouldn't tell me a word about where he'd been and he was acting strange. But we climbed it, up to Rappel Gulch, and there he insisted on edging out on the cliff face to see if there was a way good hands with rope could get down. A gust of wind caught him and he fell.

That's it, Elisa. I've been too ashamed to tell you all these years and I'm ashamed now. I think it's made me crazy. Because when I went to see Mr. Maryboy about his stock getting onto our grazing over on the Checkerboard Reservation, we got to yelling at one another and he got his rifle down and I shot him and then I shot the policeman to get away. I checked on the penalty I can expect and it's life in prison, so I'm going to take the quick way out of it and set an all-time record getting

down that 800-foot cliff into Canyon del
Muerto.

Remember I love you. I just got
crazy.
Your big brother, Eldon

Leaphorn read it again, refolded it carefully,
replaced it on the seat. He took out his handkerchief, pushed down the lock lever, wiped off the
leather seat where he might have touched it, and
slammed the door.

He drove a little faster than was smart down
the track, anxious to get out before somebody
spotted Demott's body. He didn't want to meet a
police car coming in, and if he didn't, the dry
snow now being carried by the wind would
quickly eliminate any clue that Demott had had
company. He was almost back to Window Rock
before a call on his police monitor let him know
that the body of a man had been found up
Canyon del Muerto.

He turned up the thermostat beside his front
door, heard the floor furnace roar into action,
put on the coffeepot, and washed his face and
hands. That done, he checked his telephone
answering machine, punched the button and listened to the first words of an insurance agent's
sales pitch, and hit the erase button. Then he
took his coffee mug off the hook, got out the
sugar and cream, poured himself a cup, and sat
beside the telephone.

He sipped now, and dialed Jim Chee's number in Ship Rock.

"Jim Chee."

"This is Joe Leaphorn," he said. "Thanks for the message you sent me. I hope I'm not calling at a bad time."

"No. No," Chee said. "I've been wondering. And I've been wanting to tell you about an arrest we made today in our cattle-rustling case. But by the way, have you heard they found a man's body in Canyon del Muerto? Deke said it was near the Nez place. He said it's Demott."

"Heard a little on my scanner," Leaphorn said.

Brief silence. Chee cleared his throat. "Where are you calling from? Was it Demott? Were you there?"

"I'm at home," Leaphorn said. "Are you off duty?"

"What do you mean? Oh. Well, yes. I guess so."

"Better be sure," Leaphorn said.

"Okay," Chee said. "I'm sure. I'm just having a friendly talk with an unidentified civilian."

"Tomorrow, you're going to get the word that Demott killed himself. He jumped off the cliff above the Nez place. About like diving off a sixty-story building. And he left a suicide note to his sister. In it he said he got into a quarrel with Mr. Maryboy over some cattle and shot him. Shot you while escaping. He told Elisa that he didn't kill Hal. He said Hal had called him from Farmington a week after vanishing from his birthday party, offered to delay signing the mining lease he had cooking for a year if Demott would climb Ship Rock with him the next day. Demott agreed. They climbed. Hal fell off.

Demott said he kept it a secret because he was ashamed to tell her."

Silence. Then Chee said, "Wow!"

Leaphorn waited for the implications to sink in.

"I'm not supposed to ask you how you know all this?"

"That is correct."

"What did he say about Nez?"

"Who?"

"Amos Nez," Chee repeated. "Oh, I guess I see."

"Saves you a lot of work, doesn't it?"

"Sure does," Chee said. "Except for when they find the rifle. Body near the Nez place, rifle nearby I guess. Nez recently shot. Two and two make four and the ballistics test raises a problem. Even the FBI won't be able to shrug that off."

"I think the rifle doesn't exist," Leaphorn said.

"Oh?"

"It's my impression that Demott didn't want to involve his sister. So he didn't want the Nez thing connected to the Maryboy thing because with Nez, you have his sister indicted as an accessory."

"I see," Chee said, a little hesitantly. "But how about Nez? Won't he be talking about it?"

"Nez isn't much for talking. And he's going to think I pushed Demott off the cliff to keep Demott from shooting him."

"Yeah. I see that."

"I think Demott did this partly to keep the Breedlove Corporation from strip-mining the ranch. Ruining his creek. So he left the world a suicide letter certifying that he was on Ship Rock with Hal a week after the famous birthday. Add that to Hal signing the register a week after the same birthday."

"One's as phony as the other," Chee said.

"Is that right?" Leaphorn said. "I would like to sit there and listen while you try to persuade the agent in charge that he should reopen his Maryboy homicide, throw away a written point-of-death confession on grounds that Demott was lying about his motive. I can just see that. 'And what was his real motive, Mr. Chee?' His real motive was trying to prove that accidental death that happened eleven years ago actually happened on a different weekend, and then—"

Chee was laughing. Leaphorn stopped.

"All right," Chee said. "I get your point. All it would do is waste a lot of work, maybe get Mrs. Breedlove indicted for something or other, and give the ranch back to the Breedlove Corporation."

"And get a big commission to the attorney," Leaphorn added.

"Yeah," Chee said.

"Tomorrow, when the news is out, I'll send Shaw details about the suicide note. And give him back what's left of his money. Now, what were you going to tell me about cattle rustling?"

"It sounds trivial after this," Chee said, "but Officer Manuelito arrested Dick Finch today. He was loading Maryboy heifers into his camper."

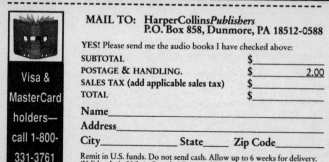